WHEN YOU HAD ME ADAPTING

ROMANCE REHAB SERIES
BOOK 2

JESS CHRISTINE

E-book ISBN: 979-8-9904385-2-1

Paperback ISBN: 979-8-9904385-3-8

Cover designed by Paige Moreland (@lpmdraws)

Copy / Line Editing by Kristen Hamilton at Kristen's Red Pen (@kristenreadswhat)

Proofreading by Tina Otero

Chapter Images by Paige Moreland (@lpmdraws)

Formatting by Kalie Gerwig | Good Girl Author Services

To my fellow tortured therapists—Jenna, Lauren, Maya, Rachael, and Stephanie.

Thank you for making the bad days bearable and the good days even better.
I feel so fortunate to call you my friends!

PLAYLIST

Please click the link or scan the QR Code below for the link to the Spotify Playlist created for *When You Had Me Adapting*

DEAR READER

When You Had Me Adapting is the second interconnected standalone in the Romance Rehab series. While it can be read on its own, I recommend the books to be read in order to avoid any potential spoilers from book one.

Please note that it is intended for individuals 18+ due to the mature language and open door/explicit sexual content.

It also includes death of a parent (off-page), on-page descriptions of loss and grief, mentions cheating, and miscommunication. Your mental health is my priority, so if these topics are upsetting to you please proceed with caution.

CONTENTS

DICKTIONARY

For those readers who want to skip the smut or go straight to it, do with this list what you will.

PROLOGUE

LACEY- 10 YEARS AGO

"I thought I'd find you up there," Jace calls from my parents' backyard. He carefully begins to climb up the side of the house to meet me. I'm sitting on the flat part of the roof above the screened-in porch—right outside my bedroom window. He pauses once he's safely on top to pull his camera to his eye, and a flash lights up the night surrounding us. Lowering it, his face drops when he sees mine is streaked with tears. "What's on your mind, Pixie?"

I shake my head and swipe my fingers under my eyes a few times. "I can't believe you leave tomorrow." I sniffle. My hands move against the soft, flannel blanket I'm sitting on, drying my fingertips. The heaviness in my chest that I've been feeling for the past few days returns.

He carefully balances along the roof until he gets to where I am and takes a seat. "I'll be back in a year," he reassures me, gently wiping away any remaining tears. Taking my chin between his thumb and forefinger, he slightly tilts my face toward his. Our lips meet and butterflies fill my stomach. I don't think I'll ever get used to kissing him. His kiss erases all of the sadness and all of the fear threatening to break my heart. It instantly puts me at ease, and I allow myself to melt into him.

When he pulls away, the heartache returns so quickly that it knocks all the oxygen right out of my lungs.

I nod my head, trying to hold back the tears threatening to break free again. "I know, I know, and I'm so proud of you." I pause and attempt a small smile. Lying down on my back, I cover my face with my hands and inhale deeply.

"Talk to me," he says, lying down so we are shoulder to shoulder, our backs flat against the thick blanket. Both of us are looking up at the stars spread across the summer sky.

"It's nothing," I lie.

"Yes it is. I want to know what's going on in that mind of yours." His fingers interlace with mine, and he squeezes my hand.

"I got in a fight with my mom earlier. She thinks the long distance plan is a bad idea. Told me I needed to stop thinking about this with my heart and use my head." I take a deep breath. "God, she was so annoying, J. Apparently she had lunch with your mom and Poppy's mom today. They must have talked about you the whole time because when she got back, she wouldn't let up. And then when I started crying, she told me to *stop being so dramatic.*"

He scoffs. "You aren't dramatic."

"Try convincing my parents of that." I shake my head.

"So, what is your heart telling you?"

"That I've had you next door since before I was born and now you won't be here." I blink, and a tear escapes from the corner of my eye. I wipe it away quickly. "I don't want to lose you." The words are no more than a whisper on my lips.

"Lose me? You'll never lose me," he assures me.

"And how do you know that?" I roll onto my side to face him.

"Because I've loved you since I was eight years old." He turns towards me. Our faces are so close they're almost touching. His features are illuminated by the glow of the moonlight. "I'm scared, too, you know. I don't want to lose you either," he says.

"Lose me? Yeah right. I hate to break it to you, but you're stuck with me until the end of time."

"I hope you're right. I don't want Lori to get in your head and scare you into the arms of one of those meathead bozos from school." He tucks the loose strands of my hair behind my ear. "Especially Alex. I'm leaving, and what if—"

"She won't. It's just her way of mothering me."

"I don't like that she has you doubting us, and I haven't even left yet." I blink, a few tears falling free. I don't know why my mom says the things she does. My dad tells me it's her way of protecting me, but I'm not so sure. I lean toward him and place my lips on his.

"I love you. Don't worry about my mom. I'm sure after a few weeks, she'll move on to something else to bother me about. She always does."

"And Alex?"

"You know I can't stand Alex. He and Beau are literally the jock versions of Tweedledee and Tweedledum." I laugh, trying to ease the tension. "Gosh, don't tell Poppy I said that. She would kill me if she knew I was making fun of Beau."

He smiles. "Your secret is safe with me."

"What secret?" I hear from my window.

We both sit up and turn to see Poppy attempting to crawl onto the roof with a bag thrown over her shoulder.

"Look, you two, I know you're in love and all, and it's, like, super cute, but I swear to god." She pauses to fix her footing and then continues, "I swear to god, if you are now keeping secrets from me, I'll never forgive either of you." She lets out a squeak as she lands on the shingles with a thud. Cautiously, she scoots over to where we are and sits to my right.

"I'm sure there are certain parts of our relationship you want us to keep secret," I tease, throwing her a wink.

"Yeah, if you could keep it PG when I'm around, that would be awesome," she says dryly.

"Well, then you might want to go home because I was about to take Lace into her room and—" I slap my hand over his mouth before he can continue.

"Yes, please stop," she deadpans.

His lips curve into a smile under my hand, and then I feel his tongue shoot out of his mouth and wet my palm.

"Jace!" I wipe my hand on the blanket. His chest rumbles with laughter. I wish I could bottle it up and listen to it forever.

"It's been ten months and I'm still not used to the two of you putting your tongues on one another." She attempts a smile, but it looks more like a grimace.

"What has you third-wheeling tonight, Pop?" he asks.

"I know, I know. It's y'all's last night and whatever." She rolls her eyes. "But I couldn't let you leave tomorrow without a proper send-off."

"Y'all need to stop acting like I'm leaving forever." He shakes his head and runs his free hand over his head, making sure not to let go of mine with the other.

"Well, you got this fancy schmancy job in D.C., so excuse me if I'm worried you will forget about your two best friends when you're busy being some fancy schmancy photographer," Poppy says, digging through the bag.

Jace squeezes my hand a little tighter, and I try to push her words as far out of my mind as they can possibly go. His eyes meet mine, and he offers me a reassuring smile like he knows what I'm thinking.

"I was just telling Lacey I could never forget about her, and I won't forget about you either. Also, it's not a job. It's an unpaid opportunity to get some experience."

"Yeah, experience with real professional photojournalists.

Don't sell yourself short. You're one of fifty rising college freshmen to get selected. That's a really big deal, J," I say. And it is. It's a really big deal, and I don't know why he's so modest about it. One graduating senior from each state, and he was picked for Georgia.

He smiles sheepishly and shrugs his shoulders.

"You're getting an opportunity that will help you find the Bixito Parrot one day. And that's extraordinary. I'm so proud of you," I add.

"You really think I'll find it?"

"I know you will," I say, giving his hand a squeeze. "It's your dream, and if anyone can do it, you can."

"Maybe. Really though, next year is going to fly by, and once it's over, I'll be back here with both of you at Farrington U." He plants a chaste kiss on my lips.

"I feel the need to remind you that Lacey was my first friend when I moved here, so if you decide to break her heart, I'm picking her." Poppy's tone is playful, but I know she's dead serious. He shakes his head, and I give my best friend a little shove.

"Wow." Jace laughs. "Have I ever told you that you're a great friend? Thank you."

"Well, you know me. I'm a real girl's girl." She pulls me into a side hug and squeezes me tight.

"Noted, but you both have nothing to worry about. I swear. I'll be back here before you know it. It's just a step toward reaching my goals."

"Good, because I would hate to hate you," she says with a wink. The knot in my gut tightens. I know Jace loves me, and I know I love him, but what if it's not enough? What if my best friend is right? What if my mom is right? Why does everyone else think he'll hurt me?

My head and heart are fighting an internal battle. One is telling me to tell him to follow his dreams, trusting that everything will be okay. The other is listening to everyone else and wanting to selfishly beg him to stay.

"Are your parents home? Colt let me in," Poppy says, distracting me from my spiral.

I shake my head. "No, they're at dinner with my dad's boss or something. Colton's probably hiding in his room playing video games. Why?"

"Because I raided Dad's liquor cabinet." Her eyes dance with mischief as she pulls a green bottle from the bag and uncorks the top. "Cheers to the three musketeers," she yells as loud as she can, giggling and lifting the bottle into the air before taking a huge swig. Her whole body shivers and she visibly gags. "Shit, it's terrible."

She passes the bottle to me, and I read the label. "This is absinthe, Poppy. I think it's meant to be mixed with something."

She shrugs. "I couldn't steal his good shit. He would've noticed."

I tilt the bottle up despite my better judgment. The liquid burns my throat as I swallow. "Fuck, this *is* terrible. Jace?" I cough out.

He takes the bottle, throws it back, and immediately chokes, causing the three of us to burst out laughing. He hands the bottle back to Poppy, who replaces the cork and tucks it into her bag.

I lean over, put my head on his shoulder, and grab Poppy's hand with my free one. "I love you both so much."

"I love you both more," Poppy chimes.

"I love you both the most." Jace squeezes my hand twice and kisses my forehead.

Man, this totally blows.

"Oh, shit!" Poppy screams, slapping my leg and pointing up towards the sky. "A shooting star! Quick, make a wish." Her eyes slam shut.

"You two don't really still believe in wishing on stars do you?" Jace laughs.

"Shhhh," Poppy says. "Make a wish before it's too late."

I feel him squeeze my hand, and I glance over to find his eyes shut. A smile is spread across his face.

I close mine for a long minute, wishing Jace and I make it through this next year. Pressure builds under my eyelids. I open my eyes to find him staring at me, causing the tears to flow down my cheeks. Quickly wiping them away and forcing a smile, I ask, "What?"

His crystal blue eyes are full of warmth and assurance. His face says everything I need it to without ever speaking a word. Deep in my gut, I hope he's right because I don't ever want to do life without Jace Jackson and Poppy Collins by my side.

Somewhere in the distance, a police car siren fades and a dog barks. The sound of crickets chirping fills the quiet night. The air is warm and still. The three of us sit in silence for a while, soaking up what feels like the final moments of our friendship.

No, not final. Jace will be back in a year. I still have Poppy.

"Okay, love birds, I'm getting eaten alive by mosquitos." Poppy slaps at her shin. "I'm going to let you two have your night." She turns over onto all fours and starts to crawl back towards my open window, the bottle in the bag clanking against the roof as she crawls. "Jace, you better not leave without telling me bye," she shouts as she falls back into my room.

"I wouldn't dare."

"Bye, babe," I say.

He watches until she disappears out of view and then pulls me between his legs. His arms wrap around me and his chin rests on my shoulder, allowing his breath to tickle my neck. Goosebumps erupt down my arms.

"So, what did you wish for?" I ask.

"If I tell you, then it won't come true."

"And I thought you didn't believe in wishing on stars," I say. He squeezes my sides making me giggle.

"I don't, but you do, and it makes you happy." I shift so I can see him. He looks so handsome. A boyish smile erupts across his face. My eyes gloss over, and as if he is reading my mind, he leans forward and kisses me. His tongue swirls around mine and those butterflies return. He pulls away and rests his forehead against mine.

"Long distance can work, Lace. We'll talk every day. We'll make time for one another."

"And if it doesn't?"

"It will," he says.

"Jace, promise me if it doesn't work…if for some reason we're no longer in each other's lives…that you'll still try to find the Bix. Promise me all the heartbreak won't be for nothing."

"Long distance will—"

"Swear it," I cut him off.

"I pinky promise." He lifts up his pinky finger and I lock mine around his. "But long distance is going to work. I promise that too."

CHAPTER 1: BOATS AND HOES
LACEY - PRESENT

I made the mistake of Googling him. For nearly a decade, I have succeeded in avoiding him, but this morning I finally caved. Seeing him a week ago at Poppy's graduation party really fucked up my head, and as much as I've been telling myself I hate him, the vision of him walking into the party won't leave my brain.

He looked older than he did at eighteen, but I guess that's what happens when you haven't really seen someone in a while. Gone was his boyish frame, and instead he looked like a grown-ass man. His black hair was longer than it was in high school. A short beard covered his face. He was all muscles, tan skin, and tattoos. *Fucking tattoos.* When did he get tattoos? His ocean blue eyes pierced right through me. He was dressed casually in dark jeans and a black T-shirt that showed off his corded arms. His always present camera was still in his hand.

I knew it was him the instant he walked in. It's hard to forget the guy who broke your heart into a million tiny pieces. Ten years worth of heartbreak and hatred hit me like a semi-truck.

I should've been focused on celebrating my best friend

getting her master's degree, but then he walked into the room and took all of my attention. He took my breath away, but not in the way you read about in a romance novel. No, this was more like I had been sucker punched so hard my lungs were depleted of all oxygen. The room started to spin the moment he hugged Tanner and Logan. I needed air. I couldn't breathe and so, I ran.

The only thing that got me through the night was copious amounts of champagne and Poppy. But now, it's been a week, and reality is starting to set in. He's back, and realistically, I don't know how much longer I can ignore him.

At twenty-seven, I shouldn't care what he's been doing. I shouldn't want to know how he spent his days after he ripped my heart out, but here I am, staring blankly at the dozens of links that popped up the minute I typed in his name. Well not his name, but his nickname. *Jacks.* That's what Tanner and Logan called him at the party. *Jacks Jackson.*

I click on the first one and scan the words. Unable to believe what I'm reading, I click out and tap the next one. It confirms what the first one revealed.

I click out and scroll up and down, scanning the screen. It's a mix of social media and articles all highlighting his accomplishments. The third link appears to be to an interview with *The Atlanta Journal-Constitution.* My finger hovers over the words: *Photographer Jacks Jackson's Motivation For His Latest Discovery Might Surprise You.*

I take a deep breath. I'm not sure I want to read it. I'm not sure I can handle what I think it'll say, but dammit if I'm not a little curious.

He fucking did it. I'm not surprised. Of course he did it. I shouldn't care, but I can't help but wonder if part of him did it for me? I shake the thought from my brain. *No, that was always his dream, not mine.*

"Lacey!" Poppy shouts from across our small apartment, breaking me out of my internal dilemma and interrupting my research. I quickly panic-throw my phone across the room like a teenager hiding porn from her parents. It hits the wall with a loud thud. *Shit.*

"Please come with us," she yells, her voice getting closer by the second. "You can't hide in there forever." She barges through the closed door of my room. I immediately try to hide under the blankets, pretending to sleep.

"I know you're not asleep. I just watched you pull the covers over your head," she says dryly, obviously not amused by my antics.

I peek out from under my comforter. She's standing in my doorway with her arms crossed, wearing a bright pink bikini and denim shorts. Her dark brown hair is pulled up into a messy bun, and sunglasses sit on the top of her head.

"Please come," she begs. "The guys rented a boat. You invited Gray. It's going to be fun."

We've had this day planned since before Poppy's graduation party, but then Jace showed back up. I pull the covers back over my head with a loud, exasperated breath. I don't want to risk him being there, and I definitely don't want to see him half-naked in a bathing suit. I don't want to go, especially after what I just read. I want to stay home alone and read.

I peek out again, and my best friend hasn't moved. She has her phone out, her thumbs tapping away at the screen. My cell pings and then pings again and again. I roll out of bed and stomp over to where it sits on the floor. *Thank God the screen isn't shattered.*

I swipe up on the phone and am instantly met with all of those links again. *I can't believe he fucking did it.* My breath hitches as I spy the interview link, but I push the thought from my brain and swipe out of the browser quickly. I click on the little white and green message app. Three separate text messages are waiting for me.

TANNER:

<<Boats and Hoes GIF>>

GRAY:

This is my first Saturday off in months. Why is Poppy telling me you don't want to come on the boat anymore?

LOGAN:

I promise he won't be there.

"Do I want to know how your phone ended up over there?" she asks.

I don't answer her and instead, I walk back over to my bed. I plop down onto my mattress with a huff. "You texted everyone?" I roll my eyes and let my body fall back. My head completely misses my pillow and hits my wooden headboard with a thunk. "Ouch." I frown and rub the spot that's now throbbing.

"Well, you weren't listening to me. He's not coming. The guys didn't invite him."

"Really? They're cool with telling their best friend he can't hang out with them because of me? I mean you and Logan haven't been together that long. I know you love one another, but why would he pick me over Jace?"

"Because I don't really want to see him either. You aren't the only person he hurt, you know."

The edges of her mouth fall. I know she's right. Jace didn't just break my heart, but he broke Poppy's too. I lost the boy I thought would be my happily ever after, and she lost one of her best friends. For a split second, I think about telling her what I found, but then I change my mind. Saying it out loud will make it real, and I'm not ready for any of this to be real.

"Look, this is all really new, and I know neither of us were expecting to see him at my party or to find out he's friends with Logan, but unfortunately, they're friends. I love Logan and I love you, so please, can we go have some fun? He's not coming."

"Does Tanner know about all the drama?"

"No, you asked Logan and me not to say anything and we won't until you're ready."

"I appreciate that."

She offers me a smile. "I'm not going to allow him to make you go back into hiding. We aren't doing that again. You've been doing nothing but wallowing since he showed up at my party, and it's time to get out of bed. You need to do something other than work and read. I'm finally done with school, so let's go have some fun. I think the sunshine will do you good."

"Fine," I grumble.

"Yeah?"

"Yes, I'll come. Just make sure you pack some sunscreen. I'm worried you might burn after not seeing the sun for the last six years."

"Ha. Ha. Ha. Very funny. Joke all you want, but all the studying paid off. In a month or so, we get to work together which is what we always wanted." She turns around and heads into our living room.

I begrudgingly swing my legs out of bed and begin to move around my room, getting dressed in my new black bikini. I throw a sheer cover up over the top of it and dig through my jewelry box. I'm looking for my paperclip chain and having no luck when another piece catches my eye. I pull out a delicate gold necklace that holds a small, oval locket. It was a gift from my brother, but I haven't worn it in years.

I grab my phone and click on his name. The last text is dated over a month ago, and I remind myself I need to do better at staying in touch with him.

Thinking about you today! Miss you!

COLT:

Miss you too. I should be home after summer
ball is over. Mom is already planning a
dinner.

Should we skip it and maybe grab dinner just
the two of us?

COLT:

Tempting, but no way she'd allow it. I'm
pulling up to the gym. I'll call you when I can.

Can't wait!

I place the locket around my neck and add a second
dainty silver chain. Looking into the mirror, I double-check
my appearance before packing my bag with sunscreen, my
favorite sunglasses, and a towel.

I hear a knock at the front door and walk out of my room
to see Poppy wrapped up in Logan's arms. His best friend
and Jace's roommate, Tanner, is standing behind them in the
doorway, sporting an aqua tank top and swim trunks covered
in bright pink, purple, and yellow tropical leaves. His blond
hair is tied into a bun on the top of his head.

"Hey, buddy," Tanner says through a cheeky grin. He
walks past the happy couple and playfully punches my
shoulder.

"I know we agreed to be friends, but you don't have to be
so weird," I remind him.

Tanner lets out a laugh, grabs me in a headlock, and playfully rubs his fist into the top of my head, completely messing
up my hair. "I thought you liked it weird, Lace." He throws a
wink and cocky smile in my direction as I swat him away.

"What are you wearing? You look like a neon sign and a
frat boy had a baby."

"You really do wonders for a man's ego," he says with a
laugh.

"So, who's all coming today?" I ask, walking over to the mirror to fix my hair.

"I already told you. It's us four and Gray," Poppy answers me. "Right, guys?" She looks straight at Logan.

"Don't worry. Jacks won't be joining us," Logan says.

"I don't know if I'm ever going to get used to y'all being friends with him or you calling him that," Poppy says with an awkward laugh.

"Me either," I agree.

"Are you ever going to tell us what happened?" Tanner pries.

"No," I answer. "You can ask him. He's your friend. I don't want to talk about it." I play with my hair, pretending to fix it a little more. Deep down, I know I should talk about it, but who am I to ruin Jace's friendship with Tanner? Poppy told me Logan has barely spoken to him, and I don't know how to feel about that.

"Gray said she'd meet us there," Poppy says. "So we can head out whenever."

"Wait, who's Gray again?" Tanner asks.

"She's the physical therapist at Dogwood Manor and a good friend of mine. Poppy's met her a few times. She's cool and makes one hell of a margarita."

"And why is she coming? I thought we were going to have a little double date." He pretends to pout. My face must say exactly what I'm thinking because his frown quickly turns into a big goofy grin. "Don't look so disgusted," he says through fits of laughter. "You're too easy to tease. You know that?"

"Ugh. You see? This is precisely why I invited her."

I glance over at Poppy and Logan. Logan moves a piece of fallen hair behind Poppy's ear before leaning down to whisper something only she can hear. She giggles. They're completely lost in their own little love bubble. I exhale and look back at Tanner.

"Those two over there," I gesture in our friends' direction, "are going to be so enamored with each other today that the last thing I need is to have only you to talk to."

"And what if Gray is *enamored* by me?" He wiggles his eyebrows.

"Highly doubtful."

"Well, like I said, always doing wonders for my ego." He chuckles. "Y'all ready to head out?"

The four of us head down to Logan's truck. I guess I *am* going on a boat today.

CHAPTER TWO: FLAMINGO COVE

JACE

"**P**oppy is Logan's girlfriend, and he's whipped as fuck. If she doesn't want you there, then I don't think you should come."

The conversation I had with Tanner this morning plays over and over in my head like a bad commercial jingle.

How the fuck did I end up here?

I run my hand down my short beard and take an extra long sip of my coffee. One week ago, I saw Lacey for the first time in nine years, and she looked stunning. Her long blonde hair was in loose curls cascading around her shoulders. She was wearing a green dress that hugged her hips and dipped low enough to show off the perfect curve of her tits. Her lips were plump, pink, and looked as kissable as they did the last time I saw her. She was pretty at eighteen, but in that green dress she was a fucking knock-out.

When her eyes met mine, it felt like maybe fate had finally intervened, which is a weird thought, but if anyone could make me believe in fate and wishing on stars, it's Lacey.

Instead of running towards me, she ran away, and then Logan asked me to leave.

"If Poppy doesn't want you there, then I don't think you should

come." That's what Tanner said this morning. If I'm honest, I'm not surprised. She made it clear she took Lacey's side over mine and she no longer wanted me in her life. Ten years of friendship out the window in one text message. I just still don't understand why I'm being painted as the bad guy.

I don't have many people in my inner circle, but five years ago Tanner forced himself to be my friend and introduced me to Logan, Donovan, and Enzo. Our group of five was formed, and the rest is history. I'm not going to let what happened a decade ago ruin the friendships I have now.

I jump up from the table and head to my room. I dig through the drawers until I find a bathing suit and pull it on. I grab my keys and head to the marina.

I realize my plan is full of holes as soon as I turn into the parking lot. Tanner headed out a full hour ago, which means they're probably already floating in some cove somewhere, and I have no way of knowing which one. I shoot him a text, but it won't deliver. Wherever they are, there must be no service.

Lake Allatoona is huge, and the marina is packed with people renting boats and water sports equipment. I walk up to the counter where a kid no older than sixteen stands.

"Hey, man, I need to get out on the lake. Do you have anything left to rent?" He clicks through the computer.

"Um, it looks like we have one more pontoon. It seats eight. How many people are in your party?"

"Anything smaller? My friends left an hour ago and I was hoping to go meet them. It's just me."

"Oh, um, I have a pedal boat."

"Nothing faster? I don't know where they are and I'm going to have to look for them. Maybe a jet ski?" He looks at me like I'm insane. *I feel insane.*

"No, sir, all the jet skis have been rented, but I could possibly find their boat. All of our rentals have trackers on them. What's the name of the person who rented it?"

"Logan Peterson or Tanner Mitchell." He taps on the keyboard and then radios to someone. I drum my fingers on the counter impatiently. I know I look completely unhinged, but with every passing minute, I want nothing more than to be on the boat I was told to stay away from.

"We located the boat in Flamingo Cove, which is like a thirty minute pedal boat ride from here. I can rent it to you for $55 an hour."

"$55 an hour? You're joking."

"No, sir, that's the rate."

I massage my temples and take a deep breath.

"Fine." Taking out my wallet, I hand him my credit card.

I follow him down to the rocky beach where the pedal boats are kept. He unties my boat and attempts, and fails, to give me decent directions to Flamingo Cove. I buckle my life vest and push the boat into the shallow water before climbing in. I begin to pedal.

At 6'4", my knees are up to my chest in this thing. I'm sure I look ridiculous, and while I know Lacey hates me, hate is the furthest emotion from how I feel about her.

So much for the image of a knight in shining armor riding in on a horse. Instead, I'm going to pull up to their boat sweating my ass off from having to pedal myself across the lake. I rip my life jacket and T-shirt off because it's unnaturally hot out here. The life jacket isn't helping my image, and I'll be damned if Lacey is going to see me looking even more pathetic than I already do. She may want nothing to do with me, but I can at least try to arrive looking good.

I wish they had a jet ski; it would have made what I'm about to do so much cooler.

CHAPTER 3: DEATH WISH
LACEY

Logan and Tanner kept their word and Jace isn't here. We're anchored in a small cove with a few other boats. The sun beats down on us and for the first time today, I'm glad I came. A mix of country and rap music fills the air as it bounces off the surrounding boats and water.

Poppy and Logan are cuddled up on a giant float tied to our large pontoon. Tanner is attempting and failing to flirt with Gray. I'm seated on the bench seat drinking her famous homemade margaritas and laughing at his shameless efforts.

It feels like summer and I love it.

"Could you rub some more sunscreen on my shoulders?" I turn around and grab the yellow and white tube before handing it to Gray. I move my hair to the side.

"I can do it." Tanner practically leaps at me.

"Hard pass," I deadpan.

"Oh, come on, buddy, I've seen you naked. I can't rub a little sunscreen on your shoulders?" He wiggles his eyebrows and then throws me a wink.

"Don't be gross, Tanner. We were drunk, and it was one time."

"Wait, you two slept together? I need to hear this story."

Gray takes the sunscreen from me and starts rubbing the cool white lotion into my skin. "Okay, so spill. How did I not know about this?"

"What's there to tell? Lacey couldn't resist my good looks and charm, so I brought her home and rocked her world." He jumps up on the edge of the boat and flexes his muscles.

I choke, and the sip I took sprays from my mouth. "Is that what you think happened?" I turn and lean over the side of the boat, sitting up on my knees. "Poppy!" I yell. "Do you remember how I described my night with Tanner?"

Poppy sits up on the big float and adjusts her sunglasses. "I think the word you used was"—she pauses for dramatic effect—"mediocre." Gray and I burst out laughing.

"Ouch!" Logan laughs.

"I'm hurt, Lacey. Truly." Tanner throws me a big pout and grabs his chest like I've shot an arrow through his heart. He falls off the boat with a big splash.

"Oh, stop. You and I have both since agreed it was a mistake and we're better as friends," I yell down at the water. I watch as he swims and jumps up on the float, almost flipping it.

"I know we are, buddy; don't worry." He flashes me a cheeky grin.

I turn back around. "He's such a child."

"I'm gonna need you to give me more details," Gray laughingly replies.

I shake my head, thinking back to the night we first met the guys at The Local. If I had known who Tanner was, I would have never left the bar with him. "Poppy and I met Logan and Tanner the same night. She had just found out her spring externship was canceled, so I took her out to forget about it." I laugh at the memory.

"The '90s party?" Gray asks.

"Yep. After one too many tequila shots, we ended up

leaving with the guys. I regrettably hooked up with Tanner which is why you've never heard about him."

"And y'all stayed friends?"

"Oh, god no. Poppy and I snuck out the next morning and honestly never thought we'd see them again, but then she ended up getting an externship at the school Logan works at. They fought their feelings for a while, but then ended up falling in love. Tanner and I decided to put our night behind us for the sake of the two of them."

"How have you seriously never told me about this?" she asks over the rim of her cup.

"Well for starters, most of Poppy and Logan's relationship was a gigantic secret, but also, you're always too busy working." I laugh. "This is the first time we've hung out in months."

Her jaw slightly clenches and she exhales. "Ugh. I know, but student loans don't pay themselves." She tips her cup up. "Oh shit, I'm empty. Do you need a refill?"

"Sure."

Gray stands to grab the pitcher of margaritas. "Jesus, some idiot is out here in a pedal boat alone and isn't wearing a life jacket." She points her finger and laughs.

I stand to see what she's talking about. About fifty yards from our boat, a man in a pedal boat is headed right for us. "You've gotta be kidding me." My grip tightens around my cup.

"Right? Some people really must have a death wish. It's insane out here today. He's going to get himself killed."

My heart starts to race.

"Oh, but he's cute. Maybe we should rescue him and invite him on board," she says, taking a sip from her cup.

I wish she was wrong, but she isn't. The man in the tiny boat is shirtless and gorgeous. A sprinkle of dark hair covers his chest. The sun reflects off the sweat running down his toned abs. Tattoos cover his forearms. He looks fucking delicious, and I hate that I think that. I hate that my body still reacts to him like it did at seventeen. *Fucking traitor.* At least my head and my heart know better.

I flip around. "Logan, I thought you said he wasn't coming." I jump up on the edge of the boat to get a better look and throw my hand in the pedal boat's direction.

"Don't look at me." He puts both hands up defensively.

"Tanner?" I practically shout.

"Same here, Lace."

"Wait, who's that?" I hear Gray ask behind me.

"My ex and Tanner's roommate." My eyes stay glued to the tiny boat moving through the water. He's close now, and I can make out his perfect fucking face. I'm hit with the same emotions from a decade ago: anger, betrayal, embarrassment, and utter heartbreak. You'd think after ten years all those feelings would be gone, but instead they're bubbling back up to the surface like they never left. Maybe they didn't? Maybe I got really good at convincing myself they had.

"What?" she asks, obviously confused. "I thought you just told me you and Tanner slept together." I glance in her direction and her eyes bounce between Jace, Tanner, and me. "Wait, is this why you didn't want to come today?"

"It's really the funniest story. Tell her Lacey," Tanner shouts, pushing me completely over the edge.

I down my margarita in two large gulps. I wish I could escape. I wish I hadn't come. I don't want to have the conversation we need to have in front of everyone. Not today. Not now. I attempt to move back into the boat, but the surface is slick. I feel my feet slip out from underneath me. My arms flail out to the side. I try to find something to grab onto, but there's nothing but the smooth side of the boat. A loud shriek escapes my mouth as I fall. My body hits the water with a splash. Lake water burns my nose and fills my mouth.

I come up for air and see the ridiculous boat floating right towards me.

"You okay, Pixie?" Jace reaches out his hand as I try to compose myself. I wipe the water from my face.

"Don't call me that." I swat his hand away and cough. His mouth droops into a small frown.

"Come on, let me help you." He tries reaching out his arm again and offers me a small smile. "Please."

"No, I'm fine." I swim towards the large float where our friends all sit. Tanner pulls me up and I run my hands through my soaked hair, gathering it all to one side.

"What are you doing here, Jacks?" Logan asks the question we're all thinking.

"Y'all are my friends too." He gestures toward both of the guys. "We can all coexist, can't we?" He looks at us with pleading eyes.

My eyes find Poppy's, and she shakes her head.

"Can someone please help me understand what's happening?" Gray asks from the side of the boat.

"Come on, it's been ten years. We can't do this forever. I live with Tanner. I'm friends with Logan. It looks like we're stuck with each other." He sounds desperate, and a part of me likes watching him beg. I look around the boat and I realize everyone is wanting me to make the final call.

"Fine," I agree. Poppy's eyes go wide, and I give her a reassuring nod.

"Fine?" she mouths. I nod again.

"You can stay." I look back at Jace. His fucking smile and those blue eyes make me feel something low in my belly I definitely shouldn't feel.

He hurt me. He hurt me. He hurt me.

"Just stay out of my way, and I'll stay out of yours." I stand and dive back into the water.

CHAPTER 4: I HAD SOME HELP

JACE

I watch as Lacey swims toward the ladder on the back of the boat, and when she pulls herself up out of the lake, my eyes lock on her body. She has more curves than she did nine years ago, and fuck if I don't want to trace every inch of them with my fingers. Water drips between her breasts and down her stomach. I have to adjust myself under my swimsuit so my dick doesn't make a show of my attraction to this girl.

Georgia summers are hot, but watching her move in that tiny black bikini, without being able to touch her, is making me feel like I've fallen into the pits of hell.

I need to cool the fuck down. She wants nothing to do with me, and as much as I want to know why, I know she's not going to talk to me in front of a bunch of people. I need to get her alone.

The sun hits the gold and silver chains around her neck and immediately makes me question everything I thought I knew. I rub my hands over my eyes like it'll somehow make my vision better. *Is that really what I think it is?*

"Move your boat to the back and I'll help you tie it off," Tanner yells, breaking my thoughts. I hear a loud splash as he jumps in the lake and swims to meet me. I pedal the boat close to the pontoon and throw the rope towards my roommate. He catches it and ties a knot. I carefully stand, climb out, and get up onto the boat where my ex sits with a girl I've never met.

"Hi, I'm Gray," the brunette says.

"Jace, but I go by Jacks," I say, offering her a wave. Lacey lets out a laugh, but doesn't look in my direction.

"I work with Lacey, and once Poppy's license gets approved, I'll work with her too."

I nod my head. "Cool, so are you all nurses?"

"We aren't nurses. We're therapists," Lacey says.

"Oh, right. I knew it was something like that. Dad told me you worked at a nursing home, but I couldn't remember."

Gray studies Lacey and me, trying to figure us out.

"Assisted living facility," Lacey corrects me.

"Isn't it the same thing?" I ask.

She diverts her gaze down to her phone and away from mine.

"Technically, no," Gray explains. "The residents at a nursing home require constant care. Dogwood Manor has different levels of care, but most of our clients can do a lot independently."

"I gotcha. So, what kind of therapists are you?"

"Well I'm a physical therapist, Lacey is an occupational therapist, and Poppy is a speech therapist," Gray explains.

"Cool. So, Lacey, what does an occupational therapist do?" I look at her, hoping she'll talk to me. She looks up, and I'm surprised to find her eyes aren't full of hatred, instead looking like they're full of pain. For a second I think she may answer my question, but then her phone pings and she looks away.

"You want a drink, man? We have beer and White Claws." Tanner is digging around in a large, turquoise cooler. On the lid, a large version of Logan and his pickleball team mascot is surrounded by other various stickers.

"Sure, a beer is fine." I walk over and grab the can from his hand. "I tried texting you, but it wouldn't go through. You think I should leave?"

"My phone is dead. And no. You're here now, so you might as well stay and hang out," he whispers.

I nod, tip my beer up, and swallow hard. Tanner walks over and spins the volume control on the radio. "I Had Some Help" by Post Malone blares through the speakers.

"So, tell me the funny story about how y'all know each other?" Gray yells over the music.

"Tanner grew up playing lacrosse with my cousin, Archie," I explain.

"Yeah, and five years ago, I needed a roommate, and Jacks did, too, so Archie introduced us. While Jacks traveled for work, Logan subleased his room for a bit. We've all been friends since," Tanner says.

My eyes shift over to Lacey. She's looking at Tanner while he speaks, and for a split second, I think I see her eyes fill with tears. I wonder if she knows what brought me back here. There's no way, because if she did, then I would have seen her five years ago, *right*? Then again, she could know and maybe she really hates me that much. She quickly covers her eyes with her sunglasses and goes back to scrolling on her phone.

"We didn't know Lacey and Poppy knew Jacks until Poppy's graduation party last weekend. Funny how fate intervenes..." Tanner continues to explain the situation with a big grin on his face.

"Interesting," Gray says. "So, how did this never come up?" she asks hesitantly, her eyes jumping to Lacey and then back to me.

"I travel a lot for work. I've been out of the country for the past year off and on, so I had no way of knowing Poppy and Logan had started dating. Lacey, Poppy, and I knew each other a long time ago. The girls call me Jace and the guys call me Jacks."

"Oh, my god. So y'all thought he was two different people?"

"Yeah," Lacey says. She's still staring at her phone, pretending to avoid the conversation all together.

"I really should stop missing girls' night." Gray laughs. "So, what do you do for a living, Jacks?"

"I'm a photographer."

"What, no way. That's so cool."

I nod and take another sip of my beer. Lacey stands and walks past me like I'm not even there. I try to think of something to say, but nothing seems right. I know she doesn't want to talk to me, but maybe if I keep trying, she'll let me back in.

"Don't be modest, dude," Tanner starts. "Jacks is—"

"Just a photographer," I interrupt him. He throws me a look and then sips from his can, but he doesn't try to finish his sentence. My eyes settle back on Lacey who's filling her cup. The gold chain shimmers around her neck and it's confirmed. She's wearing exactly what I think she's wearing, but why? Before I can stop myself, and because I need an answer, I stand and move to where she's standing by the cooler.

"Can I help you?" she asks, taking a sip from her cup.

"I was just grabbing another drink."

She lets out a long sigh and goes to walk away.

"Wait," I beg, knowing I need to say something. Anything. She freezes, but doesn't turn around, so I continue. "I like your necklace."

She slowly turns and meets my gaze, giving me a quizzical look. Her hand finds the locket, and she rubs it between her fingers. "Thanks. It was a gift from my brother."

"Colton?" My heart deflates in an instant. She thinks Colton bought her the necklace?

"Yes, Jace. The one and only brother I have. I know you've

been gone a long time, but I didn't acquire any more siblings while you were away." She shakes her head and starts to walk back towards the others.

"Wait, I—" I start, but Gray interrupts me.

"Jace, will you take our picture?" she asks.

"Huh?" I look at her confused.

"Will you take our picture?" She hands me her cell phone. "Come on Lacey!"

Gray and Tanner move together on the back of the boat. Lacey squeezes in close to Tanner. Jealousy consumes me as I watch my roommate throw his arm around her.

"Wait, we want to get in it," Poppy yells. I hear a splash, and then before I know it, both she and Logan are in the boat and walking over to join the group. I'm used to being behind the camera. I usually prefer it, but seeing the five of them sit there like the cast of *Friends*, while I take the picture, totally blows.

"Say, summer," Poppy yells.

I click the camera button on Gray's phone. *Fuck, I definitely shouldn't have come.*

CHAPTER 5: NEVER TRUST A TEN YEAR OLD

JACE - 9 YEARS AGO

I'm not sure what I'm doing because Lacey made it very clear eight months ago she wants nothing to do with me anymore, but I can't help myself. I'm home for the first time in a year, and I want to talk to her and see if I can get to the bottom of what happened. More than anything, I want to see her. I want to wrap my arms around her and tell her how much she means to me. Convince her I love her and miss her so fucking much. I've played this potential conversation in my head over and over for months, and I think I have a plan.

I spent countless hours scouring the internet for the perfect gift and finally found it. A gold locket with two small birds sitting on the limb of a tree to symbolize us engraved on the front. It's perfect. I spent the better part of the past couple of days looking for the perfect photo to put inside and writing her a note.

My stomach fills with nerves. I feel like my future is riding on having this conversation, but she hasn't even agreed to talk to me yet. I shake the feeling. This is going to work. It has to work. I just have to give her the gift and then hope she shows up later tonight.

I place the small velvet box in the bottom of the bag and

do my best to top it with tissue paper like I've seen my mom do before. I slide the letter I wrote her down one side. Checking myself in the mirror one final time, I head out of my bedroom and down the stairs of my parents' house. It's early, but I know she has a busy day ahead of her, and I'm hoping to catch her before she leaves for her graduation ceremony.

"Where are you running off to?" my mom asks from the kitchen island. She's seated on a barstool, sipping her morning coffee and reading a book.

"Out. I'll be back in a bit."

"Not so fast. What are you holding?"

I quickly shove the purple gift bag behind my back, but it's useless because I know I've been caught.

"Come. Sit. Tell me why you're holding a present." She pats the barstool next to hers and the corners of her mouth tip into a small grin.

I stride over and set the gift down on the granite counter top and let out a deep breath before sitting down. "I got Lacey a graduation gift."

My mom hums over the lip of her coffee mug, her eyes urging me to continue.

"I'm hoping I can talk to her and it might break the ice. I saw it and immediately knew she had to have it." I play nervously with the handles of the bag.

"Whatever happened between you two?" she asks wistfully, grabbing the bag. She fixes the tissue paper for me and instantly makes the gift look ten times better.

I shake my head. "I wish I knew. I'm hoping once the dust settles after her graduation, then we can talk and sort things out."

"So, I take it you won't be joining us for the girls' graduation party later?"

"I'm not invited. The invitation was addressed to you and Dad. The RSVP card listed two people. They don't want me there."

My mom's hand finds my back and she rubs methodic circles. "I'm so sorry, honey. I know how much they mean to you." She wraps me in a huge bear hug. "I'm sure it's just a misunderstanding and you two just need to talk. Want me to see if you can come to the party? I can call Lori and ask."

"No, don't call Lori. I need to handle it, and I don't want to ruin her day." My eyes begin to sting with tears and I pull away abruptly before I completely lose it all together. "I'll be back in a bit." I grab the gift bag off the counter and head towards the door.

The minute I step outside, my eyes search the street for Lacey or Poppy. Being home and this close to the people who were once my best friends feels weird. I'm about to step off my parents' front porch when Poppy walks out of her house and stops dead in her tracks. I lift my hand and wave. She looks me up and down, but she remains expressionless. Her hand starts to rise and for an instant I think she may wave back, but she stops herself, shakes her head, and heads toward her car.

Lacey's house is directly next to mine. I make my way across our yards and up the concrete path leading to her front door. Taking a deep breath, I knock three times. No one answers. I lift my hand to try one more time and it swings open, revealing Lacey's little brother. His sandy blond hair is a mess and he's wearing a SpongeBob T-shirt, gym shorts, and gaming headphones.

"Can I help you?" he asks, drawing out the final word of his question.

"Hey, bud, is your sister home?"

"You know she hates you, right?" He laughs and then scowls. "But no, she's not here." *Damn.* I see he hasn't changed a bit since I left and he turned ten.

I glance over to the driveway where I see Lacey's car parked behind her dad's truck. "Colton, her car is here. Are you sure she isn't upstairs? It's really important I talk to her. I have something I need to give her."

"Yeah, I'm sure."

I let out a disappointed sigh. "Okay, well do you know when she'll be home?"

"Nope." His eyes shift down to the bag. "I can give it to her if you want."

"It's okay. I can bring it back another time." Before I can react, he grabs the bag from my hand. "Colton, it's important." I try to grab it back from him, but he takes a step deeper into the house.

"And I'll be sure she gets it."

"Colton," I scold. "This isn't funny."

"Don't worry. I'll give it to her."

"You promise?"

"Yep," he squeaks out and then slams the door in my face. *Fuck.* I guess I have no other choice but to trust a ten year old.

CHAPTER 6: DON'T
GET OLD. IT'S A BITCH
LACEY - PRESENT

"I made a pot of coffee," Poppy shouts from our kitchen as I hop around my room stuffing my leg into one half of my scrub bottoms. "Want me to pour you a cup?"

"You know I can't stand the stuff; it's too bitter," I yell back.

Or rather drinking it makes me feel bitter.

I grab my name badge off my dresser and clip it to my top. I pull my hair into a high ponytail as I walk out of my bedroom. "Have you seen my sneakers?"

"How you find anything in your room is a miracle." Poppy laughs, turning to look at me. "They're by the door."

"Organized chaos, remember?" I fill a tea kettle with water and place it on the stove. I walk over, grab my mint and lilac Hokas, and lace them up.

"So, are we going to talk about the boat?" She sits down at the table and checks her watch. "You don't have to leave for thirty minutes."

"Remind me why you're awake again?"

"My mom and I have our spa day today." She smiles over the rim of her coffee mug.

"That's right. A spa day sounds so nice." I finish putting on my shoes and walk into the kitchen to begin packing my lunch. "How was Logan's yesterday?"

"So good. He surprised me with a date to the botanical gardens and then dinner at this super good restaurant downtown."

"That sounds like fun. It's weird how little I see you now. What time did you get in last night?"

"It wasn't too late. Maybe around eleven. I tried to come to talk to you, but it sounded like you were already asleep."

"I think I fell asleep at eight. Which restaurant did y'all eat at?"

"A place called Del Bar, but oh my goodness stop distracting me. We need to talk about the boat and Jace."

"The boat was fun. We should do it again," I say, knowing it's not what she wants to talk about, but I don't have the energy to talk about him today. I don't want to think about his infuriating smile or how his ab muscles formed a perfect v-shape that disappeared below the waistband of his swimsuit. That's what I did yesterday while I nursed my hangover from said boat, but now it's time to go to work.

"Lacey…" The tea kettle starts to scream, and I grab a thermos from the cabinet. I continue to ignore her as I walk through my ritual of crafting the perfect London Fog.

"You know, *eventually*, we're going to have to figure this out. I don't want him around either, but by some weird twist of fate I fell in love with Logan, and Jace is one of his best friends. I'm afraid we're going to have to learn to tolerate one another."

"I mean, do we? Maybe we could ignore that he exists. I'm sure he'll be gone for work again soon anyway."

"I don't know. The guys made it seem like he's home for at least the summer. I mean, Logan's mad, but Tanner still doesn't know what happened, and he's starting to ask questions."

"I told Tanner on Saturday he can ask Jace what he did. I'm not going to ask them to stop being friends with him, but just because they are doesn't mean I have to be. If they want to be friends with someone like him, that's on them."

"I get that, but I think he's going to keep showing up. You know I love you and I'll never forgive him for treating you the way he did, but I think we really need to figure this out. There are going to be times where you, him, and I will all be present."

"Okay, but can we figure it out when we have more time? I need to get gas on the way to work."

She offers me an understanding smile, stands and walks over to the fridge whiteboard and writes *TALK ABOUT JACE!* in big letters.

Noted.

———

"Ms. Clara, it's Lacey. You ready for occupational therapy?" I knock on the door of room 307.

"Come in, dear," she hollers from the other side of the door.

I walk into the small apartment. Framed pictures of Ms. Clara's grandchildren cover the walls above a worn plaid covered couch. I spy her sitting on the edge of her bed, wearing a hot pink mumu covered in different colored hearts. The covers are bunched up, the fitted sheet barely hanging on to the mattress. Her short, white curls are flattened on one side. She's taking her medications from a tiny white cup while one of the nurses stands over her watching. She turns her head and smiles.

"Oh good, you're here. Please tell Marie I don't need to take all of these damn pills."

I slap on the biggest customer service smile I can muster. "Now, Ms. Clara, you know those help you to feel good."

"Girls, don't get old," she deadpans. "It's a bitch."

Marie takes the white cup and gives me a look that tells me my favorite resident is definitely in one of her moods this morning before moving past me and onto the next patient.

I walk over, grab her walker, and place it in front of her. Then I search the space for her shoes. "Did you have a good weekend?" I ask.

"It was the same as it always is." She laughs. "Ethel and I played bridge. She cheated and I lost."

I help her put on her shoes and assist her when she stands. We both walk toward the bathroom. "I thought Wren told me y'all were having some type of luau party? Did you go?"

She scoffs. "Honey, it was a party full of old people. I have better things to do than be reminded about how old I am. You tell Wren we ladies have been talking, and we think some young eye candy would help liven the place up a bit. I'm sure she could organize a show or something." She winks at me and then moves her walker into the tiny bathroom.

I swallow down a laugh.

With my help, Ms. Clara moves through her morning routine. Once we're finished, I assist her in moving to her favorite chair.

"Would you mind handing me my book before you leave?" She points across the room to a well-loved paperback sitting on her bedside table. A Fabio-looking man in an unbuttoned shirt and a kilt is on the cover. His shoulder length hair is blowing in the wind. *Go, Ms. Clara.* I hand it to her without a word.

"Thank you, dear. Us old ladies gotta get some somehow."

I turn and head toward the door trying to keep my face neutral. "I'll see you tomorrow."

The Tortured Therapists Department

307 has requested a Magic Mike strip tease at the next party!

WREN:

Noted.

GRAY:

CHAPTER 7: WE HATE JACE FOR NO FUCKING REASON CLUB

JACE

"Hey, Dad," I say, walking toward where he stands, unloading a backpack from the trunk of his car.

"Hey, kid." He wraps me up in a big hug and kisses my cheek. "Ready to hike?"

"Yeah." Bending down, I tug on the laces of my hiking boots, making them a little tighter. "You've been here before?" He nods, and I look around to see a dozen groups of people spread around the parking lot. Most of the groups are young couples. Some of the men have toddlers on their shoulders. A few even brought their dogs.

There's a tug at my heart, but I ignore it.

"Is it usually this busy on a weekday?"

"Hawk Landing is popular, but it seems everyone had the same idea we had today." He chuckles. "It's a pretty day for a hike with your old man."

"Definitely." I stand to meet him.

"What's on your mind?" he asks. "You seem a bit distracted."

"Work."

"Miss it that much?" His voice is low as we begin to walk

toward the trailhead. It's no secret he wishes I would settle down and stay closer to home.

"I do, but I also think it's been nice being home and around people I know."

My dad laughs. "I thought you liked being alone all the time."

"Very funny." We move over to the right to let a man and his dog coming from the other direction pass by us. The golden retriever lunges in my direction, throwing itself on the ground and rolling to expose its belly. I bend down with a laugh and give it a few good scratches before the owner tugs him away.

"Before I forget to mention it, Joe called yesterday."

"Oh, yeah? What's he up to?"

"He needs help tearing down an old barn. Apparently, he reached out to Archie, but he's not giving him a firm answer. You think you could drive up there and help him with it?"

"When?" I ask through gritted teeth. Joe is my dad's older brother and the family nut. After his divorce, he moved to South Carolina and lives in the middle of nowhere. I'm pretty sure he spends most of his time preparing for the zombie apocalypse or searching for UFOs. Archie is his only son, and while we were always close, he and his dad don't get along.

"He seemed flexible. Just give him a call. It would mean a lot to me. I'd help, but this sounds like a young man's job."

"Of course."

"Thank you. So, what else is new with you, kid?"

"Not a whole lot. Enjoying the break from work and being home. Actually, do you remember Lacey Sims?"

"Remember her? You two were inseparable. It's hard to forget the kid who practically lived at your house for nearly two decades." He shakes his head.

"Yeah, so anyway. You remember my friend Logan, right?"

"Is he the one with glasses or the one with the hair that's too long?"

"The glasses." He nods. "He's dating Poppy Collins, so I ran into her and Lacey a little over a week ago."

"I see the girls and their parents from time to time, but you know it was never the same once your mom passed and I moved. She was the glue that held us all together."

"I didn't realize you had seen her."

He's quiet for a moment.

"Dad? When did you see Lacey and Poppy?"

"Oh, you know, around. It's not a very big town, Jace." I wonder why he's just now mentioning this to me. I mean, I've never asked, but you would think if he ran into them he would have brought it up when I visited or called. Then again, the few times my parents tried to talk to me about her, I told them I didn't want to. It was too painful, and I couldn't bear hearing how happy she was when I felt so miserable.

"Were they happy to see you?" He smiles, causing the corners of his eyes to crease.

"Well, not exactly." I shake my head and take a deep breath. "Actually, they both seem to still want nothing to do with me." I chuckle, stepping over a large root in the ground.

"I never understood what happened between you three. You know, your mom always thought you and Lacey would end up together even after all that mess. She used to go on and on about how some people were just destined to be together."

My heart clenches. A distant memory of my mom reminding me everyone has a soulmate and Lacey was mine plays in my head. I shake it away.

"Any chance she has something to do with all the thoughts about work and the future this morning?" he asks.

"I don't know. I mean, no. Of course she doesn't. We were together a long time ago." Her green eyes flash in my mind, and I quickly try to push them away. "I feel like I've worked so hard to reach my goal and I did it. I guess it has me thinking, what now? I love being a photojournalist, but I'm tired of not sleeping in my bed every night. You know?"

"You've been running for a while. I wondered when you'd get tired."

"Running?" I duck under a low limb and continue down the path. "What's that supposed to mean?"

"When you told your mom and me you were going to pursue environmental biology and photography at Georgetown, I was incredibly proud of you. We both were, but your mom always wondered—and I guess I did, too—if you pursued it so you didn't have to come back and face reality here. So you didn't have to face Lacey."

"No, I pursued Georgetown because it was a phenomenal opportunity, and without it I wouldn't have been as successful as I've been with my career in the last six years." My gut tightens as the half lie slips out so easily. While Georgetown was a phenomenal opportunity, I decided to pursue it the night of Lacey's graduation party.

"And then we lost your mom five years ago," his says, voice cracking. "And even though you have the apartment, you never come home."

"That's not true," I snap. "I'm home now, aren't I?"

My dad stops walking. "I'm not trying to fight with you. That's not what I'm saying. It feels like you could have gone to school anywhere. You could have chosen to photograph anything, and yet you chose to photograph birds in the middle of the Amazon."

"Those birds aren't just any birds."

"I know, and I'm very proud of you. You were the one who said you were tired. I know you love your job. I have accepted that I only get to see you once in a blue moon, but maybe you're feeling tired because it's time for something different. It's okay to not want to do what you've been doing. It's okay to want a change."

The problem is my dad isn't wrong. I have spent the last ten years avoiding this place. After my mom died, I tried to come home more for my dad's sake, but even those visits were few and far between. Too much pain and heartbreak woven into every corner.

"I've made you mad and it wasn't my intention," he says.

"No, I'm sorry. I don't know what I want these days. I love my job, but it's becoming apparent I'll never have that"—I gesture toward a man and woman holding hands and walking ahead of us—"if I decide to continue."

"And that's something you want?"

"With the right person, yes. And before you say something, I don't mean Lacey."

He smiles and lets out a chuckle.

"Maybe do some research. You're good at that. See what jobs are out there. You might be surprised by what you find."

"I don't want you to get your hopes up. There might be nothing."

"I know. Selfishly, I love that you're even considering being home more, but as your dad, I know I can't make you stay. Trust yourself. If it's meant to be, it'll be." He pats me across the shoulders.

We continue along the trail for a while longer in silence. The trees are lush with green summer leaves. It's warm today despite the time and tree cover. Birds chirp and water rushes in the distance. I pause occasionally to take photos of some of the flora and fauna. We pass over small creeks and rocky paths. It's not a super difficult hike, but a moderate one. The ground is covered with enough roots you have to pay attention to where you're stepping.

"Do you think you'll ever settle down again?" I ask.

"Me? I don't know. Your mom was the center of my universe. I don't know if I ever could. I'd feel like I was cheating."

"She'd want you to be happy," I say.

"She'd want you to be happy too." My chest tightens, and I run my hand over the tattoo on my left forearm. It's hard to be happy when the one person who made you the happiest you've ever been wants nothing to do with you.

"I was thinking about going to stop by the cemetery when we're done here. You want to come?" he asks, his eyes full of hope that I might actually take him up on his offer.

"Oh, man, I would, but I have plans. Let's do it another day?"

"Yeah, okay. Another day." His face falls into a frown, and guilt consumes me.

———

"We'll have a beer tower, a large cheese pizza with extra cheese, and an extra large Bruno's special," Tanner orders for our table. The waitress smiles, grabs our menus, and walks away towards another table.

"Would you look at her ass?" Tanner says, slapping my arm with the back of his hand and biting down on his knuckle. He leans back, keeping his eye on our waitress's swaying hips, almost flipping his chair.

"I see you haven't changed a bit since I've been gone."

"Not in the slightest," Enzo adds.

"So, how long are you hanging around for this time, Jacks?" Donovan asks.

"I'm not sure."

The waitress places the beer tower and four glasses in the center of the table. It's ninety-six ounces of amber liquid, and it looks fucking obnoxious.

"Thanks, beautiful," Tanner says with a wink.

She rolls her eyes and walks away.

"Down boy," Enzo quips. He grabs the glasses and starts to fill each one to the brim, passing one to each of us as he finishes.

"You suddenly wouldn't be unsure because of Lacey, would you?" Tanner asks.

"No. What would she have to do with anything?"

"Someone's defensive." Donovan laughs.

"No. It's just she made her decision ten years ago, my plans don't have anything to do with her. If you must know, I'm considering jobs near or around Atlanta."

"I thought you loved your job?" Tanner finishes his beer and begins to fill his glass again.

"I do, but I'm all my dad has. He's getting older, and I can't be here for him if I'm in the middle of the Amazon rainforest or the Sahara desert." Thoughts about my mom flood my brain and I try to shake them away, but it's no use. I swallow down the guilt that follows.

The waitress returns with two large pies and places them in front of us.

Tanner grabs a slice and impulsively stuffs it into his mouth, "Oh, fuck, fuck, fu—" He spits the bite of pizza onto his plate. "Fuck, that's hot as shit." He grabs his beer and finishes it in three large gulps. "Shit, I think I burnt the roof of my mouth off."

"It's hot," the waitress deadpans before walking away again. Donovan, Enzo, and I burst out laughing. Tanner scowls.

I take a swig of my beer and place a slice piled high with sausage, bacon, pepperoni, and pickled jalapenos on my plate.

"So, what would you do instead?" Tanner asks, after he recovers.

"I actually found a cool one this afternoon. The Center for North American Wildlife Conservation is in Atlanta. They're looking for a director of photojournalism."

"You? In an office? Having to interact with people? On a daily basis?" Tanner gasps dramatically.

"I'm not a complete loner. I put up with you three and Logan, don't I?"

"Speaking of. Where is Logan tonight? Too in love to leave Poppy for one evening?" Donovan asks, grabbing a slice of pizza.

"Not sure. He said he couldn't make it," Tanner says. He glances in my direction and by the look on his face I can tell he's probably thinking the same thing I am.

I take a long sip of my beer, trying to hide how his absence makes me feel. Logan is one of my best friends, and while I'm happy for him and Poppy, it feels pretty shitty that he's barely spoken to me since I got back. I don't know what the girls told him, but given he's dating the vice president of the *We Hate Jace For No Fucking Reason Club*, it's clear he's probably joined the club too.

"For the record, you're gone so often that I'd say you barely have to put up with us," Tanner jabs, changing the subject. I offer him a thankful smile.

"Yeah, I thought the big perk of your job was you getting to be alone in the woods. You really want to give that up?" Donovan asks.

"What exactly do you think I do for a living?" I chuckle. "I'm not hiking into the middle of the Amazon alone. I like adventure, but I'm not an idiot."

"I'm just saying the Amazon rainforest and an office in Atlanta are two very different places," Donovan explains.

"I'd still get to do the parts of my job I enjoy, but it would be on a smaller scale."

"Interesting," Enzo says. He squints his eyes in my direction like he's studying me and it makes me feel a little uneasy.

"What? You don't think I'm capable of a job like that?" I laugh.

"No, that's not what we're saying. You're the smartest guy we know, and after the last year you've had, they would be lucky to have you. Just want to make sure it's what you truly want," Donovan says.

"How's the wedding planning coming?" I ask, suddenly tired of everyone's attention being on me.

"It's going to be magical." Donovan grabs Enzo's hand and looks lovingly at his fiancé.

"Who's shooting it?"

"Forever Yours Photography. We had asked Logan and T about you doing it, but we were unsure when you'd be back."

"You don't want me shooting your wedding." I take a swig of my beer. "I can photograph elusive wildlife all day, but people…y'all know that's not my thing."

"That's what I said," Tanner agrees, slapping me across the back.

"I'm happy to be a guest."

"So, if you do apply for this job, does that mean you would be looking for a more permanent place than y'all's bachelor pad?" Donovan asks.

"Always working aren't you." I laugh.

"Hey, I'm just saying if you take a job in Atlanta, you might want a house, and if you do, I'm your guy," Donovan chuckles.

"You will be the first realtor I call." I take another bite of pizza. "Don't hold your breath though. I said I was considering it. I haven't applied for anything yet."

CHAPTER 8: IS THIS HELL?
LACEY

The Tortured Therapists Department

I was thinking we should start having dinner
together once a month.

WREN:

Isn't that what we already do with the rest of
the team?

No, this would be different. Like just us five.

CHLOE:

Sounds like fun. When do y'all want to do it?
I'll have to see if someone can watch Ava.

You could bring her.

CHLOE:

Thank you, but I could use a girls' night. I'm
sure my mom can help.

POPPY:

Should we invite significant others too? I'd
love for y'all to meet Logan.

WREN:

I'm very single, but if Logan has any cute friends, I'm not opposed to them coming.

GRAY:

LOL! I think everyone is single but you, Poppy. But YESSSS to cute friends!

POPPY:

Great, I'll tell Logan. You good with that Lace?

Sure.

POPPY:

Awesome! Is this Sunday too soon?

GRAY:

I'm in! I work at the hospital until 3, but should be good to meet up with y'all after.

POPPY:

Cool! Logan said he can host and Tanner can cook.

GRAY:

Are we sure we want Tanner to cook? Does he know how? LOL!

WREN:

Like THE Tanner, Lacey?

GRAY:

Wait, you know about Tanner? Was I seriously the last one to know they slept together?

WREN:

That's what happens when you work all the time.

GRAY:

POPPY:

Apparently he's the best cook out of all the
guys.

CHLOE:

I can do Sunday. Let me know what I can
bring.

———

The summer sun beats down on my body, causing a drip of sweat to run down the center of my cleavage. I dip my hand into the cool pool water and splash it onto my skin.

Man, this summer is going to be really fucking hot.

"Come in the pool and hang out with me," I say. I sit up on the unicorn shaped float I'm lying on and take off my black, bug-eye sunglasses to look over at my best friend. "Tell Logan you'll text him later. It's Saturday and I barely see you anymore. We have the apartment pool all to ourselves. Who knows when this will happen again!"

Poppy stands and walks over to the edge. She sits so her feet hang in the water. Her phone is still in her hand.

"So…" She winces. "Tanner invited Jace to the dinner thing tomorrow at Logan's."

"Of course he did." I pull my sunglasses back over my eyes and fall back onto the float. "What did I do to deserve this? Who in the universe must you fuck so your ex doesn't come waltzing back into your life claiming to be best friends with your best friend's boyfriend and the last guy you slept with?"

Poppy laughs. "It's definitely a mess."

"It's more than a mess. I mean, is this punishment for something I did? Did we die? Is this hell?"

"Stop it, Lacey." She kicks her feet, splashing cold water against my skin.

"I knew this would happen. I just wanted it to be the girls.

I've waited so long for you to be out of your study hole and finally get to hang out with me, Gray, Wren, and Chloe. Now it's turning into a whole thing."

"I'm sorry. That was my bad. I got excited and brought the guys into it without thinking."

"No, that's not what I meant. You asked and I agreed. I wish he wasn't their friend."

"Me too. It would make things easier," she says. I sit back up and put my feet back in the water.

"I'd be totally cool with the girls from work and Logan's friends turning into some fun little found family, but selfishly, I don't want Jace to be a part of it."

Her eyes find mine and she clears her throat. "He *was* our found family once."

"Please, don't go there," I say. "He hurt me so badly. I just wanted him to love me, and while D.C. was the final straw, he'd been pulling away for months. He promised long distance would work and then he shattered his promise and my heart. That's not how you treat people you claim to love."

"I know babe."

"I don't understand why this is so hard for me. It's been ten years. He shouldn't affect me the way he does. I shouldn't care."

"I get it. Beau was absolutely awful to me, and I let his words control my life for years. You were in love with Jace, and he broke your heart. You have a right to feel any way you're feeling, but I think you are going to have to deal with those feelings sooner rather than later."

I close my eyes and breathe in the warm summer air. I know she's right, but it doesn't feel fair.

"You're not even a little bit interested in talking to him and hearing what he has to say?" she asks.

"Are you?"

"I mean, well, I don't know. I've known him since I was seven, and then all of a sudden he was gone. And, babe, I know what he did was awful, but it was ten years ago. Maybe he's changed."

Has he though? Do people really change? I thought for sure seeing him again wouldn't make me react this way. I thought I had moved on a long time ago, grown up, and forgotten about him and what he did. But then he showed back up, and it was apparent my feelings hadn't changed at all. Why would he be any different?

"Lacey."

"Yeah?"

"You're in your head about this. I'm not suggesting you date him again. I'm not even suggesting we should be friends with him again, but I'm wondering if maybe we can find a way to tolerate each other for the sake of everyone in this 'fun little found family.'"

"Are you mocking me?" I let out a pathetic attempt at a laugh.

"No, but it seems like maybe we should have matured enough in the last ten years to have a conversation with him. I mean, Logan missed boys' night Thursday."

I shake my head. "I didn't ask him to skip out on things because of me. Please don't put that on me. Logan can do whatever he wants. If he didn't go to boys' night, that's on him."

"You're right, but hearing about what Jace did to you brought up a lot of the shit he dealt with with his dad. He just ended their toxic relationship and it's still really fresh. You didn't ask him not to go, but you did ask us not to tell Tanner."

I jump in the water and disappear under the surface until my feet hit the rough concrete at the bottom of the deep end. My heart echoes off the walls of the pool. The last thing I want is to have to rehash what happened a decade ago. With one foot, I catapult myself back up to the surface like one of those synchronized swimmers. My head shoots up above the water and Poppy is staring at me, annoyed.

"Nice. Please continue to run from your problems."

"Technically, I was drowning my troubles away." I smirk.

"We have to figure this out. I've given you space, but it's time. Logan and I are getting caught in the middle, and it sucks."

I make my way over to the edge of the pool and climb out using the ladder. I grab my towel, wrap it around my body, and drop into a chair. "That's not my intention," I say.

She turns to face me and rests her arms on the concrete lip of the pool. "I know it's not, but we can't keep this up. Whether we like it or not, he's back."

"Okay. Fine. I'm leaving for Orlando on Tuesday, but when I get back I'll handle it."

"Good. And what do you want to do about this dinner tomorrow?"

Her phone pings. She grabs it, looks down at the screen, and then back up at me. "If you don't want to go, you don't have to. You just need to let everyone know."

"Are you going?"

"Yeah. I want to get to know the girls better."

I think about this for a minute. I'm not going to miss out on dinner with my friends because Jace got invited. I mean, I planned it. It was my idea. All the girls from work are coming, so there will be plenty of people to talk to. Donovan and Enzo will be there too. The boat went fine and there were a lot less people. *It will be fine.*

"Okay, then I'll go too. We can all coexist at dinner tomorrow night."

"You sure?"

"Yes, I promise to behave," I say, the corner of my mouth tipping into a grin.

CHAPTER 9: PEPLUM TOPS AND GLADIATOR SANDALS
LACEY - ELEVEN YEARS AGO

I'm standing in front of my closet trying to decide what to wear. Beau's annual end of summer bonfire is tonight. I'm nervous as hell and want it to go perfectly. My crush will be there, and I plan on telling him I like him. That is, if I can muster up enough courage to admit my feelings.

I haven't told anyone yet, not even Poppy. Mainly because the realization absolutely freaks me out. It's just not any guy —it's our best friend. I don't know when it happened or why it happened, but it did.

Poppy walks in wearing a floral-print dress, a pink statement necklace, and lace wedges. Her dark brown hair is in the perfect sock bun.

"Hey, babe, you look hot," I say as she wraps me in a hug.

"Thanks," she says, letting go and doing a little twirl. "Why aren't you dressed yet?" She plops down on my bed.

I breathe out. "Nothing seems good enough." I move the clothes around in my closet.

"Why? It's just the bonfire. We go every year."

"We're about to be juniors and I don't have a boyfriend.

The whole school will be there. I can't show up looking lame."

"Since when do you want a boyfriend?"

Since I figured out I want Jace Jackson.

"I don't know, but it doesn't matter. What matters is I have nothing to wear."

"You literally have triple the clothes I have. Anything you wear will be fine." I'm not sure she's right. I'm full of nerves. I know I need to tell him and her, but what if I mess everything up? The three of us are a trio—a packaged deal.

Grabbing both of my options, I flip around so she can see them. "Should I wear this peplum top with the aqua bubble necklace or this lace top with the white bubble necklace?" I ask, trying to distract myself.

"Definitely the peplum top," she says. "What shoes were you thinking?"

"My gladiator sandals?"

"Perfect," she squeaks. "Jace said he could drive, so he should be over soon." She looks down at the Michael Kors watch Beau gave her for her birthday. My stomach fills with butterflies at the thought of Jace. I fight the urge to tell Poppy about my plan and quickly get dressed.

"Girls, Jace is here," my dad yells from downstairs.

"One second," I call back, running my straightener through my hair one more time before unplugging it. I pause in front of my floor-length mirror. Poppy joins me, and we pose for a quick mirror selfie before heading downstairs to where Jace and my dad stand by the front door.

Jace looks so good tonight. He's in a pair of dark jeans, white sneakers, and a T-shirt that reads, "Well, This is Hawkward." I laugh to myself when I read his shirt. His short dark hair is styled perfectly. As we step off the last step, he brings his camera to his eye and captures a picture of the two of us.

"Y'all ready to go?" he asks.

"Yep," Poppy says, walking by him and out of the house.

His ocean blue eyes find mine and his face erupts into a big smile, making my heart start to beat faster.

"You look beautiful, Pixie," he says.

"Thanks." I feel my cheeks heat. "I like your shirt."

"You might be the only one." Embarrassment laces his words.

"It's because no one else is as fun as us." He smiles, and I want to melt right there on the entryway floor.

"Alright, Jace, have the girls home no later than midnight," my dad lectures. "And no drinking and driving."

"You got it, Mr. Sims."

"Bye, Dad."

We walk out the door, and when we make it to his Jeep, Poppy is already riding shotgun. I climb into the back and he cranks the engine. The ride to Beau's isn't very long, and Macklemore blares through the speakers. The wind rips through the vehicle as we drive down a back road. I can't stop fidgeting, and my palms are so sweaty. *Shit, I need to calm down.*

He turns onto a driveway lined with cars and parks. Poppy jumps down and yells something about finding Beau. Jace swings my door open and helps me out of the Jeep.

"Want to take a walk?" he asks.

"A walk? You don't want to go to the party?"

"You know this isn't my thing. I can't stand Beau or his friends. I don't know what Poppy sees in him."

"She always sees the best in people and thinks they can change. I tried telling her he's still the same asshole he was when we were kids, but she swears he's different now."

"I don't trust him," he says.

"I don't either, but I trust her."

I follow him around the front of the house. Beau's family owns a bunch of property perfect for a bonfire. They don't have neighbors, so we can essentially do whatever we want out here and no one will ever know, especially since Beau's parents are never home. The house is enormous—a giant monument erected in the middle of a perfectly manicured lawn, reminding everyone of how much money they have. In their front yard, a huge oak tree sits next to a small pond.

"Let's swing," I say, taking off toward the wooden swing hanging from one of its limbs.

"Wait up," he yells.

I sit down on the swing and feel him walk up behind me. I consider telling him how I'm feeling, but then he puts his hands on my back and begins to push me gently. My brain scrambles and my breath hitches with his touch.

"I can't believe school is already starting back next week. I'm so not looking forward to having Ms. Norris for home-room. I think she actually takes it seriously," I spit out.

He doesn't respond, and I feel myself begin to still. His hands are no longer on my back, and when I look over my shoulder he's backing away from me.

"You okay?" I ask.

"Did you know you're my favorite person?" he asks softly, looking into my eyes. He moves to the tree and sits with his back against the trunk.

"You're one of my favorite people, too, J," I say, jumping down and walking towards him. "What made you tell me that?"

"I've just been thinking a lot lately. You're the only person I can be myself around. You don't mind when I go quiet."

"Yeah because sometimes I need the quiet too." I sit down next to him and give him a little nudge with my elbow. On the outside, I'm trying to stay cool, calm, and collected, but on the inside, butterflies are swarming my stomach and my heart rate is beginning to pick up its pace.

"I know you do. I guess what I'm trying to say is. Damn, I'm more—" he cuts himself off.

"You're freaking me out. What is it?" I ask. He grabs both of my hands and looks me deep in my eyes. The light of the sun is barely visible above the horizon. The faint glow of lightning bugs is beginning to show in the distance. It's only him and me. Poppy and the rest of the party are in the backyard, nowhere nearby. I squeeze his hands, encouraging him to continue.

"Lacey, you're my best friend in the entire world. I'm about to start my senior year, and I don't know where life will bring me after that, and when I look back on high school, I don't want to have any regrets."

"Okay." I try to remain calm, but I'm pretty sure the butterflies in my stomach are doing a full out acrobatic routine.

"And I guess I wanted to tell you that you mean more to me than anyone else ever has, and I think I've known for a really long time that I love you."

"I know you love me," I joke.

"No, I don't love you like I love Poppy. I love you like if I have to wait another minute to tell you how I really feel my heart might burst out of my chest. I love you like you are the one person in the world I was meant to be with." Words keep pouring out of his mouth, and I'm frozen. He looks at me like I'm the only girl he's ever seen, and my heart is beating so rapidly, I think it might burst. "And I know we're best friends, but isn't that what people say? That you should be friends first. And, well, I've known you my whole life and I want to give us a shot. I want to see if we could be more than friends because I love you." He's smiling now. "Gosh, I'm sorry I keep saying it, but it's true and I've just waited so long to tell you and—"

"Hey, Jace?"

"Yeah?"

"Will you kiss me?"

"You sure?"

"I've never been more sure about anything in my life."

He pulls me onto his lap so we're facing one another. He

moves a strand of loose hair behind my ear and then cups both of my cheeks with his hands. Our lips find each other in an instant.

Kissing Jace Jackson is everything I dreamed it would be and more. It's the type of kiss you read about in fairytales. It's my past, present, and future, and I know the minute it happens nothing will ever compare.

CHAPTER 10: DRINK UP, BUTTERCUP
JACE - PRESENT

Lacey walked into Logan's place thirty minutes ago, and I haven't been able to stop myself from staring. She's wearing a short black skirt and a cropped white T-shirt that has the word "chaotic" in small black font across the front. She's still wearing the locket, and it's taking everything in me to not confront her about it. She looks fucking gorgeous, and I'm quickly realizing if she ever gave me a second chance, I would take it in a heartbeat.

I pull my camera up to my eye and the flash goes off, brightening up Logan's living room and catching the attention of the emerald-eyed beauty sitting across the room from me. The redhead she walked in with says something and Lacey's laugh fills the apartment. It's everything I remember it being and more.

"Stop staring at her," Enzo says, walking over and sitting to my right. I offer him a small smile. "What happened between you two?"

"That's a great fucking question."

He shakes his head. "You really don't know?"

I take a deep breath. "Not really. I was eighteen and Lacey was seventeen. I had just moved to D.C. for a year to start The

Young Photographers Program, and the next thing I knew, it was all over. Lacey ended it, and then both girls blocked my number. Blocked me on all their socials. It was clear they wanted me out of their lives. I tried once to see her and it was an epic fail." My eyes find the necklace again, and I watch as she slides the locket up and down the chain. "Anyway, I got into school and then I stopped coming home. Stopped trying to contact her."

"Really? I mean I've only hung out with them a few times, but the blonde seems like she takes no prisoners. She terrifies me a bit if I'm honest. How do you not know what happened?"

Lacey lets out another melodic laugh and takes a sip from her gin and tonic. My heart deflates. Growing up, Lacey never backed down from anything. She was the fearless one of our group. Always encouraging Poppy and me to follow our dreams and take chances. The only thing I've ever known her not to fight for was *me*.

"Get it while it's hot," Tanner calls from the door, walking in from the balcony with a tray of burgers and hot dogs fresh off the grill and interrupting our conversation.

I shrug my shoulders. "Took me by surprise too. Let's eat, shall we." We both stand and walk towards the kitchen.

A line has already formed, and everyone is taking turns filling their plates. Lacey walks past me, her scent immediately taking over the air. She smells like summer—coconut mixed with tropical flowers. It's intoxicating.

"You're up man," Enzo says behind me, breaking me from my trance.

I take two large steps forward to close the gap and fill my plate with a burger and fries. I grab another beer from the fridge and head out of the kitchen. My eyes shift to the living room, and I quickly realize there is nowhere else to sit. There's one seat left and it's next to Lacey. I freeze. My eyes find hers, and for a minute, I half-expect her to tell me to fuck off.

"Want to sit with us?" She giggles, taking a large sip from her gin and tonic.

It's clear she's tipsy, but she's offering for me to sit next to her and I'm going to take it as a win. I eat mostly in silence. The conversation mostly centers around Donovan and Enzo's upcoming wedding in July.

I consider trying to talk to her. Maybe offering to go on a walk or go sit on the balcony to see if we can put whatever she has against me behind us, but then she stands to make another drink. She stumbles, reminding me she's been drinking and tonight isn't the right time.

I want to talk to her, but alcohol shouldn't be involved. I catch her waist with my arm and accidentally push up her tiny shirt, so my forearm connects with the bare skin right under her bra. Our eyes meet and her breath catches. I slowly let my fingertips graze the soft skin of her abdomen as I release her and she stands.

"You good, Pixie?"

"Fine," she says. "I thought I told you to stop calling me that."

"Right, sorry." I watch as she turns and heads back into the kitchen. She methodically walks through the steps of making her cocktail, and when she's done, she walks out and announces loudly, "Who's ready for a game?"

I stand and start collecting empty plates from everyone around the apartment.

"What did you have in mind, Lace?" Poppy asks, handing me her plate.

"Never have I ever," she says, walking into the living room and plopping down on the couch next to Tanner. "Come on, it'll be fun and we can all get to know each other a little better."

Everyone agrees. "Great," she says, her whole face

lighting up with a wide grin. "Does everyone have a drink? Because you have to drink every time you've done the thing. Who wants to go first?"

Tanner raises his hand.

"Let's hear it, T," Logan says.

"Never have I ever kissed a dude." All the girls, Enzo, and Donovan take a sip.

"Alright," Enzo says. "Never have I ever gotten a tattoo."

I take a sip and so do a few other people in the room.

After a few more rounds, Gray, the girl I met on the boat, says, "Okay, it's my turn. Never have I ever slept with a guy in this room." Donovan and Enzo groan and take another swig of their beers. Poppy and Lacey clink their glasses together and tip them back.

The blood drains from my face and the room begins to spin. Lacey and I took it pretty far when we were younger, but never all the way. We had always talked about being each other's first, but we never did. *Who the fuck did she sleep with?* My eyes dart around the room and land on her sitting next to Tanner. Her eyes are wide, and her cheeks are tinted red.

"We never slept together," I announce before I can stop myself.

"Yes, Jace, I'm very aware. Thank you for clarifying that for the group," she deadpans. Her eyes shift around the room. "Is it my turn?" she asks. The room is painfully silent, and everyone is staring at the two of us.

"So then why did you drink?"

"Huh?"

"Why did you drink?" I repeat my question because I can't help myself.

"It's none of your business, Jace," she says.

Gray mouths "Sorry" in her direction, and everyone is giving each other looks like they know something I don't.

"You know what? This was fun, but I gotta head out. Early

day tomorrow at the office," Tanner says, shifting in his seat and pushing up from his thighs to stand.

"You're kidding me?" I say, putting the puzzle pieces together. "You slept with my roommate?" My eyes dart to Lacey and then back to Tanner.

He meets me eye to eye. "Bro, before you get mad," he starts, "I didn't know she was *the* Lacey. It's a popular name."

My brain tries to process this information and it can't. Lacey and Tanner. Tanner and Lacey. *Is this why they didn't want me on the boat?*

Tanner shrugs his shoulders and offers me a grin. "We're good, right?" He throws his hand in the air like I would actually give him a high five for sleeping with my ex.

"Unfuckingbelievable. You can't be serious. Did everyone know except for me?" I scan the room, and by the looks on everyone's faces, it's apparent they all knew. I shake my head.

"Oh get a grip, Jace," Lacey snaps. "You have no right to be mad at either one of us."

"Yes, I do. He's supposed to be my best friend and you're..." I pause because I know I shouldn't finish that sentence in front of everyone we know. "Well, you're you."

She scoffs. "Just because we dated when we were kids doesn't mean you own me. I can sleep with whoever I want." She takes another large sip of her drink.

I stand there, stunned. Tanner looks down at Lacey and back to me. "Okay, well, like I said, I gotta head out. This was fun. We should do it again," he says, moving towards the door.

"But he's my best friend." My voice comes out more defeated than I intend. "I mean, fuck, Lacey. How's that supposed to make me feel?"

I can feel the eyes of everyone in the room on me. She crosses her arms.

"Oh, my apologies for not thinking about your feelings when I slept with Tanner. It must really hurt to know I could move on like you never existed. I wouldn't have any idea what that feels like." Her voice cracks and she swallows hard. The hurt I saw behind her eyes the day on the boat returns.

"What are you talking about?"

"Oh, please, cut the act and just own up to all the shit you put me through."

"Let's keep playing. It's your turn, Lacey," Gray says, obviously trying to save the night.

She takes a deep breath. "No, I'm done playing games. If this is going to work, they deserve to know what happened, Jace. Tell them or I will." Her words are slurred. She stands and slightly rocks back and forth.

"Lacey, why don't you and I go talk in private?" I say, looking around the room. I don't know what she's getting at, but I know this doesn't need to happen in front of everyone we know. She's obviously drunk, and while I don't want to have this conversation after she's been drinking, she's not giving me much of a choice. She shakes her head and looks like she might cry. She quickly blinks away her tears and downs her cocktail.

"Never have I ever cheated on someone," she says. She looks me dead in the eye, gesturing at me with her hand. "Drink up, buttercup."

What. The. Fuck?

CHAPTER 11: GOOD NEWS! I'M NOT THE PT
LACEY

The Tortured Therapists Department

WREN:

How are you holding up after tonight, Lace?

I think I'm still in shock.

GRAY:

I'm really sorry. I wasn't thinking and honestly
didn't know Jace didn't know about Tanner.

It's not your fault. It would have all come out
eventually. I just wasn't expecting him to
deny what he did.

POPPY:

Logan and I are on our way home!

CHLOE:

Well, we believe you and that's what matters.

WREN:

Exactly. He can deny it all he wants, but we
got your back.

GRAY:

Hell yeah, we do!

Thanks everyone. Poppy, y'all don't have to come here. I think I'm going to take a bath and read the new book I just downloaded.

POPPY:

Too late and we're bringing you a surprise!

I set my phone down and turn on the tub. I pour some lavender bubble bath into the water and mindlessly watch as the bubbles begin to form.

I walk out into my bedroom and grab my e-reader. I carefully place it on the bamboo tray sitting on top of the tub and grab my "smells like him calling you a good girl" candle. It was a total impulse buy, but the woodsy scent is my favorite. I undress and check the water. Most people would complain it's too hot, but that's just how I like it—the hotter, the better.

The minute I climb into the bath, my muscles instantly relax. I take a deep breath, letting the scent of lavender and wood fill my nostrils. Then, I pick up my e-reader and begin to read.

I get stuck on the three little words on the top of the first page.

I hate him.

I read a lot and exclusively romance. I know where this is headed, and for the first time it annoys me, and I'm not sure why. The main character of my book is beautiful and smart and of course the man she hates is incredibly handsome and swoony. I usually eat this shit up, but tonight I'm rolling my eyes.

I fully intended on having an adult conversation with Jace when I got back from Orlando, but then he got angry about me sleeping with Tanner. It's not like I did it behind his back when he and I were still together. He has no right getting upset. I'm not his. He made sure of ruining that a decade ago.

The minute I outed him for cheating on me, I regretted how I did it, but it was too late. I was on my third drink of the night and acted impulsively. I don't know why I was so surprised he denied it. It's like, deep down, I wanted him to prove me wrong. Prove that he had changed.

I massage my temples where a headache is beginning to form. While the events of the night sobered me up, I'm still feeling slightly woozy from all the drinks I consumed. I close my eyes, letting my head rest on the back of the tub.

A knock on my bathroom door startles me. "Pop?"

"Yeah, can I come in?"

"Sure."

Poppy walks in with a sad look on her face. She's holding chocolate ice cream and fries. "Logan thought you might need some cheering up. Want me to put it in the kitchen for after your bath?"

"Would you judge me if I ate it now?" I laugh.

"Not at all." She hands me my comfort snack and then heads toward the door. "I'm sorry about tonight," she says, pausing with her hand on the door frame and looking over her shoulder. "I know you wanted it to be so much better than it was. I'm sorry I pressured you to talk. I was really hoping he had changed."

I dip a fry into the chocolatey goodness and pop it into my mouth. The salty, sweet mixture dances on my tongue, and I instantly start to feel a little better. "It's not your fault. Maybe next time we do something with just the girls."

She nods her head in agreement and walks out, shutting the door behind her.

———

My alarm blares the next morning, and despite my bath and my attempts to relax, I barely slept. I quickly throw on scrubs, make my London Fog, and head out the door towards my black Mini Cooper. Traffic is worse than usual and my head is pounding. By the time I walk through the doors of Dogwood Manor, I feel on edge.

"Good morning," Margaret, my boss, sings as I walk into the therapy gym. "Do you have a minute to chat before your first patient?"

I look down at my watch. "Um, sure, let me clock in real quick."

"No need to have this eating into your productivity. It'll only be a minute."

"Okay." I grit my teeth and try not to come completely unglued at her statement. "What's up?"

"I spoke with Janet, and you're all set to leave for the conference tomorrow. Unfortunately, she said we can cover your hotel and the conference fees, but they can't reimburse you for the plane ticket or food."

"But I'm leaving tomorrow."

"I know, and I'm sorry. I emailed her about it weeks ago, and she just got back to me. I'm honestly surprised she approved the hotel. You know how corporate can be." She laughs off her statement like it's no big deal.

I nod and try to reign myself in. "Thanks for trying." I offer her a forced smile. Not only did I not get paid for our little chat, but this trip will cost me more than I had hoped. I take a deep breath and walk towards a computer to start my day.

After I clock in, I make my way through the building to my favorite patient.

"Hi, Ms. Clara, it's Lacey," I say as I knock and open the door.

"Good morning, hun." Her voice is a little groggy. "Can

we do this later? I'm not quite ready to do physical therapy this morning."

I take a deep breath and force a smile. "Good news. I'm the occupational therapist, so no PT will be happening now."

She grumbles something under her breath I can't make out.

I walk over to where she lays in her bed. A pink, knitted blanket is pulled up to her chin.

"Are you feeling okay?"

"Oh, yes. I didn't get a whole lot of sleep and need to rest a little longer."

"Ms. Clara, you know we need to do therapy today. How about we get it over with? I'm tired, too, so I'll make it an easy day."

A knock on the door echoes through the small space.

"Come in," she calls.

Gray walks through the door with a huge smile on her face.

"Not another one of you," Ms. Clara huffs out.

"Oh, sorry, I didn't realize you were in here. My seven thirty canceled. I thought I'd stop by and see if Ms. Clara wanted to do PT a little early."

Ms. Clara lets out a groan. "I was just telling your friend here I'm not in the mood for PT."

"That's a bummer. I had a fun session planned," Gray chimes.

"Girls, when you're as old as I am, you need your beauty rest. Now, please let me sleep. We can do this nonsense later." She tries to dismiss us with a wave.

Gray clears her throat, trying to stifle a laugh, throwing me a look. "I'll let you finish OT and I'll see you later?"

"If you must," Ms. Clara groans. Gray turns and walks out the door.

I move around the room, grabbing Ms. Clara's brush and her favorite pink bedazzled shoes from the closet. "Do you want to change?" I ask, eyeing her hot pink mumu covered with embroidered cats.

"There is not a soul in this building I care to impress."

I giggle. I hand her the brush and watch as she slowly brushes through her white curls. I place her shoes on the floor next to her feet. "Here you go. Let's get these on, and then we'll be on our way."

She rolls her eyes and reluctantly slips both of her feet inside. I grab her walker and help her stand.

The two of us begin to move toward the door. "So, why do you think you didn't get a good night's sleep? Any pain?"

"Oh no, honey, I'm fine. My book was just too good. I couldn't put it down."

"Ms. Clara!" I laugh. "You had me worried something was wrong."

"If you ever want to borrow it, you're more than welcome. My granddaughter brought it to me last week. *A Court of Something and Something*," she snickers. "Goodness, this old brain of mine can't remember, but it surprised me. I didn't think fantasy would do it for me, but don't knock it until you try it. The Tamlin character truly is the bee's knees."

I giggle to myself knowing how it all ends but not wanting to ruin it for her.

"Wren suggested I read those too. Just wait until the second book. It was my favorite."

"Oh, I can't wait."

We round the corner of the hallway and are met by boxes stacked up high outside an open apartment. "Looks like you're getting a new neighbor," I say.

She rolls her eyes. "Probably some old bird like me. The last thing this place needs is another old lady. Where are all the young men? Did you tell that Wren girl what I suggested about the—"

"Good morning," a distinctly southern voice says from the door, interrupting our conversation. We all look up to see a gray-haired man standing in the doorway. He seems to be around eighty and is dressed impeccably in slacks, a short-sleeve buttoned-down shirt, and loafers. His wrinkled skin is a deep tan. Ms. Clara comes to a sudden stop.

"Good morning," I say with a big smile. "Welcome to Dogwood Manor. I'm Lacey, and this is Clara."

His eyes rake up and down Ms. Clara. Her cheeks turn the same shade as her mumu.

"It's nice to meet you, Clara. I'm Eugene."

"It's nice to meet you." Before I can process what just happened, she begins to move toward the therapy gym. "Come on, girl," she snaps.

"Hope to see you around, Clara," I hear him shout behind us.

We walk the long hall in silence until we make it to the gym. We enter the space filled with therapy equipment and she stops walking.

"The next time I tell you I want to wear this blasted mumu around the building, get the nurse to have my head checked. I bet he thinks I'm a hundred years old." Her face flushes with another wave of embarrassment. "How mortifying to run into a man who looks like that, when I look like this."

"You look fabulous," I assure her.

"Don't lie honey. It's not very becoming."

The Tortured Therapists Department

New guy in 330 had 307 BLUSHING during her session!

I got scolded for not making her change out of her cat mumu.

WREN:

Her cat mumu is my favorite! 🐱

GRAY:

Damn! I knew we should have co-treated.

Ha! I don't need Margaret on my ass about billing today. I have enough to worry about.

GRAY:

CHLOE:

Glad to know the residents are seeing more action than me.

Ugh, right?

POPPY:

Can't wait to start! These residents seem like so much fun.

CHLOE:

This caseload is killing me. Any news on your license?

POPPY:

No I'll try to call again today.

CHAPTER 12: SOULMATES
JACE - 9 YEARS AGO

"Y'all could have gone to the party," I say.

"We did. We just didn't stay," my dad corrects me over a bite of pasta. "You're finally home and we wanted to spend time with you." He offers me a smile.

"Are you feeling okay, sweetheart?" my mom asks, eyeing my plate. "You've barely touched your dinner."

"Oh, yeah, I'm fine," I lie, moving the spaghetti around. The truth is I'm nervous. I dropped the gift and card off at Lacey's house this morning, and I've been worried all day Colt wouldn't give it to her. I also know if tonight doesn't go my way, I'll be leaving.

My parents' eyes find each other from across the table, sharing a knowing look. I need to get out of here quickly. If they start asking me questions, then I might second guess all of it, and I need to see this through. I pop up from the table abruptly.

"Dinner was delicious," I say, walking my plate over to the trash and swiping its contents into the bin.

"You sure you're okay, kid?" my dad asks.

"Yep, I gotta run out, but I'll be back." I move through the house hoping they don't press me with follow-up questions. I quickly change and brush my teeth. Standing in front of the mirror, I try to fix my hair. Nervousness pulses through my body, and my gut tightens at the thought that she might not show. For all I know she's moved on, but I have to try. I have to ask her why she ended things. I have to tell her how I feel.

I make my way back downstairs. Hearing music coming from the kitchen, I pause. My parents are wrapped up in each other's arms swaying to some George Strait song. Dishes are still spread across the counter, long forgotten. Even after twenty-three years of marriage, they both look at each other with so much love. If there are soulmates, there is no doubt they are each other's.

Lacey flashes in my mind followed by the pain associated with the last eight months that won't go away. My nerves return in full force. I'm not sure what I'm doing, given that she cut me out of her life completely, but I need to know why she wants nothing to do with me. I have to at least try to talk to her.

Was it something I did? Or did her mom finally get in her head? I know I made mistakes, but the program took up more of my time than I thought it would. I got so hyperfocused on what I was doing in D.C. that calls and FaceTimes were missed. I should've kept my word and I didn't.

"I'll be back later," I say as my dad spins my mom around the kitchen. She gives me a little wave as I head out of the door. The street is lined with cars, and the party next door is in full swing. The sound of music and voices drifts off the front porch.

I make my way down the narrow path separating our houses. Checking my watch, I realize I'm a little early, but there's no going back now. I pop the latch on the fence and move into her backyard. If she accepts my offer, then she should appear on the roof in about ten minutes and I'll climb up to join her.

I stay hidden, near the gate, hoping no one sees me. I

don't want to cause a scene; I just want to talk to her and see what happened. See if she'd consider giving me another chance. A warm yellow glow comes from inside the house, and through the windows I can see people celebrating the girls' graduation.

I hear the door swing open. The sound of party conversations and music gets louder and then is instantly muffled as the door slams shut. I consider leaving, but then I hear her laugh.

She's here. She came.

"If you would give me a chance…" A male voice I can't quite place stops me from moving into view.

She laughs again and so does he.

I move my position slightly to get a better vantage point. Lacey and Alex, Beau's best friend, are hand in hand. My head begins to spin at the realization she didn't come outside to see me. *Of all the people in the world. Why is she with him?* A photo she posted after we broke up pops into my head. *Fuck.* Is he the reason everything went to shit?

A smile takes up her whole face. He spins her around, saying something I can't quite make out from where I'm at and then he pulls her in for a kiss.

The minute her lips meet his, I stumble backward. The sound of my blood rushing through my veins fills my ears. My heart pounds against my ribcage, thumping loudly. *I need to get out of here. This was a bad idea.*

I flip the latch and disappear beyond the gate. I move quickly, not wanting her, or anyone else for that matter, to see me and I don't stop until I'm back in my bedroom.

I slam the door shut behind me. Falling onto my bed, I'm overcome with heartbreak. Tears begin to fall down my face.

It's really over. She's moved on with Alex.

CHAPTER 13: MY CRUNCHWRAP SUPREME CAN WAIT

We are officially on day three of the silent treatment. Logan won't answer any of my texts or calls. Our apartment isn't very big, but Tanner has somehow figured out a way to avoid me at every turn. Thanks to Lacey's revelation the other night, I'm starting to doubt if applying for the job in Atlanta is the right call. I didn't cheat on her, but it seems as though everyone believed her over me. It's left me questioning if it's worth sticking around.

I'm on my way to meet Enzo for a run. While I'm thankful he's not icing me out like everyone else, I'm not sure what to expect from him. If I'm honest, I considered canceling, but he seems to be the only person willing to talk to me, and I'd love to know what everyone is thinking.

I pull into the gravel lot and spot Enzo leaned up against his car near the top of the trail. Parking next to him, I grab my phone and earbuds and jump down from my Jeep.

"Surprised you still wanted to meet up this morning," I say, offering him my hand.

"Figured if we were running, we wouldn't really have to talk," he says. His lips turn up at the corners and he grabs my hand, pulling me in for a one armed hug. "How are you holding up?"

"I don't know, man. No one will talk to me. I was planning on applying for the job in Atlanta, but I haven't. It feels like everyone would be happier if I left again." I pull my leg up behind me to stretch my quad.

He nods. "You and Lacey definitely took everyone by surprise."

"I didn't do it." I switch legs, pulling my ankle to my ass.

"That's what you keep saying."

I offer him a pathetic smile. It's clear he's not quite sure what to believe, and I know there's no sense in trying to convince him. I need to convince Lacey.

"Not that my opinion matters," he continues, stretching into a lunge. "Or that you asked for it, but I don't think you should make this decision based on anyone but what you want. The other night you said you were wanting to settle down to be closer to your dad and she has nothing to do with that."

My heart clenches because I know he's right. It's been five years since my mom has passed, and I know I haven't been the best son. Rarely home when she was alive and then even less once she died. The thought of losing my dad and being out of reach pops into my head.

I shake the thought and try to focus back on what he's saying.

"You're right. I wish there was a way to work all of this out."

"Have you tried talking to Poppy?"

"No, I don't have any way to get in touch with her. Logan won't respond to any of my texts or calls. Why would she?"

"Logan is gone for her. If you talk to her and get her on your side, then maybe he'll follow."

"But how?" I exhale.

"Maybe text her. Tanner should have her number.

Donovan and I want you to be happy. We're both not completely convinced Lacey's lying about your past, but we also aren't convinced you did it either. You two are going to have to work it out in your own time, but until then, I'd start with Poppy."

I lean my head back and take a deep breath. "Your unwavering confidence in my integrity means so much to me."

He laughs and puts his hands up. "Hey. What you did at eighteen is not for me to judge."

I shake my head. We both walk towards the trailhead.

"You ready to go?"

"Let's do it. Five miles, right?"

"Yep. And thanks, man."

"Don't mention it."

"No, I meant thank you for treating me like a person today. I know you don't believe me, but you kept our plan. I wish I could say the same for everyone else."

"I'm getting married in July; not even you could make me skip my cardio." He lets out a long laugh and takes off down the trail. I fix my earbuds in my ears, start my music, and follow behind him.

———

"Tanner, can you come out and talk to me?" I bang on his bedroom door. His car was parked outside, so I know he's home from work. "At least let's try to hear each other out and put this behind us."

His door swings open and he pushes past me into the living room where he crashes onto our sofa. His arms are crossed and his face gives nothing away.

"I didn't—" I try to begin, but he interrupts me.

"Can I start?" he asks. I nod and he continues. "Look man, I need you to know I didn't know who she was when I brought her home. If I had known she was *the* Lacey, then I would have never slept with her."

"I know you didn't do it intentionally," I say. "Fuck, do I even want to know how many times it happened?"

"It happened once, and I promise it'll never happen again."

"Why didn't you tell me?"

He shrugs. "I almost did a few times, but I was worried about how you'd react. I feel terrible. I don't know the whole story, but I know she means a lot to you. If I had known who she was, I would've never crossed that line. You have to know that. I would never jeopardize our friendship."

"I know you wouldn't."

"If it makes you feel better, it definitely wasn't my best work. I mean shit, dude, she called me a mediocre lay. It obviously meant nothing, and while I won't deny that she's attractive, there was no chemistry. We're meant to be friends. Nothing more."

"You're sure?"

"Fucking swear it, dude." There is a beat of silence as I consider what my best friend is saying. Tanner was there for me when he barely knew me. When Archie gave me his number, I didn't know what to expect. I had never lived with anyone before and honestly wasn't looking forward to it. I was distraught about my mom when I moved in, and Tanner forced me to talk about her. I don't think I could have gotten through those first few months without him.

"I know it wasn't intentional, so I can't be mad at you. You didn't know, and I don't own her. She was right the other night. She can sleep with whoever she pleases, even if that's you. I have no right to be mad."

"You believe me?"

"Yeah, I believe you." His shoulders noticeably relax.

"Thank fuck." He laughs. "I've been avoiding this conversation for days. You sure we're cool?"

"Yeah, we're cool. How could we not be? She and I aren't anything. Not even friends."

His eyes roll at my statement and he takes a deep breath. Standing, he grabs his keys off the coffee table like he's about to leave.

"Wait, where are you going?" I ask.

He freezes. "Taco Bell. I'm starving from stressing about this conversation, so now that we're cool, I'm gonna go grab dinner. Want something?"

"You don't want to talk about Lacey saying I cheated on her?"

"Not really. I know you didn't do it."

"You do?"

"First of all, you're a good guy. Even younger and dumber you wouldn't have it in him to cheat on a girl. Second, if you had, you would have told me, and you said you didn't know what happened."

"You've been avoiding me for days and you knew I was telling the truth?"

"Dude, it's obvious you still like her, maybe even love her, and I was fucking terrified to face you after you found out I slept with her. I thought I was a dead man." I'm not completely sure I believe what I'm hearing. I don't respond to his accusation either. *Is it obvious?*

"But none of you will talk to me."

"Oh, that's because everyone else believes you cheated." He chuckles. "And they're pissed you aren't owning up to what they think you did."

I run my hands down my face. "This is fucked, man."

"Want to talk about it?" He sits back down with a huff. "I guess my Crunchwrap Supreme can wait," he mumbles under his breath.

Not a day has gone by in the last ten years that I haven't thought about the day Lacey ended things with me. You don't get over heartbreak like that. At eighteen, I thought she was my future. Hell, at eight, I thought she was my forever, and then it all came crashing down. I take a deep breath.

"The girls and I were neighbors and best friends growing up. Poppy was the sister I never had and Lacey, well, fuck, I was in love with her before I even knew what love was. The summer before my senior year and the girls' junior year, we finally stopped fucking around and admitted we were into one another."

He nods and I take another deep breath.

"My senior year, I got accepted for this year-long photography program in D.C. with this phenomenal photographer. The plan was for me to complete it and then come back and start college with the girls. About four months into the program, Lacey called and told me she felt like we wanted different things. I begged her to give us a chance, but she was adamant things were over. I tried reaching out to Poppy, but she ignored all of my calls and instead texted me she was done with me too. Neither of them would talk to me."

"She didn't accuse you of cheating?"

"No, she just kept saying she knew we wanted different things. I had no idea what she meant."

"And that was it?"

"Yeah, a few weeks after the phone call, she posted a picture with Poppy and these two guys from our high school, Beau and Alex. Beau was Poppy's boyfriend, and Alex was Beau's asshole best friend. I always knew he had a thing for her and so I figured he had something to do with what happened."

"So, you think she cheated on you?"

"No, her heart is too good. I knew she hadn't cheated, but I do think I was gone and busier than I thought I would be. We were young. Long distance was hard, and he was there." I let out a laugh. "In a moment of desperation, I liked the post and commented something dumb. Then, I attempted to call her and Poppy way more than I should have. I'm sure they thought I was a lunatic, but I was in love with her. After that, both of them blocked me on all of their socials and their phones. I tried talking to her once when I was home. I dropped off a letter and asked her to meet me. The same night, I found out she was with Alex from the picture, and she looked happy, so I threw myself into work and school."

"Fuck, man, but why do they think you cheated on her?"

I shrug and roll my neck, running my hand down the back of my head. "Beats me."

He nods. "I'm sorry, dude. I believe you, but Logan's going to be harder to convince. Poppy's word is gold, and you know how he feels about cheating, especially after the shit his dad pulled when he was a kid."

"Yeah, so how do I convince them I didn't do it?"

"Hell if I know, man, but we'll think of something."

"Did you pack your toothbrush?"

"Yes."

"A regular bra? You don't want to have just a sports bra all week."

"Yes, Poppy, everything is packed. Besides, we're less than five minutes from the airport. What would you do if I told you I hadn't packed a bra?"

"I could give you mine."

I laugh hard. "Right, because my double Ds would fit so nicely in your B cups."

"I'm just saying one time when I went out of town, I forgot to pack a bra and I had to go buy one and it was terrible. Almost ruined the whole trip."

"I'm going to Orlando. I'm not going to Mars. I think if I forgot to pack something, I would be able to run to the store and find it."

Her phone pings.

"Could you check that for me?" She pulls off of the interstate and down the exit ramp.

"Huh. Unknown number and all it says is 'Hey!'"

"Weird. Probably the wrong number." She shrugs her

shoulders. I set her phone back in the cup holder. "Are you excited for a little vacation?" she asks.

"It's not a vacation. I'll be sitting in conference rooms learning about how to be a better occupational therapist. We have a half day in Disney and the rest of the time we'll be networking and learning."

"Yeah, but Disney sounds fun."

"I guess, if you're into waiting in lines, dodging toddler meltdowns, and boob sweat." I laugh. "You and Logan have any plans?"

"The usual. Trying to soak up the last few weeks before I start at Dogwood Manor."

"I'm glad you two worked out. Him bringing me chocolate ice cream and fries the other night was so thoughtful. I wish I could find someone like him."

"You will. I know it." She smiles.

She turns into the airport, drives around the curve in the road, and pulls into one of the spots lining the sidewalk outside to the departure doors. "You get back on Friday morning, right?"

"Yep, I'll text you the flight information, but I think I'll land around eight."

She shifts into park and leans over the center console to give me a hug. "I know it's been a stressful couple of weeks for you. Try to have fun, and I'll see you Friday."

"I'll do my best." I climb out, grabbing my suitcase and bag from the backseat.

"Fly safe. Love you," Poppy shouts through the window as I walk away from her car.

"Love you more," I shout back, throwing my hand up in a wave.

I make my way through the sliding doors of Hartsfield-Jackson International Airport. To no surprise, the security line moves slowly and the airport is incredibly busy. By some miracle, I manage to make it to my gate with thirty minutes to spare. I check my phone, and my battery is sitting at fifteen percent. Shit. I dig in my bag until I find my charging cord and survey the terminal for a place to plug it in. I spot one empty chair next to a wall outlet and make a beeline for it.

A handsome stranger arrives at the chair the same time I do. He has auburn hair and green eyes. A smile flashes across his face, a dimple appearing in his left cheek.

"Oh, sorry," I say.

"Oh, no, that's my bad. You take it," he offers.

"Thanks." I clumsily try to pull my suitcase and bag close to me. I sit down and notice he's still standing to my left and staring at me.

"I'm Lacey."

"Chris," he says, putting out his hand to shake mine. The woman seated to my right stands to leave.

I nod my head towards the chair she previously occupied. "Care to join me?"

He grins and makes his way over.

"So, Chris, where are you headed?" I ask, trying to break the now very awkward silence hanging between us.

"Same place as you I imagine."

"And how would you know where I'm going? Are you stalking me?" I laugh as I plug my charger into the wall and attach it to my phone.

"No." He shakes his head and points toward the television screen above the desk where one of the gate agents is talking to a young family. In big, bold, white letters *Orlando* is displayed. Of course we're headed to the same place. Everyone at this gate is. *Real smooth Lacey.*

"Oh. Right." I laugh despite myself. "You headed to visit the mouse?"

"Oh, no, well I think I'll be headed there one day, but I'm an OT, and I'm headed to a conference."

"An OT? An old tailor?" He laughs at my pathetic attempt

for a joke. "No, wait I know. You're an observant tele-marketer?"

"Occupational therapist." He shakes his head at me. "And what do you do?"

"I'm giving you a hard time. I'm an OT too." I smile and tuck my hair behind my ear.

He laughs loudly, and a few people sitting across from us glance over our way. An announcement asking for volunteers to check their luggage comes over the speakers and interrupts our conversation.

I quickly stand with my bag. "You mind saving my seat? I'm going to have my bag gate checked. Unless you wanted to take your bag too?" I nod toward the black roller bag sitting to his right.

He shakes his head. "No. I'm keeping my things with me. I don't want anything getting lost."

"Suit yourself. I'm going to take advantage of them checking my luggage for free. Guard my chair with your life."

He lets out another chuckle, and I feel his eyes on me as I cross the carpeted floor toward the gate desk. I return to my still empty chair and plug my phone back in. Settling back in my seat, I scroll on my phone, waiting for my boarding zone to be called.

"Any chance you're in 15D?" he asks.

"Huh?"

"Your seat on the plane? I'm in 15E."

I shake my head. "I'm afraid not. I'm in 10A." I pull my e-reader from my bag and swipe it open to the enemies to lovers story I keep failing to connect with.

"Should we exchange numbers?" he asks.

"Huh?"

"Your number? You know I'm headed down by myself, so I thought maybe we could grab a drink or something?"

"Oh, yeah, sure. I'll text myself from your phone." He hands me his cell, and I quickly type my number in and shoot myself a text. I hand it back to him and pick up mine. My lips curl into a devious smile as I save his number. I turn the phone around so he can see.

"You saved my number under 'Cute Stalker'?" He chuckles.

Maybe Orlando will be just what I need after all.

CHAPTER 15: B.Y.O.H. (BRING YOUR OWN HONESTY)

JACE

>   Hey!
>
>   Can we talk?

POPPY:

Sorry, I don't know who this is. I think you may have the wrong number.

>   Oh, sorry, it's Jacks.

POPPY:

Sorry, I don't know anyone named Jacks.

>   It's Jace. Please talk to me.

I told Poppy it was me two hours ago and I haven't gotten a response. I arrived at the park thirty minutes ago to go for a run to try to clear my head, but it's no use. I need her on my side if I'm ever going to convince Lacey I didn't cheat on her. I turn the music up louder on my phone, trying to drown out my thoughts. I round the corner of the path and feel my phone vibrate. I pull it out and swipe up on the screen.

POPPY:

Logan and I will be at his place tonight. Want to join us for dinner at 7?

Yes! Absolutely. Can I bring anything?

POPPY:

Just your honesty.

Done.

POPPY:

Do NOT make me regret this.

I slip my phone back into my pocket and finish my run. Tonight isn't going to be easy, but at least they agreed to talk to me.

———

LOGAN GREETS ME AT HIS DOOR WITH A SCOWL. HE MOVES TO the side and silently gestures for me to come in.

"Hey, man. Thanks for having me over."

He grunts and walks toward Poppy in the kitchen.

"Hey, Jace," she yells over the roar of the blender. "We made tacos, so I convinced Logan we needed margaritas too."

"Sounds good to me. Can I help you with anything?" She shakes her head and goes back to moving around the kitchen. I see her give Logan a look, and he clears his throat.

"So, Jacks, how are things?"

I can't help but scoff a little. "Well, they've been better."

He lets out a small chuckle, and I'm thankful for the break in the tension between us.

"Margarita anyone?" Poppy walks out of the kitchen holding two glasses of lime green liquid. "I thought we could eat and then we could talk?"

"Fine by me."

"Same," Logan agrees, taking one of the glasses and swallowing down a large sip.

The dinner is painfully quiet as we all eat in silence. The loudest thing in the room is the elephant in the corner weighing all of us down. I finish the last bite of food and push the plate back a bit so I can rest my arms on the table.

"I know what you both think happened, but I need y'all to know I didn't cheat on her."

"Jace—"

"No, Poppy, let me get this out. Please." She inhales deeply and then blows out a long breath.

"Go ahead," she says.

"I was completely blindsided when Lacey dumped me, and if I'm honest, I don't know if I fully got over the pain it caused. She was and still is the only girl I've ever loved, and you were like my sister. When I lost both of you, it crushed me."

She sets down her fork and her eyes find mine. "How do you think I felt? She's been my best friend since I was seven, and she trusted you. We both trusted you. You should have seen her." Her head falls into her hands and she rubs her eyes. "Jace, it was awful. She stopped eating. I had to drag her out of bed every morning so she didn't flunk out of high school. I guess I knew there was a chance you wouldn't come back, but I never thought you would cheat on her."

"But I didn't cheat."

"Stop lying!" she yells. Logan reaches over and grabs her hand. "What am I supposed to believe? She lied to me all those years ago? That's a hell of a lie to keep up for ten years. I told you that night on the roof, I'd choose her, and I meant it." Logan opens his mouth to speak, but Poppy cuts him off. "I mean, god, when she got back from D.C., it was heart—"

"What do you mean when she got back from D.C.?" My mind fumbles over her words. *Lacey was in D.C.? When? How? Why?*

"Don't do this. Don't lie. You said you'd be honest tonight, so just be honest."

"I really don't know what you're talking about." I run my hands through my hair and exhale. "This is beginning to feel like we've been living in two very different realities. The way I remember it, I got a call out of the blue in September, and she told me she and I wanted different things. She wouldn't talk to me, wouldn't hear me out. Told me we were over and that was it. The next thing I knew, you had texted me something similar, and then y'all posted that picture with Beau and Alex. Poppy, I was devastated."

She looks up at me, eyes wide.

"No, that's not what happened." She shakes her head. "Lacey went up to visit her cousin, Mariah, in Virginia over fall break. She was going to surprise you. She said she saw you in a coffee shop near your apartment. Said you were with another girl. They called me after. Mariah was so convincing. She said it was clear y'all were more than friends, and Lacey agreed. She was so upset."

Lacey was in D.C.

I search the corners of my brain for a memory, but I was so busy with the program then that I can't remember who she could have possibly seen me with. I didn't have many friends in D.C.; I was there to work toward my goals. I had friends back home. I had Lacey. Why would I have wanted anyone else?

"Is it possible she was mistaken?" Logan asks hesitantly, squeezing his girlfriend's hand.

"No, Mariah agreed with her. They were both so sure." Her eyes flick back to me. "Jace, y'all hadn't been talking very much. You were busy. She was lonely. When she saw you with someone else, it broke her."

I try to wrap my head around her words, but I can't.

"What is it going to take for you to both believe me? I

can't go back in time, but I need you to know I didn't cheat on her. You've known me since you were in the second grade. Logan, you are one of my best friends. Have I ever once lied to either of you before? Why would I be lying now?"

"No," Logan says.

"Exactly," I say. "I didn't cheat on her."

"I want to believe you, but I don't know you anymore. It just doesn't make sense," Poppy says, standing from the table. She walks over to the dishwasher where she loads her plate.

"But you knew me then. Come on. Growing up, did I ever lie to you?"

"Well, no." She lets out an exasperated sigh. She grasps the edge of the sink with her hands and rocks back, shaking her head.

"I would never lie. To her or to either of you. Fuck, Poppy, you were like my sister. Logan, you and Tanner are like my brothers. Tell me what I can do to make this better. Please. I'll do whatever it takes."

Poppy turns to face me. Her eyes dart back and forth between Logan and me. He stands and walks to meet her in the kitchen. He places his plate in the dishwasher and then whispers something in her ear.

Think Jace. Fucking think of something.

"What if I talk to her? Convince her to hear me out. Maybe she remembers something that will help me remember who she saw me with."

"She's not going to talk to you on her own," Poppy says. "After the other night, she's afraid you're going to continue to lie to her."

"Please." My voice sounds desperate. "At least let me try. If she doesn't believe me, then I'll back out of all of your lives. It'll be like I never came back."

"That's not what we want, Jacks," Logan says.

Poppy bites her lip and twirls a piece of her hair around her finger.

"Fine, I'll help you talk to her, but that's it."

CHAPTER 16: WHAT'S KICKIN CHICKEN?

LACEY

CUTE STALKER:

Want to meet up for a drink in Atlanta
tonight?

I might be able to clear my schedule 😊

CUTE STALKER:

How about 8 pm?

"What has you looking so happy?" Poppy asks as I throw my luggage into the back of her car and slide into the passenger seat.

"A cute guy I met at the conference," I say coyly.

"Holy shit, Lace! Spill." She turns on her blinker, and I click my seatbelt across my lap. She pulls into the flow of traffic and starts to drive towards the interstate. My phone pings again. How I'm feeling must be written all over my face.

"I haven't seen you like this in years. Don't leave me hanging."

"I don't know. We met at the airport on the way down to

the conference. Neither of us knew anyone, so we started hanging out."

"And?" She draws out her question and wiggles her eyebrows at me.

"And nothing. We hung out at the conference, drank ourselves silly in EPCOT, and now we're meeting up tonight for drinks."

"Lacey!" She slaps my leg.

"Truly, it's nothing. We had like one moment on the little boat ride in the Mexican restaurant where I thought he might kiss me, but he didn't. We had a good time, and it was fun to get away from here and forget about all the drama."

My phone pings again, and I let out a laugh.

"For *nothing*, he sure is making you laugh."

"He sent me a video of these people drinking in EPCOT, and I'm afraid we were much worse off. Anyway, enough about that. How are things here?"

She doesn't respond immediately. Instead, she leans forward and turns off the radio, so we're now sitting in complete silence.

"Jace had dinner with Logan and me."

"Oh, how was that?" I look at my nails, feigning indifference, but my gut twists at the idea that she would have dinner with him, especially after the other night.

"Interesting..." She comes to a stop at a red light and turns to face me. "He didn't know you went to D.C."

"Yeah, I know."

"What do you mean you know? I thought you caught him with a girl?"

"I did. He just didn't see me."

"Please explain." The light switches to green, and she begins to drive again.

"I don't know. I walked into that coffee shop, and he was with some other girl. Mariah was with me and instantly yanked me out and back to the train. I was embarrassed and felt so silly that I planned to surprise him. Fuck, I had planned to lose my virginity that trip. You remember? So, I called him when we got back to Mariah's and ended things. I told him we obviously wanted different things because we did. He wanted the blue-haired chick I saw him with, and I wanted him."

"Lacey—"

"I know what you're thinking, but I didn't lie to you. I told you he cheated and we broke up. That's what happened."

"Lacey—"

"What?"

"I think you should hear him out."

"Why? So he can continue to lie and make me feel like I'm crazy? You heard him the other night. He's not going to admit to it. He's not going to apologize for breaking my heart." I turn the radio back on and the car fills with "Please Please Please" by Sabrina Carpenter.

"Lacey!" Poppy slams the volume knob with her palm returning us to silence. "Talk to him. Figure this shit out. I'm done being in the middle of it. I don't know who to believe anymore, and I'm exhausted and so is everyone else."

"I called him out the other night, and while I admit I should have gone about it a different way, he lied in front of everyone. Then he convinced you and Logan to talk to him, and it sounds like he continued to lie." I take a deep breath. "I know what I saw. It's not like I was the only person who saw it. Mariah did too. Do I need to call her so she can remind you what happened? I didn't lie to anyone. He's lying and trying to save face in front of his friends."

She inhales deeply. "You need closure. The past ten years, I've watched you with guy after guy, and I supported you through it. You compare everyone to Jace. No one is good enough. They're all below average lays you forget about the next day. Maybe if you talk to him, it'll give you the closure you need to move on and find someone worth your time."

"You taking his side was not on my BINGO card for today." The knot in my stomach tightens. She knows what he did to me. Why is she believing him over me?

"I'm not taking sides. This is getting out of hand. If he really cheated on you, then he deserves an Oscar for the performance he gave the other night at Logan's. And if he didn't, then, we, well you, have let it take over your life for the past ten years. I love you, but the two of you need to sort this out."

"You're my best friend in the entire world, and he was the love of my life. You remember the aftermath of D.C." My voice cracks and tears roll down my face. "I know everyone thinks I'm dramatic, but I'm not that good of an actress. He broke my heart. Do you really think I would lie to you? That I'd intentionally ruin your relationship with him?"

"No, and I know he did, but maybe it was a misunderstanding. I don't know what to believe anymore. Please talk to him. Put this behind you, so we can all move on."

"Okay," I say quietly.

"Good. I'll share his contact."

"Great." I turn the radio back on, and we don't talk for the rest of the drive.

———

POPPY SHARED JACE'S CONTACT THE MINUTE WE WALKED INTO our apartment. I have been sitting on my bed for fifteen minutes staring at his number, contemplating what to say. Nothing seems right. *"Hi?" "Hey?" "Howdy?" "What's kickin' chicken?"* I type and delete each one. I fall back into the pile of clothes on the top of my bed and begin to type.

Hello.

Well, that was fucking brilliant.

JACE:

Sorry, I don't have your number saved. Who
is this?

> It's Lacey. Poppy said you wanted to talk.

JACE:

Hey, Pixie. Why don't you come over tonight
and we can sort through things?

> Stop calling me that. I have a date tonight.

JACE:

A date?

> Yes, a date. Not that it's any of your
> business.

JACE:

Tomorrow then? 1 pm? Want to grab coffee?

> You and I don't have the best track record at
> coffee shops. Can we meet somewhere else?

JACE:

My apartment?

> Okay.

I hear a soft knock on the door, and I drop the phone onto the bed. I walk over and open the door to find Poppy standing in the doorway.

"I thought you were going to Logan's?"

"I couldn't leave knowing we fought." She wraps me in a hug and squeezes me tight. "I'm sorry. I love you."

"I'm sorry too." She releases and looks at me. "You were right, you know?"

"About what?" she asks.

"I've been holding onto Jace for ten years. Most days it's hatred, and other days I miss him so bad it hurts. He was my first love, and no one compares to what I had with him. What he ruined. I texted him and we're meeting tomorrow."

"Just hear him out. Maybe y'all can sort this out and we can all be friends again."

"Maybe."

"And if not, that's okay too. At least you'll have some closure and can move on. I'm proud of you."

"Yeah, yeah, yeah. Being an adult sucks."

CHAPTER 17: IS THIS
A FUCKING JOKE?

JACE

My phone rings, and I pull it out of my back pocket fully expecting to see Lacey's name on the screen. I was shocked when she agreed to talk to me, and part of me keeps expecting her to cancel. I swipe up and place the phone to my ear.

"Eli! How's my favorite mentor doing? It's been a minute."

"Ha. As far as I know, I was the only one dumb enough to take you under my wing."

I chuckle. "Are you back from Guatemala?"

"We are. We're actually in Atlanta for the Nat Geo charity auction tonight, and I was hoping you might be in town too?"

"Oh, yeah. I'm in town and will probably be here until at least August. What's up?"

"Are you coming to the auction?"

"No, not really my thing."

"How'd you manage to get out of it?"

"I'll never tell my secrets."

"Bastard. Could you do me a huge favor today?"

I nervously check my watch. It's eleven. Two hours until

Lacey arrives. "Depends. I have plans with an old friend. Whatcha need?"

"Well, one of the photographers who was supposed to donate something to the auction backed out at the last minute. I was wondering if I could meet up with you and maybe have you sign something?"

"The infamous Eli Miller wants my autograph. Oh, how the tables have turned," I laugh.

"Shut it, Jace. I would autograph one of mine, but I already donated two. They don't need a third."

"Alright, when? I have a bunch of prints at my apartment. Want to meet me here and we can go through them. You can pick something out and I'd be happy to donate it. My friend is coming over at one."

"Oh, I'll be long gone before then. Drop a pin and I'll head your way."

We hang up, and I send Eli my address. I sit down on the couch and crack my knuckles. I look at my watch again: eleven fifteen. My phone pings and I swipe up on the screen.

ELI:

Says I'm only 45 minutes from you. See you soon.

I lean back and shut my eyes. My mind drifts to my meeting with Lacey, and I know I have to get it right. I somehow need to convince her I'm not the man she thinks I am. My chest tightens, and I don't think I've felt this nervous in a long time. When she called me all those years ago, she was so cold and emotionless. I've replayed that conversation more times than I care to admit. I wish she would have told me the real reason she was ending things. I wish I could go back in time and assure her that I only had eyes for her, but that's not how it happened, and now I have so many questions.

Tanner walks out of his room. "You ready?" He sits down across from me putting on his shoes.

"I don't know what to expect. I'm hoping she can clue me in on what went down that day in D.C. so I can convince her that I would never betray her trust."

"It's a good sign she's coming over."

"I hope so." I rub my sweaty palms on my shorts.

"What are you going to do until she gets here?"

"I bought some food I need to get ready. Figured it might go better if I had snacks."

Tanner's face twists.

"What? You think it's a bad idea?"

"No, it's just interesting."

"Care to elaborate?"

He leans back in his chair, crossing his ankle over his knee. "I think it's funny that she has made everyone think you did this terrible thing, and you're over here making her food."

"We were young. I'm sure you did some dumb shit at seventeen too. Hell, you do some dumb shit now at thirty."

"Oh, I'm not holding it against her. Trust me. I like Lacey, but you making her snacks tells me everything I need to know about you and how you feel about her."

I don't respond. Part of me thinks I should be angry, but I'm not, and I know that sounds insane. As much as I want to hate her for not fighting for us, for giving Alex a chance, for not being there when I needed her the most, I can't bring myself to be mad at her. She means too much to me.

If anything, I'm hopeful that for the first time in ten years, we might have a chance to move forward, and that makes my heart swell. Over the last decade, there were so many times I wanted to call her but knew I couldn't. If today goes well, she may be a part of my life again, and I can't think of anything I want more.

He chuckles. "I'm going to play pickleball, and then I'm going over to Donovan's. Wanted to give y'all space." He stands and grabs his keys. "Text me when I'm cleared to come back, lover boy."

———

I open the oven and remove the pan of golden fries that just finished cooking. When we were younger, fries could fix everything when it came to Lacey, and I'm hoping that still holds true today. I sprinkle salt over them and give them a good mix.

Eli has yet to show up or text me back. I check my watch and it's twelve forty-five. To say I'm a little annoyed is an understatement. I need today to go perfectly, and I don't want Lacey to think meeting with her isn't my priority. I hear a knock and I place the fries back in the oven to keep them warm before jogging towards the front door.

I'm met with short signature blue hair, brown eyes, and a big smile.

"Jacks!" Eli throws her arms around me. "It's been too long, my friend." I hug her back and quickly release.

"It's about damn time," I laugh, looking at my watch. Twelve forty-nine. Great. This is great.

"I know. I'm so sorry I'm late," she says. "There was an issue with the rental car. I know you have plans at one. I promise to make this quick." Eli moves past me and into my apartment.

"The photos are in my room. Come on."

She follows me into my bedroom, where a dozen photographs of various animals I saw during my latest trip to the Amazon are laid out on my bed.

"Oh, wow, they're spectacular."

I nervously check my watch again while Eli peruses my photos.

"Take whichever one you want." Her eyes land on a photo

of two scarlet macaws that have their beaks pressed against each other.

She snickers. "They look like they're kissing."

I nod and try to calm my fidgeting, but I know Lacey will be here any minute.

"Do you have any of the Bixito?"

"Not with me. How do you think I got out of going tonight?"

"Fuck you," she jabs.

"This one will do. Sign it and I'll be out of your hair."

I grab a marker and sign my name in the corner. We make our way out of my room and as I round the corner I come to a complete halt causing Eli to run into my back. Lacey is standing in my doorway wearing cutoff shorts that show off her long legs and a black tank top that fits her hourglass shape like a glove. The locket still hangs around her neck. Her white high tops contrast against her tan skin, and her black baseball cap is worn and embroidered with a purple smiley face.

"Some warning would've been nice," Eli says as she pushes off my back.

"Oh, sorry, I knocked and I thought I heard someone say come in," Lacey says. "Am I interrupting?" Her eyes land behind me and shift from Eli to the door we came from.

"Oh, no, I'm the one interrupting. I'm E—" Eli steps forward and begins to offer Lacey her hand.

"I know who you are." Lacey's voice cracks as she turns and rushes from the apartment.

"Did I do something?" I hear Eli ask the question, but I'm already out of my apartment and following Lacey to her car.

"Lacey!"

She doesn't stop moving. Hell, she's almost running and I break into a jog. "Lacey, please stop!"

She whips her head around and her blonde hair moves

through the air. Tears run down her face and there is so much pain in her eyes that my heart breaks.

"Is this a fucking joke to you?"

"What?"

"Do you think it's funny to come back here and blow up all of our lives? Gosh, we were all doing fine without you. I was doing fine without you."

"What are you talking about?" She turns and starts to move toward her car. I can hear her mumbling something, but she isn't making any sense. With two large strides, I catch up to her and grab her hand. Her skin feels incredibly soft, and for a moment I don't want to let her go. I want to pull her into me and tell her it was all a misunderstanding. That it's going to be okay and now that I have her back in my life, I'll never let her go again.

"Please come back upstairs. Let's talk."

She flips around and shakes me off of her. "Why is she in your apartment?"

"Who? Eli?" My brain fumbles as I try to make sense of how Eli could have caused such a reaction.

"Eli?" She shakes her head and wipes away her tears. We are both quiet for a minute and I take a deep breath. My lungs fill with her tropical scent, and I realize we're standing incredibly close, so I take a step back.

"Yeah, Elizabeth Miller, but she goes by Eli."

"You cheated on me with your photography program mentor?" Her question throws me off guard.

"Wait, *what*?" I ask.

She takes a deep breath and crosses her arms. "Don't be smug. You know she's the woman I saw you with that day. The one you were all over in that coffee shop."

"I was all over Eli?"

"Yes, well, you two were laughing and staring at one another. Anyone could see you were into her and she was into you."

What in the actual fuck?

"I mean, Jace, you barely had time for me. You left and said we would talk everyday and we didn't. When we did talk, your calls got shorter, and we were barely texting. I tried to convince myself you were busy. That our schedules were different and it didn't mean anything, but then I saw you with *her* and it all made sense. You no longer wanted what I wanted. You wanted her, and I wanted you."

A sob escapes her throat and she swallows hard, wiping her face with her hands. She takes a few deep breaths. "And now you invited me over to talk, and I walk into seeing her walk out of your bedroom. How cruel can you be?" She shakes her head.

I knew she thought I cheated, but with Eli? Is she serious? I let out a laugh and I immediately try to stifle it.

"God, you're such an asshole. I shouldn't have agreed to this. I was doing fine hating you." She turns to leave and I grab her hand once more.

"No, shit, I'm sorry. Eli was my mentor in the photography program, and then she became my friend. We were never anything more. I swear."

"You really think that's all it's going to take for me to believe you?"

I rub my hands down my face and place them on top of my head. "Lacey, Eli is married to a woman."

Her eyes meet mine. "A woman?"

"Yes, a woman and has been for a while. I'm not her type, and she's not mine." I shake my head. "She stopped by today to pick up a photograph for an auction she's going to later. The photos were in my room, so when you walked in, she had just finished choosing one." She wipes the remaining tears from her eyes. "Don't cry, Pixie."

"I thought I told you to stop calling me that."

"Can we please go upstairs and talk? You can ask her yourself if you want."

To my surprise, she nods her head and follows me back to my apartment. When we enter, Eli is sitting on the couch holding the photo of the macaws.

"Eli, this is Lacey. Lacey, this is Eli."

Eli's eyes flair at Lacey's name and I give her a small nod. "It's nice to meet you, but I'm afraid if I stay much longer, I'll be late to the auction and my wife might kill me." I walk her toward the door and she gives me a big hug. "It was good seeing you, Jacks. Thanks again for saving my ass."

I chuckle. "Anytime." The door closes behind her, and I turn to face Lacey, who is sitting on the couch. Her brow furrows.

"Now what?" I ask.

CHAPTER 18: FRENCH FRIES AND FUCK UPS

LACEY

The last fifteen minutes have felt like being trapped on a roller coaster. I'm still processing what happened when Jace shuts the door behind Eli and turns to face me. I'm honestly not sure where we go from here. For ten years, I built up what he did to me in my head and have hated this man because I thought he betrayed me.

I play back the memory burned into my mind of that day in the coffee shop. I was so sure. Mariah was so sure. She wouldn't shut up about it. Kept pointing out all the little things I missed. And then I got home, and when I told my mom we broke up, she didn't even ask why. Instead told me I should have never tried long distance and it was doomed from the beginning. Her words solidified everything I was feeling, and I completely crumbled.

How could I have been so wrong?

"Now what?" I hear him ask. He walks over and sits in a chair across from me. "Are you hungry? I made fries."

"You made fries?"

He nods. "Yeah, I remembered you liked them and thought I might need a peace offering." He lets out a low chuckle, and I sit there, stunned. He rubs his hand over the back of his head. His eyes locked on mine.

"Hold on." He jumps up and moves into his kitchen. I hear the shuffling of what sounds like pots and pans. He walks back into the living room. His hands are full of a bowl of freshly cut fries, a plate, and a variety of dips. He sets it all on the coffee table in front of me. He didn't heat up something frozen. He actually made me fucking hand-cut french fries.

"Thank you." I bite my lip and grab one from the bowl. Squirting a little ranch on the plate, I drag the fry through it and then pop it into my mouth. He returns to his chair and watches me. *Fuck, they're good.*

My mind races, trying to come up with something to say. How do I even begin to tell him how sorry I am?

"Do you like them?" he asks.

"I'm so sorry," I say at the same time as his question.

"Oh, yeah. They're delicious," I say. I take a deep breath and rub my hands on my denim shorts before crossing my arms. "Do you mind if I start?"

He nods and leans back into his chair.

"So, let's see. The September after you left, I convinced my parents to let me go visit Mariah in Virginia for fall break. The plan was for me to take the train into D.C. and surprise you. The day of the trip, she came with me." I pause trying to remember every detail of the day. He offers me a smile and another nod. "So, we were on our way to your place and we passed by the coffee shop you had been raving about…"

"The Espresso Bean," we both say at the same time.

I take a deep breath. "Yes, The Espresso Bean. So anyway, everytime we did talk, you'd rave about the coffee and the pastries. I decided to go in and get us both a coffee." I laugh to myself. "I didn't want to show up empty handed."

"Lacey, I had no—"

"Please, let me finish." He nods and I continue. "So, we

walked in and the shop was packed with people. Mariah saw the two of you before I did. You were seated at this tiny table with a woman, who I now know was Eli. You were sitting close to one another, I remember, closer than friends would be sitting. And you were making her laugh. You both looked so happy, and I froze. Mariah grabbed my arm and dragged me out the door and back to the train before I could really process what I'd seen."

"Why didn't you talk to me?"

"I don't know." I let my head fall into my hands. "After you left, you got so busy, and I was so lonely. I felt like I was the annoying high school girlfriend not letting you live your new, cool life. You remember how it was? We would plan to talk and then we wouldn't. I felt like I was losing you, and then I saw you with her."

He leans forward onto his knees and I grab a couple more fries. "Just because I was busy didn't mean I didn't want to be with you. When you called, it felt so out of the blue. I didn't know what to do or say. I don't understand why you didn't say something about Eli then."

I stand and start pacing back and forth in front of his couch. "Because I was seventeen and emotional. I was embarrassed. I mean, fuck, I had planned on…" My voice trails off and I stop moving. I'm not sure I want to tell him what my plan had been. The embarrassment I felt that day creeps back in and makes my stomach turn. I was seventeen. I was in love and I thought I was losing him. I got it in my head we needed to connect and convinced myself sleeping with him was the best course of action. And then I saw him with her and I froze.

"You had planned on what?"

Hearing his question breaks my thoughts, and I let my eyes settle on him. He's looking up at me, his sky-blue eyes begging for me to continue.

"I had planned on sleeping with you," I say quietly. He

clears his throat, and I watch as his Adam's apple bobs up and down. "So imagine how embarrassed I was that I came all that way with the grand plan to give myself to you, and then I saw you with someone else. It was mortifying. So I called you and ended it because you had hurt me, and I didn't want to give you the satisfaction of knowing you had." I plop back down on the couch.

"I'm sorry," he says.

"You're sorry? I'm the one that fucked all of this up. I've created some huge drama because of some teenage narrative I've been telling myself for ten years. You must think I'm the worst person you've ever known."

"I could never think that." His words hang in the air, and for a second he looks at me like he did when we were teenagers. Like I am the only girl he's ever seen. I push the thought from my head. My phone pings and I look down.

CUTE STALKER:

Thinking about you! Want to grab dinner tonight?

I put my phone face down on the coffee table and look back up at Jace. "I mean, you tried to talk to me and I ignored you. Hell, I blocked you and convinced Poppy to block you too." I shake my head. "I'm just, well, I'm so sorry." Tears well in my eyes, and I try to wipe them away. "Oh, god dammit." I blink. "I got something in my eye."

He stands and strides over to where I'm sitting. "Here, let me look." He settles in next to me and our knees brush against each other. He barely grazes my cheek as he moves his fingers to my eye. His other hand rests on my upper arm, steadying himself. My skin tingles under his touch and my lungs fill with his deep, woodsy scent. My breath hitches as I allow my eyes to flutter shut. He carefully plucks something from my eyelashes. "It was a piece of fuzz," he says, causing me to open my eyes again. He studies my face and time feels frozen.

"Lacey?"

"Yeah?"

"Can I hug you?"

I hesitate for a minute before answering. Growing up, he was always there when I needed him. Always willing to give me a hug when life felt hard. My parents weren't like Jace or Poppy's parents. They were great at showing us they were proud of our accomplishments, but when we were hurt or upset, it was like my mom couldn't handle the stress of it, and my dad thought talking would fix it. Jace was always there to hold me and let me cry on his shoulder. A hug from him could make the worst days instantly better. For ten years, I've wished so many times I could hug him and now he's sitting inches away from me.

"Lacey?"

"Huh?"

"Can I hug you? It looks like you could use one."

I nod my head and his arms instantly wrap me up, pulling me in close. I let my arms wrap around him, and my body melts into his. Tears threaten to fall because he's right, a hug is exactly what I needed in this moment. His body is warm and his grip is firm. How is it that we haven't spoken in ten years and he knows exactly what I need? My phone pings again and I move a cushion away, unsure of how long I let him hold me. I grab it from the coffee table and swipe up.

POPPY:

You still over there?

I look up to find he's still sitting next to me. "So, where do we go from here?" he asks.

"I'm not sure." There's so much more that needs to be said, so much lost time that needs to be made up, but his touch has left me feeling dizzy, and I know I need to leave. I need to go home and process everything. "I mean, I've hated you for ten years. Do I just stop hating you?" I laugh, trying to make light of everything.

"Maybe we try to be friends again?" His eyes meet mine with a silent plea.

"I'd like to try that."

"Good. I've missed you, Pixie."

"I've missed you, too, J." His face breaks out into a wide grin.

———

"Poppy," I yell, swinging the door to our apartment open. "You home?"

She walks out of her room holding a duffle bag. "How was your meeting with Jace?"

"I really fucked up."

She drops her bag by the door with a thud. "What do you mean?" She raises an eyebrow.

We both move to the couch, and I recap the events of the day. By the end, tears are running down my cheeks. "I'm so sorry. I convinced you to hate him. If you never forgive me I understand. I was so sure. I never meant for this to happen."

She rubs my back in slow circles, helping me to calm down. "It's okay. It was a long time ago. He's back now, so let's focus on the future. You can't change the past and neither can I."

"You aren't mad?"

"I mean, I'm not exactly thrilled, but we both made decisions based on the information we had. I know you wouldn't have told me unless you believed it to be true, and at the time you did." She wraps her arms around me. "I chose you then, and I would choose you again. I'm glad we can all move forward. I've missed the three musketeers."

My eyes land on her duffle bag. "You going to Logan's again?"

She nods. "Do you want me to stay here? I can call him. I know he would understand."

"No, I'm okay. It was a long day. I'm probably going to curl up in bed with a book and try to process it all. Fill him in on everything, will you?"

"Of course. I'll see you tomorrow." She walks across the room and grabs her bag. She stops at the door and turns back towards me. "I'm so proud of you. I know today was hard, but I'm glad y'all talked. Love you."

"Love you more," I say as she closes the door behind her.

My head falls back on the couch, and I let out a long breath. My phone chimes.

CUTE STALKER:

Everything okay?

Shit, I never texted him back.

> Yes, I'm so sorry. It's been a weird day. Rain check?

CUTE STALKER:

Of course. Can I do anything to make it better?

> You're sweet, but no. I'm okay.

I climb into bed with my e-reader. The sun is still shining outside, but I need to decompress and relax. I open the enemies to lovers book I've been attempting to read, but after a few chapters I put it down. I can't focus. My head is spinning with the events of the day. *That hug.* My stomach knots as I think about the past ten years. How different they may have been if I hadn't assumed the worst of him. If I hadn't listened to everyone else and let my insecurities win.

I mindlessly play with the locket around my neck and

stare at the ceiling fan. Grabbing my phone, I click on my brother's name. I sit up in bed and continue to play with the necklace while I wait on him to answer. His sandy blond hair and green eyes come into view.

"Hey, Sis," he says, over lots of shouting and loud music in the background.

"Hey, bud. Is now a bad time?" I ask.

"Lacey, you there? I can't see you."

"Oh, shit. Yeah. I'm here. Can you hear me?"

"Lacey?" The video freezes and his voice sounds muffled.

"Colt?" The line drops. *Fuck.*

Colt: Sorry I'm out with friends. I'll call you soon. Promise.

Lacey: Have fun!

I throw my phone down on the mattress and pick up my e-reader again. My phone pings again, and I swipe up fully expecting to see a message from my brother. My heart stops when I see Jace's name instead.

JACE:

Tell me something I don't know about you.

Why?

JACE:

We've got ten years to catch up on.
Humor me.

I like to dip my fries in chocolate ice cream.

JACE:

Why didn't you say anything earlier? I think
we had some chocolate ice cream in the
freezer.

LOL! You should try it.

JACE:

Hold on.

A few minutes pass, and then three dots appear on the screen.

JACE:

We had some! You're right. Chocolate ice cream is definitely a top tier dip option.

No way you're eating fries in chocolate ice cream right now.

JACE:

<<selfie attached>>

JACE:

We didn't finish off the fries, so I had to try it for myself.

I'm glad you like it!

JACE:

Maybe we could grab some together sometime.

My heart starts to race when I read his text. *Together.* I'm trying to think of a response when three dots appear again.

JACE:

I meant as friends. You know, just to catch up.

Friends. My heart deflates. Of course that's what he meant. I should be thankful he even wants to be my friend. I definitely don't deserve it.

I'd like that!

JACE:

Me too.

CHAPTER 19: THE BOYS ARE BACK

JACE

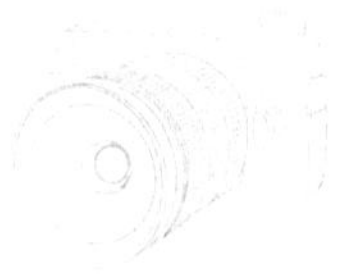

POPPY:

I'm sorry. Will you ever forgive me?

Thank you and yes, I forgive you.

POPPY:

You sure?

Positive.

POPPY:

Okay, good. I missed you.

I missed you too.

———

The warm water surrounds me, relaxing my sore muscles from my morning run. I ran longer than I usually do, but I needed to clear my head and process yesterday.

Funny how sometimes things work out exactly how

they're supposed to. If Eli had been on time, who knows how my conversation with Lacey would have gone.

I turn off the shower and wrap myself in a towel. A knock on the front door echoes through the apartment. "Can you get the door, T?" I yell through my bathroom door.

"Got it," he yells back.

I throw on a pair of shorts and a T-shirt and walk out to see who it is. Logan is sitting on the couch talking to Tanner and drinking coffee.

"Hey, man. I didn't know you were coming over this morning," I say, looking down at my phone to check the time. It's nine thirty.

"Figured I should come and apologize for being a shit friend the past couple of weeks," Logan says, taking a sip from his cup.

"I'm gonna go jump in the shower and let y'all talk," Tanner says. He stands and walks into his room, closing his door behind him.

"You didn't have to do that," I say, walking into the kitchen to pour myself a cup of coffee.

"Yes, I did," he says. I walk back into the living room and sit across from him.

"Look, man. After the party, Poppy told me what happened. When I heard you had cheated, it pissed me off and reminded me of my dad. All I could see was my mom when Poppy was telling me about Lacey. It wasn't fair for me to project my own shit on you."

"It wasn't, but I get it. Your dad's a piece of shit, and you thought I did the exact same thing he did."

"Yeah, but I should've known better. At the graduation party, you said she broke your heart, and then you denied it when she accused you of it. I should've believed you. I let my emotions get the best of me, and I'm sorry."

"I'm not going to lie, you surprised me. I know you love Poppy, but I think of you like my brother."

"I know. It was really fucked up. Poppy and I are still so new. I went into protective mode, I guess, because I want to make her happy. She and I both feel awful."

I rub my hand down my face and take a long sip from my mug. "I get it. You love her."

"Yeah."

"I'm happy y'all found one another." I offer him a smile.

"Does that mean we're cool?" he asks.

"Yeah, we're cool," I say. "Honestly, I should probably thank you for falling in love with Poppy. If you hadn't, I wouldn't have them back in my life."

"They both mean a lot to you, don't they?"

"Yeah. I mean you were at dinner with me and Poppy the other night. She was like my sister, and Lacey is the only girl I've ever loved."

He nods. "Why did you never mention them to me before? I mean, I've known you for a long time."

"It's never really been my style to talk about this sorta thing. Plus it was so long ago, it never came up. The only reason Tanner knew I had an ex named Lacey was because I mentioned her once when we were talking about my mom."

Tanner walks out of his room. "Did y'all kiss and make up?" he asks, chuckling.

"Yeah," I say. "We're cool."

"Thank fuck," he says. "Glad to have the boys back together."

"Me too." The past couple of weeks have felt so out of control. Relief washes over me at the thought that the air is finally clear around everyone who means the most to me. I take a swig of my coffee and exhale.

"What are y'all doing today?" Logan asks. "Poppy's shopping with her sister."

"I was planning to play pickleball with Enzo," Tanner says. "Y'all want to make it a doubles game? I think Donovan is busy, so it'd be the four of us."

"I'm in," I say. "Probably should kick Logan's ass for being such a dick to me."

"Ha!" Logan says. "I said I was sorry. I didn't say I'd let you win.

CHAPTER 20: "THAT'S WHY THEY CALL IT A JUNGLE, SWEETHEART."

LACEY

Sunday

JACE:

How are you doing?

> I still feel completely awful. I'm so sorry that I
> did that to you. You?

JACE:

I actually feel good about it all. I'm really glad
we talked.

> Me too.
>
> How was your day?

JACE:

Good. Logan and I cleared the air and then
we played pickleball with Tanner and Enzo.

> That sounds like fun. Did you win?

JACE:

Ha! No way. Logan and Tanner are too good.
What did you do today?

I went shopping with Poppy and her sister.

JACE:

I haven't seen Olive in years. How is she?

Fine, same as she was when we were younger. She's married and has a cat named Karma that she's obsessed with.

JACE:

Karma?

Yeah, like the Taylor Swift song.

JACE:

I'll take your word for it. Is it safe to assume she's still your favorite artist?

Hard yes! You still listening to nineties country?

JACE:

Yeah, it reminds me of Mom.

Tuesday

JACE:

What's your favorite movie?

Why?

JACE:

I told you we had a lot of catching up to do.

It's still Romy and Michelle's High School Reunion. No movie will ever compare.

JACE:

I should have known that.

It's been a long time. Are you still watching Indiana Jones and the Temple of Doom?

JACE:

You remember my favorite movie?

You only made me watch it one million times.

JACE:

I did not.

You did too! "That's why they call it a jungle, sweetheart."

"Okey dokey, Dr. Jones. Hold on to your potatoes."

"Nothing shocks me. I'm a scientist."

JACE:

Are you just googling quotes?

No, I wish. They are permanently imprinted on my brain.

Thursday

Have I told you I'm sorry today?

JACE:

Have I told you to stop apologizing?

I just feel so bad about everything.

JACE:

I know you do, but I don't want you to feel bad. We both made mistakes back then.

I'm really glad we're becoming friends again, J. I missed you a lot.

JACE:

I missed you too.

CHAPTER 21: PREDICTABLE
LACEY

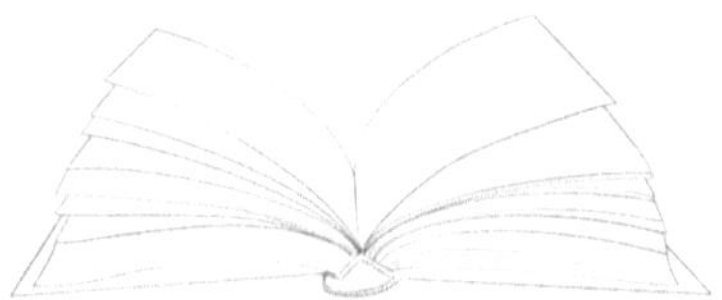

"Lacey, don't make me remind you again that all your paperwork needs to be done by the end of the day," Margaret says the minute I walk through the doors of the therapy gym.

"You got it," I say, forcing a smile and silently groaning.

CUTE STALKER:

We still on to meet at 6?

Perfect!

Shit. I look at my schedule. A miracle is going to have to happen in order for me to get through all of my patients and the pile of paperwork I have to do before I leave. I run out of the gym and head towards room 307.

"Ms. Clara, it's Lacey." I knock on the door and when I hear her voice I swing it open. She's sitting in a chair, already dressed, and reading one of her books. "Happy Friday! You're up bright and early."

"I have a date today," she says.

"A date?"

She sets her book down. "Eugene asked me to meet him

for coffee in the dining room this morning. So I had Marie help me get ready."

"Is that so?" I check my watch. "And what time is this coffee date happening?"

"At eight thirty, so I'm going to need you to make your therapy quick. I have places I need to be."

"You got it." We make our way down to the therapy gym and I help Ms. Clara through an upper body exercise routine.

"You're getting stronger," I say when she finishes it.

"Does that mean I'm almost done with this nonsense?"

"Not quite yet." I laugh. "It's not that bad, is it? At least you get to spend your mornings with me."

"Honey, I didn't work out in my twenties, so what makes you think I want to work out in my eighties?" She eyes the clock on the wall.

"We still have ten minutes. I promise you won't be late." She rolls her eyes. I lead her through a few more sets of exercises. When our ten minutes are up, I help her stand and accompany her to the dining room.

When we arrive, the air smells like a mix of coffee, syrup, and bacon. The man I met a couple of weeks ago is seated at a table for two. He smiles when he sees her.

"Alright dear, that's enough. I can take it from here," she says, shooing me away with her hand. I watch as she slowly makes her way across the space. When she makes it to the table, Eugene stands and pulls out her chair and places a kiss on her cheek.

The Tortured Therapists Department

307 and 330 are currently on a date in the dining room.

WREN:

So cute. Which mumu is she wearing?

> She's not. Woke up early and had the nurse help her get dressed. Even had on some makeup.

GRAY:

STOP IT! That's precious. Maybe I'll take 415
on a walk to get some coffee and spy!

> Do it!

POPPY:

Speaking of dates… Lacey, are you excited
for tonight?

WREN:

Wait, you have a date? With who?

> Chris. The guy from the conference. I'm going to need a miracle to happen though to get out of here on time. Margaret is breathing down my neck about paperwork.

WREN:

Yeah because you never do it on time.

> It's the literal worst part of working here.

AT THE END OF THE DAY, I SIT DOWN IN FRONT OF MY LAPTOP TO finish my notes. I have forty-five minutes to complete them, and I told Chris I'd meet him at tonight's food truck festival.

"Word on the street is that Ms. Clara and Mr. Eugene are actually a thing," Gray says, sitting down next to me.

"Really, who told you that?" I ask, stopping mid note and turning to face her.

"Ms. Ethel. You know she always has all the good gossip," Gray laughs.

"Wouldn't it be so cute if they end up getting married?"

"Lacey! Focus. I need your paperwork done today," Margaret shouts from her office. I roll my eyes. Gray grabs a piece of paper and in bold red letters writes: *Please do not talk to me. I have no self-control.* She grabs a piece of tape and sticks it on my back with a laugh.

"Very funny," I deadpan. "You're part of the problem."

"Don't worry. I'm heading out. Have fun tonight." She pats the piece of paper and laughs as she walks away.

I spend the next half hour working on paperwork and signing off on notes. When I'm finished, I clock out and run home to get ready for my date. I'm cutting it close, but if I hurry, I can change and be close to on time.

I'm a little nervous on the drive over. This is our first official date, if you don't count EPCOT and briefly grabbing drinks after the conference. I can't remember the last first date I had that I was excited for, but this one feels different. Poppy being with Logan all the time has me feeling like I need to grow up and find someone too. I like Chris, and so far we've had a lot of fun together, so for the first time in a long time I'm hopeful this could be something.

When I pull into the parking lot, it's packed. There's not a spot in sight and I circle the lot a few times before I finally find a car backing out. I glance down at the clock. Six ten. *Shit.* I climb out and click into his contact to call him.

"Hey," Chris answers.

"Hi, I'm so sorry I'm late. I just parked. Work was crazy, but I'm here."

"You're fine. I'm standing near the Cajun truck. I'll see you in a few." We hang up and I make my way through the crowd of people. He's standing next to a truck with a large crawfish on the side, still wearing his scrubs.

"If I had known you were going to be in your scrubs, I wouldn't have changed out of mine." I laugh.

He pulls me into a hug and plants a quick kiss on my cheek. "What are you hungry for?"

I glance around the lot where all the trucks are parked. Across the way is a blue and white Greek truck. "Do you like gyros?" I ask.

He nods and we walk over, joining the long line. The heat radiates off the asphalt and the air is a mix of different types of fried food and truck exhaust. "Gosh, it's hot."

"Yeah, starting to think you had the right idea with changing." He looks down at his black scrubs. "So, how was your day?"

"It was good. We found out a couple of the residents are dating, and they're absolutely adorable. How was yours?"

"Fine."

"That's good." There's a lag in the conversation and I shift my weight back and forth. The line starts to move. My phone pings and I look down.

POPPY:

I know you're on your date, but do you know where the caramel sauce is?

I finished it off yesterday.

POPPY:

You traitor! 😭 What am I supposed to put on top of my ice cream?

"Everything okay?" he asks.

"Oh, yeah, just my roommate," I say, putting the phone back in my bag.

Music starts to play and a few people abandon the line in front of us. After what feels like an hour, we finally make it to the front. I order a gyro with fries and extra tzatziki and he orders a gyro with fruit on the side. We pay separately. Once we have our food, we move through the crowd until we find a table.

I place a few fries on top of my sandwich and take a bite.

"Is that good?" he asks.

"What the gyro? Yeah it's delicious, you should try yours."

"No, the fries on top?"

"So, good," I say around a big bite. "Want some fries?"

He shakes his head. "I'll stick to my side of fruit."

"Suit yourself." I search my head for something else to talk about. Tonight feels different than the other times we've hung out, and I'm not sure what's going on with him. "So, do you like to read?" I ask, trying to move the conversation along.

"Yeah," he says. "It's alright."

"Oh, I love it. What kind of books do you like?"

"Mostly historical non-fiction. You?"

"Romance. I'm a sucker for a happily ever after." I smile, but he scowls. "Not a fan of romance, I guess?"

"Can't say that I am. They're a little silly, don't you think?"

"Silly?" I quickly try to fix my tone, but his comment annoys me and I'm offended. "What do you mean?"

He sips his water. "I don't know. I've always found them to be a little out of touch and predictable. I've never seen the point in believing in anything other than reality." He shrugs his shoulders.

"Interesting," I quip.

"Oh, I don't mean it's bad that you read them. It's just not a genre I enjoy."

I take a long drink of my Coke. "So, if you like history, I bet you're really good at trivia."

"Oh, I love a good trivia competition. My friends and I play a lot. It might sound lame, but I watch a lot of Jeopardy too."

"My grandpa loves Jeopardy."

"Very funny," he says with a chuckle.

"My roommate actually mentioned Bruno's, a pizza place near our apartment, was doing a trivia night in a couple of weeks and a bunch of us are going. There's a cabin up for grabs and we're going to try to win it. You should come."

"Really?"

"Unless that's too fast," I say. "My friends are cool though, and it would be super laid back."

"I don't know…that would mean I'd be having to drive back to the city pretty late."

"It's a Friday, so no work the next day. You're welcome to stay at my place with me."

"Really?"

"I wouldn't mind if you stayed. I mean if you want to." I take a bite of my food.

"I do know a lot of random history facts," he says.

"Is it a date then?"

"It's a date," he agrees.

The rest of the meal continues, and we make small talk about work and being OTs. When we finish, he clears our plates and walks me back to my car.

"Sorry if I seem off tonight. I had a hard day at work and couldn't shake it. I'm looking forward to trivia," he says.

"You're going to love my friends. None of them are big fans of romance books either."

He laughs. "Maybe I can see you before then?"

"I'd like that." He pulls me into his arms and I let him kiss me.

What are your thoughts on romance novels?

JACE:

I've never read one.

Do you think they're silly?

JACE:

No, why would I think that?

Because you're a guy.

JACE:

Do you like them?

Yep, that's all I read.

JACE:

Which one is your favorite?

When He Was Wicked by Julia Quinn.

JACE:

I'll have to check it out!

Seriously?

JACE:

We're getting to know each other again. Your favorite book seems like a good way to do that.

Full disclosure: it's spicy!

JACE:

Even better.

I'll read your favorite too. What is it?

JACE:

On The Road by Jack Kerouac. It's a classic.

Just ordered it.

JACE:

I'll let you know when I finish. Can't wait to hear your thoughts.

Deal!

CHAPTER 22: YOU'RE RIDICULOUS

JACE

Sunday

PIXIE:

Look what came in the mail!

PIXIE:

<<picture attached>>

I hope you like it!

PIXIE:

Oh BTW, Poppy's birthday is next Friday. She
wanted a pool party, so everyone's coming
over to our place around 6. You should
come!

I'll be there.

Monday

PIXIE:

Whatcha doing?

Laying in bed reading. You?

PIXIE:

Same! Poppy is with Logan again tonight.

Does that happen a lot?

PIXIE:

Yep. Which is awesome for her, but sucks
for me.

Why does it suck?

PIXIE:

It's Monday which is usually the day we
watch SBTS.

SBTS? Should I know what that means?

PIXIE:

Single By The Sea!

What's Single By The Sea?

PIXIE:

Only the best trash TV around. 20 singles go
to this super remote island and look for their
soulmate.

Ha! Like The Bachelor?

PIXIE:

OMG! It's sooooo much better!

And you can't watch it without Poppy?

PIXIE:

Nope! It's not as fun alone.

I gotcha.

PIXIE:

I think we're going to try to stream it later this
week, but I'll have to stay off the internet.
Can't risk any spoilers.

Tuesday

OMG! Did you see who hooked up last
night?

PIXIE:

Huh?

Single By The Sea. Have you not watched?

PIXIE:

You're ridiculous. No, I haven't and
neither have you.

Yes, I have. I forced Tanner to watch it with
me when he got home from work.

PIXIE:

Stop it!

I'm serious. You can ask him.

PIXIE:

I believe you, but why?

Figured you might want to talk about it with
someone. Also, I think I might sign T up to be
a contestant. Feel like he would thrive in that
chaos.

PIXIE:

Thursday

What's something you're excited about?

PIXIE:

Donovan and Enzo's wedding. Are you going?

I wouldn't miss it.

PIXIE:

Good! You'll have to save me a dance.

Deal!

PIXIE:

What's something you're excited about?

Getting to see you tomorrow.

PIXIE:

It should be a lot of fun!

CHAPTER 23: LIKE WHAT YOU SEE?

JACE

I pull into Lacey and Poppy's apartment complex at the same time as Donovan and Enzo.

"Hey, guys," I say, stepping down from my Jeep. Tonight feels different. It's the first time since Lacey and I cleared the air that we will be around all of our friends. It's been nice getting to know her again over texts the past couple of weeks, but to say I'm nervous is an understatement. I don't know why it felt easier to come around when she hated me, but it did.

Donovan, Enzo, and I walk through the gate, and I look around the pool. Logan, Poppy, Tanner, and Wren are in the pool playing volleyball. Olive, Poppy's older sister, is seated with some guy at one of the tables. She offers me a small smile and a wave. My eyes settle on Lacey sitting on the edge of the pool. She's laughing with Gray and sipping something from a pink cup.

"Happy birthday, gorgeous," Enzo yells at Poppy, who climbs out of the pool and walks over to where we're standing. She wraps both of the other men in a huge hug.

"Happy birthday," I add, handing her the gift I brought.

"Thanks, Jace. You didn't have to get me anything."

I shrug. "It's not much."

She walks over to an empty table and removes the tissue paper. She pulls out a three-pound bag of sour worms and immediately begins to laugh.

"I thought I remembered you liked them," I say.

"I do." She smiles. There's a beat of silence and her eyes find mine. "Hey, I wanted to apologize for everything in person. I know we texted, but I still feel awful."

"You don't have to apologize again. I know it was a hard time, and things were misunderstood. We were young."

"Okay, well yeah, but I'm still sorry and I wanted you to know I'm glad you're here." She throws her arms around me and squeezes me tight before letting go and ripping open the bag of candy.

"Me too."

Lacey walks up behind her and I have to stop myself from staring. She's wearing a tiny green bikini. Her hair is pulled out of her face, and her skin is sunkissed. She looks so fucking beautiful. The locket still sits around her neck.

"Whatcha get?" she asks, peering over Poppy's shoulder. "Sour worms?"

Lacey looks in my direction. "You remembered she liked them?" A couple of girls walk through the gate and Poppy runs off to greet them.

"You're surprised?" I ask.

"No, I mean, I don't know. It's been a long time."

"There's a lot I remember about you, too, you know?"

"Is that so?"

Her voice trails off, and silence fills the space between us. I go to say something but am interrupted as Tanner runs and jumps into the pool, shouting "Cannon ball" at the top of his lungs. Lacey lets out a laugh as she looks over her shoulder in his direction.

Unintentionally, I pull off my shirt at the exact moment

she turns back to face me. Her eyes noticeably move down my body before she quickly tries to divert her stare.

"Like what you see?" I tease.

"Oh, what, huh, no," she says, flustered. Her cheeks turn a light pink. "I zoned out for a minute." She turns and makes her way back to the pool. Her suit barely covers her ass, and I allow myself to stare for longer than I should. "You coming, J?" she asks, looking back at me.

Fuck.

———

"Wait, Lace. You gotta tell us about Chris," Gray says after she swallows down a bite of her burger, catching my attention. We're all sitting around a few of the poolside tables.

"Yes, tell us all about the conference guy," Wren adds.

"What do you want to know? The date was fun, and he's great. He lives in the city, so with work it makes it hard to plan dates, but I'm seeing him tomorrow."

"Do you have a picture of him?" Wren asks.

Lacey grabs her phone and taps a few times before turning it towards the girls.

"Oh, he's cute," Gray says.

"Right?" Lacey says. "So cute." All the girls giggle, and her cheeks turn a light shade of pink.

I take a swig of my beer, my shoulders tense as they talk. I know I have no right to feel jealous, but the last thing I want to hear about is the guy Lacey is dating. I'm not sure how I keep ending up in these situations: Alex, Tanner, and now Chris. I try to remind myself that we said we were going to be friends, and this is what friends do.

"It's nice to be with someone who can understand what it's like to be an OT," she continues.

"But do you have anything else in common with him?" I ask.

"Of course I do," she says. "Actually, I invited him to trivia night next week, so y'all can all meet him."

"Trivia night?" I ask.

I feel everyone's eyes shift to me.

"Oh, shoot," she says. "We made the plan before you and I settled things. You're welcome to join us."

"I don't want to intrude."

"No, man. That's my bad. I meant to mention it, but then things got stressful at work and it slipped my mind," Tanner says.

"Yes, come! You were the captain of the quiz bowl team in high school," Poppy says. "We could use someone who actually knows what they're doing. Winner gets a weekend stay at this cool cabin over the Fourth of July."

Logan chuckles. "I'd like to think I know what I'm doing."

Poppy leans in and kisses him. "Oh, you definitely know what you're doing."

"Get a room," Tanner shouts, tossing a crinkled up napkin at them and causing the group to break out in laughter. Logan throws Poppy over his shoulder and takes off toward the pool. She lets out a loud shriek, and water splashes all over us.

"So anyway…" Lacey begins, wiping water from her face. "It'll be great. Chris is a huge history buff, so between the two of you there's no way we'll lose."

The rest of the group agrees, but I'm torn. My stomach twists at the thought of seeing her with another person. The memory of Alex kissing Lacey pops into my head. "I'll think about it. Shoot me the details and I'll see if I can make it."

"Good." She smiles.

"Poppy and Logan, come on. It's time for cake," she yells.

CHAPTER 24: THAT'S A WEIGHTED QUESTION

LACEY

"**W**hat did you think about Jace being there tonight?" I ask as Poppy, Logan, and I make our way back to our apartment. Our hands are full with the aftermath of the night, and I'm exhausted.

"I think it was good he came," Poppy says. "I'm glad we can all put the past behind us and move forward. How are you feeling?"

That's a weighted question. How am I feeling? At seventeen, I was sure Jace would be my forever and then D.C. happened. My world as I knew it came crashing down, and I spent the last ten years heartbroken and hating him for what I thought he did. And then as quick as it ended a decade ago, he proved me wrong. He never cheated. I was the one who fucked it all up.

My mind drifts to him tearing off his shirt. His toned abs and those tattooed arms.

"Lace?"

"Huh?" I look up to see Poppy and Logan staring at me. We're standing in front of our apartment door and I have no memory of getting here. Like my body was's on autopilot while my mind was somewhere else entirely.

"You gonna unlock the door?" she asks, gesturing to the door knob.

"Oh, yeah, sorry." I set down the container of leftover food I'm holding and fumble for my key. I slide it in and swing the door open. They move past me and I follow.

"Are you ever going to answer my question?" Poppy asks as she moves around the apartment putting everything away.

"Yeah, you kind of spaced out there," Logan adds. "You good?"

I shake my head. "Oh, yeah, I'm fine. Just tired and a little tipsy. What did you ask?"

"I asked how you were feeling about Jace being at my party?"

"Oh, I don't know. I guess fine. Seemed normal. Glad he could make it." She stops moving and looks at me with a smirk. Logan lets out a little laugh.

"What?"

"Nothing," she chimes.

"Don't nothing me. What?"

"Nothing. I'm glad y'all are trying to be friends again, that's all. Come on Logan, I'm ready for bed."

"You're lucky it's your birthday or I would make you tell me what you're thinking."

"Love you, Lace," she says, giggling as they walk towards her bedroom, hand in hand. Logan leans over and places a kiss on the top of her head and then they disappear. There is a tug on my heart as I watch them walk away. Will I ever find someone who loves me that much?

"I love you more," I chime, looking down at my phone to check for text messages from Chris, but there's nothing. I make my way into the kitchen and grab a cup from the cabinet. My phone pings and I swipe up.

JACE:

Tonight was fun! Thanks for the invite.

I quickly fill up the glass with water and head to my room so I can text him back. I'm getting dressed in my pajamas when my phone pings again.

JACE:

I think I will come next week to trivia, so shoot me the details when you can.

It's next Friday at Bruno's. Starts at 6. I'm really glad you're coming!

I crawl into my bed and snuggle deep into my pillows. Three dots appear on the screen and then disappear. Why am I watching his text messages like a teenager with a crush? I don't have a crush on him. Even if I did, why would he ever give me another chance?

JACE:

Can I ask you a question?

Sure.

JACE:

What was your favorite birthday (has to be one I missed)?

Twenty was a good one.

JACE:

What made it special?

Poppy was back from Europe and she surprised me with ice skating. We snuck little bottles of peppermint vodka and spiked our hot chocolate. We spent the whole day together and had the best time. We even took pictures with Santa!

<<Santa photo attached>>

JACE:

You look happy.

That day I was!

JACE:

So Poppy went to Europe?

Yeah for a year with fuck face. It ended awful and they broke up.

JACE:

I bet you missed her.

I hesitate before I respond. My freshman year of college was the loneliest I have ever been. Jace was supposed to be back and we were supposed to be at Farrington together. Then, Poppy left to follow Lord Fuckwad around Europe, and I was alone.

My parents were too busy with my brother and my dad's job to notice how sad I was. When I did try to talk to them, I was met with lectures about how I needed to grow up and focus on getting my degree.

The only thing that made it bearable were my Friday calls with Annie, Jace's mom, and I don't know if I can handle that conversation tonight. I inhale deeply. We said we would try to be friends, but how much should I let him in?

I did. Night, J.

JACE:

Sweet dreams, Pixie.

CHAPTER 25: THIS FUCKING GUY
JACE

The parking lot at Bruno's is slammed with cars when my Uber pulls into the parking lot. I hop out and make my way through the front door of the restaurant.

My eyes land on Lacey the minute I walk in. She's seated at a table with Logan, Poppy, and some guy I've never seen before. Her hair falls around her shoulders in loose curls, and her whole face lights up as she laughs at something the guy next to her says. I freeze and realize this must be the infamous Chris. I suck in a deep breath. We agreed to be friends again, and part of that is meeting the men she brings around. I know it's true, but it doesn't make this easier.

I feel a hand slap across my back and I look over my shoulder to find Tanner followed by Wren and Gray.

"You ready to dominate trivia, dude?" he asks, squeezing my shoulders. We all begin to walk towards our friends.

"Yeah, can't wait," I manage to choke out. Lacey stands when we approach, and I get a better look at what she's wearing. Her white workout top is fitted and hugs her tits perfectly. The locket is still hanging around her neck like the universe is taunting me. Her skirt is light purple and fits her like a second skin.

"Hey, everybody." She smiles. "This is Chris. Chris, this is Jace, Tanner, Wren, and Gray."

"It's nice to meet you all," he says, putting out his hand, shaking mine and then Tanner's. We all sit around the table and I take a seat directly across from Lacey.

"So, Chris, Lacey said you know your history," I offer, trying to be cordial.

"I think I do."

"Good," says Poppy. "I want that cabin. We have to win."

"Welcome to Friday Night Trivia. I'm the one and only Legendary Leonard, and I'll be your host this evening. If your group will be participating, please make your way to the bar, give me your team name, and pick up your answer sheets. We'll begin shortly," our trivia host says over the mic. Some eighties tune begins to blare through the speakers.

"What should our team name be?" Poppy asks. "I'll go get the stuff and turn it in."

I've never been good at this sort of thing. The first thing that pops into my head is Parliament, the name for a group of owls. Owls and trivia go together, right? *Shit, that's bad, but it's all I got.* I begin to offer my suggestion, but I'm interrupted by our waitress.

"Hi, I'll be taking care of y'all tonight. What can I get you to drink?"

"Well, *hello* beautiful," Tanner says, raking his eyes down her body.

"Settle down, pretty boy," the waitress says, pulling out a notepad and immediately looking annoyed.

"You think I'm pretty?" he flirts.

"It wasn't a compliment. What can I get you to drink?"

The rest of the table is deep in conversation about the trivia team's name. Lacey laughs at something Chris says, and my stomach rolls. I turn my attention back to the interaction between my roommate and the waitress, who looks like she could eat him alive.

"Sounded like one," he presses.

"Tanner, stop flirting and help us pick a name," Gray says. Logan and I both choke on a laugh. The waitress's cheeks turn a deep red and she looks around the table.

"We'll take a couple pitchers of Miller and waters all the way around," I say. The waitress nods and quickly moves away from us

"You jealous, Gray?" Tanner says in a cocky tone, turning to face her.

"Gross," she says flatly.

"Focus, y'all. We need a team name," Poppy says.

Tanner clears his throat. "I vote Dink and Balls."

"We can't name ourselves that," Chris says.

"Why not?" Lacey asks. "It's the name of their pickleball team."

"It's pretty inappropriate."

"I think it's funny. They have the cutest mascot. It's a pickle and he's got little pickleballs as balls." She laughs.

"Suit yourselves," he says, sounding like a pompous asshole.

"I'm cool with that," I say. Chris's eyes shoot in my direction, and I stop myself from saying anything else. *This fucking guy.* Lacey offers me a small smile.

"It's perfect," Poppy adds, standing up and running towards the bar.

She returns with a pencil and an answer sheet. The music continues to play, and the conversation around the table is a mix of updates about work and strategizing how we're going to win the cabin. Chris stays mostly quiet, and I can't seem to figure out what he and Lacey have in common. Lacey brightens up the whole room while Chris somehow dims it.

"Where are Enzo and Donovan?" I ask.

"Out of town, but they fully expect us to win so they can come to the cabin," Lacey says.

"Of course they do." I laugh.

"There are more of you?" Chris asks with a chuckle.

"Yep, Donovan and Enzo are getting married soon, and Chloe was going to come, but her sitter canceled at the last minute," Lacey explains.

"Have you all known each other for a long time?"

"Some of us have known each other longer than others," I say, my eyes shifting to Lacey's. Fuck, she looks beautiful tonight. I don't know what I was thinking sitting directly across from her.

"What do you—" Chris begins, but he's interrupted.

"Alright folks, it's time to get tonight started." The music fades as Leonard begins to talk. "Please take a moment to put your phones away. Cell phones will not be tolerated, and your team will automatically forfeit if I see a phone being used at your table." The restaurant fills with the sound of people putting away their phones, and I place mine in my pocket.

"Okay, now that we've addressed the cell phone policy. There will be seven rounds of questions tonight. Each round will have three questions. I will ask a question, and you will have until the end of the song to turn in your answers. You decide how many points you wager for each question. We're going to start this off with a bang—or should I say a POP! Your categories for round one are pop hits, poppin' bodies, and popular sports."

Poppy frantically jots down each category onto the slip of paper in front of her. Our waitress returns and drops off the first round of beer and grabs our pizza orders. "Okay, so when he asks the question, I'll write our answer and run it up to him. We gotta be quick, so everyone be ready," Poppy lectures.

"Yes ma'am," Lacey quips, saluting Poppy with her hand.

Logan, Tanner, and I all stifle a laugh.

"Stop it. I really want to win this," she says.

"We can tell." Tanner chuckles. "Seems like Logan's competitive nature is really rubbing off on you."

"Is not," Poppy argues.

"I beg to differ," Lacey says, nudging Poppy with her elbow.

Poppy giggles, and Logan leans over and places a kiss on her forehead. "My girl knows what she wants, and she wants that cabin."

"We got this," I say, offering them a smile. I let my eyes explore the restaurant. There are at least ten other tables participating in trivia night, and each one looks more intense than the last. We definitely have our work cut out for us.

"Okay, your first category is pop hits. This song, originally released in 2019 and then re-released as a single in 2023, is now Taylor Swift's most streamed song of all time." Another eighties song starts to blare through the speakers.

Lacey and Poppy whisper-scream "Cruel Summer" at each other, and Poppy scribbles it down.

"Are we sure?" Chris asks.

"Yes," both girls say in unison, and I can't help but chuckle.

"Chris, I'm no Taylor Swift fan, but I imagine the girls know what they're talking about. Want to wager three points, ladies?" I ask.

Lacey offers me a big smile, and Poppy jots down a three on the slip of paper. She stands and runs toward the front of the restaurant.

"I was just saying that she has a lot of popular songs," he tries to argue.

"It's okay. We know when we're right, and we're never wrong about Taylor Swift. You'll see," Lacey teases, but Chris doesn't look amused.

Poppy returns with a cocky smile. "We were right," she

says, plopping down in her seat next to Logan and cutting her eyes in Chris's direction.

The music fades out, and our host comes back on the mic. "Alright. The second category is poppin' bodies. If you were to crack the joints of your finger, what three joints would you be popping?"

Both Chris and Lacey's faces light up. "Quick, give me the paper, Poppy," Lacey practically shouts.

"Distal interphalangeal joint, metacarpophalangeal joint…" Chris begins. Lacey is scribbling them down as the rest of the table watches her and him work together to come up with the answer. I fucking hate it.

"Shit. What's the third one?" Chris asks. They search each other's faces like the answer is somehow going to appear on the other's forehead. The knot in my gut tightens. I have no right to feel this way. I know I don't, but I hate seeing her with this guy. I barely know him, but it's obvious she is way out of his league.

Lacey looks back at the paper and reads it to herself a couple of times before a wide smile spreads across her lips, and she begins to write again. "Proximal interphalangeal joint," she whispers.

"Yes, that's it," he says, slapping the table.

"Y'all good with two points?" she asks. We all nod, and she jumps up from the table and runs the paper to the front. Jealousy pulses through my body, and I take a long swig of my beer, letting the ice-cold liquid cool me down.

"No way any of the other tables got it correct," Chris boasts.

"I guess we'll see," Tanner says. Lacey returns with a big smile on her face.

"Okay, last question of round one. The category is popular sports. This sport was invented in 1965 by Pritchard, Bell, and McCallum." "Don't Stop Believing" is fed through the speakers, and our whole table is filled with blank stares and blinks.

"Does anyone have any idea?" Logan asks.

"Not a fucking clue, man," Tanner adds.

"Would be really nice if we could use our phones right about now."

"Don't you even think about it," Poppy scolds, her finger shooting in my direction.

I throw my hands up. "I wouldn't dare, but I have no clue what he's talking about." I shake my head.

"Could it be basketball?" Chris asks.

"Basketball has been around a lot longer than 1965," I say.

"True," Lacey says. "So, think of some newer sports."

The other tables are all noticeably quiet, and I know we need to get this answer right.

"It's pickleball," Wren says, so quietly that I can barely make it out.

"What?" Logan asks.

"The answer is pickleball," she repeats.

The corners of Tanner's mouth tip up. "Hell yeah, Wren." He puts out his hand for a high five, and she hesitantly meets him with hers. "How did we not think of that?"

"Hurry, Poppy. Write it down," Gray says. She writes quickly, placing our final point next to the ten-letter word. She pops up and runs toward the front as the last notes of the song play.

CHAPTER 26: PIXIE?

LACEY

Empty metal pizza trays and beer glasses litter the table. Our waitress stops by to refill our water cups and begins to clear off the used dishes. The restaurant is empty other than the trivia teams and the staff that is starting to wind down for the evening.

"Last call," our waitress says.

"One more round?" Jace asks. A large, handsome smile erupts across his face. Most everyone agrees and the waitress disappears toward the bar.

"Okay, folks, we have made it to the last round of our game," Leonard announces as he plays a sad sound effect over the speaker. He begins to recap each team's score, and it's a close game.

We are currently in a three-way tie for first place with the Trivia Terminators and the Quiz Daddies. If we want the cabin, we have to get every point this round.

"This round is for the lovers." Some nineties love ballad begins to play in the background. There's a dramatic pause, and I watch as Logan's eyes find Poppy's. I turn my gaze to Chris, but he's finishing his last slice of pizza and doesn't even look in my direction. When I turn to grab my beer, I find

Jace's eyes locked on me, and I allow myself to stare back. Warmth pools deep in my belly and my heart rate quickens. I know I shouldn't be staring, but I can't help myself.

"Book lovers, movie lovers, and music lovers," Leonard says, finishing naming the categories.

"You okay?" Jace asks, causing me to break my gaze and stand abruptly.

"Oh, yeah. I'm great. Just thinking about what we have to do to win the cabin. I, um, I'm going to run to the bathroom, do one of y'all want to come with me?" I turn to my friends. All three girls stand at the same time.

"Hurry back," Tanner yells as we begin to move away from the table. "We've got asses to beat."

I roll my eyes and the four of us finish making our way to the restroom. The door swings open and I make a beeline for the sink. My hands grip the laminate countertop and I try to shake away the leftover feelings from the stare contest I just had with Jace.

"Chris seems nice," Wren says, running her hands through her red hair.

"Oh, yeah, he's great. I'm glad y'all like him."

"He's definitely the safe choice," Gray adds.

"What's that supposed to mean?" My eyes find her in the mirror and she shrugs.

"Nothing. He seems fine," she explains. "Safe. You know?"

I don't know what choice she's referring to. Chris is nice. He has a good job. After years of making the wrong choice, the safe choice feels like the right one. Plus, choice would mean I have other options, and I definitely don't. I shake off her words. Poppy walks out of one of the stalls and begins to wash her hands. "What do you think about Chris?" I ask.

Her eyes dart toward Wren and Gray.

"What? None of y'all like him, do you?" I question my friends.

"No, no one is saying that. He's fine. If you're truly happy with him, then I'm happy." She dries her hands with a paper towel and walks past me towards the door. We all follow her out.

I sit back down next to Chris and the final round of trivia begins. "Our first category for our lovers round is book lovers. This series by Julia is set during the regency era and features stories about siblings Anthony, Benedict, Colin, Daphne, Eloise, Francesca, Gregory, and ____?"

The answer pops into my head immediately, but before I can get the name out, I watch as Jace grabs the answer sheet from Poppy and jots something down.

"Come on, man. Now's not the time for you to try to answer questions," Logan says.

"Yeah," Poppy adds. "Everyone knows Lacey's the reader."

"Okay, then." He hands me the piece of paper with a cocky grin, and I read his answer. *He got it fucking right.*

"How'd you know?"

"I read," he says, like none of us should be surprised.

"You knew the answer?" Chris questions.

"Lacey recommended one of the books in the series, so I started with book one," Jace says. "I'm about to finish book two."

"You're reading the whole series?" I ask.

"Well yeah, you can't read a series out of order, and I haven't made it to book six yet, so I hadn't mentioned it." My mind tries to wrap around what he's admitted.

"This is a very sweet moment, but if I don't take the answer up, then we're going to lose. You sure he's right, Lace?" Poppy asks.

I nod and watch as she puts a three next to our answer and then jumps up to turn in the question.

"If you need book recommendations, I'm sure I can give you a few you would actually enjoy," Chris says.

"What makes you think I didn't enjoy Lacey's recommendations?" Jace argues.

"It's a chick book. Is it not?"

"I wasn't aware books were gender specific. You should read it," Jace says and then throws a wink in my direction. I feel my cheeks blush, and I instantly feel Chris's hand on my knee. I shift my legs enough to make him pull away. *I need to get a fucking grip.* Jace is my ex. I'm dating Chris.

"It's time for question number two, lovers. This time we are heading to the movies. This 2008 rom-com features Matthew and Kate as they get a second chance at love and look for buried treasure."

"*Fool's Gold,*" Logan and Poppy say simultaneously with a laugh. Poppy scribbles it down with a two and runs it up to the front.

"We're so close to the cabin being ours," Poppy says when she returns. "We're two for two."

"Hell yeah!" Tanner high fives Jace and Logan.

"Alright, it's time for our last category, music lovers. Once the final song ends, I will tally up the final scores. Good luck, and now for your final question. This song topped the charts in 1974 and was later featured on the soundtracks for *Reservoir Dogs* and *Guardians of the Galaxy.*"

"Tanner, you watch Marvel movies. Do you have any idea what he's talking about?" Jace asks.

"I think it's 'Hooked On A Feeling,' but I'm not positive. Does anyone else have an idea?"

"When does that play in *Guardians of the Galaxy*? I think you're thinking of a different song," Chris questions.

"No, I'm a huge Marvel fan. I've seen that movie at least thirty times. It definitely plays when they're at the—"

"Prison," Wren finishes Tanner's sentence.

"Exactly," Tanner says, smiling at Wren.

Chris opens his mouth to say something, and I interrupt him before he can. "Quick, Poppy, write it down and run it to the front. The song is almost over." She does what I say and disappears.

"Well?" Chris asks when she returns.

"I'm not sure. He wouldn't tell me." We all sit in silence as the music fades from one song to the next and wait for our host to announce the winners.

After a few songs, Leonard is back on the mic and listing off the standings. He begins with tenth place and slowly moves up the list toward first. The tension at our table is palpable.

"In third place, Trivia Terminators." The table to our left groans.

"Folks, it appears we have a two-way tie for first between Dink and Balls and Quiz Daddies."

Our table and theirs erupt into cheers as everyone stands. Chris puts both of his arms up for a double high five and my hands find his. His fingers lace with mine, and he pulls me in for a quick kiss. My head turns to find Jace's eyes locked on me over the edge of his beer. His jaw tightens, and his Adam's apple bobs in his throat. If I didn't know any better, I would think he was jealous. I feel my face twist with confusion, quickly trying to hide it.

"Alright, settle down. Settle down. It's time for the tie breaker. The final question is for our two first place teams only. You will have until the song ends to get me your answer. If you both answer correctly, then the winning team will be whoever gets their answer to me first. Are you ready?"

There's a pause as everyone settles back into their chairs and waits for the question. Most of the other teams have left, but a few still remain watching to see who takes home the grand prize.

"Your category is rare wildlife."

Jace and my eyes lock across the table. I hear Poppy let out a little squeak of excitement.

"Native to Mexico, this bird, known for its small size and

unusual color, was recently rediscovered in Brazil by a group of scientists and dedicated wildlife photographers."

"The Bix," Jace and I say at the exact same time.

"You know?" he asks.

"Know what?" Gray says. The rest of the table is staring at the two of us.

"I might have googled you," I admit. My cheeks heat.

"What did you say?" Chris asks.

"Holy fucking shit," Tanner says as a large smile spreads across his face.

"Wait, do you know what it is?" Wren asks.

"Can someone please give me the answer? The other team looks like they have an answer," Poppy says, frantically.

"You want to do the honors?" Jace asks. I grab the piece of paper from Poppy and jot down "Bixito Parrot." Standing quickly, I turn to head toward where Leonard sits. Out of the corner of my eye, I see a flash of pink. I turn my head and see a brunette wearing a pink dress heading toward the bar. We both make it to the front at the same time. Leonard laughs as we both slam our answer sheets onto the small table.

"Congratulations to our winners, Dink and Balls!"

Cheers erupt from our table as I flip around and I let out a loud scream. The brunette scoffs. *We did it*. We won the cabin. I skip back toward my friends and straight into the arms of Jace. He wraps me up tight and spins me around. I let my arms wrap around his neck, and his woodsy scent takes over my senses. My arms erupt with goosebumps, and for a split second I forget where I am.

I hear someone clear his throat, and when I look over Jace's shoulder, my eyes find Chris. Jace sets me down, and I straighten out my clothes, unsure of what just happened. Making my way around the table, I pull Chris into a hug.

"So how did you two know the answer?" he asks, pulling away.

"Um, well, Jace was part of the team who found it last year."

Chris's eyes widen, and Jace shrugs.

"Wait, what? I had no idea you actually found it," Poppy says, moving towards Jace and wrapping her arms around him. "And to think how obsessed you and Lacey were when we were younger, and then you grew up and actually found it!" Poppy giggles.

"Y'all have all known each other a really long time?" Chris questions.

"Yeah. Pixie and I have known each other since we were in diapers," Jace explains.

"Pixie?" Chris's face contorts at the sound of the nickname, and my cheeks heat.

CHAPTER 27: BULLIES, BOOKS, AND BIG NEWS

JACE - TWENTY YEARS AGO

"**N**erd alert! Nerd alert!" Alex yells from the top of the tall red tower on the playground. I hang my head and look at the ground trying to ignore them like my parents told me to, but it's hard.

A loud thud comes from inside the yellow tube slide, and Beau appears in the opening followed by Alex.

"Hey, science dork, cool shirt," Beau says, shoving my shoulder and causing the book I'm holding to fall onto the ground. I quickly pick it up. My eyes look down at the T-shirt I'm wearing. It's blue and has a picture of a large red macaw with the words "Feelin' Macawsome." My mom bought it for me, and I thought it was cool until now.

I move toward the swing set and take a deep breath. I should be able to stand up to them. I'm a year older than they are, but I'm small for my age and they're big for theirs.

"Hey, guys," I try, but it's more of a squeak.

"Hey, guys," Alex repeats in a high-pitched voice.

Since August, Beau and Alex have made fun of me every day at recess, and I'm so sick of it. I'm not into sports like they are, and they think they can make fun of me because of it.

"Hey, Jace, over here," Lacey's voice calls from one of the

swings. Poppy, our new neighbor, is on the swing next to her, and they're waiting on me. Yesterday, I challenged them to a "who could swing the highest" competition, and today is the day I kick both of their butts.

"It's so weird they hang out with you," Beau says as we approach the swings.

"Lacey, how are you friends with him?" Alex asks. "Don't you think it's weird he's so obsessed with birds?"

Beau and Alex begin running around me with their arms outstretched, flapping them up and down like wings—both squawking and laughing. Poppy sits quietly watching them, but Lacey jumps off her swing and charges them, her blonde pigtails bouncing as she does.

"Look at his dumb shirt," Alex says.

"And his animal book," Beau adds.

"Stop being such jerks. His shirt is cool, and I gave him that book. Maybe one day you two will learn to read," she yells, sticking out her foot and tripping Alex as he runs by her. "Oops!" She giggles.

Beau helps Alex up and they both stare, stunned by the tiny girl who just brought Alex to the ground.

"I think it's cool he likes birds and animals because I like them too." She crosses her arms. "Especially the pixie bird."

"Like a fairy?" Beau asks. "Dude, you like fairies?" He looks over at me.

I don't say anything. I just smile and watch Lacey.

"So lame," Alex says through fits of laughter.

"It's not lame," Lacey argues. "The pixie is really cool, and it's not a fairy. Jace is going to find it one day, and the two of you will never do anything that cool."

"Find it one day?" Beau asks.

"Yeah, find it? Because it's not real?" Alex laughs.

She turns around and sits back down on the swing. "Come on, Jace. I bet I can go higher than both you and Poppy. See you never, Beau and Alex." She giggles and sticks out her tongue. They stomp off, and I take a seat next to her.

"I can stand up for myself," I say, feeling a little embarrassed.

"I know you can, but no one is mean to my friends."

"Well, thanks." Her eyes find mine, and for the first time, I notice they're green.

"Of course, and the pixie is really cool," she says. "Poppy, you're going to love it. Jace is super smart and knows a lot of cool animal facts. For his birthday last year, I got him this book and it talks all about the pixie."

"You know it's called a Bixito Parrot, right? I call it the Bix for short. Not the pixie." I start laughing and so do her and Poppy.

"I like pixie better," she says.

"Me too." I grin. "Now, you ready to lose?" Both girls laugh, and we all start pumping our legs as hard as we can.

———

"HEY, DAD?" HE'S SITTING ON THE COUCH, AND MY MOM IS IN the kitchen baking cupcakes for our school bake sale that's tomorrow.

"Yeah, kid? What's up?"

I sit down next to him and he mutes the TV.

"Can I ask you a question?"

"Sure. Everything okay?"

"Oh, yeah, I'm fine."

"You sure? You were awfully quiet at dinner. Barely touched your sloppy joe."

"I was just thinking, I guess."

"Thinking?" He smiles at me. "What's on your mind, bud?"

"How do you know when you're in love with someone?"

"Woah! Hitting me with the tough questions tonight,

aren't we? You've got plenty of time to worry about that. Let's try to get through the third grade first. Don't you think so?" He pats my knee and unmutes the TV, but I don't move.

"No, Dad. I need to know. This is important. Tell me."

He takes a deep breath. "Okay, I guess we're having this conversation." He mutes the TV. "Um, I think it's different for everyone. For me, it was a bunch of small moments with your mom. Our first kiss."

"Ewww, don't be gross."

He chuckles. "Well, you wanted to know. It was also the way she saw me for who I was and stuck by me no matter what. I knew deep in my gut she was my person. One day, I realized I didn't want to do life without her, and the rest was history. Does that make sense?"

I nod, not really sure what he means, but I think I get it.

"Why do you want to know?"

"Because I think I'm in love."

A huge grin erupts across his face, and for a second, I think he's going to laugh, but he doesn't.

"Annie, you may want to get in here. Jace has some big news," he yells.

CHAPTER 28: THERE'S A FINE LINE BETWEEN LOVE AND HATE
LACEY - PRESENT

Chris has barely spoken a word since we got in the Uber and left trivia. Poppy and Logan keep trying to make small talk about the Fourth of July weekend, but he's not biting. He's sitting next to me silent, like he's pissed. It's a little annoying. Actually, it's a lot annoying, and I don't know what it all means.

The Uber comes to a stop in the parking lot of our apartment complex, and the four of us climb out and head up the stairs. Poppy, Logan, and I make our way into the apartment, but Chris pauses outside the door.

"You're coming in, right?"

"I'm not sure," he says. He's standing there with his hands in his pockets and his shoulders slouched.

I step back outside and close the door behind me. I reach out and try to touch his arm, but he moves away from me to lean against the metal railing of our landing. Both hands remain firmly in the pockets of his pants.

"Did I do something?" I ask. My mind immediately revisits the hug with Jace after we won. Is that why he's acting so mad? People hug. Friends hug. Fuck, strangers hug. Surely, he can see it was just a hug. Right?

It was just a hug. Right?

"That Jace guy likes you."

His words stay suspended in the humid air surrounding us.

"No, he doesn't."

"Yes, he does, and I think you might like him too."

I shake my head. "You're wrong. Up until two weeks ago, I hated him."

"There's a fine line between love and hate, Lacey."

A laugh spills out of me and I shake my head again. "No. Do we have a history? Yes. Are we friends? Maybe, but he's just another guy in our friend group." I move toward him, but he doesn't move. He doesn't try to invade my personal space at all, and I hate it.

"He calls you by a nickname. He reads the books you like. You don't think it means he sees you as more than a friend?"

"The nickname is something stupid he's called me since I was seven. It's not like he calls me baby or babe. It's an inside joke from when we were kids."

"And the book thing?"

"I don't know. Maybe he likes romance books." I shrug and try to laugh, but he continues to stand there stiff as a board with his mouth in a thin line.

"Look. You and I haven't talked a lot about our past relationships, but I'll tell you anything you want to know. Please let's go inside. I'm tired, and I was really looking forward to you staying over."

The corner of his mouth tips up slightly.

"Does that mean you're coming in?" I reach my hand out, and to my surprise he takes it in his.

Disappointment fills me with how underwhelming the gesture feels. My skin doesn't react to his touch at all. In fact, both of our hands feel a little sweaty from the heat and my gut reaction is to let go, but I don't. I will myself to push that idea as far out of my head as I can and lead him through the door instead.

———

My alarm blares, and I look over to find the other side of my bed empty. After Chris followed me inside, we fell asleep. We didn't revisit the conversation that happened outside the apartment door. When I asked him if he would be coming with all of us to the cabin, he gave me some noncommittal response about having to check with work.

We brushed our teeth, changed into pajamas, and then fell asleep without even a foot graze under the covers. It's now six thirty and I don't know at what point he left because I might as well have been sleeping in my bed alone. I breathe out and rub my hands over my eyes. Scanning the screen of my phone, the green and white message app is topped with a little red five. I swipe up, and I'm met with message after message from Jace.

JACE:

Tonight was a blast!

JACE:

I can't believe the Bix was the winning answer!

JACE:

How long have you known I found it?

JACE:

The Bix I mean.

JACE:

Shit, sorry. I know it's late. I hope none of these woke you.

I let out a giggle. He was always cute when a little flustered.

> You didn't wake me.

JACE:

> Good morning, Pixie!

> Morning!

> I've known about the Bix since the day we went out on the boat. I'm really proud of you.

JACE:

> Why didn't you say anything?

> Because I didn't know if you wanted me to and us being friends again is still so new.

My phone rings, and Jace's name is displayed across the screen. I sit up in bed and smooth the comforter around my legs.

"Hello." My voice sounds groggy, so I clear my throat and try again. "Hello."

"Hi, Pixie."

My stomach does a flip at the sound of the nickname coming out of his mouth. My eyes find the clock on my bedside table.

"Everything okay, J? I'm about to start getting ready. My boss asked me to work today."

"Oh, yeah. Right. I wanted you to know that when our team found it, you were the person I wanted to call. More than anything, I wish we could have shared that moment because it felt like it belonged to you and me."

The line is silent for a few moments, and I have to remind myself to start breathing again.

"Anyway, I, um, I'm glad you know about it now and

yeah, I guess I wanted you to hear me say that versus reading it on a text."

"Thanks for telling me. Are you really reading the entire *Bridgerton* series?"

"Sure am. Did you read the book I recommended?"

"I did. I finished it a couple nights ago. It was a beautiful book. I actually enjoyed it more than I thought I would. Did you know it's also Jess's favorite book in *Gilmore Girls*?"

"Can't say I did. Is that a good thing?"

"Definitely. I'm firmly in the Team Jess camp." I laugh.

"I'm glad you read it. I'll let you know when I get to book six."

"Good. I gotta get ready for work. Talk to you later?"

"Bye, Pixie."

He hangs up and I drop my phone on the mattress. I sit there for a few minutes longer trying to wrap my head around the past twenty-four hours—the hug, the stolen glances, the erratic text messages, and then the phone call. I throw my legs out of bed and get through my morning routine, and it's not until I start my ignition that I realize I haven't heard from or thought of Chris since I saw Jace's texts.

CHAPTER 29: SHE HAS A BOYFRIEND
JACE

I look over at the time and it's six forty-seven. Not only did I text her like a psycho last night after trivia, but I called her before seven in the morning. What's wrong with me?

I make my way out into the kitchen to find Tanner sitting at our table eating a bowl of cereal and playing on his phone. His head pops up in my direction when he hears me. Through a large bite of Froot Loops, he says, "Last night was awesome." He swallows hard. "Did you see the pictures Logan sent of the cabin? Fucking sick dude."

"No, I haven't had a chance to look." I rummage through the fridge and pull out a carton of eggs, some cheese, and spinach to make an omelet. I crack three eggs into a bowl and begin to whisk them with a fork.

"That hug you got from Lacey was something," he says.

"I guess."

"What do you mean you guess? If Chris hadn't cock-blocked you, I would have put money on you two kissing."

"She has a boyfriend."

He laughs, "You think that lame ass guy is her boyfriend?

No fucking way dude. They've been on a few dates. She's way out of his league."

"You don't know what you're talking about."

"All I'm saying is she's way too cool to be with a guy like him. Plus, she seemed pretty interested in looking at you last night. Don't think we didn't all notice you two eye fucking the hell out of each other."

"You have no idea what you're talking about. She wants to be friends, and I'm happy I've been invited back into her world."

He scoffs and takes another bite of his cereal.

"What?"

"It's just—" My phone begins to ring, and it's Eli calling.

"Sorry, I gotta take this." I abandon my breakfast and walk back to my room, swiping up on the screen.

"Hey, Eli. What has you calling so early on a Saturday?"

"Shit. Sorry. It's just before one here."

"I didn't realize you were out of the country."

"Just a little holiday in Paris with Lily. Anyway, that's not why I was calling. Ryan called me with an opportunity I thought you might be interested in."

"I'm listening."

"They're putting a team together to do a piece on the Great Barrier Reef. We would leave at the beginning of September, and would be gone for six months, maybe longer. It seems like a lot of the Bix crew has already signed up to go. I told him I would talk to you and convince you to come."

I run my hand over the back of my head. Six months in Australia sounds awesome, but I'm not sure it's what I want. My friends know I've been wavering on returning to my job, but no one at work has any idea.

"Can I think it over?"

"Oh, um, yeah. Ryan needs to know by the end of July. I know it's no Bix, but I really hope you do it. It would be great to have everyone back together, and we could really use another photographer as talented as you."

"Definitely. We'll talk soon."

We hang up and I walk back out of my room to finish making my breakfast.

"What was that about?" Tanner asks.

"It was Eli calling. A job came up in Australia and she wants me on the team."

"You gonna take it?"

"I'm not sure. Don't get me wrong, it sounds awesome, but I'd be gone for six months. Maybe more."

He nods and sips his coffee. "Have you applied for the job here?"

"No, but it's on my list of things to do this week. If it's even still available."

"When does Eli need an answer?"

"End of July."

CHAPTER 30: TOUCAN
PLAY THAT GAME

LACEY

The Tortured Therapists Department

GRAY:

Lacey, how do you keep getting Margaret to
agree to let you go on vacation?

Because I'm the favorite! 

CHLOE:

We all know Gray is the favorite.

Yeah, because she works more than all of us
combined.

GRAY:

Very funny.

It's amazing what she will say yes to when
you ask (and have the coverage).

GRAY:

Y'all try not to have too much fun
without me.

We make no promises 

CHLOE:

Speaking of coverage… Poppy you're still starting on Monday right?

POPPY:

Yep! I can't wait!

Logan turns onto a gravel road. The truck fills with the sounds of rubber on loose rocks, and I place my e-reader back in my bag. Chris has been incredibly quiet the entire ride up, so I spent the time reading. The past week and half, things have been off between us. He didn't seem interested in talking about it, so we didn't.

Instead, we swept the whole trivia night under the rug like it never happened. I told myself that my lack of excitement when he agreed to come with us to the cabin was due to shock, but after this short road trip, I'm starting to think part of me doesn't want him here. I hope he cheers up once we get there, or this is going to be a very long weekend.

The road winds back and forth for a few miles before the homes start to come into view. Every house is large and beautiful. Between houses, views of the lake and the setting sun peek through the trees.

Logan pulls around a curve, and our home for the weekend appears on the right. Wren's car and Jace's Jeep are already parked in the driveway. We would have been here earlier, but I had to work a half-day. Logan honks the horn and puts his truck in park.

"Holy shit, this house is stunning," Poppy says, opening the passenger side door and climbing down.

She's right. It's breathtaking. The house before us is a large Craftsman with all the rustic charm you would expect from a lake house nestled in the North Georgia mountains. Large wooden beams, cedar shake siding, and stacked stone give it a cabin feel. The sage green paint of the siding contrasts perfectly against the warm wood and stone. Large pine and oak trees tower above it. Although there are neighboring houses close by, it feels like it could be the only house for miles. The sun is beginning to set, and the sounds of crickets start to fill the warm night.

"If this is what the front looks like, I can't wait to see the view of the lake," Logan says.

"Fuck, I hope the mosquitos aren't this bad the whole weekend," Chris grumbles, slapping his leg and helping Logan pull our luggage from the bed of the truck.

I finish collecting my suitcase from where he set it on the driveway and make my way towards the front of the house. Jace swings the large double doors open, causing me to freeze. He's wearing a backwards hat, a T-shirt, and khaki shorts that hit above his knees showing off his toned thighs. A large smile erupts across his face when our eyes meet.

"Hey, Pixie. Can I help you with that?" In three long strides he moves toward me and reaches for my bag.

"Toucan play that game." I chuckle reading his tee. "I like your shirt."

"So, where's Chris?"

"Helping Logan unload the truck," I point behind me.

The corners of his mouth fall, and he turns with my suitcase in hand. I follow behind him up the stone steps and through the front door.

The interior of the cabin can only be described as cozy. The floor plan is open with a stunning kitchen complete with a large light-colored granite island and black cabinets. A wooden table that sits ten is in the center of a large dining room. It looks handmade. The wood is decorated with natural knots and imperfections. A deer antler chandelier hangs above it. On one of the walls an enormous stack stone fireplace reaches from floor to ceiling and two worn leather love seats frame the space. The entire back wall of the house is glass and shows off the view of the lake.

I spin around at the sound of the front door shutting. Poppy, Logan, and Chris are all standing in the foyer.

"So, there are four bedrooms and a couple of pull out couches," Tanner begins. "We figured Logan and Poppy could take the main suite down here. The rest of the bedrooms are upstairs. Lacey, do you and Chris mind sharing a bathroom with Donovan and Enzo when they get here tomorrow?"

"Fine with me. Chris?"

He nods.

"Awesome, and then Wren, you can take the fourth room. Jace and I will take the pullout couches in the rec room."

The group disperses to claim their beds. Chris follows me up the staircase, holding both of our bags. Our room is one of the smaller spaces, but just as homey as the rest of the house. The bed is covered with a red plaid duvet, and little black bears decorate every lamp and throw pillow.

"Is everything okay?" I ask once we're behind the door and away from all of my friends.

"Yeah, I'm great. Looking forward to having the weekend off work," Chris says.

"You sure?" I step toward him, reaching out to rub my hand down his arm. He takes a step back and I take a deep breath. "Look, this is going to be a really long weekend if you act like you're mad at me the whole time. Is this still about Jace?" My voice is slightly raised.

"Let's not be dramatic. I'm fine."

"Dramatic? What's that supposed to mean?"

"You're making something out of nothing. I'm fine. This weekend is going to be fun. Let's go back downstairs before everyone starts wondering what's keeping us up here." He walks out of the room, leaving me standing there, wondering why I thought him coming was a good idea.

Wren meets me at the top of the stairs.

"You good?" she asks.

"I'll be fine." I roll my eyes. "Is your room decorated with black bears like ours?" I laugh.

"Moose." She giggles. "Or is it meese?"

We make our way down the staircase. The boys are all on the back deck huddled around the grill, and Poppy is sitting on one of the couches in front of the fireplace. She's holding a paperback, and I smile to myself when I realize it's one of the recommendations I sent her.

"Are you finally going to read a book? I love that one."

"I read," she deadpans.

"Yeah, textbooks and research articles," I jest.

"That's only because I was in grad school. Now that I'm done and can actually relax, I figured I would start with the list you gave me."

"Well that one is one of my favorites, plus it's super spicy. I think you'll like it."

"Wren, have you ever read it?" Poppy shakes the book in Wren's direction.

"No, I read mostly fantasy with a touch of romantasy when I'm in the mood."

The doors off the dining room slide open, and Jace walks inside. The smell of the burgers and the sound of laughter wafts through the open doors. I watch as he makes his way into the kitchen and over to the fridge. He has to be the only man alive who could make a shirt that silly look this good. His arms are covered in black ink, and for the first time since he's been back, I find myself wanting to study them and discover what's there.

I feel Poppy push her hand against my knee, and when my eyes shift back to my best friend, I find her studying me like she knows something I don't.

"So, Lacey, you sure you're okay?" Wren asks, kicking her legs up and covering herself with a big red blanket covered in little black trees.

"Yeah, why?"

"Our rooms share a wall, and I could have sworn I heard you and Chris fighting?"

"Ugh, no. I don't know what his deal is. Maybe he's hangry or tired."

"So things are good between the two of you?" Wren asks.

"Yeah? How's the sex?" Poppy probes.

"Non-existent." I try to laugh off my answer, but both of my friends wince.

A loud crash comes from the kitchen and my shoulders tense. My eyes flit toward the kitchen, and Jace is standing there with his eyes locked on me. When my eyes find him, he quickly drops to the floor to pick up whatever fell.

I watch as Jace stands and heads back for the deck. The door slides shut and I feel my shoulders relax.

"Y'all haven't slept together?" Poppy asks. "I mean, he spent the night after trivia, so I assumed you had. What's going on?"

I let out a groan. "I don't know. We've kissed, but that's it. He says he wants to take things slow."

"Okay, that's weird as fuck," Wren says. "I mean, y'all are exclusive, so what's his hold up?"

I shrug. "We're not exclusive. We haven't had that conversation either. I think he thinks Jace and I still have a thing for each other. He's been acting all pissed off and jealous since trivia night." I roll my eyes.

Poppy and Wren's eyes find one another.

"What?" I ask.

"I didn't know y'all when you were together before, but you two definitely are giving off a will they or won't they vibe," Wren says, her voice hushed.

"No. We're trying to be friends again. That's ridiculous."

"Is it?" Poppy asks. "I mean, you were both so in love, and then you weren't. It kinda feels like the universe is giving y'all a second chance. I mean he looks at you like he still loves you and you look at him like—"

"Stop," I yell, slapping her knee. "Maybe you shouldn't read that book. It's giving you too many ideas."

———

JACE:

I wasn't trying to eavesdrop. I'm here if you
need to talk.

CHAPTER 31: NO WAY I'M MEDIOCRE AND HE'S NOT

JACE

I slept like shit last night. Both pull out sofas are in the same bonus space above the garages. Between the thin, uneven mattress and Tanner's snoring, it would have been impossible to sleep on a good night. After hearing that Chris and Lacey haven't slept together, my mind raced all night with what ifs about her and me. I tried texting her, but she never responded.

I couldn't exactly decipher her emotions about all of it, and that was a new experience for me. For seventeen years, I could always read her. Growing up, she would give me a look and I would instantly know if she was happy or sad. I would know exactly what she needed. Last night, I couldn't read how she felt and it bugged the hell out of me.

So, I decided to clear my head with some fresh air and the sunrise. A run was exactly what I needed.

I climb the front steps of the lakehouse and check the time on my phone. It's six thirty. I sneak back through the front door and start a pot of coffee before jogging up the stairs to grab a quick shower. The warm water pelts my muscles and eases any tension that remains there after my run. It's going to be a long weekend if I have to keep sleeping in that bed.

I let my mind drift to Lacey. She looked beautiful yesterday. Long blonde hair, green eyes, and curves for days. I feel my dick harden at the thought of her, and I instantly turn the knob from hot to ice cold. I can't have those thoughts. We're trying to be friends again. She's here with someone else. I run my hand down my face.

Get it fucking together.

I shiver under the water and slam the knob off. Stepping out of the shower, I wrap my waist in a towel. I make my way back into the spare room and dig through my bag. Tanner is still out cold, and I chuckle as his snores fill the very quiet house. Everyone else must still be asleep too.

I locate my bathing suit and pull it on. I grab the book I've been reading, head back out into the hallway, and down the stairs. The smell of coffee fills the air and I breathe it in, anticipating my first morning cup. I round the corner and freeze dead in my tracks. Standing next to the coffee pot with her back to me is Lacey. Her hair is in a messy bun on the top of her head. She's wearing tiny cotton shorts covered in little purple hearts and a black tank top that hugs every bit of her curves. She's stirring a spoon in a mug.

"I made that pot of coffee for me," I tease. Lacey's shoulders tense when she hears my voice. Her hand stills, and she turns to face me with a sleepy smile. My eyes immediately dart down her body, and I realize she's not wearing a bra. *Fuck.* I do my best to redirect my gaze, but her pebbled nipples are pressing against the thin fabric of her top, and it's impossible not to stare.

"I don't drink coffee," she says. "I'm making a London Fog."

"A London Fog? Like a café au lait, but with tea, right?"

"Yeah, tea, steamed milk, and a little vanilla. How did you know?"

"Someone told me once." I shrug. "I thought you loved

coffee?" In high school, she and Poppy couldn't start the day without some absurd drink from the local coffee shop.

"Wait, is that *Romancing Mr. Bridgerton*? You finished book three?" She gestures at the paperback I'm holding.

"It is. I'm already about halfway done." I flash the book in her direction. "I like how Colin and Penelope were friends first. Reminds me—" I stop myself.

"What does it remind you of?" she asks. Her eyes lock on mine.

"Nothing, so why don't you drink coffee anymore?"

"Because of you." She giggles and turns around to finish making her drink.

"Me? What did I do to coffee?" I walk over to where she stands. Mere inches are between us. Her tropical scent fills my nostrils, and I have to place my hand on the counter to steady myself. Her gaze finds mine, and more than anything, I wish I could touch her.

"It's seriously such a dumb reason." She picks up her mug and walks toward the sliding glass doors that lead to the deck. "Care to join me? The sugar is in the cabinet to the right of the microwave." She smiles over her shoulder. She may not drink coffee anymore because of me, but she still remembers how I take mine.

I quickly pour my cup. Finding the sugar exactly where she said it would be, I add two packets before giving it a quick stir and meeting her on the deck.

"So, why exactly is it my fault you don't drink coffee?" I chuckle and narrow my eyes. I take a seat in one of the Adirondack chairs next to her.

"Well after I thought I had caught you cheating in that coffee shop, I may have vowed never to drink it again." She laughs. "I don't know. I guess it reminded me how bitter I was about everything that happened." Her cheeks turn a slight shade of pink and she shakes her head. "God, being young can make you do the dumbest shit."

"You haven't drank coffee in ten years."

"No," she says, wincing. "I told you it was dumb, especially since now I know you didn't cheat and the whole thing was made up in my head. Talk about dramatic." She laughs at herself, but I sense there is more to her statement than she wants to let on.

"I don't think you're dumb or dramatic. We were in love, and you thought I betrayed you."

"Well, I bet you didn't do anything because of me in the last decade. If anything, you've been off doing amazing things. Discovering the Bix. Gosh, I still can't believe you did it. I'm so proud of you." My heart swells at her words. How do I tell her everything I did in the last ten years was because of her?

"Gooooood morning." Tanner yawns, stretching out his arms and walking through the door. "Y'all ready to celebrate our country's birth?"

"I'm gonna go upstairs and find Chris," Lacey says, standing and taking her mug with her. She offers me a small smile before disappearing back through the door. Tanner takes her chair.

"Wait! You forgot your book," he picks up the paperback I set on the table.

She reappears, grinning from ear to ear. "It's not mine, it's Jace's." She spins and is gone again.

"How fucking interesting." He looks at the cover of the book. "You know there's a show you could watch, right? Why are you putting yourself through the misery of reading these?"

I snatch the book from his hands. "Well for one, Lacey told me to read them, and for two, I didn't know there was a show."

"You gonna tell her how you feel or are y'all gonna keep the miscommunication thing going for another ten years?" He lets out a loud laugh.

"What's that supposed to mean?"

"Dude, tell me you don't love her and I'll shut up. But don't fucking lie to me because you look like Logan does when he gets around Poppy. You're reading books for her."

"What does it matter? If I say I love her, which I'm not confirming to you, she's hated me for ten years, and now she wants to be friends." I shake my head. "Plus there's a real chance I'm leaving for Australia soon, and I'm not going to hurt her again."

He scoffs. "I thought you were looking into that other job? What happened to your plan to stay?"

I take a large sip of coffee and roll my neck. "I applied, but I haven't heard anything yet. It's been over a week. There's still a lot up in the air."

"Right, like the girl you love is dating someone else."

"They have nothing to do with it."

Tanner grins and shakes his head. It's apparent he doesn't believe me, but what else can I say. The truth is she is with someone else. I might have overheard that they haven't slept together, but it's none of my business. The best I can do is be her friend again.

"That guy won't be around much longer."

"Oh, yeah? You don't know that."

He shrugs. "No way I'm mediocre and he's not."

I throw a playful punch, and he runs away laughing and wiggling his eyebrows at me. *Dumbass.*

I don't know if he's right about Chris, but I know he's right about me. As much as I've let my brain go there in recent days, I know it's not what Lacey wants, and that's okay. I finally have her back, and I don't want to lose her again. My phone pings, and I swipe up on the screen.

Yesterday 8:00 PM

I wasn't trying to eavesdrop earlier. I'm here if you need to talk.

Today 7:45 AM

PIXIE:

No worries! Maybe next time don't make it so obvious.

Promise me you'll find me if you need to talk.

PIXIE:

Pinky promise.

CHAPTER 32: DANCING VAGINA

LACEY

After tubing all morning, we went back to the cabin to pick up Donovan and Enzo, eat lunch, and take a break from the heat before heading back on the water.

The boat is anchored in a small cove near the cabin. The sun is starting to move lower in the sky, but unfortunately the heat hasn't diminished at all. It has to be the hottest day we've had all summer. The only reprieve is the lake water and so that's where most of the group is—floating on various shaped floats.

Chris has surprisingly loosened up, and I wonder if it's the booze or if he actually might be turning a corner and putting whatever he thinks is going on with Jace out of his head.

"So, Donovan and Enzo, are y'all ready for the big day?" Logan asks.

Both men smile. "I can't believe in two weeks I'll get to call this guy my husband," Donovan gushes, pulling Enzo in for a kiss.

"I didn't realize you all were getting married so soon," Chris says, looking at me. I sip my beer and try not to look at

199

him. I have a plus one, but after trivia I wasn't sure I wanted it to be Chris. I told myself if this weekend went good, I would invite him to come with me. I still don't know what I want to do.

"Who's in the wedding?" Jace asks.

"My sister and Enzo's brother. We wanted to keep the wedding party small."

"And then Tink and Peter are the flower girl and ring bearer," Enzo chuckles.

"Your dogs?" Tanner asks before sipping from the can he's holding.

"Dogs?" Enzo gasps for dramatic effect. "Tink and Peter are our children."

I have to swallow a laugh imagining their dogs walking down the aisle. Tink is an old English mastiff, and Peter is a yorkie.

"Dogs at a wedding?" Chris asks. His face contorts into something resembling disgust.

"Why not? It's their wedding. They can do whatever they want," I argue.

He shrugs. "I don't know. Aren't weddings supposed to be formal? Dogs are so dirty. You aren't concerned about them ruining your day?"

Donovan and Enzo look at each other and back at Chris.

"Well, I think it's a great idea. I've always wanted a dog," I say. "Peter and Tink are very cute children, and the day wouldn't be complete without them there." Chris doesn't respond. Donovan offers me a thankful smile.

"We got Tink this little tutu, and Peter has a bow tie," Enzo tells the group. Donovan's eyes stay locked on his fiancé, and you can tell he's so in love. That feeling of jealousy, or maybe it's longing, returns deep in my gut. I wonder if I will ever find someone who will love me that wholly.

"That's precious. Gray and I were talking the other day. It was so nice of you to invite us. We are a good time at a wedding," Wren giggles. "One of the girls from work, Jasmine, got married, and we had to cut Gray off from the champagne at the after party. I'm pretty sure she was doing the splits by the end of the reception."

"I didn't know you were coming," Tanner blurts out. Everyone turns to face him.

"Of course they're coming. We invited them the night we met them." Donovan laughs. I look toward Wren, and she's gone quiet. Her eyes are locked on Tanner, and I wonder for a moment what that's about.

"So, where's the honeymoon?" Poppy asks, breaking the awkward silence.

"We aren't doing one right away," Enzo says.

"Yeah, with Enzo's work schedule, we had to postpone it until his winter break," Donovan adds.

"I get that," Logan says. "Where are you going?"

"Bora Bora," Enzo answers. "It'll be the perfect weather, and it's an adult only resort, so after having to be around middle schoolers for four months, it'll be a nice and relaxing break from work."

"I'm going to grab another water. Anyone else want a beer or anything from the cooler?" Jace asks, swimming toward the ladder hanging off the back of the boat.

"I'll take a beer," Chris says.

"Me too," Tanner and Logan say at the same time.

"And me," Poppy says.

"I'm good," Wren chimes in.

"Let me help you," Chris offers before swimming toward the boat.

My gaze follows both men toward the ladder. Chris pulls himself up and onto the boat first. My stomach twists at how little the view does for me, and I'm not sure why. He's attractive, fit, and smart. He has that dimple when he smiles, but my body stays neutral. No dancing vagina, not even one pathetic butterfly in my stomach.

Jace pulls himself out of the water next, and every thought I was having about Chris empties from my head. At the sight of him, my body erupts with feelings. The muscles in his arms flex, and I cross my legs to dull the very present feeling dancing between my thighs. *Fuck.* The sun reflects off the water rolling down his chest and abs. I want to look away, but I can't. He runs his hand through his dark hair and I realize I'm very attracted to the handsome, tattooed man I'm supposed to be friends with.

"Earth to Lacey," Poppy chimes, splashing me with water and breaking the thoughts I shouldn't be having. "Whatcha looking at?"

"I'm trying to make sure the guys get out of the water safely."

"I'm so sure," she says dryly.

"What? I am!"

"What's going on?" Wren asks, paddling her float closer to us.

"Lacey is eye-fucking her man and trying to pretend like she isn't." She giggles and so does Wren.

"Shut up, I wasn't looking at Jace." I laugh, splashing water in her direction.

Both girls stop laughing abruptly and look at me. I realize the name I said was all wrong.

"I mean Chris. I wasn't eye-fucking Chris."

"What an interesting slip of the tongue," Poppy says, eyeing me. Her eyebrow quirks up, and I know she can see through my bullshit. I'm here with Chris, not Jace. Jace is my ex. Jace and I will never be anything more than friends. I made sure to sabotage the hell out of any chance we had at being together ten years ago.

"Don't," I warn. "It was an accident. It meant nothing."

"Whatever you say." Wren offers me a small smile. I hear a splash, and when I look back at the boat, Chris is headed straight for me holding two beers. He hands one to me.

"What did I miss?" he asks looking at both of my friends. Their reactions to my mistake are still painted on their faces.

"Oh, nothing," Poppy lies.

"Lacey was telling us about the last book she was reading," Wren adds.

I offer them a thankful smile before popping the top on the can and taking a large sip.

We all hang in the water for a little longer, and when the sun starts to dip below the trees, we make our way back up to the boat for sandwiches, more drinks, and fireworks.

I settle on one of the bench seats as far away from Jace as I possibly can get. Chris makes his way over to me, sandwich in hand, and takes a seat next to me. I try to nestle into the crook of his arm, but he moves away. "Not in front of your friends, okay?" he whispers, so only I can hear him.

My face falls at his inability to show me any physical affection, and for a split second I wonder if I don't turn him on either. I straighten up, now very uncomfortable. The first firework erupts above us, and I take a moment to look around the boat. Poppy is in Logan's lap. Enzo's head rests on Donovan's shoulder. Tanner and Wren sit on opposite sides of the front of the boat. Jace is in the captain's chair in front of me, and my eyes settle on his back. Fireworks continue to go off above us, but my eyes stay locked on him instead.

TANNER DOCKS THE BOAT, AND I'M THE FIRST ONE OFF. I WALK lazily up the ramp toward the house. I can hear Chris behind me, talking endlessly about some political something with Logan, and I can't bring myself to listen. My bag is thrown over my shoulder and my flip flops are in one hand. The night air is filled with a melody of drunk laughter, stray fireworks in the distance, and something I think must be a frog.

Footsteps make me turn around, and Jace is a couple of

strides behind me, holding a cooler. We walk back up to the house side by side, neither of us talking. The walk feels longer than it is, the silence deafening. For some reason I'm nervous, and I don't know what to say or do.

"Did you have fun today?" he asks, his mouth turning into a gorgeous grin. His face is illuminated by the lights coming from the house. Something deep in my core warms and I try to push it away, but I can't.

"Yeah, it was a blast, but I'm exhausted. Probably going to see if Chris wants to head to bed."

His jaw slightly ticks at the mention of Chris, but he doesn't say anything else. We walk into the main level of the house, and I let my bag hit the floor by the dining room table. He moves to the fridge and starts unloading the cooler.

"Here, let me help you," I offer, joining him. We start clearing out the leftover drinks and food in silence. I'm trying to think of something to say when both of our hands grab for a can of beer at the same time. The touch of his fingers on mine sends a shock up my arm and creates a feeling deep in my core that I'm not sure what to do with. He turns to face me. His blue eyes bore into me, and I want so badly to know what he's thinking. Donovan and Enzo walk in laughing, causing me to let go of the can and to take two steps back.

"Is there any beer leftover?" Enzo asks.

"Oh, um, yeah," Jace says, turning away and throwing the can in Enzo's direction.

"Thanks, man."

Jace flips back towards the fridge, and when he does, his eyes find mine for another split second. He makes quick work of cleaning the cooler out, and I move to the other side of the kitchen, putting much needed space between us.

Tanner walks in with the rest of the group, holding a wireless speaker. The upbeat music fades and "Remember When" by Alan Jackson begins to play on full volume. My eyes dart to Jace's, and his face is immediately covered with sadness. His gorgeous smile is nowhere to be found.

"Turn it off, T," I shout.

"Huh?" he asks, his body rocking back and forth like he's still out on the water. Time seems to slow, and I don't understand what he's not understanding.

"I said, turn the fucking song off. Or turn it. Do something. Just stop playing it, please."

Tanner's eyes meet mine with confusion, and he pulls out his phone, tapping the screen. The song stops, and when I look around the room, Chris is staring at me with his mouth agape.

"You good, Lace?" Wren asks, her eyes full of concern.

"I'm fine. Are you okay, J?" He walks out of the room without a sound, and I follow him. I hear Chris call my name, but I ignore him.

CHAPTER 33: REMEMBER WHEN
LACEY - 5 YEARS AGO

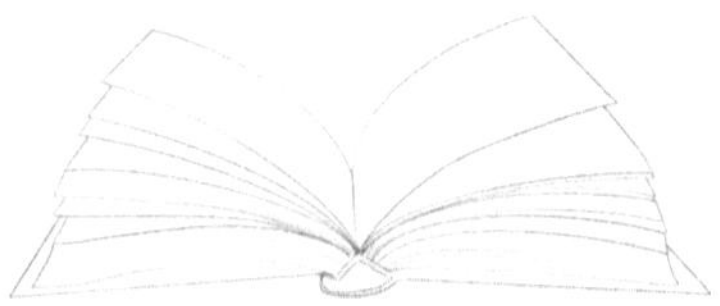

I'm standing in my childhood bedroom, and I'm wearing a black jumpsuit. Black. The color that makes up most of my wardrobe, but today I hate it.

My eyes have been red and puffy since my dad called me three days ago to tell me Annie Jackson passed away. The emotional roller coaster of the past few days hit me when I least expected it.

I spoke to Annie last week, and she was so positive. She assured me everything was going to be okay, and then without a bit of warning, she was gone. Tears start to well up in my eyes at the thought of the last words she said to me: "I love you, honey." I take a few deep breaths and stop the tears from running down my face. She would not want me crying over her. She told me as much during our weekly calls.

I finish applying my waterproof mascara and try to think about a happy memory with Annie. A lot of the memories are intertwined with memories of Jace. I hate him for tarnishing some of the happiest days of my life. Annie was everything my mom isn't. She was a ball of sunshine and positivity. Everyone she interacted with could feel the warmth and love that radiated off of her.

My bedroom door clicks open, and Poppy walks in wearing a black dress and heels. Her hair is curled and pulled back out of her face. She crosses the space between us and wraps me in a hug. We both begin to sob.

"Today is going to be a hard day, but we're going to face it together. You're sure about going?" She pulls back and wipes under her eyes with her fingers.

I nod. "I think so. I mean, I know he'll be there, but she would have wanted me to come. You too. We will keep our distance and sit in the back like we said. No need to stir up drama. Annie wouldn't have wanted that."

"You really think she never told him about y'all's weekly chats?"

"Not that I know of. She said she would tell him when the time was right, but I never really knew what she meant. Always called them our little secret because she knew how lonely I was. You know Lori is always too busy to bother to talk to me beyond what's scheduled on the Sims' family calendar."

"She loved you so much, Lace." Poppy squeezes my hand, and tears threaten to fall again. I turn and grab a tissue.

"She never pushed me about him either, just respected that something happened between him and me. One time I asked her why, and she said with all the confidence in the world that she knew one day we would figure it all out, and then we never brought him up again." I take a deep breath. "Fuck, life isn't fair. She was one of the best people I knew. Why her?"

A tap on my door makes us turn around. My mom is standing in the doorway, expressionless. Her makeup is perfectly done, not one strand of her blonde hair out of place. Not even Annie Jackson dying could make this woman crumble. "Goodness, Lacey, pull yourself together. No need to make today more dramatic than it needs to be."

I take another deep breath and plaster a fake half smile across my face.

"Will you girls be riding with us?" she asks.

"No ma'am. We don't want to make the day harder on Jace, so we're gonna go separate and sit in the back."

"Suit yourselves." She turns to leave and yells, "Colton, we're leaving in five. Please put your shoes on and wear the sports coat I bought you." Colton grumbles something from down the hall.

"Is she fucking serious?" Poppy asks.

"You know Lori. She thinks showing any emotion is too much, so she shows none at all and expects the rest of us to follow suit."

"It's baffling. Annie was one of her best friends. I can't imagine being that stoic if I ever lost you. They'd probably have to commit me," Poppy says.

"Yeah." I shrug and sigh. "I don't think she's cried once. Just pretends like nothing bad happened and goes into robot mode. She caught me crying last night, and instead of comforting me, she rolled her eyes and reminded me to steam my jumpsuit. And then, when I didn't do it immediately, she proceeded to do it for me. How are your parents?"

"They're both a mess. Mom keeps making casseroles for Richard and can't stop crying. Dad's been over at their house all week, watching TV and spending time with them."

"This sucks," I say. Tears stream down my face and my body begins to shake. A wave of grief washes over me.

Poppy grabs my hand and squeezes it hard. "I know, but we're going to get through it together. Like we always do." I wipe the tears from my face and grab my purse off my bed. We head towards the door.

———

THE CHURCH IS COLD AND QUIET, OTHER THAN THE WHIMPERS and sniffles that fill the space from Annie's friends and family. I do a quick scan and don't see Jace anywhere, but it doesn't look like any immediate family has been seated. Poppy's family is seated a couple rows behind the reserved pews with mine. I do another scan of the room, but he's not here. Not yet.

I breathe deeply, feeling like a coward. I've played with the idea of trying to talk to him since I heard about his mom. Two nights ago, I almost worked up enough courage to walk across the street and knock on his door, but when I walked outside and saw his Jeep pulling away, I realized going over there was a terrible idea.

Poppy must see me scanning the crowd because she grabs my hand and whispers, "If we run into him, it's going to be okay. We loved Annie too. She would have wanted us here."

I nod because I know she's right. I check the time on my phone. "Hey, I think I'm going to run to the bathroom." Poppy nods and follows me.

We stay quiet until we're inside. A brunette woman, around our age, is washing her hands at the sink. She's wearing a tight, black mini dress that hits her mid thigh. Black pumps adorn both of her feet. She smiles in our direction and pulls out her phone. We move past her into separate stalls.

After I finish using the bathroom, I head towards the sink. The brunette is still there, applying more mascara and red lipstick.

"Excuse me," I say, reaching for a couple paper towels. She smiles again and makes her way to the door. "You ready, babe?" she asks, stepping out of the bathroom. The sound of her voice trails down the hall followed by a very familiar male's voice right before the door shuts.

It's been five years, but I would recognize his voice anywhere. Poppy's eyes find mine as she exits her stall, and I feel frozen. I knew he would be here. It's his mother's funeral for fuck's sake, but I didn't prepare for hearing his voice or seeing him like I should have.

"Was that who I think it was?" she asks.

I nod.

"So that woman must have been?"

I nod again. Poppy twists her hair around her finger and she searches for the right words.

"Fuck, what are we doing here?" I ask. "I can't go back out there. What if he sees me?" Panic bubbles up my throat.

"This isn't about him, Lacey. This is about Annie." Deep down I know she's right, but I can't face him. Not today. A familiar country song begins to play, and it sounds like a song Annie would have picked. "Come on, let's go. It sounds like it's about to start," she urges.

"I'm staying in here until it's over," I say, panicked.

"Staying where? In the bathroom?"

"Stay with me please."

Poppy shakes her head and wraps me in a hug. Tears stream down my face. She holds me for a few long minutes before stepping back and grabbing my hands.

"Okay, Lace. I'll stay with you."

CHAPTER 34: I WAS THERE
JACE - PRESENT

I make it upstairs to the room I'm sharing with Tanner. I'm trying to slow my breathing, but all of the emotions of losing my mom are bubbling to the surface. Five years ago, that song played as our friends and family gathered to honor the life of the greatest woman I've ever known.

"Jace, wait. Are you okay?" Lacey asks from the door.

I flip around to face her. My eyes are full of tears. "How did you know to tell him to turn it off?"

There's a beat of silence.

"Can you please explain to me how you knew that song would upset me?" I sound breathless.

"Because I was there."

I start to pace. "You were there?"

"Of course I was." Her voice is low and tentative.

"No." I shake my head. "No, I looked for you that day. Fuck, you were the only person I wanted to see, and you didn't come. I'm sure of it. You weren't there." I sit down on the edge of the bed. My head falls into my hands. She moves across the room to join me.

"Poppy and I both came. I was devastated, J."

The words fall out of her mouth, and I don't believe what I'm hearing.

"You know Annie meant so much to me," she says. "The day of her funeral, I was there, but Poppy and I had run to the bathroom before things got started. There was this beautiful brunette at the mirror. When she left the bathroom, I heard you and her talking in the hall, and I panicked. I wasn't sure you wanted me there, and I didn't know how to face you, so I stayed in the bathroom until it was over. I hid, and I'm so sorry. I'm so sorry she's gone. I'm so sorry I wasn't there for you. I'm so sorry for everything."

Tears stream down her face, and my hands find her cheeks. My thumbs swipe softly under her eyes, clearing away the tears. I wrap my arms around her and pull her into me and we both begin to cry harder.

"I can't believe it's been five years," I say through sobs. Her arms wrap around my neck, and she pulls me in firmly against her.

"I know. I wish I could go back and change it all. I wish I could have been there for you. I'm so incredibly sorry."

We sit there for a few long minutes and hold each other. Five years too late. Neither of us try to break our embrace. I'm not even sure what we're grieving. Losing my mom or losing each other.

I hear someone clear his throat near the door, and Lacey pulls away. I turn and see Chris standing there watching us. His face is covered with confusion. Or is it frustration? I quickly try to wipe my face with the back of my hands. She puts more space in between us, wiping away her tears.

My eyes find hers, and that's when I hear Chris mumble something under his breath and walk away.

"I'm so sorry, J." She stands, and follows him back to their bedroom.

LACEY

"What the hell was that?" Chris asks when I walk into our room, still wiping my face.

"It was the song that played at his mom's funeral."

He lets out a harsh breath and crosses his arms across his chest. "What the hell am I supposed to do with that?"

"What do you mean?" I stand there, a little stunned that he's so mad.

"I agreed to come this weekend with you knowing he'd be here. Knowing he likes you. And then you follow him upstairs, and I walk in to find you practically sitting on his lap."

"I wasn't on his lap."

"You might as well have been."

"No, I followed my friend upstairs because I knew hearing that song would be hard for him. Hell, it was hard for me to hear. Hearing it brought up all the emotions associated with her death. I was comforting my friend."

He scoffs.

"Don't scoff at me. I loved Annie."

He scoffs again.

"I think you should leave," I say, my voice firm.

"What?"

"I said I think you should leave. This isn't working anymore."

"And why do you think that is?"

"Maybe because we have now slept in the same bed twice and you haven't even tried to touch me. Not even grazed my toes with yours. What kind of man doesn't want to touch the girl he's dating?" I can hear my voice getting louder, but I don't care. "You've barely paid me any attention since the trivia night. I honestly don't even know why you agreed to come."

"You know, I'm beginning to wonder the same thing. God, you couldn't even hide staring at him tonight on the boat. I might as well have been invisible."

"That's not true. I tried to snuggle up to you and you pushed me away."

"Please lower your voice. You're causing a scene."

"No, I'm not going to lower my voice to make you more comfortable. You're trying to put this all on me, but I think you know this isn't working anymore for you either. We don't have anything in common. You find my personality over the top and my interests silly. And I find you boring and rigid."

He walks over and grabs his duffel bag, throwing it on the bed. "So you're ending things with me, so you can go be with him."

"Where did you get that from anything I just said?" I let out a loud breath and walk into the bathroom slamming the door behind me. Gripping the edge of the counter, I take a few deep breaths and try to compose myself. I stare into the mirror, trying to collect my thoughts. If he can't understand why I would want to be there for my friend, then he needs to leave. I'm not going to quiet myself for him. He shouldn't have come. I don't know what I was thinking.

I walk back out of the bathroom and he's zipping up his bag, grumbling something to himself.

"The Uber will be here in twenty minutes. I'll get out of your hair so you can go fuck your teenage crush." He throws the duffel bag over his shoulder as he walks out the door.

I follow him, yelling, "Fuck you" as he descends the stairs. I turn on my heels and head back into the bedroom, slamming the door behind me. I collapse on the bed and grab a pillow. Covering my face, I silently scream. *What a douchebag.*

The worst part is that he isn't even completely wrong. I couldn't take my eyes off Jace tonight. The world could have been burning down around me and I couldn't look away. Then that song played and my heart broke. I didn't hesitate to follow him because I knew wherever he was going is where I needed to be.

CHAPTER 35: MAKE A WISH

JACE

Lacey hasn't come out of her room since I heard her yell "Fuck you" at Chris. I have to admit it made me laugh. That was the girl I fell in love with as a kid. Always willing to speak her mind and stand up for herself and her friends.

Poppy and Wren both went and checked on her after he left and assured me she was okay. They told me to give her space, so that's what I'm doing. I'm sitting downstairs while she's upstairs, and the rest of our group is down on the dock drinking and having a good time.

I've been staring at our text message thread for the last hour weighing my options. The girls said she needed space, but if I know her, like I think I do, what she wants right now is a hug.

I stand quickly before I have time to change my mind and make my way up to the door of her room. I pause for a few seconds before lightly tapping my fist on the wood.

"Poppy, I told you I'm fine. Please let me—" she says before the door swings open. Her breath hitches and she stands there with her mouth slightly parted. Her blonde hair is wet like she just showered, and she's wearing the same shorts and tank top she had on this morning. A thin line of her stomach shows between the hem of her shirt and waistband of her shorts. Her e-reader is in her hand. My eyes immediately find her peaked nipples, and I quickly divert my gaze back up to her emerald eyes.

"Oh, Jace. It's you," she says. "I thought you were Poppy."

"No, just me." I rub my hand over the back of my head. "I guess I was worried about you and wanted to come make sure you were okay. Thought you could use a hug or someone to talk to."

"Oh, no, I'm fine." Disappointment settles deep in my stomach because I was banking on getting to hug her.

"Not my first break up, if you could even call it that." She laughs. "And it probably won't be my last." She shrugs and rocks back and forth on her heels.

"For the record, I wasn't a big fan of Chris. I mean who doesn't read romance novels?" I offer her a smile and she laughs again. "I found a cool spot earlier—want to check it out? Maybe we could talk?" I gesture over my shoulder. "If not, I get it, I understand the importance of needing to decompress alone, but I thought maybe…"

"I'd love to."

She sets her e-reader on the dresser by the door. We walk down the hall toward my room. "Where are you taking me?"

"You trust me, Pixie?"

"I'm trying to," she says. Her honesty makes me pause for a split second. I know she knows I didn't cheat, but it's what she believed for a decade, and I'd be an idiot if I thought the last ten years could be wiped away after one month. I walk over to one of the windows, slide it open, and climb out before leaning back inside and offering her my hand. She takes it, and I pull her through to a flat part of the roof. My skin heats under her touch and I don't want to let her go. She releases her grip once both feet are safely on the shingles.

"It's like when we were kids," she says with a hint of nostalgia in her voice.

The corners of my mouth tip upward and my head floods with memories of us sitting on the roof outside her window. "I thought you'd like it." We both sit down. There's a noticeable space between us, but we're close enough that when I rest my forearms on my knees, my elbow brushes against the side of her legs that she has pulled up to her chest.

"You know I was planning on coming to find you tomorrow," she admits.

"Oh yeah?"

"Well, yeah. I pinky promised I would find you if I wanted to talk." She shrugs. "And I wanted to make sure you were okay after the song."

Technically, she promised to find me if she needed to talk, but I don't correct her. My heart quickens at her admission. All I've wanted for a decade was for her to want to talk to me and now she does.

"I was trying to get my head on straight before I rejoined the group," she says.

She moves to lay on her back and looks up toward the night sky. I join her. The pop of a firework sounds in the distance, and Tanner's loud laugh comes from somewhere below us.

"How many nights do you think we spent out on the roof looking up at the stars?" she asks.

"No idea, but those were some of my favorites. It's like it was our own little world away from all the noise."

"It was, wasn't it?"

"You know when I was on a project and I needed some space to think, I would find a place away from the team and look up at the night sky. It always helped me quiet my head."

"What are the stars like in other parts of the world?" she asks.

"Magnificent. Especially in the really remote places with

no light pollution. There seems to be millions that cover the sky. You would love it."

"I can only imagine." Her voice is wistful. She turns her head to look at me, and I meet her gaze as she sits up suddenly. She pulls her legs back up to her chest. Her hands move up and down her crossed arms.

"Do you remember how scared Poppy was when we first started meeting outside my bedroom? I think the first three times she yelled at us from my bed to come back inside." Lacey laughs. There were so many nights over the last ten years I wished I could hear her laugh. So many nights I wished she had been laying next to me looking up at the stars, but she wasn't.

"Can I tell you a secret?" I ask, sitting up to look at her.

"Please do."

"I was as scared as she was, but I didn't want you to know." I wince, and she laughs again, slapping my leg.

"Why wouldn't you tell me? We could've stayed inside."

"Because I'd follow you anywhere you asked me to go." Our conversation stills, and she moves a little closer and rests her head on my shoulder. Our hands are so close that there is only a whisper between them. My heart rate quickens, and for a split second, I have the urge to kiss her forehead, but I stop myself.

"Jace?"

"Yeah?"

"Did you ever think we would get the chance to be friends again?"

Friends. The word hits me like a punch to the gut.

"Honestly, no. When I walked into that graduation party, you were the last person I thought I would see there. You?"

"No. I mean I thought about it over the years, but it was more like what I would say to you when I finally had the chance. There were a couple times before your dad moved." She lets out a sigh. "One time, I saw your Jeep parked in his driveway, and I almost worked up the courage to knock on the door, but I didn't do it."

"Why not? I never knew you to be afraid of anything."

"With you it's always been different. It sounds so silly now, but I did everything in my power to avoid you. Too many feelings, I guess."

"What do you mean?"

"I don't know how to explain it." She takes a deep breath. "My biggest fear was losing you, and I guess when it came true, I didn't know what to do or how to handle it. It was like I broke. I stopped fighting because I could no longer function. The feelings were too much for me, so I blocked you and pretended like you never existed because that was easier than accepting the fact that you broke my heart."

"I get it. I threw myself into school and work so I didn't have to deal with losing you either."

Our fingers barely touch, and it sends a shock up my arm. She quickly moves her hand and sits up so we are no longer touching. I wonder if it's because she felt it too.

"So, what else have you been up to in the past decade? Any girlfriends?"

Her question throws me, but I try to remind myself that this is our second chance at friendship and nothing more.

"Oh. No. My last serious relationship was with a girl named Amber. We were together when Mom died and I think we stayed together longer than we should have because of it."

"The brunette I saw in the bathroom that day."

"Yeah, I don't think either of us were ever fully in it, but then Mom died and I wasn't in a great place. She didn't end it because she didn't want to dump the guy who just lost his mom, and I didn't end it because I didn't care either way."

"I get that. I'm sorry again about hiding in the bathroom."

"I'm glad you were there." I nudge her shoulder with mine. "So what about you? Any exes I should know about other than Chris?"

She shakes her head. "Oh, well there was one guy. I think you know him," she giggles out. "Tall and blond. Lives with you. God, what was his name?"

"No idea." I laugh. "Come on, no other guys ever caught your eye?" The vision of her kissing Alex pops into my head and I shove it away.

She swats me with her hand. "Not really. My dating history is mostly a bunch of first dates that went nowhere. If you walk away first, you can't get hurt, you know?" Her voice is playful, but underneath it I can hear sadness too.

"Chris was the first guy I introduced to any of my friends, but I don't even think he qualifies as an ex-boyfriend. We hadn't even talked about being exclusive. I knew he wasn't the one for me, but I think part of me saw what Logan and Poppy have and I wanted that. Figured that maybe if I stuck it out we'd get there one day."

Another moment of silence stretches between us and I think about pulling her towards me, but she stares up at the sky. The dim moonlight highlights the features of her face and the slope of her nose. She's so fucking beautiful.

I turn back towards the dark night. "Look!" I point up above us. A shooting star flies across the sea of black. "Hurry and make a wish." Her eyes shut and I do the same. I repeat the wish I said a decade ago. When I open my eyes, Lacey is looking right at me.

"Did you just tell me to wish on a shooting star?" A smile erupts across her face.

"What did you wish for?"

"No, you know how it works. You tell your wish and it's all over. Ruins the magic," she says.

"Come on, I'll tell you mine, if you tell me yours."

She lets out a laugh and begins to stand. "Guess you're gonna have to stick around, J."

"What do you mean?"

"I promise to tell you mine when it comes true."

CHAPTER 36: S.H.I.E.L.D.

JACE

I barely slept last night. I swear Tanner's snoring was louder than the night before. I finally got out of bed at five and started my day with a long run. After the rooftop chat, I needed to clear my head.

I walk back through the front door and head into the kitchen to start a pot of coffee, but when I get to the coffee maker, I find it's already brewing. A mug and two sugar packets sit on the counter next to it. I look around the room and see that Lacey is sitting on the back deck, her blonde hair tied on top of her head. My face breaks into a wide grin.

I jog up the stairs and grab a quick shower before returning downstairs to make the cup of coffee she left for me.

"Care, if I join you?" I ask, sliding the door open and finding her reading.

"I was hoping you would," she says with a smile. She sets her e-reader down and takes a sip from her mug. "How'd you sleep?"

"Awful," I admit. "Tanner snores like he's eighty, and the pull out bed mattress is too thin. You?"

"Like a rock. My bed is like sleeping on a cool cloud," she

replies on a laugh. "It might be the most comfortable bed I've ever slept in. Plus, it was nice to have it all to myself."

"Yeah, yeah, yeah. Really rub it in, why don't you?" I take a sip from my mug. "Thanks for the coffee, Pixie."

"Oh, it was nothing. I woke up wanting to try some." She holds up her drink and I realize there is no tea bag hanging from it.

"You're drinking coffee this morning?"

She nods. "Yeah, it felt right."

"And?"

"I still like my tea, but it's not as awful as I remember." Her lips curve upward, and I wonder if she's talking about me or the drink. She picks up her e-reader again and begins to read. We sit there for a while drinking our coffee in silence and enjoying each other's company.

The lake water is still, and morning dew covers the surface of the wood deck. I feel at ease with her next to me, and I know deep in my gut that this is what was always missing. I have seen some of the most magnificent places in the world and photographed some of the most extraordinary animals, but nothing compares to sitting next to Lacey.

"So, whatcha reading?" She cuts her eyes at my interruption.

"It's an enemies to lovers book and the enemies are finally becoming lovers, so shush." Her eyes dart back down to the page.

"The enemies are becoming lovers? That's a thing?"

"Yes," she says, not looking up from the book.

"Can I see?" I stand and grab her e-reader. She lets out a shriek.

"He tastes as delicious as he looks." I begin to read out loud. "He deepens our kiss, taking one of my breasts in his—"

"Go get your own book." She tries to grab it back, but I

hold it above my head, and even though she's 5'7", she can't quite reach it. She may be tall, but I'm taller.

"Let me read it, Lace." I spin around and start reading out loud again. "Taking one of my breasts in his hand, he flicks my nipple—"

"No, give it back." She's jumping now, and I can't help but continue to tease her. It's obvious she's not wearing a bra, and the swell of her tits bounce with every jump. It's fucking torture to watch.

I put it behind my back, and she wraps her hands around me to try to grab it. We playfully wrestle back and forth for a few minutes. She begins to tickle me and I burst out laughing. "You're gonna have to do better than that if you want it back," I tease through heavy breaths, trying to tickle her back one handed.

Our bodies are wrapped around each other. I can feel her breath on my neck and I'm surrounded by her sweet scent. We catch each other's stare, and for a split second, I think about kissing her.

"Whatcha doing?" Poppy sings.

Lacey's body tightens and I can't help but smile. She slowly turns to find our friends standing in the doorway. Her cheeks are a deep pink. She finds the device and yanks it out of my hands before standing up straighter.

"How long have you two been there?" she asks.

"Long enough," Logan says.

Lacey looks back at me and shakes her head with a playful grin. "I'm gonna go get ready." She pushes by them. Poppy lets out a little giggle and takes a sip of her coffee before following after her. Logan steps out on the deck. "Want to share what that was about?"

"I was giving her a hard time." I laugh.

"You sure about that?"

I exhale and grab my coffee mug. "You sound like Tanner."

"It just seemed like maybe it was more than that," he adds.

"Man, I wish." We move over to the railing of the deck. He leans forward on his elbows.

"Why not tell her how you feel?"

"Because I finally have her back in my life and I don't want to lose her. If I don't get the job in Atlanta, then I'm going to have no choice but to leave again. The Australia job would be at least six months, and that's if everything goes according to plan. I want to tell her, but I need to make sure it's the right time. Make sure she and I are on the same page. I need her to know I'm serious about our future. You know?"

He nods. "Can I help in any way?"

"No man, but thanks." I take a sip of coffee. "I'm gonna go get ready." I turn and walk back into the house.

———

TANNER:

Logan said you need our help

What's happening?

LOGAN:

After our conversation, I filled T in and we decided we're going to help you get her back.

Tanner changed the name of the group to S.H.I.E.L.D.

Group name change? Really?

TANNER:

Gotta have a cool name if we're doing this

And what exactly are we doing?

LOGAN:

Helping you get Lacey back.

LOGAN:

What's S.H.I.E.L.D.?

TANNER:

It's like the Marvel CIA

And what does that have to do with anything?

TANNER:

I changed what it stands for

TANNER:

Strategic Heartbreak Intervention, Emotional-Support, and Love-Creating Division

You're an idiot.

TANNER:

But I'm your idiot

Is this necessary?

LOGAN:

100%

TANNER:

You need us man

CHAPTER 37: WHO'S NAME RHYMES WITH FACE

LACEY

"**Y**ou and Jace seem to be getting close," Poppy says as we walk back into my room. She throws herself on my bed.

"Yeah, I'm glad we're working through things and becoming friends again."

"Lacey."

"What?" I dig in my suitcase. "Should I wear my black bikini or my red one?"

"Why does it matter? Are you trying to impress some-one?" The corner of her mouth tips upward.

"No, I wanted my best friend's opinion."

"Well then my opinion is that if you were trying to look hot for a certain someone, who is at this cabin, and whose name rhymes with face, then I would go with the red one. Your ass looks good in that one."

"You know that's not what I meant," I deadpan, throwing the black top at her head.

"Seriously though, what's going on? You two seemed very close this morning." She quirks her eyebrow up at me. "And you admitted to eye-fucking him yesterday on the boat."

I walk into the bathroom to get changed. "Hell if I know,"

I yell from behind the door. "It's all very confusing if I'm honest."

"Go on."

"Well you know our history and then he showed up looking like… well he showed up looking like he looks, but I hated him." I pull on my bottoms. "Then everything got sorted out and we started texting here and there to catch up, and then trivia happened." I fix the triangular top over my tits and tie the string around my back. "And I don't know, Poppy, it's like I'm sixteen again with a huge crush on my best friend and I don't know how to tell him."

I walk out of the bathroom, brushing through my hair. "Please say something," I beg.

"Gosh, it kinda feels like we've been here before, except this time you're telling me about it."

"You're hilarious."

"The two of you always thought you did such a good job hiding your feelings for each other. Did you ever wonder why I didn't even blink when you told me y'all kissed at that bonfire? It's because I fucking knew you two loved one another. You both are about as subtle as the main characters of a Disney movie."

I dig through my suitcase, find a pair of denim shorts, and pull them on.

"It's because I know you better than I know anyone else. And I know I haven't seen Jace in a decade, but you two still look at each other the same way you looked at each other in high school," she says.

"And what should I do? Pretend like the past decade didn't happen and tell him I want to try again?"

"That would be the mature thing to do."

"Shut up."

"The past decade didn't happen babe. It was made up in your head, so forget about it."

We make our way back downstairs. Her words circle in

my brain over and over. I try to push them away. Now is not the time. I'll deal with Jace Jackson and my feelings later.

The rest of the group is waiting for us on the deck as we make our way outside.

"Y'all ready for a boat ride?" Enzo asks, lifting a cup into the air. The group cheers and heads toward the dock.

———

MY BODY IS EXHAUSTED, BUT MY MIND WON'T SETTLE. THE DAY out on the lake was full of tubing and drinking. I should be asleep, but I'm not.

I turn over and stare at the clock on the bedside table. It reads one fifteen. I swing my legs out of bed and tiptoe down the hall and then the stairs to find a cup of water. I round the corner towards the kitchen and stop in my tracks. On one of the small loveseats in the living room I see Jace's feet hanging off one end.

I try to keep quiet as I move toward the cabinet and carefully pull a glass down. I press it up against the water dispenser, and the loud sound of ice falling fills the house.

"Shit," I say in a hushed voice trying to make it stop and frantically hitting the water button.

"Lace, is that you?" I flip around to see him sitting up.

"Sorry, I didn't mean to wake you. I couldn't sleep, so I was coming to grab some water."

"Yeah, I can't sleep either," he breathes out and stands. He's shirtless, his gym shorts hanging low on his hips. *Fuck me.*

He walks into the kitchen and grabs a glass from the cabinet and moves over to where I'm standing. I freeze as he invades my space and I swallow hard.

"Lacey?"

"Um, yeah?"

"You mind scooting over so I can get some water too?"

"Oh, yeah, my bad." I take a few steps back.

"So what's keeping you from sleeping, Pixie?"

You.

"I don't know. There's a lot on my mind I guess." I sip my water and move to one of the barstools.

"Enlighten me."

"It's nothing. Boring even." He walks over and takes the barstool to my left. I think he might continue to press me on what's in my head, but he doesn't. "What has you awake at this hour?" I ask.

"Let's see. Tanner's snoring, and the mattress up there is so thin I can feel every spring, so I figured I'd try a couch, but these are more like love seats and I'm too tall," he laughs. "I don't think sleep is in the cards for me tonight." He moves his head from side to side stretching his neck.

"You could sleep with me." The words spill out before I can think about stopping them.

His head flips in my direction and his mouth forms into a sexy grin. "Sleep with you?" The word *you* hangs between us.

"Well, yeah. I mean I'm afraid if you have to endure another night of sleep on the pull out bed, you might end up needing physical therapy or something. We can't have that."

What the hell am I thinking?

"You sure?"

"Yeah. We're both adults. I have a comfortable bed and you don't. It would only be one night. I can stay on my side if you can stay on yours."

Fuck, I don't even believe me.

He takes a long sip of his water, and I watch as his Adam's apple bobs up and down. Tension crackles between us.

"After you, then." He gestures towards the stairs and I quickly move past him. He follows close behind me.

We make our way up to the room, and I climb in on the left side of the bed.

"You sure you're good with this, Pixie?"

"Oh, yeah. This isn't weird at all." I snuggle deeper under the covers. *What the hell am I doing?*

He makes his way to the other side of the bed and climbs in next to me.

"Can you put my phone on the bedside table?" he asks, handing me his cellphone. I place it next to mine and turn off the lamp. I stay on my side, facing away from him. I try to will my eyes to shut, but being this close to this man in the dark shouldn't be allowed. The spot between my legs begins to throb, and I have to squeeze my thighs together. I feel him shift in the bed and his foot brushes mine. A jolt of electricity shoots up my body causing goosebumps to explode across my skin.

I roll onto my back, and when I glance over at him, I can faintly see that he's also on his back, staring at the ceiling.

"You know we've never done this before," I say.

"We never got the chance before, but I'm glad we're getting it now," he says.

Our fingertips brush against each other. We lay there for a few long minutes, letting our fingers touch and neither of us moving away. The room is quiet, and I wonder if he can practically hear me screaming in my head for him to take me. I wonder if I asked him to kiss me or to touch me, if he would.

I open my mouth to ask the question, but he breaks our connection and flips to his side. "Night, Pixie."

"Night, J."

CHAPTER 38: SPILL THE TEA, BOYS
JACE

The sun peeks through the blinds and wakes me up. I'm on my side, and Lacey is tucked up against me. Both my arms are wrapped around her. Last night I thought about taking it further than innocent hand-holding. Shit, I don't even know if you could call it hand-holding, but I know I was really fucking happy it happened.

I breathe her in, knowing I shouldn't lay like this much longer. I have so much I need to do before I tell her how I feel.

It kills me, but I slowly let her go and slide out of bed, trying my hardest not to wake her. I make my way into the bathroom, ensuring the door to Enzo and Donovan's room is locked before undressing and climbing in the shower.

My mind instantly drifts to Lacey and how she felt in my arms. My morning wood gets harder, but instead of turning the water to ice, I let the warm shower wash over me while I stroke myself to the thoughts of what I wish I could have done to Lacey last night. When I finally find my release, it's her name on my lips.

I hear a loud knock on the door.

"Jace! Do you need something?"

"No," I yell over the roar of the water.

"You sure, I thought I heard you call for me?"

Fuck.

"Oh, no, wasn't me." I run my hand down my face. I quickly finish up my shower, shut off the water, and dry off. I walk out of the bathroom and find her sitting on the edge of the bed.

"Good morning, Pixie."

"Morning." Her eyes trail my body.

"Like what you see?"

"I don't hate it." Her mouth quirks into a sexy grin, making my dick twitch underneath my towel. She stands and moves past me toward the bathroom. "You sure you didn't call out my name?" she asks, pausing in the doorway.

"Yeah, wasn't me."

"So weird, I could have sworn…" Her voice trails off behind the door as it closes behind her, and I have to silence the laugh threatening to break free. The shower turns on and that's my cue. I head back to my original room to throw on clothes and then head downstairs.

I type London Fog into the search bar and begin collecting the ingredients from around the kitchen. I follow each step precisely—making sure it's perfect—and when I'm finished, I head back upstairs to Lacey's room.

I gently knock on the door and enter. She's moving around the room packing her suitcase, and she turns to face me.

"What's that?" she asks, eyeing the mug.

"A London Fog."

"You made me my drink?" Her eyebrow hitches slightly. She walks over and takes it from me.

"It's the first one I've ever made, so I hope it's good." She takes a large sip and lets out a sound that makes my cock harden instantly.

"It's perfect, J," she says, taking another sip and letting out another moan. *Fuck.*

"Good," I manage to choke out. "I'm going to go get packed up." I turn quickly and walk out the door. Tanner is laying on his bed scrolling on his phone when I walk in our room.

"Did you really sleep downstairs last night?" he asks.

"No."

He looks up from his phone screen and sits up in bed. "Well if you weren't in here and you weren't down there, where the hell did you sleep?"

"In a bed."

"Which bed?"

"Lacey's."

"Dude, you slept with her?" His voice is loud, and I gesture for him to lower his voice. "You slept with her?" he repeats in a whisper.

"We shared a bed, but that's it."

"Dude!"

"It's not what you think. She found me miserable in the living room and took pity on her friend."

He rolls his eyes and shakes his head. "So what's step one in getting her back?"

"Already in action. I made her favorite drink this morning and brought it upstairs for her to drink while she packed." I smile to myself. Two days ago, I had no idea what her favorite drink was, but this morning I learned how to make it. The sound she made when she took a sip from the mug replays in my head and I try to shake it away. *God, what I'd give to hear it again.*

"I think we're going to need to do better than that." Tanner's eyes look ridiculous and he pulls out his phone. His fingers are moving a mile a minute.

"What are you doing?"

"Helping you," he deadpans as he continues to type. My phone begins to vibrate.

S.H.I.E.L.D.

TANNER:

I have an idea on how we can help Jacks get his girl back

TANNER:

But I think you're going to have to get Poppy's help

TANNER:

You think she would help us

LOGAN:

Good morning to you too.

LOGAN:

Depends. What's your idea?

Do I get a say in this?

TANNER:

No

LOGAN:

No.

TANNER:

Can y'all kick Lacey out of your car

I look at Tanner. "I'm standing right next to you. This is fucking stupid man."

"No it's not. If we text, she can't hear us talking about the plan," he whispers. I roll my eyes.

LOGAN:

I mean sure, but who would she ride with?
The plan is for me to take the girls back to
their apartment.

TANNER:

She'll ride with Jacks and get some much
needed alone time 😏

And how will you two dumbasses convince
her to do that?

"I drove you here. Who are you going to ride with?" Tanner looks up at me and then gestures back at his phone. I let out a long breath. Why is he so fucking annoying? I walk away from my roommate and plop down on my bed before beginning to type again.

Tanner, I drove you here. Who will you ride
with?

LOGAN:

We could tell her it's supposed to rain and
that we need the back of the truck for our
luggage? We put everything in the bed on the
way up.

TANNER:

Fucking brilliant dude

TANNER:

I'll make Wren drive me home

What makes you think she'll agree to that?

TANNER:

There won't be room in your Jeep with you
two love birds and all your luggage

LOGAN:

I'm on it!

I look over at Tanner, and he's smiling like a fucking idiot. I can't deny his plan is genius. We're two hours from home, and I can't think of a better way to spend the drive back than with Lacey.

I finish my cup of coffee and head back downstairs to help with the final tasks that need to be completed before we leave the cabin. Logan and Enzo are standing in the kitchen talking. Donovan rounds the corner carrying his luggage.

"Have you talked to Poppy and Lacey about the weather?" I ask.

"Not yet. Poppy was finishing up getting ready," Logan says.

"What about the weather?" Enzo asks.

"Oh, we might have to rearrange who is riding with who because it's supposed to rain," Logan explains.

Donovan walks over and looks out the window. "There isn't a cloud in the sky. You sure?"

Logan and my eyes meet each other. I quickly try to direct my gaze elsewhere, but Donovan catches us.

"Wait, what's going on?" he asks.

"Nothing," I answer too quickly.

"Spill the tea, boys." Enzo laughs.

Tanner walks back into the kitchen. "Mornin' fellas," he says. "What are y'all talking about?"

"Logan and Jacks were about to tell us why they think it might rain later," Enzo says.

Tanner starts to laugh. "Might as well let them in on it. We could probably use their help."

I look around the space and none of the girls are nearby. "Logan and Tanner are helping me get Lacey back," I say.

"We want in," Enzo says.

"Yeah, what's the plan?" Donovan asks.

I fill them in on the car plan and they agree to go along with our little ruse. Tanner adds both of them to the group text. We finish taking out the trash, and Logan starts the dishwasher. Poppy rounds the corner, and Lacey and Wren make their way downstairs.

"Could y'all help me with my luggage?" Poppy asks. Logan nods and heads toward their room, pausing to place a kiss on her forehead. Wren walks an armful of towels over to the laundry room and starts a load.

"Is there anything else we need to do before we head out?" Lacey asks.

"No, I think we got everything," Donovan says.

Logan appears, holding Poppy's luggage and sets it by the door. "Wren and Lacey, are y'all's things upstairs?"

They nod.

"I'll go grab it," Tanner shouts, running by all of us and up the stairs.

S.H.I.E.L.D.

TANNER:

Show time baby! Let's FUCKINGGG go!

I silently chuckle to myself. If this works, I'll be shocked.

"Lacey, you mind riding back with Jacks? It's supposed to rain, and I don't want our stuff to get wet in the bed of the truck," Logan says.

Lacey and Poppy glance at each other. "Rain?" Poppy asks.

"Yeah. Are you sure?" Lacey adds, walking over to the window and looking up at the very blue and very clear sky.

"Yep, my app says it's supposed to hit on the drive home. I don't want to chance it."

She looks at me skeptically. "If I ride with you, then who will Tanner ride with?"

"Wren," Tanner says, stepping off the bottom step and making his way over to the door.

Wren's face immediately falls and she glances over to the other girls.

"Tanner isn't going to bother Wren for two hours. Donovan, y'all have more than enough space for Tanner, right?" Lacey says.

"Sure do," Enzo says.

"Are we sure it's even going to rain?" Poppy asks, looking down at her phone. "My weather app shows—"

Logan grabs her and pulls her in for a kiss, cutting off her statement.

"On second thought, Lacey, you may need to ride with Jace regardless of the weather." She winks at Logan and giggles.

"It's settled then. I'll ride with Jace and Tanner will ride with Donovan and Enzo," Lacey says.

CHAPTER 39: I GOT YOU

LACEY

Waking up with Jace's arms around me was interesting. I honestly don't know what to think about full on spooning with him, but it happened and I definitely didn't hate it. I pretended to be asleep, and when he snuck out of bed, I wished he hadn't. It was a stark reminder he is my friend and the cuddles were purely accidental.

I walk my luggage over to Jace's Jeep, knowing it's not going to rain, but a little intrigued as to why everyone was making such a big deal about the weather. He helps me load it in the backseat, and then we both round the car to say bye to our friends.

"Jace, you think we can get a group picture before we all head out?" Poppy asks.

"Sure thing. Y'all get in front of the house." He jogs over and begins digging in his trunk.

Locating his camera, he walks over to the front of the cabin. I know I'm staring, but there is no harm in looking at him. He's wearing a black T-shirt, gray sweatshorts, and a backwards hat. His tattooed biceps and forearms are exposed.

Poppy walks over to where I stand and nudges me. "You

gotta little drool on your mouth," she whispers, gesturing to the corner of hers with her thumb.

"I don't know what you're talking about."

"Liar. You're very obviously checking out the photographer."

"No, I'm not. I was thinking about how unfair it feels that he looks like that now. Doesn't it?"

"What do you mean?"

"It's like he made it his life mission to get even hotter to spite me. It has to be my punishment for ruining everything."

"Oh, yeah definitely not checking him out," she says sarcastically. "Come on, let's go take the picture."

We walk over and find our places among the group in front of the house. I squeeze in between Wren and Tanner.

"Everyone move in close," Jace says, gesturing at the group.

Poppy jumps in front of Logan and he wraps her up from behind, kissing her on her neck. She lets out a squeal, and I try to push the thoughts of having what they have out of my head. Jace brings the camera to his eye.

"Wait, are you not going to get in the picture?" I ask.

He drops his arms and his ocean blue eyes find mine. "Oh, um, I can."

"You gotta be in the picture."

His mouth forms into a devastating smile, and he jogs back over to the Jeep, grabbing a tripod. When he finishes setting up the camera, he pushes between Tanner and me. I'm immediately surrounded by his scent, and he smells delicious. He wraps an arm around my back, and the feeling I had between my thighs last night returns. *Goddammit.* Jace counts down from five and I try to push every thought I have about him out of my head, but it's no use.

We take a couple more pictures for good measure and when we're done I head toward Jace's Jeep. Wren and Poppy flank either side of me.

"I'd say don't get wet, but there's no fun in that." Poppy giggles.

"Shut the fuck up."

She slaps my butt and makes her way to Logan's truck. "Love you, Lace. See you at home. Bye, Wren."

"Love you more," I yell after her. Wren wraps me in a hug.

"Thanks for saving me from Tanner." Her cheeks turn a rosy shade of red. "You really helped me dodge a bullet."

"Of course." I pull away from her. "I'll see you tomorrow."

"I want every last dirty detail of your little car ride."

I roll my eyes as she walks away. I swing the door open and climb into the passenger seat. My head swirls with thoughts of last night again. How his fingers barely brushed mine and how desperate I was for him to touch me somewhere else. Anywhere else. How his corded arms were wrapped around me, holding me like I was a life raft in the middle of the ocean. How, after he got up to shower, I considered following him into the bathroom. But why would I do that? We're only friends.

The driver side door opens, snapping me from my train of thought.

"Ready to go, Pixie?"

"Let's do this." I try to tug on my seatbelt, but it's stuck and I can't get it across my body. "Shit, it's stuck."

"Damn it, I thought I fixed it. Here, let me help you." Jace reaches over and grabs my seatbelt, tugging firmly until it releases. The weight of his body on mine and his woodsy scent makes my whole body come alive. He pulls the belt across my body and clicks it into place. Just as quickly as he invades my space, he leaves it, leaving me as disappointed as I was this morning when he climbed out of bed.

Rummaging through my bag, I grab my e-reader and begin to read. If I can keep my eyes on my book for the next two hours, then I won't be tempted to stare at the man in the driver's seat. I won't think about how much I like the weight of his body on mine. And I definitely won't think about how much I liked laying in his arms this morning.

Jace starts the ignition and turns on some music. Zach Topp pours through the speakers filling the silence. We back out of the driveway and follow our friends down the gravel road. We are the last car in our caravan of four.

My eyes stay locked on the screen as we make our way around each curve of the mountain. I peer over for a split second to see him singing along to the song. His thumbs drum on the steering wheel to the beat. I quickly divert my gaze back to my book.

As we continue, I realize there seems to be more twists and turns than I remember. I look up and find none of our friends' cars are anywhere to be found.

"Did we lose the rest of the group?" I ask. He rounds a large curve in the road and my whole body flushes with heat.

"I need to stop and get gas," he says. "We can get home this way too. The closest gas station is a little out of our way."

I nod and my skin erupts with goosebumps, but not the good kind. I fidget with the air vents in front of me trying to get more air.

"You good?"

"Um, yeah, I think so." I put my e-reader down and take a big swig from my water bottle, but nausea immediately over-whelms me. I try to close my eyes and breathe through it, but it's no use. My jaw starts to tighten and my stomach does a somersault.

"Fuck, pull over!" The words are rushed, and I slap my hand over my mouth. His wide eyes meet mine as he swerves off the road and onto the shoulder. I throw the door open and jump out. My feet barely hit the dirt before I empty the contents of my stomach all over the ground. *Fucking hot, Lacey. Really fucking hot.*

I bend over with both hands on my knees. I try to take a

deep breath, but another wave of nausea hits me like a truck. I begin to heave, my body retches, and that's when I feel him behind me. One of his hands gathers my hair out of my face and the other rubs slow circles on the small of my back as he soothes me.

"It's okay, Pixie. I got you," he says.

I finish getting sick and slowly stand, wiping my mouth with the back of my hand.

"Goodness, I'm so sorry."

"Don't be. Are you okay?"

"Yeah." I quickly scan my body and realize a small spot of vomit on my T-shirt. My face burns with embarrassment. "Fuck me."

"Huh?"

"Oh, nothing." I quickly move to the back of the Jeep and he follows me, hovering closer than he should, like he's worried I may get sick again and he'll need to jump into doing whatever it is he did before.

I swing the back door open, dig through my suitcase, and locate a new T-shirt and my toiletry bag while trying to ignore how close we are and how good it felt to have him take care of me.

I grab the bottom of the shirt I'm wearing but realize his eyes are glued to me. "Um, I need to change my shirt." I spin my finger in the air.

"Oh, yeah. Of course." He takes a step back before flipping around and facing the other direction so I can change. I quickly change tops and stuff my newly stained shirt deep in my bag so he doesn't see it. I don't know why it matters. He literally just held my hair while I threw up breakfast. I let out a low grumble.

"You decent?"

"Yes." I grab my overnight bag and make my way back to the passenger side of the Jeep, careful not to ruin my shoes.

We both climb in. I pull on my seatbelt and it glides easily.

I send a silent thank you to the universe. The last thing I need is him leaning over me to buckle me in when I have vomit breath.

"Didn't want me to see you topless?" he teases, clicking his own belt into place.

"Are you saying you wanted to see me topless?" I cut him a look before laying my head on the headrest and shutting my eyes.

He lets out a low chuckle and starts the engine. "You good if we try to make it to the gas station?"

"Oh, yeah. I think the mix of the sharp turns and my book made me nauseous. I'm fine now, just going to try to relax."

"I'm sorry I took us this way."

"You didn't do it on purpose," I laugh, keeping my eyes closed. "Thanks for holding my hair and rubbing my back and all that. You didn't have to, and it was nice that you did."

"I told you I got you, plus it's not the first time I've had to take care of you when you were sick," he remembers, chuckling.

"Oh, my god. How could I forget? Four wine coolers at fifteen was not my brightest move." I squint my eyes open and turn my head towards him.

"No, it wasn't, but I'll always take care of you. I didn't mind back then and I don't mind now." His words settle in my brain and I try not to think about what they could mean. I roll my head back to center and close my eyes.

"You know my parents still don't know about that night." I laugh. "Mom would probably lose it on me if she ever found out."

"You think she'd still get mad about something that happened twelve years ago?"

"Well, not mad, but you know she doesn't handle that kinda thing well. Would probably lecture me about how I need better life choices or something. Me drinking at fifteen really plays into her whole *Lacey's a mess* narrative. She hasn't changed much since you last saw her."

"So, I'm guessing that means you two aren't very close."

"I don't know. It's complicated. You know Lori. Everything has to be planned and on the calendar, so unless she plans some family dinner or it's an obligatory holiday, I don't talk to her much. Part of me hoped I'd see my parents more once my dad retired, but the opposite has happened. Colt moved to Texas for school, so unless the prodigal son is in town, then we don't get together."

I feel his hand squeeze mine and my eyes shoot open. A spark flies up my arm, making my heart flutter. As quickly as I can, I shake him off. Silence fills the car and his hand returns to the steering wheel.

What are we doing?

The gas station comes into view and I take a deep breath, relieved that my stomach held it together and I'll be able to get some much-needed space between us.

Jace parks the Jeep at one of the pumps, and I make a beeline to the bathroom with my toiletry bag. It's a single stall and surprisingly cleaner than I expected it to be.

At the sink, I splash some cold water on my face and try to gather my thoughts. Grabbing a few paper towels, I gently dry my face. My hands rest on the edge of the sink, and I give myself the pep talk. *Get it together, Lacey. He's your friend. He's being nice. He doesn't want to be more than friends. You just puked in front of him for Christ's sake. Be fucking normal.*

I brush my teeth, fix my hair, and double check that the rest of my clothes are clean before heading back to the car. I slide into the passenger seat and throw my bag in the back. Grabbing my e-reader, I pull my knees up to my chest and try to get comfortable for the long ride ahead.

Jace slides in with a wide grin plastered across his face, holding two plastic bags.

"What's that?"

"Things for you," he says, placing the bag next to me in my chair.

I take a minute to dig through it. Ginger ale, off-brand saltines, Dramamine, a Coke, and a bag of mini red and pink Starbursts are all piled inside.

"I wasn't sure if you were still feeling sick, so I got you options. Also they didn't have any coffee or tea, so I figured a Coke would help if you wanted caffeine."

"How did you know I liked these?" I lift the Starbursts out of the bag.

"I have my ways."

"Hmmm." I eye him and pull out the Coke. "Did you not want anything?"

He digs through the second bag and pulls out a Coke, a bag of chili-cheese Fritos, and some gum. He places it all in the center console and puts the bag at my feet. "Speaking of you feeling sick, I think you should probably put the book down. We're not quite off the windy roads yet." He plucks my e-reader from my hands and puts it on the backseat.

"Fine, but then what will I do for the next hour and a half?" I grumble.

"I guess you're going to have to talk to me." His face curves into a wicked grin.

CHAPTER 40: CAR CONFESSIONS
JACE

Lacey lets out another little grumble, and I turn my head back toward the road ahead. Out of the corner of my eye, I see her adjusting her chair.

"So, Pixie, what's Colt doing in Texas?"

"He moved out there for school. Got a scholarship for baseball at UT and is loving it."

"Are y'all still close?"

"Sorta. I try to check in with him as much as I can. I tried him a couple times this summer and he was supposed to call me back, but he hasn't."

"That sucks."

"I know he's busy."

"I don't think he likes me much." I chuckle, remembering all of the times Colt and I crossed paths over the past ten years. My eyes flit to the necklace that still sits around Lacey's neck, and for a second I think about telling her it was from me, but I change my mind. I don't want to complicate things for them or for us.

"Goodness, he was so young and so cute back then. I'm pretty sure he offered to beat you up." She laughs. "I'm proud of him, and you know Mom and Dad are elated he's playing college baseball. He's made all their dreams come true."

"Are they not proud of you too?"

She's quiet for a minute, and when I look over at her, she's staring out the window, lost in her thoughts.

"What's on your mind?"

"Family's hard. Don't get me wrong; I love my parents, and I know I had it easier than most growing up. But sometimes, I feel like I'm too much, you know?"

"What do you mean?"

"You know, like I'm not the super composed beauty pageant queen my mom wanted. I'm messy and say what's on my mind. I'm dramatic and loud. Sometimes I think she's disappointed I didn't turn out the way she hoped I would."

"I don't think you're too much."

Silence hangs between us, and I think about grabbing her hand, but I stop myself.

"I know your dad has to be so proud of you and your career. Your mom would be. She used to tell me all the—" She quickly takes a sip of her Coke and lets out a very fake cough.

"What was that?" Our eyes find each other for a split second, and hers are full of something I can't quite place.

"Huh?"

"You said my mom used to tell you. What did she tell you?"

She takes a deep breath. "Promise not to hate me."

"I could never hate you."

"Okay, well that's not true." She bites her lip. "And you have to promise not to be mad at your mom. She was going to tell you, or at least I think she was, but then she…"

"Died."

"Jesus, Jace." She slaps my arm. "Don't say it like that."

"Well she did, so I technically can't be mad at her. Come on, tell me about it."

"Okay, well after we broke up, I saw your parents often."

"That makes sense. Our parents were friends and we were neighbors."

"Yeah, but it was more than me waving hello. Like I would talk to your mom a lot."

"What do you mean?"

"Like every Friday on the phone starting my freshman year of college until she passed away." She says the sentence so fast that I'm not sure I heard her right. I know once I started college I wasn't around very often, but I talked to my parents almost daily, and Mom never mentioned talking with Lacey.

"See I told you. You hate me," she says.

"I don't hate you. I'm a little surprised, but I don't hate you."

She pulls out the bag of mini Starbursts and pops a few into her mouth.

"Why did she call you every week?" I try to keep my tone even. I'm not mad. I honestly don't know how to feel about it.

"My freshman year, I was really lonely. You were out of my life, Poppy was gallivanting around Europe with that asshat, and my parents were so wrapped up in work and Colt that I felt like I had no one. I came home one weekend and ran into your mom. She asked me how college was going, and I lost it in the middle of the driveway. I mean, like, really lost it. Full on ugly cry." She pauses. Any doubt I initially had about this revelation leaves me. Mom took care of her when no one else was around. I reach out and place my hand on her thigh, encouraging her to continue. To my surprise, she doesn't move away.

"So anyway, she held me in the driveway and let me cry. Let me get it all out and then when I was done, she double checked she had my phone number. Every week after, she would call me on Fridays and ask me about my week. Encourage me to go out and meet people. Listen to me laugh or cry. It meant so much. During my darkest time, she was my light."

"Wow, I had no idea."

"I know, but she told me she would tell you when the time was right and then she got sick, and I'm so sorry." Her voice cracks and her eyes gloss over. I squeeze her thigh.

"Y'all talked about me?"

"Well sorta. Not really. After a few of our first calls she brought you up and told me you were doing well. Told me you had gotten into Georgetown and that she was so proud of you for following your dreams."

That makes me smile.

"Did she know what happened between you and me?"

"No. I never told her, and she didn't push. She would tell me she knew one day you and I would sort it all out and then we would go on talking about something else."

"I'm glad she was there for you when no one else was. She was good like that. Knowing what everyone needed. I wish so badly she was still around."

"Me too."

"You know I haven't been back to her grave since she died," I admit, disappointed with myself for not being able to visit her. Lacey places her hand on top of mine. Our fingers wind together. *Holy fuck, Lacey Sims is holding my hand.* I try to compose myself.

"Why not?"

"I don't know. Too many things I guess. I feel so guilty I wasn't here when she died."

"I didn't know you weren't there. That had to be so hard."

"Yeah, I was out on location for a project, and it took Dad a whole day to get ahold of me. I came home as quickly as I could, but it was too late. She was gone and I didn't get to say goodbye."

She squeezes my hand. "I'm so sorry."

"It is what it is. I entered the apartment lease with Tanner for Dad's sake, but it didn't change how often I was home. I stayed away because it was easier. If I'm honest, I'm scared to go to her grave. Scared of all the feelings it'll bring up."

"I understand. Is that who the sunflowers are for?" She lets go of my hand for a minute and gently traces the petals of one of the flowers tattooed on my right forearm.

"They were her favorite flower."

"It's beautiful." Her fingers trail back down to my hand, and she intertwines my fingers with hers once more. "I know how much you loved her." I glance over and her eyes are glossy.

"Have you visited her?" I ask.

"Yeah. I try to go on her birthday if I can, but with work it doesn't always work out. Your dad goes a lot. I've run into him a couple of times."

"Am I the worst son in the world for not going?"

"No, she's your mom. I think it makes sense that it would be hard to go, but I also think it would be really good for you to visit her. Talk to her. Have you ever thought about going with your dad?"

My stomach sinks.

"He always asks if I want to go, but I never take him up on it. The thought of seeing him sad at her grave is too much."

She nods her head and lets out a little hum. "They were so in love, weren't they? Gosh, to have a love like theirs. That's the dream."

"All Your'n" by Tyler Childers starts to play, and I take a moment to take Lacey in. The sun casts a warm glow into the car, and her hair falls over her shoulders—it's somewhere between straight and wavy. Our hands are still locked together like two puzzle pieces always meant to fit. She hums along to the song.

I know without a shadow of a doubt that we could have a love like my parents did.

"It really is," I say. "I can't imagine losing your person and never getting to see them again. He doesn't talk about it a lot, but I know it's still so hard for him, and I don't think I could bear seeing him break down above her tombstone."

"You know, if you wanted me to go with you to see your mom I would," she offers.

"You wouldn't have to do that."

"I know, but just like you got me, I got you. If you ever want to go, just say the word."

"I'd like that." Her thumb begins to rub soft circles on the back of my hand.

"I think she would too," she says.

"I'm headed out of town tomorrow for a few days. Do you remember my Uncle Joe?"

"The conspiracy theorist?"

"Yes, him. He needs some help at his cabin, so I was voluntold to go." I chuckle. "Maybe when I get back we could do it."

"If you want to, we could. Or if you still need more time, that's okay too." She squeezes my hand gently. "I'm here whenever you're ready."

We drive the rest of the way home in silence. Lacey drifts off to sleep, but I don't let go of her hand. She doesn't know it yet, but if I have it my way, I'm never letting go of her again.

CHAPTER 41: INTERRUPTIONS
JACE

"Pixie, we're home." I let go of her hand and gently brush the side of her face, causing her to stir and her eyes to blink open.

"Oh shit, how long was I out?" She rubs her eyes and stretches in her seat.

"A little over an hour."

"You could have woken me up."

"Nah, I'd much rather you sleep than puke." I chuckle and she gives my arm a little shove.

"Very funny. Well, thanks for the ride home. Did I sleep through the rain?"

"What rain?"

"You know the rain that kept me from riding with Poppy and Logan." Her mouth curves into a sexy grin, and I know we've been caught.

"Oh, um, I guess it held off. You know those weather apps. They're never right."

"Interesting," she says, raising her eyebrows. She starts gathering up her belongings off the floorboard, and I jump out and grab her bags from the back. We make our way across the lawn and up the stairs to her front door.

"You didn't have to walk me."

"I don't mind."

There's a beat of silence, and I'm not sure what to do next. The plan is to woo her and get my shit together before I tell her how I feel. She's run from me before because she was worried we didn't want the same things, and I want to make sure this time there is no doubt in her mind that I want her.

I should stick with the plan, but she's standing inches from me. Her lips are a soft shade of pink and look so damn kissable. The air is tight with tension and I can see it in her eyes—she wants me too. Her gaze dips to my mouth. I drop her bags on the wooden deck and she takes a half step closer to me.

Fuck the plan.

I move toward her and brush her hair out of her face. Her breath quickens. I lean down to close the remaining gap between us.

"Oh, shit! Sorry." Poppy's voice interrupts the moment we almost shared. I turn to see her and Logan standing in the now open doorway staring at the two of us. My eyes flick back to Lacey, who has taken a step back. Her cheeks are a deep shade of pink.

"Alright, well thanks for the ride," she says, grabbing her things and moving past me and our friends.

"Lacey, wait." I try to stop her, but she keeps moving deeper into the apartment and then I hear the sound of a door closing.

"I'm sorry. I didn't realize you two were out here," Poppy says.

I rub my hand over the back of my head and push past her. "Which room is hers?" I ask.

Logan points at a closed door. I cross the living room toward her bedroom. Leaning against the door frame with my left hand, I knock erratically with my right. My heart is beating rapidly, and I've never been more sure of what I'm about to do.

"Geez, Poppy. I'm fine," she yells from behind the door. It swings open, revealing gorgeous emerald eyes. Her mouth opens in surprise to me standing there.

"Jace, what are you—"

I don't let her finish her sentence because, I'll be damned, we are not getting interrupted again. I reach forward to move her hair behind her ear and take her face in both of my hands. I pull her towards me, and when our mouths finally collide, my whole body comes alive. She lets out a small moan, and fuck if it's not the prettiest sound I've ever heard. Her lips part at the feel of my tongue and I slightly tug on her hair, giving me more access to her mouth. She tastes like strawberry Starbursts.

We stumble into her room and our kiss becomes desperate. I swing the door shut behind me. Lacey's hands move up the back of my shirt, her fingers digging into my skin. I pull her in tighter, and her hips grind into me, causing my dick to strain against my shorts.

"Fuck," I let out. My hands find her hair and I knot my fist in it, causing her to let out another moan against my lips. I walk her backwards until her body presses up against a wall. I push my hips forward and she meets my pace.

Our mouths continue to tangle. Her leg wraps around the back of mine, pulling me in closer, and the feeling is too much. It's too good. I realize if I don't stop this soon, I'm going to come from this kiss alone, and that can't happen. Not with her. I try to will away the feeling, try to slow the kiss, but then she grinds against me, moaning again and saying my name.

My body jolts as I find my release. Warm cum coats the inside of my boxers. *Fuck.*

I quickly back away from her, knowing I need to get out of here before she realizes what happened. I swallow the embarrassment. My eyes find hers. She's still leaning up against the wall. Her green eyes are hooded, and her lips are swollen and wet from our kiss. She looks fucking sexy as hell, and my brain rattles off a thousand different things I wish I could do to her, but for now, I need to leave. I need to get cleaned up and then get my shit together so that there is no doubt in her mind that she's the one I want.

"Jace. That was…" Her chest rises and falls with heavy breaths.

I close the distance between us and press a kiss to her forehead. "See you later, Pixie." I turn and walk out of her room before she can stop me. I hear Logan say my name as I walk back through the living room, but I don't stop until I make it to my Jeep.

S.H.I.E.L.D.

LOGAN:

I thought the plan was to sweep her off her feet first. What exactly did I just watch?

You watched? Weird.

LOGAN:

Alright asshole, want to tell the class what happened or should I?

TANNER:

What happened

DONOVAN:

Did the car plan work?

LOGAN:

I'd say it worked.

ENZO:

What happened?

I don't kiss and tell.

TANNER:

Letsssss fuckkkkkinnngggggg go dude

TANNER:

So what now

I don't know. I left. I need to get my shit together and show her what a future with me is like, and I need to do it before the end of the month.

ENZO:

How can we help?

Logan, can you check with Poppy and see if Lacey still likes dahlias?

LOGAN:

On it.

I back out of the parking lot and head to my apartment. The entire drive, my head is consumed with thoughts of Lacey—the way her hands felt on my body and the taste of her tongue. I waited ten years to kiss her again, and I would gladly endure every lonely night I faced in the last decade if it meant I could do it again.

Fuck, I wish I could have stayed. Laid her down on her bed and worshiped every bit of her body, but then I had to come in my shorts and ruin the moment. I try to remind myself that even if that hadn't happened, I have things I need to do before we go further.

I walk through the front door of my apartment and find Tanner sitting on the couch watching *Iron Man*.

"I can't believe you kissed her," he says, pausing the movie and sitting up a little straighter. "How are you feeling? Want to talk about it?"

"Nope." I turn and head to my bedroom, shutting the door behind me.

CHAPTER 42: DO IT FOR THE PLOT
LACEY

I remember kissing Jace Jackson, or at least I thought I remembered what kissing him was like. When I broke up with him, I grieved not being able to kiss him again and then promised myself to forget. Buried the feelings his kiss gave me deep inside me so I could try to move on, but it didn't work.

For a decade, I've been searching for someone that could make my body come alive the way he could and I never found it. It didn't matter who they were or what we did, it always felt less than, mediocre, not good enough, or bland. They became a name added to the list of men who, despite their best efforts, couldn't make me come.

And then he came back into my life like a goddamn wrecking ball, and I don't know what to do with this new information because kissing him was nothing like I remembered it being. It was so much better. And then that mother-fucker kissed my forehead and left me up against my bedroom wall breathless and with the taste of him still on my tongue.

Now, I'm standing in my bathroom, looking in the mirror,

and wondering what in the actual hell just happened and how I feel about it.

My hair looks freshly fucked, which is completely unfair because he left before I got off, and to be honest, it wouldn't have taken much more for me to come right there, dry-humping him while standing.

I replay the kiss in my head. Him leaning on the door frame. His backwards hat and those piercing blue eyes. His tattooed, brawny arms wrapped around me, pulling me against him. His hand tugging on my hair.

Fuck, I liked when he pulled my hair.

His dick straining in his shorts against my most sensitive spot. It felt big. I think I remember it being big. I mean, I may never have slept with him, but I wasn't a prude. We did other stuff but never went all the way. *God, why can't I remember what it looks like.*

I splash some water on my face and wipe it away with a towel. *Dammit, why am I trying to visualize his cock? Get it together. It was just a kiss.*

My phone vibrates on the counter and startles me from my thoughts.

The Tortured Therapists Department

WREN:

Lace, did you stay dry on the way home?

POPPY:

Yeah, Lace. Did you stay dry? Because I'm dying to know what the fuck I just witnessed.

GRAY:

Wait, what did I miss?

CHLOE:

What happened?

WREN:

Poppy, what did you just witness?

POPPY:

I'll let Lacey share with the group.

I walk out of my room to find Poppy sitting in our living room reading the book she started at the cabin.

"Where's Logan?"

"He had to go help his mom with something."

"Are you serious?" I ask, shaking my phone in her direction.

"Am *I* serious?" She marks her page. "Girl, are *you* serious? What the fuck was that?"

"I don't know." I let out a long breath and make my way over to the couch. I sit opposite her and let my face fall into my hands. "Did y'all see the whole thing?"

"Well, not everything," she explains. "He shut the door pretty quickly after he kissed you."

"It was hot, right?"

"Really hot."

"What do you think it means?" My phone pings.

GRAY:

You really can't leave us hanging like this.

WREN:

I'm guessing that means you did in fact
get wet?

CHLOE:

Is this some weird sexual innuendo?

GRAY:

Yeah, why does Wren keep asking if you
got wet?

Poppy giggles at her phone.

"This isn't funny. You interrupted us outside, and then he

barged in here like some sort of sex god and made me almost come on his leg with a fucking kiss."

"You know, I feel like someone once told me that if a guy almost makes you come on his leg, clothed, then you should have sex with him ASAP." She smirks. I equally love and hate her for using my own words against me. I glare at her, and my head falls onto the back of the sofa. "Come on, do it for the plot," she laughs.

"But he left, and, like, not to toot my own horn, but I know that kiss wasn't bad. It was really fucking hot. So why did he leave?"

"Maybe he panicked?"

"You think?"

"What happened on the car ride here that led to that?"

"Nothing. I mean, we slept together last night and—"

"Wait, you slept with him at the cabin?"

"Well, not like slept with him slept with him, but yeah, we shared my bed because his mattress sucked, and apparently Tanner snores."

"Why am I just now finding out about this?"

"I don't know, because it wasn't that big of a deal."

She squints her eyes at me. "You sure about that because that kiss looked like a pretty big fucking deal?"

"I don't know. I'm confused. We slept together, and I woke up to him holding me, and then he snuck out of bed and left me laying there thinking it was an accident and not what he wanted, but then in the car I got sick."

"Like you threw up?"

"Yeah, and he did the whole hold my hair and rub my back thing and then made sure I had everything I needed, which was really sweet."

Poppy takes a deep breath. "Go on."

"And then the conversation got really deep and at one point he put his hand on my thigh and I didn't fight it because I liked it, but then I held his hand."

"Is that so?" she teases.

"And then I fell asleep and the next thing I knew we were here and you interrupted the almost kiss on the porch and then he barged in here and kissed me and I couldn't remember how big his dick was…"

Poppy bursts out laughing. Her eyes go wide and she puts up her hand stopping me. "Wait, hold that thought. You brought up Jace's cock. I think I need a drink." She stands and walks into the kitchen.

"Wait, that's all you have to say?"

"I'm coming back, I just feel like I need something to get through the rest of this conversation."

WREN:

<<Bueller, Bueller GIF>>

> The short version: I puked on the way home. Jace was a fucking saint about it. We held hands. He just kissed my brains out.

GRAY:

So you did get wet? I think I understand now.

GRAY:

CHLOE:

Y'all are disgusting.

WREN:

OMG! He kissed you?

> He did. Hottest kiss of my life.

CHLOE:

Meanwhile, I'm at work and just walked into 506 and caught 440 giving him a handy. I'm so glad everyone else is getting some today.

GRAY:

They truly do NOT pay us enough.

WREN:

No way?!

Did you tell Margaret? Maybe she'll finally let me give my presentation on safe sex for seniors.

GRAY:

Keep dreaming girl 🤭

CHLOE:

They do NOT pay us enough. But yay Poppy! I can't wait for you to start tomorrow. You're going to love it here. 😂

Poppy walks back into the living room holding two glasses of white wine. "Did you see Chloe's text? I'm dying." She hands me one of the glasses and sits back down on the couch.

"Oh, get ready—that's nothing. You will see things you'll never unsee." I laugh and take a sip of my wine.

"Okay, so where were we?"

"I was trying to remember how big Jace's dick is."

"That's right, please continue."

CHAPTER 43: NEXT STEPS

JACE

I thought about texting Lacey last night, but I wasn't sure what I should say. I left so abruptly, and I hate myself a little for it. At twenty-eight, I should be able to control myself a little better, but it's been a long fucking time, and that kiss was everything.

There is still so much up in the air with work and my plans. Maybe I shouldn't have kissed her, but then I think back to the way she looked standing there. Her green eyes, ones that put the depths of the Amazon rainforest to shame, begged me to kiss her, and I don't regret it one bit.

My phone rings, and I swipe up on the unknown number.

"Hello," I say.

"Hello, I'm calling to speak with Mr. Jacks Jackson," an unfamiliar voice comes through the phone.

"This is he."

"Hello, Mr. Jackson. My name is Roger Lucas. I hope you're having a great Monday. Do you have a moment to talk?"

"Yes, sir. How can I help you?"

"Great. I'm the president of the Center for North American Wildlife Conservation, and I was looking over your port-folio." He pauses and chuckles. "First of all, let me apologize for the delay in contacting you. We've had some recent internal changes, and I was working on getting those resolved before I dove into hiring for this position."

"That's no problem. I'm glad you called." Nervousness pulses through my veins and I try to calm myself.

"I must say, when I saw it come across my desk I was a little surprised. I've been following your discovery of the Bixito Parrot quite closely. Finding it in the wild was an impressive feat."

"Thank you. It was a lifelong dream of mine."

"So I hear. Well, I won't keep you too long, but I would like to have you down to the center this week for an official interview. It would give me an opportunity to show you around and get to know you a little better."

"That would be fantastic."

"Great. How does Friday at three sound?"

"Perfect. I can be there." I breathe a sigh of relief that I'll be back in time for the interview.

"Wonderful. I'll have my assistant send over the information and I'll see you then."

"I look forward to it, Mr. Lucas."

He hangs up the phone and I exhale. This is what I want. I want to be able to do what I love and not have to worry about being too far away. I want a future with Lacey, and a job like this would give me that.

S.H.I.E.L.D.

I got the interview at the CFNAWC.

TANNER:

Where

ENZO:

The Center for North American Wildlife
Conservation.

TANNER:

Ohhhhh got it

LOGAN:

Oh. BTW, I asked Poppy. Lacey likes purple
dahlias.

Thanks.

TANNER:

So what does this mean

It means I have an interview. He seemed
impressed with my resume.

ENZO:

How could he not be? You discovered a
whole fucking bird that hadn't been seen in
fifty years. You're as good as hired.

Maybe.

TANNER:

So what's next for you and your girl

First flowers, then maybe a date when I get
back.

DONOVAN:

Definitely a date.

I quickly look up a local florist and call in an order of Lacey's favorite flowers to be delivered to where she works. Then, I get to work prepping for my interview. Friday needs to go perfect, and I know there will be no internet at Joe's. He doesn't believe in it. Or trust it. Or maybe it's both.

I scan the CFNAWC website, and it's as incredible as I thought. Most of their work focuses on conservation efforts for North American species. Currently they have active projects centered around the ivory-billed woodpecker, red wolves, the Vancouver Island marmots, plus a dozen more. The amount of money they raise each year is astounding. I do a quick Google search on Roger Lucas. I was familiar with the name, but didn't understand how impressive his resume actually was. I feel energized and excited. This job is exactly what I want and working for him would be an honor.

My phone vibrates, interrupting my research. I close my laptop and swipe up on the screen.

DAD:

When are you leaving for Joe's?

Hopefully by 3, maybe earlier. I'd like to get there before it gets too dark.

DAD:

Thank you again for helping him. It means a lot to me.

Don't mention it.

DAD:

I was thinking about going to visit Mom in about an hour. Would love for you to come with me. We don't have to stay long.

I consider what to text him but can't find the words. Grief consumes me and I try to shake it away, but the longer I sit here staring at his text message, the bigger it feels. I lay back on my bed. I should go. I should tell him I'll meet him there, but I can't.

Sorry, I don't think I'll have time. Rain check?

DAD:

Drive safe and let me know when you get
there.

All the grief I was feeling turns to guilt, causing my stomach to flip. I don't know why I can't say yes. Why can't I make myself go with him? I flip over and re-open my laptop.

.

CHAPTER 44: SEX IS AN ADL

LACEY

I've been listening to Margaret drone on and on about the importance of completing all company training modules on time for what feels like thirty minutes. She's lecturing us about making sure we watch them thoroughly, and I don't miss her staring at me as she says it.

"Before we end today, I'd like to take a moment to welcome Poppy Collins to the team," she says, shifting the subject. "I thought everyone could go around the room and introduce themselves, and then Poppy, you can tell us a little bit about you."

Pia, our certified occupational therapy assistant, begins, and the rest of the group follows. I have to stifle a laugh because this seems ridiculous. Poppy has had dinner with everyone sitting in this room.

I zone out the introductions. My mind drifts back to yesterday and how it felt when Jace pressed me up against my bedroom wall and kissed me like our lives depended on it. I expected he would text me last night, and when he didn't, I was surprised. I thought about texting him this morning, but then I stopped myself. That kiss might have completely blown my mind, but Lacey Sims chases no man. Not even the one she wants, apparently.

"Lacey, it's your turn," Margaret says, breaking me of my thoughts.

"Oh, right. Hi. I'm Lacey. I'm the occupational therapist here. Glad to have you as part of the team," I deadpan. I take a sip of my London Fog.

Gray, Chloe, and Poppy all burst out laughing, and Margaret scowls at the four of us. "Poppy, why don't you tell us a little something about yourself. I realize you may know some of the people in the room, but not everyone knows you."

She smiles and twirls her hair around her finger. "Okay, I'm Poppy. I graduated from Farrington University in May. I love coffee and watching rom-coms. I'm so excited to be a part of an all-woman therapy team."

"Yes, well, we are proud to be one. Not that I wouldn't hire a man because I would," Margaret assures us. Muffled laughs come from every person in the room.

"Alright then, that's all I have," Margaret continues, abruptly ending the staff meeting. "Poppy, if you wouldn't mind hanging back. There are some training videos the company needs you to complete today."

Poppy nods and the rest of the team disperses to start our work day. I make my way down the hallway with Chloe and Gray on either side of me.

"God, I honestly didn't think she was ever going to stop talking about those modules," Gray says.

"Right?" I laugh. "Did y'all see her look right at me when she was giving her little lecture about watching them 'thoroughly.' Like she doesn't click through every single one like the rest of us."

"Could you imagine how low our productivity would be if we actually watched the entire video every time?" Chloe asks.

"Oh, we would all for sure be put on some sort of action plan."

"Personally, I'm glad she clarified she would in fact hire a man. I was worried she might be sexist against them," Gray says dryly, causing both Chloe and I to howl with laughter.

We stop in front of 307. "This is me."

"You still owe us all the details about the kiss," Gray says, walking backwards down the hallway.

"Yeah, yeah, I know," I say, knocking on the door. "I'm swamped this morning, but I promise to tell y'all everything at lunch." My friends both turn and disappear around the corner.

"Ms. Clara, it's Lacey. Can I come in?"

"It's open," I hear her call.

I swing the door open to find she's still in bed. She's sitting up reading a book and wearing a purple mumu covered in little shooting stars and rocket ships. A bouquet of red roses sits on her bedside table.

"Another good book?" I ask walking towards her.

"*Pride and Prejudice*," she says, marking her page and setting the paperback on her bed.

"That's not your usual cup of tea."

"No, but you can't beat a classic, and now that I've met Eugene, I don't have to just find my spice in books."

My eyes go wide and I try to control my facial expression with a smile. "Alright then, let's get to work. Are we changing this morning, or are we wearing the mumu to therapy?"

"No need to change. I'm a taken woman, and he likes my mumus."

"Great."

"If you go in my closet, I have a pair of matching shoes. Be a lamb and grab them for me, would you?"

I walk over and open the closet door. A pair of purple bedazzled shoes sit on one of the shelves. I grab them and then her walker. When I get to her bedside, she's already sitting with her feet on the floor.

"Those flowers are pretty. Did your son visit this weekend?"

"Oh, no. Eugene had those delivered on Saturday."

"Wow, someone is smitten." I offer her a smile and kneel down to help her with her shoes.

"He's more than smitten. Men are all the same, honey. When they start sending you your favorite flowers for no reason, that's how you know you got 'em. They're in love."

"I don't know about that."

"Has a man that was not in love with you ever bought you flowers?" I think for a minute. The last time someone bought me flowers was... God I can't even remember... surely it wasn't Jace. *Fuck, maybe it was Jace.* Have I really not had anyone buy me flowers since I was seventeen? How fucking depressing. Then again, I never really gave anyone the chance to either.

"Come to think of it, I guess not," I say.

"See. I told you." She slides on her shoes and then stands with a little less help than she needed before I left for the cabin.

"I think you're getting stronger, Ms. Clara. That was great."

"That friend of yours worked me to death all weekend. Where have you been?"

We begin to walk toward the door. "Oh, a group of my friends and I won a weekend at a lake cabin for the Fourth of July. Did y'all get to see fireworks?"

"We did. They did a private show over the pond. It was nice. Did you know Eugene was in the Army?"

"I didn't. That's neat."

"God, what I would have given to see him in his uniform..." We round the corner near the therapy gym at the same time the receptionist, Robin, comes from the other direction. She's holding an obnoxiously large bouquet of dahlias. Each bloom is large with a cream center that fades into lilac rimmed petals. It's gorgeous.

"Oh, good, Lacey. Just the person I was looking for. These were delivered for you."

"For me?" I ask, admiring the arrangement.

"Don't stand there like that girl. A man sent you flowers. Take them and see who they're from," Ms. Clara orders.

"You don't know they're from a man," I laugh.

"Here, let me follow y'all inside the gym," Robin says, gesturing for Ms. Clara to continue walking.

I help her over to one of the mats and then meet Robin to take the vase. I set down the arrangement on one of the office desks and pluck the little card from the middle of the flowers.

Yesterday was incredible. I can't wait to see you when I get back.

-J

Yesterday was incredible, and I haven't stopped thinking about that kiss since it happened. My stomach does a flip, butterflies erupting inside of me. Inhaling deeply, I tuck the card back into the envelope and then deep into the pocket of my scrubs. I'm at work. I need to remain professional.

"Alright, sorry about that. Let's get started," I say, grabbing a basket of towels and walking back over to where Ms. Clara sits.

Ms. Clara eyes me. "You weren't expecting those were you?"

"No, I wasn't." I pull over an adjustable table and set the basket on top. "Let's start with folding these towels."

The conversation I had just minutes ago with Ms. Clara in her room replays in my head. Surely, she's mistaken. Men buy flowers for women all of the time. Right?

"Remind me why I'm having to do laundry?" She looks at the basket and her brow furrows.

"Because it works on your range of motion and when I put the basket over here"—I roll the table to Ms. Clara's left—"and you reach for the towels with your right hand, it works on your trunk control too."

She lets out an annoyed breath and grabs a towel with her right hand. "So, are they from a man?" she asks.

"Yes." I smile, walking across the gym to find a stool to sit on. "A friend sent them."

She starts laughing. "Oh, honey, friends don't send arrangements that look like that."

I grab a stool and roll it over to where she sits.

"Is it your birthday?" She has yet to start folding the towel.

"Huh?"

"The flowers. Did this friend send them for your birthday?"

"Oh, no. My birthday's in December."

"Are you sick then?" she asks, still not beginning.

"No, I'm not sick. Let's fold that one and then grab another one."

"Someone die? Anniversary? Job promotion?" she presses. "If a friend sent them, then he must have had a reason."

"Come on, we gotta get to work." I urge, trying to push what the flowers could mean out of my head completely.

"Oh, sweet girl. You didn't know he loves you."

"I don't know that."

"Men aren't complicated. He sent you flowers for no reason. Sounds like love to me," she says, finally beginning to fold the towel.

———

The Tortured Therapists Department

GRAY:

Who is the insane bouquet of flowers for in
the gym?

Me 😌

POPPY:

That's why Logan asked me about your
favorite flower.

Your boyfriend asked you what my favorite
flower was and you didn't feel the need to
tell me?!

Did Jace ask him to ask you?

When did he ask you this question?

GRAY:

They're from Jace?

Yes. Poppy answer me.

POPPY:

Sorry. Margaret has me doing these modules
and I was getting the next one set up. Logan
said Jace asked him yesterday after the kiss.

And you didn't tell me?

POPPY:

It felt like a canon event. I didn't want to
ruin it.

307 thinks it means he's in love with me.

GRAY:

Of course she would. 😏

Apparently her and 330 are so serious she
doesn't need to "get her spice from books
anymore."

CHLOE:

💀

Honestly though, good for her. Sex IS an ADL and I hope she's getting some. Makes my little OT heart happy.

CHLOE:

You gonna ask Margaret if you can give your "Safe Sex for Seniors" presentation now?

I SHOULD!

GRAY:

She'll never say yes.

She might.

GRAY:

We're getting off topic. Back to the flowers…

POPPY:

Yes, what do you think they mean, Lace?

CHLOE:

The flowers are beautiful!

WREN:

Wait! I just walked by the gym. They're STUNNING!

I don't know what to think.

GRAY:

Must have been some kiss. Can't wait to hear all about it in an hour.

———

I'M SITTING AT A PICNIC TABLE OUTSIDE DOGWOOD MANOR waiting for my friends to meet me for lunch. I tap on the screen of my phone, trying to decide what I should say to Jace. The flowers were gorgeous, the kiss was amazing, but I'm having trouble making sense of it all.

I look up and see Wren, Gray, and Poppy heading across the lawn together. I slide my phone into my scrub pocket.

"Every patient I've had today has brought up your flowers," Gray says, sitting down across from me. "Apparently Ms. Ethel was in the gym with Pia when you got them and now everyone knows," she explains.

Poppy joins me on my side of the table and Wren sits next to Gray.

"Where's Chloe?" I ask.

"She had a swallowing eval. Told me to enjoy my lunch break while I still had one," Poppy giggles.

"I honestly could never be a speech therapist," Gray says. "Chloe never eats with us. No way in hell I'm missing lunch."

"So, Lacey, a kiss and flowers?" Wren smiles in my direction. "That's big news."

"I don't know, is it?"

"It sure seems like it. You don't think it is?" she asks.

"Ugh, I don't know y'all. The kiss was…god, it was so hot. He knocked on my door, and then when I answered it he was leaning against the frame with his hat on backwards. It was so…"

"Hot," Gray says, around a bite of salad.

"Yeah. And then he kissed me. Like barged his way into my room and pushed me up against the wall and kissed me, which, if I'm honest, I wasn't expecting from him at all."

"Sounds amazing. I don't understand what you're confused about?" Wren asks.

"Well, then all of a sudden he stopped. Kissed me on the forehead and then tore out of there like he was on fire. I honestly thought he would text me last night, but then he didn't, and then today I show up to work and he has that bouquet delivered." I take a bite of my food and stare at my friends.

"Have you tried texting him?" Poppy asks.

"No, why would I do that?"

"Lacey, the man sent you flowers."

I let my head fall into my hands. "I don't know what to make of all of it, you know. Like what do I text him? *Thank you for the flowers and for kissing me? Let's do it again soon.*"

"Do you want to do it again soon?" Wren asks.

"Yes," I answer honestly. "It's all I can think about, but he's being so confusing, and I know our history isn't great and I'm not about to have him break my heart for real this time."

"Well, I think you should at least text him thank you for the flowers. I mean he had Logan ask me to confirm they were your favorite. I think he likes you."

"Agreed," Wren and Gray say at the same time.

I pull out my phone and swipe up on the screen. My finger hovers over his name.

"Do it, Lacey." Poppy looks me dead in the eye.

Thanks for the flowers!

JACE:

You're welcome, Pixie.

"Now what?" I laugh. "I'm not going to be the one to ask him on a date. Plus, he's going out of town today, so it's not like I can see him."

"Should we plan a dinner?" Wren asks. "We haven't had one of your dinner things in a while."

"Yeah, weren't those supposed to be monthly?" Gray asks.

"Yeah. God, this is ridiculous. He is the only man ever to throw me off my game." I shake my head. "It's infuriating."

All three of them stare at me.

"Don't," I warn.

"Why don't we go out to The Local or something easy?" Poppy suggests. "Text him and see if he wants to come."

> The girls and I were talking about seeing if you and the guys wanted to go out to The Local on Friday once you're back.

JACE:

I'd like that!

> Great. I'll text the rest of the group.

"He's in," I say.

"Perfect, now all you gotta do is wear something super hot and make him beg for it," Gray says, making all four of us laugh.

JACE:

Downloaded book 6 today, so I can listen on my drive.

JACE:

This one is sad.

> It's a little sad, but it's so good! I can't believe you're still reading them.

JACE:

You recommended them. I want to know what you like.

> I recommended book 6 not the whole series.

JACE:

Made it this far. I gotta see them through!

> Are you real?

JACE:

I'm very real. Wish I didn't have to leave today!

I feel my cheeks heat, but I try to play it cool.

> When are you heading out?

JACE:

Probably in an hour. The service is non-existent at his house, so if you text me and I don't respond that's why.

> Okay. Have fun and drive safely.

JACE:

I will, Pixie. I can't wait for Friday

"You still texting Jace?" Poppy asks.

"Oh, yeah, sorry." I look up from my phone and back at my friends. "Can y'all believe he's reading the entire *Bridgerton* series?"

"Yeah," all three of them say at the same time like they aren't surprised at all.

"But why?" I ask.

"Because you mean a lot to him," Poppy says. "You always have."

CHAPTER 45: KEEPING PROMISES
JACE - ONE YEAR AGO

Since my team and I discovered the Bixito Parrot, I've been asked to complete interview after interview. I don't mind it entirely. I realize that the attention on the story will help fund programs integral to the conservation of the rare bird, but my social battery is officially drained.

I flew home a few days early to visit my dad before my interview with the Atlanta Journal-Constitution that starts in ten minutes.

My dad, the AJC, and my team are the only people who know I'm here. I didn't bother letting my roommate or friends know I was in town. It's not the first time I've done this. I needed a break from people. Needed to clear my head and decompress.

Today, though, I have to muster whatever energy I have left, put on a smile, and talk to the reporter who contacted me about doing a story on me.

I walk into some trendy tea house in the Old Fourth Ward. I scan the small room looking for the woman I googled before heading over. I find her sitting in the corner of the shop, sipping from a mug and checking her watch.

Meredith Russell is a beautiful Black woman about ten

years older than me. Her dark hair is braided and wrapped up in a bun on top of her head. She's dressed in a black blazer and a white blouse. She's the picture of class and poise. She's all business, and I'm immediately intimidated.

Glancing down at the T-shirt and shorts I threw on, I wonder if I should have dressed more professionally, but I guess it's too late. I order a cup of coffee and walk over to meet her, trying to muster up the energy and courage I need to get through one more interview.

"Meredith?" I ask. "I'm Jacks Jackson."

"Thank you so much for taking the time to meet with me today," she says, standing and shaking my hand.

"Sure thing," I say, returning the gesture.

We both take a seat at the small table. "I hope you like tea. This place is quickly becoming my favorite spot in the city. Their London Fog is out of this world."

"A what?"

"A London Fog. It's like a café au lait but with tea instead of coffee."

"I've never tried it. I prefer coffee." I laugh, lifting my cup.

"Good, I'm glad you found something you enjoy." She smiles and my shoulders relax a bit.

She places a recorder on the table and pulls a pad of paper from her expensive-looking bag. "Do you mind if I record our conversation?" she asks.

"Go for it." I nod and take a sip of my coffee. "I have to admit I was surprised you were interested in interviewing me."

She taps the record button with a manicured nail. "Really? Local boy rediscovers a bird that hasn't been seen in fifty years. Sounds like the perfect story for our paper."

"It wasn't just me. I had a team of people that helped."

"True, but if I understand correctly, it was your passion project, right?"

"I guess you could say that."

"So, take me back. When did you know this was something you wanted to try to accomplish?"

I hesitate before answering, not sure what to tell her. My mind floods with memories of Lacey Sims and me trekking through the woods, looking for the mysterious bird that defined our childhood. The night before I left to go to D.C., our conversation and the promises that were made. All but one broken. Last I heard, she was still in Georgia, although I'm not sure where. Maybe I should try to find her and tell her I found it. But how? Would she even want me to?

"Mr. Jackson?" Meredith says, drumming her nails against her notebook.

"Please call me Jacks." I smile. "Sorry, I got lost in thought. What was your question?"

"I was wanting you to take me back to the beginning."

"Right." I sip my coffee, trying to find the right words. "I've wanted to find it since I was a kid. I've always been interested in birds and other animals. When I was really young, maybe seven, a friend of mine gave me a book on lost species for my birthday." I chuckle at the memory of unwrapping the book from Lacey. "I must have read it a million times. The Bix was one of the animals featured in it. The illustration was beautiful—light purple feathers trimmed with bright green."

She nods and begins to jot down notes.

I swallow and continue. "I was mesmerized by the mystery behind it. It was like one day it had disappeared, and I knew that couldn't be the case. Entire species just don't vanish off the face of the Earth. My friend and I would spend days playing in the woods around our houses, pretending to look for it. Those were some of my favorite memories as a kid. We never found it, of course. The Bix was native to Mexico, and I guess now Brazil, but as kids we were sure we'd find it right here in North Georgia."

"Was the friend the same one that gave you the book?" she asks.

"Yeah, um, her name was Lacey. We were neighbors and very close. Anyway, in middle school, I watched this documentary about how a group of photojournalists had discovered a new plant species in Africa. It was so impressive, and I got it in my head that maybe one day I could discover the Bixito Parrot."

"So, would you say this has been a lifelong dream of yours?"

"You could say that."

"And how did you stay driven to find it all this time? I mean, I have kids. One day they want to be a firefighter, the next they want to be a doctor. Why do you think you never changed your mind?"

"Lacey," I answer honestly because fuck it. Maybe she'll read this and I'll get to see her again.

"Your friend?"

"Yes. She is the type of person who you want in your corner. She's fierce, loving, and supportive. She pushes you to be better. Before I graduated from high school, she found the application for the Young Photographers Program in D.C. She urged me to apply because she believed I was good enough to get it. I wasn't so sure, but she didn't let up until I submitted the form. To my surprise, they picked me, and because of that opportunity, my life was forever changed."

"Do you think completing the program played a part in helping you make the discovery?"

"Oh, definitely. Without the program, I would have never gotten into Georgetown, and without my degree, I wouldn't have gotten the opportunities to learn and work with the people I have since. Lacey made me promise her before I left for D.C. that I would find the Bix and live out my dreams. I made her that promise, and I guess I've spent the last nine years working to keep it."

"I won't lie, Jacks, I did my research on you. Finding the Bix, as you call it, wasn't an easy feat. The trip you discovered it on was your third attempt. I've heard you talk about how weather and close encounters with some pretty intimidating animals almost derailed the third try completely. I had no idea how dangerous the life of a wildlife photographer could be. So, why continually put yourself at risk to keep a promise you made as a kid?"

"Because I love her, and she deserves for me to keep every promise I've ever made to her. No matter how big or how small."

Meredith smiles and shakes her head. "I was not expecting to hear you say that. Thank you for sharing that with me. What did Lacey say when you told her you found it?"

"Oh, she doesn't know. We went our separate ways after I moved to D.C. We haven't spoken in a long time."

Her eyes go wide. "I want to make sure I'm understanding you. This girl and you no longer speak, but you still went on to make this extraordinary rediscovery for her."

I nod. "I know it sounds a little crazy, but I guess love makes you do crazy things." I laugh.

"I guess it does." She smiles.

The rest of the interview continues with her asking general questions about the Bix, our conservation efforts, and how people can help support the species. After an hour, she clicks off the recorder and stands to shake my hand again.

"Thank you again. It's going to be a great story," she assures me.

"It was my pleasure." I smile.

CHAPTER 46: THANK GOD FOR A GOOD VIBRATOR
LACEY - PRESENT

It's been three days, seven hours, and roughly twenty-two and a half minutes since Jace barged into my room and kissed me. I know this because I have literally thought of nothing else since it happened. Thank god for a good vibrator.

On Monday night, he called me from his uncle's landline to let me know he had made it safely, but I haven't heard from him since. I tried texting him a couple of times, but they never delivered.

Poppy left an hour ago to go to Logan's for the night, so I'm home alone again. I consider reading, but the last thing I need is to be more horny, so instead I settle for an ice cream sundae and *Romy and Michelle's High School Reunion* to distract me.

I'm halfway through the movie, but it's no use. My whole body is buzzing from all the sugar I just consumed, and I feel restless. I turn the TV off and fall back on my pillow. My phone begins to ring, and when I look down I'm surprised to see it's Jace FaceTiming me.

I quickly flick on the light and try my best to fix my hair. I swipe up and am instantly met with his panty melting smile. "Hi, Pixie."

"Hey. How'd you find service?"

"We had to run out to the store for Joe, so I don't have long. I'm sitting in the parking lot waiting on Archie to buy some beer and finally have a little signal."

"I'm glad you called. I didn't realize Archie was there."

"Yeah, he showed up yesterday. Him and Joe are miserable being around each other, so it's been a lot of fun. Hence the need for beer."

"Oh, dang. Joe doesn't have beer?"

"No, he has some homemade concoction that he claims is beer, but if I'm honest it didn't look safe to drink." I laugh. "It's been an interesting couple of days."

"How so?"

"Apparently a couple goats are missing, so he thinks BigFoot is living on his property. I'm exhausted and ready to come home." He chuckles and leans back against the headrest of the driver's seat.

"You should have made Tanner go with you. Don't he and Archie go way back?"

"Yeah, Archie introduced us, but T had to work."

"What exactly are y'all doing there?"

"He has an old barn on his land that needs to be torn down. Dad didn't want him doing it by himself, so we got roped in to come and help him. How's your week going?" he asks.

"Honestly, it could be better. Poppy's gone again, so I'm lonely."

"I'm sorry. Did she watch *Single By The Sea* with you this week?"

"She did."

He moves his hand through his hair. My thoughts drift to Sunday. We haven't been able to talk, and while I've gotten myself off from thinking about the kiss, I still don't know why he didn't stay. Why didn't he try to take it further? I know I need to ask him the question that's been weighing on my mind, but seeing him on the other end of my phone has my mind scrambling. *Why does he do this to me? Be an adult and ask him why.*

"You okay?" he asks.

"Oh, yeah." *Just spit it out for fuck's sake.* I take a deep breath. "Why did you leave so quickly after our kiss?"

His face flushes with heat and he runs his hand over the back of his head.

"You really want to know?"

"More than anything because I'm so confused. I know it wasn't a bad kiss."

"The kiss was incredible. It's all I've been able to think about," he admits.

"Then why leave?"

"Do you know how much you turn me on?"

"Well no." I shake my head. "You literally kissed me on the forehead and then ran out of there."

"Kissing you made me come in my pants like a fucking teenager." His head drops into his free hand, and he rubs his forehead. "That's what you do to me, Lacey. I shouldn't have left, but I was embarrassed."

My breath hitches at his admission, and I bite my lower lip. *Why do I think the idea of him coming in his pants is so hot?*

"I turn you on?"

"Are you kidding me? Look at you. You're beautiful, Pixie. The kiss was hot as fuck and I tried to slow it down, but apparently I can't help myself around you."

His words are doing more to me than he knows. *So much for not being horny tonight.* I move a little so that the robe I'm wearing falls from my shoulder, revealing my skin. "Does this turn you on?" I trail my hand over my skin slowly.

He swallows hard and adjusts in his chair. "Archie is going to be back any minute."

"That's not what I asked," I say, stripping the robe completely and revealing my bra. "Does this turn you on?" I run my fingers over the lace.

"Yes." His voice is low and gravely.

I pause and play with one of my nipples through the fabric. "Do you like what you see?" He watches my every move, and I wish there was a way I could pull him through the phone.

A loud knock on the Jeep's window interrupts our conversation.

"Fuck," he bites out. "Archie's back."

"Bummer," I tease, pulling my robe back on.

"You're going to be the death of me, you know that?" He lets out a low chuckle and shakes his head. "Promise me you'll wear that bra on Friday."

"Who's to say I'm going to let you see it again?"

Archie knocks again, and I can hear him say something muffled from outside the car. Jace takes a deep breath. "I really don't want to hang up."

"It's okay. I'll see you Friday night. Try not to let BigFoot eat you before then."

"Bye, Pixie."

CHAPTER 47: THE CFNAWC

JACE

"Thank you for meeting with me today," I say, shaking the hand of Roger Lucas, the president of the CFNAWC and hopefully my future boss.

"No, the pleasure is all mine, Mr. Jackson," he says with a smile. "Please, sit down." He gestures toward a leather armchair in front of his desk. "I think I mentioned it when we talked on the phone, but I was rather surprised to see your name come across my desk. Your discovery of the Bixito Parrot was nothing short of extraordinary, and your portfolio speaks for itself."

"Well thank you, but the Bix was a team effort. I could not have done it without my team."

"True, but it was your dream, correct? That's what you said in the interview with the AJC."

Shit, this guy did his research. Up until this point, I hadn't been nervous. My mind drifts to Lacey, and I wonder if she ever saw it. If she ever read it. My palms start to sweat.

"No, sir, you're correct. As a kid, some may have said I was obsessed with the Bix. All lost species really, but I was always drawn to that one in particular. I feel very fortunate to have found it."

"So tell me, why do you, a young man, with a better resume than some of my most elite photojournalists, want to come work for me?"

"My mother passed away five years ago and my dad is getting older. I'd like to settle down and be around more for him. I think I would do well in this position because it would allow me to continue a career that I'm incredibly passionate about while being closer to home. The work you all have done here is phenomenal, and it would be an honor to be a part of your team."

"And the girl you mentioned in the interview?"

"Happy to say she's back in my life, sir."

"I'm glad to hear it," he says, spinning his wedding band around his finger. "The life of a photojournalist is a lot tougher than most people think, so I've made it my mission to make sure our organization puts families first. I'm happy to hear that you're wanting to do that in your own life because, in this position, I would expect you to foster a family-first environment for your team."

"Of course. That's a big part of what makes me want to work here."

"Excellent. Why don't we tour the building and I can ask you the rest of my questions while we walk?"

"I'd like that." He stands, and I follow him out of his office. As we walk, he introduces me to some of the people I would work with, and I do my best to memorize their names and faces. It's easy to see that I would enjoy working here.

He continues the interview asking me about my experience and my time at Georgetown. Most of the photojournalists are out on assignment, but the couple I'm able to meet remind me of the people I've worked with in the past.

"I'll be in touch, Mr. Jackson," he says, shaking my hand as soon as we've made it back to the front doors.

"I look forward to it. Thank you again for meeting with me."

"The pleasure was mine."

I'm feeling good as I walk to my car. Confident even. The work the center has done for wildlife conservation is unmatched, and the thought that I could be a part of continuing their mission is exhilarating. Getting this job would mean getting to be there for my dad and getting to spend more time with Lacey.

I pull out my phone to check the time. It's four thirty. I'm supposed to meet everyone at the bar at eight. Sliding into the driver's seat, I dial my dad.

"Hey, kid. What's up?"

"Driving back from an interview."

"An interview?" he asks, surprised. "I didn't know you had an interview today."

"Yeah, I did. I'm leaving the Center for North American Wildlife Conservation. They're looking for a director of photojournalism and I applied."

"That's fantastic. How'd it go?"

"Great. He knew a lot about me and seemed really interested. Especially because of the Bix. He said he'd let me know soon, but I'm optimistically hopeful I'll get it."

"So, does that mean you'd be home more?"

"Yeah, there's still some travel involved, but not like I currently do."

"I'm so glad to hear that." He pauses. "You know I'll always support you no matter what, but selfishly I'm happy I might get you back."

The GPS on my phone comes over the speakers, interrupting our conversation.

"Thanks, Dad, but hey, I gotta run. Apparently there's a wreck or something and the GPS is trying to reroute me. I'll see you later."

"Love you, kid."

"Love you, too, Dad."

I hang up and pull off the interstate following the new

route. Unfortunately, because it's Atlanta, it doesn't seem to buy me much time, and traffic is still horrendous. By the time I pull back into my apartment complex, it's already six.

When I walk in, Tanner is sitting at the kitchen table eating dinner.

"I made pizza," he says, nodding toward the stove top. Two pizzas sit on top of the burners. I walk into the kitchen and grab a plate.

"How was your interview?"

"I think it went great," I say, placing two slices of what appears to be a meat lovers on my plate. I open the fridge, grab a beer, and meet Tanner at the table.

"Awesome, man. So, how you feeling about seeing Lacey tonight?"

"Really good. We've barely talked because my service was shit, but I was able to FaceTime her once when Archie and I ran out to the store. I almost drove straight there last night, but I had the interview today."

My mind drifts to my call with Lacey. Her bare skin was only covered by thin black fabric. The way she touched herself and teased me. I could have killed Archie when he knocked on the window and interrupted us.

"So are y'all official?"

"No. I mean the kiss changed things, but we haven't really talked about it. I originally was going to ask her on a date tonight, but then she said she wanted to do this. I'm trying to go slow and do it right. I'm hoping this job pans out, but if it doesn't I'm leaving again."

"So."

"I left before and that's when everything went to shit."

He shrugs. "Yeah, but y'all were kids. If you want her, then don't let the job stuff get in the way. I'm sure if this one doesn't work out, then you could find something else or make it work."

He's right. At the end of the day, it's her I want. I know

I'm willing to make things work no matter what job I have, but I don't know where her head is at. Would she want to do this thing long distance if that's how it all pans out?

"Who are you and what have you done with my roommate?"

Tanner laughs and sips his beer. "So, what's the plan for after?"

"What do you mean?"

"Are you bringing her back here or are you taking her back to her place?"

I laugh out loud. "There you are. Let's not get ahead of ourselves, T. I'm gonna go get ready."

"Suit yourself, but you say the word and I'll find a different place to sleep tonight. Y'all want this apartment, it's yours."

S.H.I.E.L.D.

TANNER:

Logan if I give you the signal it means you
and Poppy need to go to your place because
Jacks is going to be taking Lacey back to her
place

LOGAN:

Signal?

Don't listen to him.

DONOVAN:

Sorry we're missing tonight.

LOGAN:

No signal necessary. Poppy and I already
decided we would be staying at my
apartment tonight. The girls' apartment is all
yours Jacks.

TANNER:

So we don't need to come up with a signal

Please don't.

CHAPTER 48: SPACE

JACE

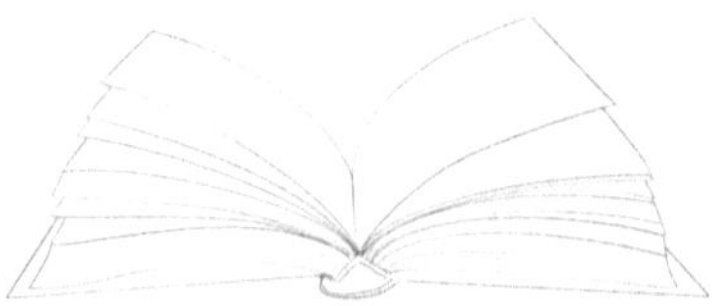

The Local is packed when we walk in. Tanner and I push our way through a crowd of people, and that's when I see Lacey sitting at a table with Poppy and Logan. She stands and waves in our direction.

Lacey's hair is in loose curls that fall around her face, and she's wearing a short, black dress. The fabric is ribbed, and the bottom hits her right at her upper thigh. It hugs every one of her curves, and it takes all of my willpower not to let my mind slip to thinking about everything I want to do to her in that dress. The locket is still around her neck and is layered with a few other chains. She's wearing white sneakers.

She looks effortlessly beautiful and so fucking sexy. I approach the table, and she immediately throws her arms around me, wrapping me in a hug.

"Hey, J," she says into my ear.

"Hey, Pixie. You look gorgeous." I kiss her cheek, and she pulls away.

Her cheeks turn a soft shade of pink, and our eyes meet. The air feels tight with tension. I don't know where tonight will lead, but I know I'll follow her wherever she goes.

"So, whatcha drinking? A gin and tonic?" I ask.

"We hadn't ordered yet," Logan cuts in. "We were waiting for everyone to get here."

"Actually, I'm kinda feeling a ranch water with tajin on the rim." Lacey slides back into the booth. "Wren and Gray should be here soon, so you can probably grab them the same thing."

"Tequila?" Poppy glances in Lacey's direction with a quirked eyebrow.

"You got it," I say. Logan, Tanner, and I make our way to the bar and order the drinks.

When we return, all four girls are sitting around the table, and I slide in across from Lacey. Her foot brushes up against mine, and I swallow hard. Sitting this close to her tonight is going to be torture. I hand her the glass bottle and she takes a long sip. Her tongue jets out of her mouth and licks the tajin off the neck of the bottle in a long, languid stroke, and my mind immediately imagines her on her knees in front of me. I take a long sip of my beer, clenching my teeth.

She does it again, but this time her eyes meet mine. *Fuck, is she torturing me on purpose?* I sit up a little straighter and adjust in the booth. I swear she lets out a little snicker before taking another long sip of her drink.

"Who's Tanner talking to?" Poppy asks, looking over towards the bar. Tanner is standing there sipping his beer and talking to an older man I've never seen before. He shakes the man's hand and then begins to walk back towards our table.

"Geez, didn't your parents teach y'all not to stare," he says.

"What was that about, T?" Logan asks.

"Anyone up for a friendly game of ping-pong?" He avoids the question and nods toward the tables in the corner of the bar.

"I'm good," Gray says. "Wren you should play."

Wren chokes on her drink and glares at her friend.

"Lace, you want to play against them?" I ask.

"Sure, why not? Wren, if I'm playing, you have to too."

Wren rolls her eyes. Tanner goes to the bar to collect the paddles while the rest of us head towards the tables.

"What are we playing for?" Tanner asks, handing out the equipment.

"Losing team has to share a dance," Wren says, looking straight at Lacey. "And the winning team gets to pick the song."

"You sure Wren? Because when Jace and I kick your ass, you're going to be stuck dancing with Tanner to 'Pony' by Ginuwine," Lacey says, laughing.

"Trust me, if I thought that was even a remote possibility, I wouldn't have made the bet."

"I kinda want to throw the game now," Tanner says, smirking at Wren.

"Don't," she warns.

We take our places and the game begins. The little ball bounces back and forth over the net, and Wren was absolutely right. Lacey can't hit the ball if her life depended on it. I'm just as bad. I keep getting very distracted because everytime she tries to hit the ball, her dress rises up in the back, giving me a perfect view of the underside of her ass.

"Shit, y'all are terrible at this," Tanner shouts across the table.

"See, I told you I didn't have to worry about a dance," Wren laughs.

"Would y'all stop?" Lacey shouts. "I'm trying my best."

I lay down my paddle and move behind Lacey. "Let me help you," I say, wrapping my arms around her and placing my hands over hers. I pull her into me and my dick strains against my shorts.

"Couldn't wait any longer to touch me, J?" she asks, causing me to inhale sharply. Her tropical scent invades my nostrils. *Fuck, she smells good.* I push my hips slightly forward against her ass and pull her in tighter. She lets out a little whimper, and I immediately want to pull her into some dark corner of the bar, but I don't.

"Cat got your tongue?" she teases, and I could swear I feel her press her ass back into me.

Before I can respond, Tanner hits the ball straight at us and our paddle makes contact with the ball sending it back over the net. This time it's Tanner who misses, and we score our first point.

"If you weren't losing so badly, I'd say you were cheating," he says, laughing.

The game continues, and I stay wrapped around her. I let my breath tickle her neck and smile to myself when I feel goosebumps erupt down her arms. Tanner hits the ball hard in our direction, and we miss it completely.

"That's our point; we win!" he shouts, turning to high five Wren. They make their way over to the DJ.

She pushes her ass into my crotch again before pulling away entirely. *Fuck me.*

"Lacey," I warn.

"What? I was warming up for the dance floor. What song do you think they're gonna pick?" she asks, looking over towards the man running the music. "Hope it's something *hot.*"

The music shifts and "Love In This Club" by Usher begins to play over the speakers. Tanner shoots me a wink.

"They have to be joking."

"Dance with me, Pixie?"

She takes my hand, and I lead her out to the small dance floor. I spin her around so her back is flush against my chest. We begin to move to the beat of the music. She grinds her ass backwards, almost ending me right here. Loud cheers come from our table and Lacey flips our friends off, causing me to laugh against her neck.

"Have I told you you look beautiful tonight?" I say, bringing my mouth to her ear, so only she can hear me.

"You may have mentioned it," she flirts, the back of her head resting on my shoulder.

I flip her around and pull her into me. My leg is between hers. Her body writhes against it, and our eyes find each other. The rest of the bar disappears.

My fingers trail down her spine. She pushes her hips forward and lets out a moan. Her head falls back, exposing her neck. I press a kiss to her pulse point. She pushes her hips forward again, making my cock harden below my shorts.

Her eyes meet mine and her mouth slightly parts. Bending down, I take her mouth with mine in a filthy kiss. Her body continues to grind against me, and my hands pull her in close. My mouth moves to her neck and then up to her ear.

"Do you feel that, Pixie? Do you feel how hard you make me?"

Her eyes find mine, and then she turns and runs off the dance floor. *Fuck.*

I glance over to our table. Logan shrugs, and Tanner shoots me a thumbs up.

"Lacey," I yell, following her. "Wait, come back."

She doesn't answer me and instead keeps moving through the crowd of people toward the back of the bar. I catch up to her in three long strides, just in time for the bathroom door to slam in my face and her to disappear behind it.

I bang on the door, desperate to know what she's thinking, worried I said too much.

"Lacey, open the door. Please don't run from me. Talk to me. I'm sorry if I—"

The door swings open. "What are we doing?" she asks, breathless. Her face is flushed and she runs her hand through her hair. "You can't talk to me like that. You can't kiss me like that. Not here. You can't make me want you this badly."

"You want me?" I smirk.

"Yes, you idiot." She lets out a long breath. "Fuck, you saying those things...I had to walk away from you before...I don't know. I just knew I needed space. We're in a bar for Christ's—"

"*You* needed space?" My breaths are ragged. "You want to talk about needing space? Do you know how hard it's been having to be around you tonight after that kiss we shared? After that phone call? How torturous it was for me to watch you lick the neck of that bottle and not think about your tongue on my cock? How difficult it's been to have you teasing me all night in that fucking dress—"

"Why do you think I wore the dress, J?" Her lips turn up into a sexy grin.

"Lacey." My tone is laced with warning because all she has to do is say the word and I'm hers.

Her green eyes lock on mine, and they're filled with desire. Her chest rises and falls. I want to push my way into this bathroom and show her exactly what that dress makes me want to do to her, but I don't move. Instead, I stand there staring at her, my breaths heavy, hoping she'll invite me in.

She steps forward and fists my shirt, pulling me over the threshold of the door and into the small bathroom. I slam the door shut and flip the lock. My lips find hers, and my hands knot in the back of her hair, tipping her head ever so slightly. Her lips part, and she lets me in. Our bodies crash up against the wall. Her hands run up my back, nails digging into my shoulders. She lets out a loud moan, and I push my hips into her, letting her feel my length. Her hands find the button of my shorts and I pull away, grazing her lower lip with my teeth.

"The first time I fuck you will not be in this bar." I grab her wrists stopping her from unbuttoning my pants and place her hands above her head. "Don't move. Let me."

She nods. Her pupils are blown, her hair a mess, and her lips swollen. I lay kisses down her neck, stopping to suck slightly on her ear lobe. I can feel her writhe underneath me.

"Can I touch you?" I ask. My hands trailing down the sides of her dress and cupping her ass. She nods.

"I'm going to need you to use your words."

"Yes, please."

"Good girl." Her breath hitches, and I slightly lift her dress. Moving her lace thong to the side, I slide a finger up her center, and she lets out another moan.

"Fuck, you're so wet for me. Should I clean you up?"

She nods frantically.

"Words, Pixie."

"Yes," she breathes out, and I drop to my knees in front of her.

I move her thong down her legs and help her step out of it before shoving it into the pocket of my shorts. I lift one of her legs and place it over my shoulder. Her hips jolt forward, begging me to taste her as I lay kisses down her thigh.

"Greedy, are we?" I tease.

"Jace, for the love of god. Fucking eat me out before someone knocks on this door and interrupts us."

Her hips thrust forward again, and I laugh against her. "I like it when you're greedy." She moans, and her eyes find mine. In one motion, I lick her from ass to clit. I let out a low groan. "Fuck, you taste good."

My tongue works her center over and over, pausing only to pay special attention to the bundle of nerves at the top. Her hands find my hair, and she rocks into my face, taking what she needs from me.

With one hand, I grip her ass, and with the other, I push one finger and then two deep inside her, causing her to clinch around me. Her leg tightens around my back, pulling me closer.

"Fuck," she says.

Her hips grind against my face, and I continue to devour her, pumping my fingers in and out, making sure to hit her most sensitive spot.

"Come for me," I command. I suck hard on her clit, and she completely unravels around me. Her body shudders as she rides out the waves of her orgasm. I lap up every bit of what she gives me, and when I'm sure she's finished, I stand to meet her.

"Jace...I...that...you were..."

"Words, Lacey." I smirk. Leaning in, I kiss her hard. Her tongue swirls around mine, and I know she's tasting herself. My dick strains against my shorts at the thought. I need to get us out of here. I need to get her home.

A loud knock comes from outside the door, breaking our moment.

"Shit," she says, flipping toward the mirror. She frantically tries to fix her dress and runs her fingers through her hair. "Give me my thong."

"You can get it back later," I tease. "I'm not done with you yet."

I pull her in for another kiss. A second knock echoes through the room, and she pushes me away.

"How the hell are we going to get out of here?"

I splash some water on my face, cleaning off my beard. "You have your phone?" I ask, drying my face with a paper towel.

"Yeah, but how is that going to help us?"

"Call Poppy and tell her you need her to come make sure the coast is clear."

"You want me to call my best friend and tell her what we did in here?"

I laugh. "They all saw us come back this way. I imagine they already have some kind of idea. Unless you'd rather I call Tanner."

Her cheeks blush, and she pulls out her phone. Her fingers type away, and three minutes later, Poppy's voice comes through the door, letting us know it's safe to come out.

"Not a fucking word," she says, walking past Poppy, who smirks at the both of us.

"I think we're gonna head out," I say, following Lacey towards the door.

"I bet you are," Poppy calls behind us.

As we leave the bar, I turn to see Tanner doing some dramatic series of hand motions and hip thrusts in our direction. *Fucking idiot.*

CHAPTER 49: WILDEST DREAMS
LACEY

Jace Jackson just went down on me in the bathroom at a bar. My body is still reeling with the aftermath of my orgasm, and my brain is trying to process what exactly happened in that bathroom.

The dance was meant to be a joke, but then it turned into something more. I was having fun teasing him, but then he opened his mouth, and I lost all control. The feeling of his cock grinding into me, his breath on my neck, and then his lips on mine was too much. I needed space between us before I did something in public that I would probably regret later.

When I walked away from the dance floor, I don't know what I was expecting to happen next, but I sure as hell wasn't expecting him to drop to his knees and devour me like I was his last fucking meal.

"Lace, the car's here." His voice breaks me of my thoughts.

He pulls the hand that he's holding toward the Uber that just drove into the parking lot. I climb in, and he slides in next to me in the back seat. His hand instantly finds my leg. It's dangerously close to touching my center, but he doesn't move it. He just draws small, teasing circles on my thigh, making me more and more desperate for his touch. *Fuck, what's gotten into me?* If he tried, I wouldn't stop him. I'd totally let him finger fuck me in the back of a stranger's car.

He leans over and kisses me tenderly, causing my breath to catch, and the rest of the world disappears for a moment. The driver clears his throat, causing both of us to straighten, but his hand doesn't move away. His fingers toy with the hem of my dress.

The Local is a ten-minute drive from my apartment, but time feels like it's moving painfully slow. I'm desperate to get out of the car and see where tonight might lead.

His hand inches up my thigh ever so slightly. The car is dark, and I wonder for a moment if I could keep quiet so the driver wouldn't know what we were doing.

I slightly part my legs and shift in my seat, silently begging him to touch me, but he doesn't. A wide, sexy grin breaks across his face in response to my movements. "So needy," he whispers.

He continues to draw small circles, teasing me and winding me tighter. I let out a frustrated breath, and he chuckles.

The driver pulls into my apartment complex, and Jace opens the door before the car stops. He grabs my hand and pulls me out, offering the driver a wave and a quick thank you as we both stumble into the parking lot. We move towards my apartment and rush up the stairs. I wrestle with the key, wondering if I should be questioning any of this. If I should stop and ask what it all means, but then the door swings open and he follows me inside. I kick off my shoes and turn around to find his bright blue eyes looking me up and down. My whole body heats under his stare.

"Lacey, I'd like—"

I take a step forward and meet him where he stands. I place a finger over his lips. "Take me into my room and show me what you'd like, J."

Time slows, and he cups my face, kissing me. It's not a delicate kiss. It's rough and sloppy, like I'm the only thing that can satisfy the hunger within him. Our teeth crash and our tongues twist together.

His hands find my ass as he lifts me up so my legs wrap around his waist. He lets out a low, guttural groan and continues to kiss me as he walks me into my bedroom, kicking off his shoes. My hands tangle in his hair, and he deepens our kiss. I love the way he tastes. I love the way his body feels against mine.

He lays me gently on top of my bed before stepping back and taking me in. His eyes are dark with desire and my core tightens. *How is this man so fucking hot?*

"Lacey, you sure you want this?" he asks.

"I want it all," I answer, wondering if he knows I mean more than tonight. I want him now and forever. I've never been more sure of anything.

He undoes his shorts and pulls his shirt over his head, revealing his toned chest and abs. The dim light from the living room illuminates him from behind. A sprinkle of dark chest hair covers his toned pecs. I follow his lead, moving my dress down my body and revealing all of me to him.

"Fuck, look at you." He steps toward the bed. "I thought I told you to wear the bra from the call."

"Oops. I must have forgotten to put it on." Leaning back on my elbows, I feel so sexy and confident under his gaze. "Come on, I showed you mine. Now it's your turn to show me yours." My eyes flit to the outline of his cock behind the boxer briefs that hug both of his thighs. A smirk erupts across his face, and he pulls them off. His dick springs free. *Fuck, it's huge.*

He crawls onto the bed and hovers over me. His lips find my neck and he sucks the sensitive skin there, causing my body to erupt in goosebumps.

"I've wanted you for so long, Pixie." His voice is a

whisper against my skin, and he rolls to his side where I turn to meet him. His hand starts at my shoulder and moves down the curve of my body. Everywhere he touches ignites. I reach out and touch him too. My hand moves down his chest to his abs, and I trace the cut lines with the tips of my fingers until my hand finds his cock.

I roll it in the palm of my hand, and I feel him shudder under my touch. I move my hand up and down his shaft a few times. My thumb grazes the head, wiping away a small bead of liquid from the tip. With his eyes on me, I move my thumb to my mouth and suck it off, savoring the taste of him.

Another groan escapes him, and he flips me to my back. "Tell me what you want."

"You," is all I can manage to say between heavy breaths.

He moves down my body, trailing kisses to every part of me and causing my skin to erupt under each touch of his lips on my skin. He pauses over one of my breasts and sucks one of my nipples into his mouth. My hands dig into the sheets, and I let out a moan.

He smiles against me and moves to my other nipple. His tongue flicks against it before he takes it completely into his mouth. Pulling away, he lets his teeth graze against the sensitive skin there. My whole body jolts and my eyes shut.

"Eyes on me, Lace," he says.

My eyes open, and I watch as he continues to trail soft kisses down my abdomen and then my hips. His rough beard tickles my skin as he moves.

"You like it when I kiss you here?"

I nod my head.

"I told you at the bar and I'm going to tell you again. Use your words."

"Yes," I say through heavy breaths.

"And what about here?" He takes a finger and runs it through my slit. "Do you like it when I play with your pussy?"

I swallow hard. "Yes."

"That's my girl," he growls, and I think I could come apart just from hearing him talk to me like this. He plants kisses down my thighs and I thrust my hips in his direction begging him to taste me again.

"I need more," I beg.

His mouth finds my clit, and I let out a loud scream as he sucks it into his mouth because fuck, this man knows what he's doing. His tongue moves through my slick center, the friction from his beard making me squirm. He pushes two fingers deep inside me. His tongue and hand begin to work in perfect unison, and I grind into him. He works my most sensitive spot, winding me tighter. His teeth ever so slightly graze my clit. The room goes completely dark as I come apart on his tongue.

He doesn't stop until I've completely come down from the high, and when he's sure I'm done, he grins up at me.

"Condom?" he asks.

"Top drawer."

He locates it and hands it to me. "Be a good girl and put it on for me, won't you?"

I nod my head. I didn't know I had a praise kink, but hearing him call me a good girl tonight is doing it for me, and I don't think I ever want him to stop.

I sit up on my knees and he meets me with his cock on full display. Tearing the foil package with my teeth, I remove the rubber from the packet. I wrap my hand around his shaft and pump a few times before rolling the condom down the length of him slowly.

I lay on my back and he lines up between my legs. He pauses before he enters me, his eyes finding mine.

"This is everything I've ever wanted. You, Pixie, are everything I've ever wanted."

"Me too, J. Me too."

He pushes forward in one motion, filling me completely.

His cock stretches me wide, silencing my moans with his mouth. Our bodies move in perfect rhythm. Our hands explore each other's bodies, and with every touch, he brings me closer to another release.

In one motion, he flips us over, so I'm on top. "Ride me," he commands, and I do as I'm told. I sit up and begin to move up and down the length of his shaft.

He grips my ass, pulling me into him. He thrusts his hips upward, causing my head to tip back. He does it again and again. His hands find my breasts and he begins to play.

"You look so pretty like this, riding my cock."

"Jace…I…fuck…"

He pushes his hips into me again. I begin to move faster and he moves with me, creating the perfect pressure. His fingers start to draw circles on my clit while his other hand finds my nipple. He rolls both between his fingers, and my whole body begins to fall. His body tenses beneath me. I collapse on top of him. His mouth finds mine, and we swallow each other's moans.

I inhale his woodsy scent and my heart rate and breathing begins to slow.

"That was…" I begin.

"Everything," he finishes.

"Yeah, everything," I breathe out. I plant a quick kiss on his lips before rolling off of him and heading into my bathroom. He follows behind me.

"Um, I'm gonna need to pee. Can you wait until I'm done?"

"I went down on you in the bar bathroom tonight—I think it's safe to assume you can pee in front of me now."

I can't help but laugh. "Did you know any of this was going to happen when you walked into that bar tonight?"

He shakes his head, removing the condom and disposing of it in the trash. "No, but I think it's safe to say all of my wildest dreams came true."

After we finish cleaning up, I walk out into the living room to look for my phone. I pull it out of my purse and start laughing.

"What's so funny?" he asks, walking out of my room—completely naked—and into the kitchen.

"I have forty unread text messages." I shake my head and lock my phone. "My friends are outrageous. I'll deal with them all tomorrow."

He fills two glasses of water and walks one of them over to me. "I had twenty-five from Tanner alone," he says with a laugh.

We head back into my bedroom and crawl under the comforter of my bed. He pulls me in tight, and my back melts into him. I know we should talk about what all of this means. We both said a lot of shit while we were in the moment, and while I know I meant every word, I don't know where he stands. Hell, I don't even know when he's leaving again. *Shit, what if he's leaving again?* I shake the thought from my head.

Without warning, my stomach growls. *How fucking attractive.* First I vomited and now this.

"You know, I was just thinking that I'm completely starving," he says, chuckling.

"No, you weren't."

"Swear it."

I snuggle deeper into his arms. "You're just saying that so I'm not embarrassed my stomach sounds like a monster."

"It does sound like a very cute monster, but I am hungry." He presses a kiss to my shoulder before sitting up and grabbing his phone. He begins swiping on the screen.

"What are you doing?"

"Well, before you texted me about hanging at the bar with everyone, I had planned on asking you on a date tonight, and given it's only ten forty-five, we still have some time to make that happen."

"A date?" My heart sinks. "You could have asked. I would

have much rather gone on a date with you than embarrass myself playing ping-pong and hanging out with everyone else."

"Tonight was better than anything I could have dreamed of. If I remember correctly, you promised me we could have chocolate ice cream and fries together, and we haven't done that yet." He flips his phone around.

A confirmation message for two chocolate Frosties and two large fries from Wendy's is on his screen. My face breaks into a wide grin. "You ordered my favorite snack?"

"I did. Lacey Sims, will you go on a date with me tonight, right here in your bed?"

"I'd love to go on a date with you, but only if we both stay naked," I smirk, and he pulls me into his lap for a kiss.

"Deal."

CHAPTER 50: GOOD BOY

JACE

The sun peeking through Lacey's blinds wakes me up. She looks so peaceful sleeping. I pull her in tighter and press a kiss to her head. As much as I want to wake her and repeat our night, I also want to show her I'm serious and want to be with her.

I slowly climb out of bed and locate my boxers.

"Jace?" she questions, rubbing her eyes with her hands. "Where are you going?"

I walk around her bed and sit down next to her.

"Go back to sleep, Pixie. I'm gonna go make us breakfast." I run my hand down her face, smoothing her wild hair. She nestles back into the pillows, and I plant another kiss to the top of her head. A sleepy smile breaks across her face and her eyes fall shut.

Once in the kitchen, I begin to inventory what the girls have. I'm not sure what they eat because the pantry and fridge are pretty much empty. It's mostly ice cream toppings, and I laugh to myself.

On the counter sits half a loaf of bread. I manage to find two eggs, an almost empty gallon of milk, cinnamon roll-flavored coffee creamer, and some whipped cream. It looks like we're having French toast.

I start the water for her tea and a pot of coffee for me. Then I whisk together the eggs and coffee creamer because the little bit of milk I found I'm going to need for Lacey's London Fog. I turn the bread in the mixture and add it to a pan on the stovetop, flipping it when it becomes golden brown. The kettle begins to whistle, and I walk through the steps of making her favorite drink.

I pour my coffee and then plate the food, topping each slice with a dash of cinnamon. I place the can of whipped cream on the tray. I'm not sure if the food is going to taste good, but it smells delicious.

Making my way back toward her room, I push the door open with my back. She's still asleep, and I pause a moment to take her in. She's absolutely stunning. She begins to stir a bit and sits up against her headboard. Her tits are on full display, and nothing but the thin sheet is covering below her waist. My dick hardens at the sight of her, but I remind myself we have all day. This morning is about showing her what life could be like with me and maybe telling her how I feel.

"Morning, J." She smiles, stretching her arms above her head with a yawn.

"Morning. You hungry?" Her eyes trail my body down to the outline of my cock. Her tongue pops out of her mouth and wets her lips. "I meant breakfast." I chuckle.

"What did you make?"

"French toast." I walk around her bed and place the tray of plates and mugs across her lap. "I couldn't find the syrup, but you had whipped cream, so I hope that's okay."

"We've been on an ice cream sundae kick lately." She laughs. Turning the can over, she places a huge dollop on top of her toast. She swipes her finger through the sweet cream and sucks it into her mouth, moaning around it.

Fuck me.

"Whipped cream is perfect," she says. Her lips form into a smile that has me questioning if I should forgo the French toast and have her instead.

"Have I told you that you're gonna be the death of me?" I laugh, climbing back into the bed next to her.

She takes a bite of her breakfast and sips her drink. "This is delicious; thank you."

"I'm glad you like it." I take a bite and thank the universe that it doesn't taste like garbage—it's actually pretty good.

"So you never said, did you finish *When He Was Wicked* while you were with your uncle?" she asks.

"Not yet, but I'm almost done. I'm really liking it so far."

"Good, I can't wait to hear what you think." She smiles at me as I take another bite of my food. She gestures toward the ink covering my left forearm. "What's that tattoo mean?"

"The camera is one of my favorites that I use in the field, and then I had my tattoo guy turn some of my favorite memories into photographs." I point to one of the photos. "This one is a family of Vancouver sea wolves. After mom died, Eli, a couple of other guys, and I went up to Vancouver to research the wolves. They're a really cool species. This was my favorite photo I took on that trip."

She smiles. "Is it a mother wolf and its cub?"

"Yeah, it reminded me of my mom."

"That's really sweet. She would have loved it. What about this one?" She points to another photo inked on my arm.

"Humpback dolphins. It was a super small team, and we went to the coast of Morocco to learn about their behavior. I related to them so much. They're pretty elusive animals and usually steer clear of people. At that time, I didn't have many friends." I chuckle to myself. "On our second boat trip out, we spotted a small pod of them, and I realized they really weren't all that alone and I didn't have to be either."

She lets out a little hum and takes another bite of her

breakfast. "I like hearing about your adventures. Is this one the Bix?" she asks, pointing to a picture of two small parrots.

"Sure is."

"And what's this one?" She points to the final photo. "There isn't an animal."

"It's the night sky above your parents' house the night before I left for D.C."

She sets her plate on her bedside table and inspects my arm.

"I found the star map of that night and had him duplicate it," I explain.

"Is that a shooting star?"

"It is."

"But I thought you didn't believe in shooting stars?"

"I don't."

"Then why do you have one tattooed on your arm?" She looks up at me, her eyes a little glossy like she's putting the pieces together. Her fingers trail over the stars permanently on my skin.

"Because that night was the last time I was truly happy."

"But you were leaving the next day?"

"That's not what I mean." I shake my head and set down my plate. "I had you that night. After I left, everything changed."

She's quiet for a minute while she processes my admission. "You got a tattoo for me?" she asks tentatively. "But I broke up with you. I completely blocked you from my life for ten years. How did you not completely hate me?"

I pull her into my lap so she's facing me. Brushing her hair out of the way, I take her face in my hands.

"I told you before, I could never hate you. I want you. For the last ten years, I dreamed about getting to touch you the way I did last night. I've fantasized about waking up to you in my bed and getting to make you breakfast. Getting to take you on dates, even if that means we just stay in, hang out, and eat our favorite foods. This is everything I've ever wanted. *You* are everything I've ever wanted."

Her lips find mine, and I open, letting her in. She tastes like whipped cream and cinnamon. The kiss is slow and tender. She runs her hands through my hair before pulling away.

"So," she begins, a little breathless from our kiss, "does this mean we're doing this? You and me. We're going to try again?"

"Oh, we're doing this." I flip her over, so she's on her back and I'm hovering above her. She meets my gaze. "But only if it's what you want too."

"You are definitely what I want, J." She smiles, then lifts her head and plants a quick kiss on my mouth. "But we're going to need to finish breakfast first." She rolls out from under me, laughing. "You're going to need all the energy you can get for what I have planned for after we're done."

She grabs the can of whipped cream and begins to add more to her plate.

"Not so fast," I say, grabbing the can from her hand. "I'm hungry, but not for breakfast."

I pull her toward me, laying her on her back. She lets out a giggle. "Don't move," I warn. I take the can and give it a good shake before placing a trail of small dollops of whipped cream from her neck down to her most sensitive spot.

I set the can aside. Starting at her neck, I move my tongue down the trail of sweet cream. She lets out a small whimper. "Don't move, Pixie." I trail two fingers through the whipped cream on one of her nipples. Bringing my fingers to her mouth, she opens immediately and sucks me clean.

"Fuck," I almost growl out, as her tongue twirls around my fingertips.

My eyes trail down her naked body. The white cream

contrasts with her sun-kissed skin. She's on full display for me and I love it. I'll never get enough of seeing her like this.

"Can you lay there like a good fucking girl and not move while I clean you up?" I ask.

"I don't know," she says, her face breaking into a wicked grin that threatens to end me right there on the spot. "I might need you to tie me up. I've never been very good at following the rules."

"Fuck, you sure?"

"Go in my closet and grab the purple scarf off my bag," she says, and I do as I'm told.

When I crawl back onto the mattress, I find her with her arms already above her head. I quickly secure them to her headboard with the silk fabric. "Is that okay?" I ask. "I don't want to hurt you."

"You aren't going to hurt me, J. I trust you." I lean forward, pressing a kiss to her lips. I move down her body, following the sweet trail, and when I get to her breasts, I take each one into my mouth. I suck them clean, spinning my tongue around each nipple. She remains still, but not quiet. Every flick of my tongue causes her to moan and my cock to throb.

I lick down her abdomen, and when I glance up, I find her eyes locked on me. Her hands are tied above her head, her breasts rising and falling with each heavy breath.

"You're so fucking pretty all tied up for me like this," I say against her skin, continuing to move down her body. She shudders under my compliment, and her breath hitches as I lick along her thigh, stopping right before I get to her most sensitive place. She breathes out my name, and her hips rock forward.

"Even all tied up, you still can't help yourself, can you?" I lick down her other thigh. "So fucking desperate for me to taste your cunt, aren't you?"

"Please," she begs, thrusting her hips again.

I run a finger down her wet slit, and she moans. I do it again, and her moans get louder.

"I fucking swear, you better stop teasing me," she warns.

"So bossy." I do it one more time, stopping at her sensitive bud and circle it with my fingertips.

"For the love of—"

I place my lips over her clit, sucking it into my mouth. I don't think I'll ever get used to how good she tastes. I work my tongue up her center, flicking it against her clit.

"Fuck...yes...more..." Her words are choppy. Breathless.

She's so fucking wet, and I lap up every bit of what she gives me with long, slow licks of my tongue. She begins to move, her hips rocking into my face, searching for friction, and I place one of my hands across her stomach, holding her still. I continue to devour her, working her most sensitive spot, until her body begins to tense and she falls.

Kissing up her body, I move until I find her mouth and kiss her deeply. "You're so fucking sexy, Pixie."

"I want to taste you," she says, breathing heavily. I untie her wrists and flip over to my back. She moves down my body, planting kisses as she moves, and when she gets to my waist, she tugs my underwear down and my cock springs free.

Taking it in her hand, she rolls both fists down my shaft, causing me to groan. "Now, are you going to be a good boy and let me suck your cock? Or do I need to tie you up?" she asks, biting her lip.

My cock grows harder. I thought praising her turned me on, but hearing her call me a good boy does something to me that's hard to explain.

"I can be good," I breathe out.

She smiles up at me, and then I watch as she dips her head. Her tongue trails up my length, the feeling of her mouth almost too much. I let out a hiss, and I feel her smile against me. She sucks me into her mouth. With one hand she fists the base of my cock, and with the other she plays with my balls.

"Fuck me," I bite out, trying to pull away from her, but she doesn't listen. I know if she continues for much longer, I'm going to come in her mouth, and while the thought of that is tempting, I want to make her come again. She continues to work me over and over. Her tongue swirls around the head, her hands working perfectly in unison with her mouth.

"If you don't stop, I'm going to come," I warn. "Come up here and fuck me, baby."

She sits up on her knees and tucks her heels under her ass. "I said I wanted to taste you, so let me taste you," she says.

Her head dips forward and she takes all of me into her mouth. She hollows out her cheeks and swallows me deep into the back of her throat. My whole body tenses at the feeling, and I come apart in her mouth. She doesn't stop until she's swallowed every last bit of me.

She moves up the bed and lays her head next to mine. "Such a good boy," she teases.

"You're such a fucking brat."

She gives me a quick peck. "Don't you fucking forget it," she says rolling out of bed and moving to her bathroom. I watch as she walks away, her bare ass swaying as she moves.

"You gonna join me, J?" she asks, looking over her shoulder.

———

I know you're crazy busy with the wedding coming up, but I was hoping you or someone from your office could help me with something.

DONOVAN:

I'm off starting Wednesday, but my partner Jaime is in all week. Give me a second and I'll share her contact.

DONOVAN:

<<Jaime Smith Contact>>

Thanks, D. I'll reach out.

CHAPTER 51: SUCH AN ANNOYING KID

LACEY

The Tortured Therapists Department

POPPY:

Lacey Danielle Sims if you do not text us back, I'm calling 911. At least let us know you're alive.

> Y'all can relax and stop blowing up my phone. I'm alive and am doing very, very, veryyyy good 😌

POPPY:

Is it safe to come home?

> Jace just left to go change and then I think he's going to come to my parents' for lunch. Colt texted yesterday. He's in town.

CHLOE:

So wait, how did y'all go from fucking in the bathroom to you bringing him home to your parents 😂

> We didn't fuck in the bathroom…

Did they tell you we fucked in the bathroom?

POPPY:

That's not what it looked like when y'all did your little walk of shame!

<<Friends friendly finger GIF>>

WREN:

Yeah, I didn't mean for you to actually do what the song said. 💀

Very funny.

WREN:

So are you going to tell us?

Girls' night tonight? My parents shouldn't take long and then I'll be all yours.

POPPY:

I'm in.

WREN:

Me too!

CHLOE:

Let me see if my mom can watch Ava. I could use a break.

Gray?!?

GRAY:

Sorry, yes! I'm at my other job. I can come. I'll bring wine.

———

We pull into my parents' house with ten minutes to spare. He parks his Jeep and kills the ignition.

"I haven't been back here since Dad sold the house," he says, eyeing the street where so many of our memories are set.

"Well, not much has changed. Poppy's family still lives across the street." I point to the white house she grew up in. "The Mcafferys moved into your parents' old place. They're nice enough, older, no kids, and an adorable cat."

Jace stares at the house he grew up in. His eyes gloss over, and I grab his hand. "Look, I know it's hard being back here, but I'm really glad you came."

"No, I'm glad I came too. It'll be good to see your family. Did you tell them I was coming?"

"I texted and let Mom know I was bringing someone. Felt like it may be more fun to surprise them with you." I smile.

Jace jumps down from the Jeep and rounds the front of the truck. "You ready?" he asks, grabbing my hand and pulling me in for a quick kiss.

"As I'll ever be."

We walk down the sidewalk toward the front door of my parents' two-story red-brick home. I ring the doorbell and straighten out the resort-print dress I put on for lunch with my parents.

"You look beautiful," he says.

"I hate this dress."

"I know, but you still look beautiful." He pulls me in and places a kiss to the side of my head.

I inhale deeply and offer him a reserved smile. The dress is fine, but it's not like my other clothes. It's the type of dress you wear when you eat at a country club. It's meant to be worn with pearls and modest heels. It was a gift from my mom, so I wore it knowing she can't comment on something she purchased. No need to hear her go on and on about how I don't dress my age, or however she thinks a twenty-seven-year-old woman should dress, when I can just wear the dress she wants me to wear.

After a couple of minutes, my dad swings the door open and greets us with a smile.

"Well this is a sight I never thought I'd see," he says, moving to the side so we can both walk in. "Jace Jackson walking into our home for lunch." He shakes Jace's hand and slaps him across the shoulders.

"It's great to see you again, Mr. Sims," Jace says, extending his hand towards my dad.

"It's been a while, son. How's your dad doing? I saw him at the golf course last month and meant to call him to grab lunch, but then life got busy." The three of us move through the narrow entryway.

"He's doing pretty good. I'll have to tell him you asked about him."

"Please do." My dad offers Jace a smile. "Grab yourself a beer, kid, and come help me on the grill." My dad disappears out the back door, and we walk into the kitchen, where my mom is preparing a salad. "Hi, Mom," I say. "You remember—"

"Jace Jackson," she says, looking up from the bowl of spinach in front of her. "Lacey told us she was bringing someone, but I never would have guessed it was you. How's Richard?"

"My dad's doing well. Glad to have me back here for a while," he says.

For a while. The words hit me like a metal rod to the chest, and I quickly try to shove any doubts I might have about him and I out of my head.

"Oh, I bet he is." She eyes the clock on the oven. "What had y'all running late today?" she asks.

"You said one o'clock, and it's twelve fifty-seven. Most people would call that early."

"Oh, don't be so dramatic. I was just trying to ask you about your day."

I take a deep breath. "So, where's Colt?" I ask, trying to change the subject, suddenly realizing I'm the only Sims child present.

"Stuck in traffic. You know your brother, always so busy. He landed this morning and went to see a friend before heading here, but now he's going to be late." She laughs and tosses a diced tomato into the bowl. I roll my eyes internally.

I grab Jace a beer from the fridge. He takes it before wrapping his arms around me. "You two going to be okay if I go help your dad?" he whispers.

I nod, and he kisses my forehead before walking out of the kitchen toward the back door. I look up to see my mother looking right at me.

"What?" I ask, sitting on one of the tufted leather bar stools lining the large island in the middle of the kitchen.

"Oh, nothing. It's interesting that of all the boys you could bring home, you brought Jace Jackson."

"What do you mean?"

She swipes a diced cucumber off the cutting board into the bowl with the side of her knife and then begins cutting a red onion. "You were devastated when you two ended things. I haven't heard you mention his name in nearly a decade, and now you're back together?"

"Things are different now."

She takes a deep breath. "I hope you're right."

"What's that supposed to mean?"

"That boy was never meant to stay around here. That's why he's been gone for so long. Gosh, when Annie was alive, she missed him so much. You really think he's going to stick around this time?"

"Can we not do this? Not today. I'm happy for the first time in a really long time, so can you please let me have this?"

"I only say all of this because I care about you. I don't want to see you hurt."

"Yeah, okay. Let me know when Colt gets here. I'm gonna go help the guys."

I head out of the kitchen toward my dad and Jace. I can hear her rolling her eyes behind me and muttering something under her breath, never pleased with my attitude. I try to shake off her words, but I can't.

"Everything okay?" Jace asks as soon as I step onto the wooden deck.

"Just Mom being Mom." I offer him a sheepish smile.

"Your mother loves you very much," my dad lectures. "She just has her own way of showing it."

"Yeah, that's what you tell me."

I walk over and sit next to Jace. He immediately grabs my hand and gives it a squeeze.

"So, Jace was telling me about how you two got back together," my dad says, flipping the chicken in front of him.

"Is that so?"

"I must say, I always liked you, son. Never understood why my daughter here broke up with you all those years ago." Jace's face breaks out in a big smile.

The door swings open, interrupting our conversation, and my brother walks out onto the deck.

"Colt," I yell, jumping up from my chair and throwing my arms around his neck.

"Hey, Sis," he says, wrapping his arms around me and spinning me around. He sets me down. His green eyes immediately find Jace.

"Oh, hell no," he says. "What's he doing here?"

"I know what you're thinking, but it's okay. We're back together."

"Together?"

"Yeah, together," Jace says, joining me by my side and grabbing my hand.

Colt shakes his head. "Lace, can I have a word?"

I nod and follow him back into the house. Glancing over my shoulder, I give Jace a reassuring smile. While everyone in my family was oblivious, and still is, to the reason we ended things, I confided in my brother.

He moves quickly toward the front door. I hear my mom say something, but we both ignore her.

He swings it open, gesturing for me to walk outside, and when I do, he follows me, slamming the door behind him.

"Please explain why the asshole who cheated on you ten years ago is sitting on the deck with Dad and you're calling him your boyfriend."

"I didn't call him that."

"No, you said you were together. What does that mean? Fuck, don't tell me you two are engaged?"

I laugh, "God no, Colt. We're together. It's really new. No label, but we're trying again, and I invited him to come because he knows what it's like for me when I'm around Mom. I wanted him here."

"He cheated on you." He begins to move around the driveway.

"No, he didn't."

He scoffs. "And how do you know? Did he tell you that? Fuck, men lie."

"Colton, while this is very sweet of you, I think you forget you're my younger brother. I'm eight years older than you, and I'm not an idiot. The woman I saw him with was the mentor he was paired with for the photography program. They weren't a couple. Mariah and I blew it out of proportion. I overreacted and ran because I was young and scared and didn't like the way being vulnerable made me feel."

"And you know this because?"

"Because I met her. She's happily married—to a woman, I might add. It was all a big misunderstanding, and I promise he's a good one. He's so good, Colt."

He stops moving and turns to face me. "I don't ever want to see you that hurt again."

"I know, but I promise he won't hurt me."

Stepping forward, he wraps me in a hug. "I've missed you."

"I missed you too, bud." I let go and ruffle his dirty blond hair with my hand like I did when he was a kid.

"Sorry I never called you back. You FaceTimed me over a month ago but I got so wrapped up in summer ball. I should've called you back or at least texted."

"It's fine. I'm just as guilty. I called you to tell you Jace hadn't cheated. I had just found out and I wanted to tell you about it. I'm sorry I made you hate him too. I'm sorry you had to see me like that. That wasn't fair to you. You were only nine."

"I don't care. I'll always protect you, Sis. You don't have to be sorry." He wraps me in another hug and squeezes me tight.

When I pull away, my hand finds the locket and I begin to move it along the chain.

His eyes dart down to the necklace and he begins to laugh. "Why are you wearing that?" he asks.

"I told you I've missed you. You're so busy with school and baseball and we never get to talk. I found it at the beginning of the summer and it made me think of you, so I've been wearing it since."

He continues to laugh and he can't stop. Tears stream down his face. I hear the door open, and when I look over my shoulder, Jace is walking out to meet us.

"I was coming to check on y'all and to make sure everything was okay, but it seems to be." He gestures in Colt's direction. "What's he going on about?"

"I've got no idea. He saw my necklace and then started laughing."

Colt takes a few deep breaths, his laughter beginning to subside. "Do you want to tell her or should I?" he says.

"Tell me what?"

Jace's eyes flit down to the locket and then back up to mine.

"Tell me what?" I raise my voice.

"The locket was from me," Jace says.

"No, Colt got me this for my high school graduation." I run my hand over the engraving on the outside of it. "The birds were supposed to be for the Grantville High Golden Eagles, which was so funny because they are very obviously not eagles, but he was only ten, so I thought it was sweet. He even put his picture inside it," I flip it open and reveal Colt's sweet, little face.

"God, you were such an annoying kid." Jace laughs, running his hand down his face.

"He's right," my brother says. "He brought it over the day of your graduation. He wanted to see you, and I was so mad at him for what I thought he did that I lied and told him you weren't here."

"Colton!"

"I snatched it from his hand and told him I'd give it to you, but I took it up to my room and opened it instead. I switched the picture, hid the letter he wrote you, and came up with the story about the birds. I'm sorry, Lace. I thought I was protecting you."

I flip around to face Jace. "You brought it over the day of my high school graduation?"

He nods.

"And you didn't think you should tell me? I've been wearing it since the day on Lake Allatoona."

"You said things were weird with your family. You missed Colt, I didn't want to complicate things for you and him."

"I mean, to be fair, Lace, you believed that I thought the

two birds sitting on the branch were eagles. I didn't have your grades, but I wasn't that dense."

I shake my head thinking back to the moment he gave me the necklace.

"You were so convincing. You told me you had been saving your allowance. I had no reason to believe anyone else would have bought it for me. "

"I'm sorry," Colt says. "It was a shit thing to do even if I was mad."

"What did you do with the letter and the photo?"

He shrugs, "Last I saw them, they were up in a bag in my closet. I was going to throw them away, but it didn't feel right."

I turn without responding. I pass by Jace, heading in the house and up the stairs toward Colt's old bedroom. I can hear both men behind me, but I don't stop. I'm on a mission to find the letter and picture I should've been given nine years ago.

I walk into his room and immediately start searching his closet for a bag. "What kind of bag?" I yell.

"Purple gift bag. Top of my closet," he shouts from down the hall.

"Would you two please lower your voices?" my mom yells. "This is not a concert venue; it's a house."

I shuffle the items on the top shelf until I find a small gift bag. I pull it down, moving the old, crinkled tissue paper out of the way, revealing an envelope with my name scribbled across the front and a tiny picture of teenage Jace and me.

I grab both and storm out of the room past my brother and Jace. I head straight into my room, slamming the door behind me. Sitting down on my childhood bed, I tear the envelope open. With shaking hands, I unfold the paper and begin to read.

Pixie,

Meet me in our spot tonight at 8 so we can talk and

figure this out. I'm sorry I got busy. I'm sorry I didn't call like I should have. I love you more than you will ever know. Please talk to me.

Yours forever,
Jace

"Can I come in?" Jace asks, pushing the door open and tapping his knuckles against the door frame.

"Please."

"Are you mad?" he asks, climbing onto my bed and pulling me between his legs. He wraps me up in his arms.

"No. He was young and you were right. It's been hard having him so far away." I lean my head back onto his chest. "I wish I would've known. I wish I could go back in time and change it all."

"I know, but we can't. All we can do is move forward, and I'm glad we're getting the opportunity to do that together now."

"Did you come that night?" I hold up the letter.

"I did. Waited down there for a few minutes and then I saw you with—"

"Alex." My hand covers my mouth as the name falls from it.

"Yeah." His voice sounds defeated.

I turn to face him, sitting with my legs tucked underneath me. "What exactly did you see? Fuck, were you in the bushes or something?"

He swallows hard. "I saw you come outside with him smiling. He was holding your hand and then y'all kissed. I got out of there as fast as I could. You seemed happy, and I knew then that it was really over."

"It was just a kiss." I think back to the night and shake my head. "It wasn't what you thought. Beau's older brother had given him a bottle of some fancy vodka, and he spiked the punch. I didn't like them. Beau or Alex. But Poppy was so blinded by her love for Beau that she couldn't see how mind-numbingly awful they were. Alex was a thorn in my side my entire senior year. Everywhere Beau went, he went, and everywhere Poppy went—"

"You went."

"Yeah. So we somehow became this little foursome." I roll my eyes at the memories. "God, they were so terrible and so dumb."

He nods. "Oh, I remember."

"Anyway, we were all a little tipsy from the punch, and Alex decided he was going to shoot his shot with me, I guess. He pulled me out to the backyard and kissed me before I really realized what was happening. God, Jace, I hated it. I pushed him away. Told him he was insane if he thought I wanted anything to do with him. It was the worst kiss I've ever had, and that's saying something because I've had some really bad kisses."

He laughs, and I feel my shoulders relax a little. He pulls me back into his lap.

"But I guess you were already gone and didn't see that part?"

"No, I left thinking you were happy with Alex of all people." He chuckles. "I should've known better. I told my parents that night about Georgetown."

"You decided on Georgetown that night?"

"Yeah. I knew there wasn't a place here for me anymore. Coming home reminded me too much of you, so I threw myself into work and school. Convinced myself that maybe if I could find the Bix, it would somehow bring you back to me. That you would hear about it and come back into my life, even if it was for a fleeting moment, and I'd get to see you again. Get to tell you I did it."

Tears begin to run down my face. "I'm sorry. I wish I could go back and change everything."

"It's okay; you didn't know I was there. Colt took the bag from me, and I wanted to believe he would actually give it to you. I should've known better," he says. "I'm sorry. I should've tried talking to you."

He pulls me into him, and I press a kiss to his lips. "Where's the picture?"

I hand him the small photo of him and me as kids. His arms are wrapped around my back, and we look so happy.

"May I?" he asks, undoing the clasp of the necklace.

I nod. He pops out the photo of Colt and replaces it with ours. "Much better," he says, closing the locket and placing it back around my neck. My mom's voice echoes through the house, calling for us.

"We better get back down there. Lunch was almost ready, and I'd like to do something before I bring you home."

"Do we have to?"

"Yes, Pixie. Come on."

We walk down the stairs hand in hand. As we round the corner, we find my family sitting at the perfectly set table, waiting for us to join them.

"Well, it's about time," my mom says.

"Sorry," I say, sitting in one of the chairs. Jace sits next to me.

"Honey, will you say grace?" She looks over at my dad, who nods and then begins to recite the same prayer he's said before every meal my entire life. Once he's finished, my mom begins to pass around the plated food. I place a piece of grilled chicken on my plate and then pass the plate to Jace.

"How's work going, Lace?" my brother asks.

"It's good. Margaret, my boss, can be a little much sometimes, but I really like it. Actually, Poppy started last week, so that's been fun."

"That's great. I played golf with her father the other day," my dad adds. "He was telling me she was starting soon."

I put a scoop of salad onto my plate. "We're really excited to get to work together."

My mom hums over a bite of chicken but doesn't look up from her plate.

"How's Austin?" Jace asks, looking at my brother.

"It's good. I've been up in Massachusetts playing summer ball."

"Colton's the ace pitcher," my mom beams.

"That's cool. I thought you played for UT," Jace says.

"Oh, I do. This is for the Cape Cod Summer League. Gives scouts a chance to come see what we can do."

"I see. You think you're going to get drafted?" Jace asks, cutting into his chicken.

"We'll see. I'm hopeful."

"It'll happen, Son," my dad encourages.

"So, how'd you manage to get a weekend off?" Jace asks.

"This damn blister has made me miss two starts now." Colt lifts his left hand and looks at his middle finger. "I got approval from my coach to come home while it heals."

"A blister?" I ask.

"It's a very serious injury for pitchers," my mom says. I can't help but laugh. Before my IUD, I was expected to act like nothing was wrong while my uterus tried to kill me every month. Colt gets one tiny blister and has to come home to heal.

"She's right, Lace," my brother says. "I put a lot of pressure on this finger when I pitch and risk a lot of pain and infection if I were to play."

"Well, whatever the reason, I'm glad you're home."

The rest of the conversation continues to center around Colt and baseball. I stay mostly quiet, preoccupied with the necklace around my neck and thoughts of what the last decade may have looked like if I had known it was from Jace.

A knot forms in my stomach at the thought that nothing would have been different because eighteen-year-old me would've probably read the letter and decided not to go. Too dramatic and too immature to even consider having a conversation.

"You okay?" Jace leans over and whispers in my ear.

I nod and sip my iced tea. When we finish eating, I get up and place my plate in the dishwasher. My mom walks over, placing hers next to mine.

"What was all the fuss about before lunch?" she asks in a hushed tone.

"It was nothing," I lie.

"Didn't seem like nothing," she says unamused. "Why don't you three go spend time with your father and I'll clean up the mess in here?" She picks up a sponge and begins to clean a dish sitting in the sink.

"Lacey and I can clean up," Jace offers from behind us.

"I can help too," Colt adds.

"That won't be necessary. Jace is our guest, Lacey hates to clean, and your finger is injured," she says.

"Well then I can clean up," Jace says, offering her a smile. "You three go spend time with each other."

My mom breathes deep, rings out the sponge, and dries her hands. "Thank you," she says, walking away and leaving the three of us in the kitchen.

"You don't have to go in there," Colt says. "I'm sure it's going to be more baseball talk." He offers me a sheepish smile and rolls his eyes. "They probably want to know more about all the MLB scouts that aren't calling."

"It'll happen." I squeeze his upper arm. "You sure you won't be mad? I don't know how much more I can take today."

"Not at all. Stay and help Jace clean up. I'll call you when I'm back in Massachusetts and we can catch up."

"You promise to call me this time?"

"Yes," he assures me. "Plus I'll be home again one more time before fall semester starts. I'll even carve out a whole day for my favorite sister."

"I'm your only sister."

"Still my favorite," he says, turning to walk out of the kitchen.

"Oh, Colt," I yell behind him.

"Yeah?"

"I'll be sure to keep your finger in my thoughts and prayers."

He shakes his head and laughs before turning and heading into the living room.

Jace and I load the dishwasher, clear the table, and wipe down the counters. When we're finished, I lean back against the island, watching Jace load the leftovers into the fridge.

"Thank you for helping," I say, drying my hands and placing the towel back on its designated hook. He walks back to where I stand and leans on the counter, his arms caging me in.

"I don't mind."

"Sorry if today was weird." His ocean-blue eyes find mine.

"It wasn't."

I laugh. "Yes, it was."

"I'm glad you know about the necklace."

My hand finds the locket and I move it up the chain. "Me too. I think I've had enough Sims family fun to last me for a while. You ready to head out?"

"You sure? I know you miss Colt."

"I'm positive. Didn't you say you wanted to do something before you dropped me off?"

He pushes off the counter and leans back against the counter across from me. "I was wondering if we could stop at my mom's grave."

"Oh, Jace..." My heart simultaneously breaks and swells

with pride. I know he's never been, and part of me wonders why today, but I don't question him.

"We don't have to," he begins, looking down at the hardwood floors. "I didn't mean to blindside you with that. I know it's close by and—"

"You didn't blindside me." I step forward, wrapping my arms around his waist. "I think we need some new rules. If this is going to work this time, we need to talk to one another. When we were kids, we talked about everything. We didn't let fear get in the way of confiding in one another about how we felt or what we wanted to do. I don't want to lose you again, so we talk." I rub my hands up and down his back. "Promise me you'll talk to me. No more assumptions. No more apologies. If you want to go see your mom, you don't have to apologize. Of course I'll go with you."

He plants a kiss to my forehead. "Deal, Pixie."

"Pinky promise?"

"Pinky promise." He links his pinky with mine.

CHAPTER 52: HI, MAMA
JACE

I pull through the gates and follow the paved drive over to where we laid my mom to rest. Her grave is situated under a large oak tree. My grandparents are buried to her left, and to her right is the plot of land my dad bought for himself. It's a harsh reminder of why I need to get this job at the center, and I hate it. The thought of one day losing him, like I lost her, makes a knot form in the pit of my stomach. I park the Jeep and look over at Lacey. She's sitting staring out the window holding the large bouquet of sunflowers we bought on the way.

I kill the ignition, and she turns to look at me. "You ready?"

"I don't know," I answer honestly. I'm not sure what I'm doing here. I don't know what to do. It feels like it's been too long, and the guilt of never coming before consumes every part of me. Being back on the street where I grew up made me miss her, and so I thought maybe it was time to rip the Band-Aid off.

"What are you unsure about?" she asks, taking my hand in hers. Her thumb draws soft circles on the back of my hand, calming me.

"I feel guilty about never coming before. I don't know how to do this." She offers me a soft smile.

"We'll do whatever feels right. If you want to talk to her you can, or if you want to sit in silence we can do that too." She squeezes my hand tightly. "I'm right here and will be the whole time unless you tell me otherwise."

I consider her words and nod my head. Tears prick the back of my eyes, and I try to swallow the pain down.

"You ready?" she asks.

We both climb down from the Jeep and she walks around the front, handing me the flowers and taking my other hand in hers. We walk across the grass toward the headstone engraved with the name Anne Jackson.

"Hey, Annie, I brought someone to see you," Lacey says, reaching down to remove some old flowers from her grave. My eyes fill with tears at her words, and I wipe them away as they fall down my face. Lacey walks back to my Jeep and puts the old flowers in the back so we can dispose of them later.

She returns, takes a seat in front of the small plot, and pats the ground, encouraging me to join her. Taking a step forward, I lay the sunflowers at the base of my mom's headstone. "Hi, Mama." It comes out in a whisper as I brush my hand across the top of the rough stone, close my eyes, and try to calm the tears that continue to fall.

I sit down next to Lacey on the manicured grass. She grabs my hand again and lays her head on my shoulder. We sit there for a long while, neither of us speaking. The sun is warm on my back, and there's a slight breeze. A few cars pass by with other people going to visit their lost loved ones. A squirrel hops across the lawn, and the air fills with the sounds of chirping birds from the tree above.

Lacey breaks our silence. "What's on your mind, J?"

I take a deep breath. "There is so much I wish I could tell her, but I feel ridiculous saying them to a rock and not her."

"Why don't you try telling me then?" She nuzzles into me,

and I instantly feel a little calmer. A little more comfortable with continuing to speak.

"I wish so badly we could have wandered over to the old house today after lunch with your parents. I wish I could have walked in and found her in the kitchen baking something and Dad watching TV."

She lifts her head off my shoulder and her green eyes find mine. "I wish we could have too. What else?"

"I feel so guilty this is the first time I've been here since she died. I feel like a coward, always too scared to feel the feelings associated with coming here. I feel like the world's worst son never taking my dad up on his offers to visit with him."

"You aren't the world's worst son," a deep voice says. I turn to see my dad walking up behind us, a large bouquet of flowers in his hand and his eyes already a little glossy.

"Dad?" I stand quickly, brushing off the back of my shorts. I glance down at Lacey and then back over to him, wondering if she's the reason he's here. "How'd you know I'd be here?"

"I didn't," he says. "I come every Saturday to make sure she has fresh flowers."

Lacey stands. "Hi, Mr. Jackson."

"Hey, sweetheart." He walks over and wraps her in a hug. "It's so good to see you."

"You too."

"So, how's my girl?" he asks, looking toward the headstone and placing his flowers next to mine.

I look over at Lacey, and she's studying my dad and I. "I think I'm going to give you two a minute. I'll be over by the Jeep, if you need me."

I watch as she walks away.

"I'm glad you're here, kid," my dad says.

"Me too." A sob breaks free. The tears begin to fall and I can't stop them. There's no use. "I'm so sorry, Dad."

He wraps me in a hug and holds me while I cry, like he

did when I was a kid. "You don't need to apologize," he assures me.

"But I do." I take a step back. "You've asked me to come here with you so many times and I never did. I've been so absent despite having the apartment. You were right at the hike. I've been running. Running from losing Lacey and then when we lost Mom, I ran from that too. I don't know how to do this. How to be vulnerable. How to feel these feelings."

"You're doing it now, though, and that's what matters," he assures me. He takes a seat in the grass. "Sit with me?"

I sit down next to him and he pats me on the back. "You know, after she died, I came up here every day for the first year. The pain of losing her was overwhelming, and coming here and talking to her put me at ease. Sometimes I would sit here and cry. Beg her to come back to me. Other days, I would tell her about you. She would have been so proud of you, Jace."

I let his words settle. My heart clenches. "I miss her so much. After my trip to Vancouver, I actually dialed her number, wanting so bad to tell her about the family of wolves we had photographed. It rang a couple times before I realized she wouldn't be picking up. She couldn't. She was gone."

"I saved a couple voicemails, and on the hard days it helps to listen to them. What made you want to come today?" he asks.

"Lacey."

"It's good to see y'all are friends again."

"We're more than that. We're giving it another shot."

"Mom would've loved to hear that."

"I think so too."

"You know, on your mom's first birthday after she died, I came up here expecting to be alone, but I wasn't. When I got here, Lacey was here."

I turn and look behind me. She is leaning against my Jeep, her blonde hair blowing in the slight breeze. She seems lost in her thoughts, and for a second, I wonder what's on her mind. "She mentioned she had come before."

"She was singing your mom 'Happy Birthday' and had brought cupcakes." He chuckles again. I laugh at the thought of my girl throwing my mom a birthday party.

"Lacey," I call, gesturing for her to come over.

"What are you two laughing about?" she asks, walking toward us.

"I was telling Jace about the birthday party you threw Annie here." My dad's face breaks out in a wide grin, and hers turns a deep shade of pink.

"You're amazing," I say as she sits down next to me. I grab her hand and bring it to my mouth, planting a kiss on the back of it.

"Annie was special and she deserved to be celebrated." She smiles.

I see a flash of red in my periphery, and when I look up, a cardinal is perched on the top of the headstone. I smile. "You know, some people say cardinals are lost loved ones visiting us," I say, pointing to the bird.

"They definitely are." Lacey smiles.

The three of us sit there for the next hour, sharing stories about my mom. With every memory shared, I feel my shoulders relax and a little more at peace.

"Alright, you two, I'm gonna head out," my dad says, standing. "Lacey, please tell your parents I said hello. It's always so good to see you, sweetheart." We stand to meet him, and he hugs us both.

"Jace, I'm so proud of you, Son. I know today was hard for you. If you ever need to talk, you know I'm here for you." His words hit me straight in the heart.

"I love you, honey," he says looking back towards the stone. The cardinal is still perched there, and I smile at the thought that it could be my mom.

I wrap my arm around Lacey's shoulders and pull her tight into my side. "Thank you for coming with me," I say.

"Always, J. You don't have to do this stuff alone." I lean down and press a kiss to the top of her head. I check my watch and realize it's beginning to get late.

"You ready to head home? I know you have the girls coming over."

"I could cancel. I know it's been an emotional day," she offers.

"No, I could use some time to myself to process it all. You hang with the girls and we can do something tomorrow."

Her mouth falls a little, but she nods her head. "Okay." We both say our goodbyes to my mom, and for the first time in five years, I feel a little lighter. Hand in hand, we head back to my Jeep, and I drive her home.

CHAPTER 53: THE INVISIBLE STRING IS REALLY INVISIBLE STRINGING

LACEY

"I'll call you tomorrow?" Jace asks, breaking the kiss we just shared in front of my apartment door.

"You sure you're okay?"

"I'm better than I've been in a long time," he says, peppering my face with kisses and making me laugh. "And you, Pixie, have everything to do with it." His lips find mine again. His tongue swirls around my mouth, and I let out a small moan. The thought of calling off the girls' night crosses my mind, but I know Jace, and I know he needs time to process things. I pull back and those blue eyes capture mine.

"Have fun with the girls." He gives me one more chaste kiss before spinning around and heading down the stairs towards his Jeep.

I watch him as he goes, leaning on the metal railing and smiling to myself. It feels surreal that we're back together and we've fallen back into each other's lives so easily. It's like nothing ever happened.

Once his Jeep disappears down the street, I turn and walk into my apartment. Poppy is sitting on the couch intently scrolling on her laptop and drinking from her favorite coffee mug. I check my watch and shake my head. Only my best friend can drink coffee no matter the time of day and still sleep.

"Whatcha looking at?" I ask, eyeing her and setting my keys by the door. "I haven't seen that look on your face since before you graduated."

"Oh, nothing," she looks up from the screen and shuts her computer. "Just some mindless scrolling." She twirls a piece of hair around her finger and offers me a sheepish smile. There's a weird pause before she sets the laptop on the coffee table and pulls her legs to her chest.

"How were your parents?"

"Same old, same old." I shrug, sitting down across from her on the sofa. My body sinks into the pillowy cushions. "I accepted a long time ago I'll never change Lori Sims, but that doesn't mean some of the shit she says doesn't get under my skin. Dad was fine, all business, per usual. And oh, my god —" I sit up, grabbing at the locket around my neck. "Did you know this was actually a gift from Jace and not Colton?"

"No way." Her eyes land on the necklace. "But I thought Colt got it for you because he thought the birds were eagles." She laughs.

"I know. I can't believe it, but I guess it makes more sense now." I run my fingers over the metal. "All this time it was from Jace. The crazy part is I hadn't worn it in years. I found it the day we went on the boat and decided to put it on because I couldn't find the other necklace I was looking for."

"Damn, the invisible string was really invisible stringing." She laughs, sipping her coffee. "That's sweet. How did Colt end up with it then?"

"Apparently, Colt snatched it from Jace when he brought it over." I let out a laugh. "You know Colt always has to act like my big brother even though he isn't." I shake my head. "There was a letter too. He wanted to try to work things out. Asked me to meet him the night of our party on the roof, and then he saw Alex kiss me and thought I had moved on. He decided to go to Georgetown the same night."

"Oh, my god, I forgot Alex kissed you. So gross."

"Right?" I laugh.

"You think if you had gotten the letter, you would've gone?"

"Honestly, I don't know. Maybe, maybe not. I was still so mad at him. That was the night you told me about Europe with Beau. Alex kissed me. I was in such a weird headspace back then that I don't know what I would have done."

"Maybe it was all meant to happen this way." She shrugs. "Me meeting Logan. Jace coming back into your life when you least expected it."

"Maybe."

"So, what did your mom say this time?"

I let out a groan. "She wasn't amused that Jace and I are back together. Thinks he's not meant to stay here. Like he's some vagabond." I pause and roll my eyes. "For someone who thinks I'm dramatic, she sure knows how to be."

"Does that mean he's officially your boyfriend?"

"We didn't label it. We agreed we want to try again and see where it goes."

"And do you think he'll leave again?"

"I don't know. Maybe, but I think if he does, we can make it work. We haven't had a chance to talk about it. After we left lunch, we stopped by Annie's grave. I know we need to talk about what comes next, but today was a hard day for him and he needed some space to process his mom. For now, I'm really happy."

She nods understandingly. I glance down at my watch. "Shit, they'll be here soon. I need to grab a quick shower. You want to order the food?"

"Thai?"

"Yeah, but the good Thai place, not the one we got last time."

———

I walk out of my bedroom to find Wren, Chloe, and Gray are already here with drinks in hand.

"It's about damn time," Gray says when she sees me.

"It was a long day. I didn't realize y'all were all here." I walk over and pour myself a glass of wine from the opened bottle.

"Food will be here any minute," Poppy says, checking the app on her phone. I sit down next to her.

"How was the hospital, Gray?" I ask. "You got done sooner than I thought you would."

"Oh no, we came over to hear about you and Jace. I'd love to hear about Gray's second job, but unless she can offer us something as scandalous as fucking in the bathroom at The Local, it'll have to wait," Wren says, smiling mischievously.

"She's right, Lace. You owe us the dirty details of what happened." Gray smiles over the edge of her wine glass.

There's a knock at the door, and Poppy jumps up to answer it. "Hold that thought; that's the food." She moves across the living room to the door and takes two bags of takeout from the delivery driver. Thanking him, she kicks the door shut with her foot and returns to where we all sit.

She sets all of the containers on the coffee table and sits crossed legged on the ground. "Okay, I'm ready, tell us what happened."

My friends all listen intently as I detail the night at the bar and what happened after.

"I'd like to take credit for this finally happening." Wren giggles. "If it hadn't been for Tanner and me picking such a *hot* song, you two could still be pretending like this wasn't incredibly inevitable."

"You're a good friend," I tease. "It was weird seeing you and Tanner get along so well. I thought he drove you crazy."

"He does. It's amazing who you'll tolerate after some tequila." Wren laughs. "I'm glad you're getting some."

"It feels like more than just sex though," I say. "I mean don't get me wrong, the sex is mind-blowing, and part of me hates myself when I think about all of the bad one-night stands I've had when I could have been having Jace, but I don't know, it feels like—"

"Love?" Poppy cuts me off, smirking.

"Maybe." I feel my cheeks heat. "But that's insane, right?"

"Not necessarily," Chloe says. "Y'all have a past, and just because you were apart for a decade doesn't mean your history was erased."

"Yeah, I don't think you ever actually fell out of love with him," Poppy says. "You were mad and hurt, but you've loved him since we were kids."

Deep in my gut I know they're right. It seems crazy, but I love Jace and I think I've loved him my entire life.

"So when do you see him again?" Gray asks.

"Tomorrow, maybe. He said he would call me."

My phone pings and I grab it, secretly hoping it's him.

57189:

Good Vibrations Summer Sale is LIVE! Take up to 50% off your favorite toys and make this summer even hotter! Shop Now www.goodvibrations.com

"Is that Jace?" Poppy asks.

"Oh, no. Apparently Good Vibrations is running a summer sale." I laugh and sip my wine. "Anybody need a new vibe?"

"Maybe you should buy your new boyfriend a present," Gray teases.

Chloe gets up and grabs the bottle of wine. "I'm excited for the wedding," she says, changing the subject. She returns and tops off all of our glasses.

"I didn't know you were coming to the wedding," I say.

"I'm Gray and Wren's plus one," she laughs.

"Can you believe those assholes didn't give us a plus one?" Gray asks. "We persuaded Enzo to agree to us each having half of a plus one. He said it was the best he could do."

"I'm glad you're taking a break from work and coming," I say. "How will the hospital and the clinic manage without you next weekend?"

"Very funny," Gray deadpans.

"What's everyone wearing?" Wren asks.

"I still need to get a dress," I admit.

"Girl, the wedding is next weekend," Poppy says. "How do you not have a dress yet?"

"I know, but I haven't had time."

"You're going to have to get something really hot," Gray says. "Especially now that you'll have a date."

The conversation continues about dresses and Donovan and Enzo's wedding. My phone pings again, and when I look down I smile when I see who the text is from. My friends' voices fade into the background.

JACE:

How's girls' night?

Fun!

JACE:

I miss you.

I miss you too.

My cheeks heat as I hit send. I might as well be seventeen again, hiding my phone under my desk and texting him in the middle of algebra.

"Lacey." Poppy's voice catches my attention.

"What?" I look up from my phone and all four of my friends are staring at me.

"Who are you texting over there?"

"Oh, shut up."

Laughter fills our small living room. The rest of the night is filled with more wine and catching up. We talk about anything and everything. I'm so thankful to work with a group of women I can also call my friends. At some point, we decide snacks are a good idea, and Chloe makes a batch of chocolate chip cookies.

"So, anyway, I don't know what I'm going to do," Wren says around a cookie. "They said we all have to move out by the end of October."

"Can they terminate your leases like that?"

She shrugs, "I guess so. They sold the building and the new owner is bulldozing it."

"That sucks. I'm so sorry babe," I say.

"Would you consider a roommate?" Poppy asks, twirling her hair around her finger. Her eyes flit over to me.

"Maybe," Wren says. "I'm so used to having my space and living alone, so that might be strange, but I also realize my current apartment was a steal and the chance of me finding something similar for what I'm currently paying is slim to none."

"I'm sure something will come available," Poppy assures her.

"Yeah, I'd say you could move in with me, but my studio is the size of a shoe box," Gray says.

"You're always welcome in my guest bedroom," Chloe offers. "But I know living with a toddler isn't for everyone."

"Or our couch," I add.

"Thanks, but I'll find something. Just let me know if you hear of anything."

After another hour or so, Wren, Gray, and Chloe all Uber home, leaving me and Poppy alone.

"I'm really happy for you," she says, cleaning up the empty cookie plate and takeout containers from the coffee table.

"I'm really happy," I say, honestly.

"You didn't say, but did you remember correctly?"

"Remember what correctly?"

"The size of Jace's dick," she laughs, heading toward her room.

"Good night," I yell across the apartment.

"Night. Love you."

"I love you more."

CHAPTER 54: GOOD VIBRATIONS
JACE

The past week has been better than I could have ever imagined. Almost every night Lacey was either in my bed or I was in hers.

Roger called two days ago to offer me the job at the CFNAWC, and I accepted it immediately. I haven't told Lacey yet because I haven't found the right time. I don't just want to tell her about the job; I want to tell her how I feel, and it needs to be perfect. I also haven't turned down Australia, and I'm not sure why.

Lacey and I decided sometime last week to forgo our separate hotel rooms for the wedding and get one together. She's been in the bathroom for close to an hour, and I keep checking my watch, knowing we need to leave soon or we will be late for the ceremony.

"You about ready?" I call through the door. I hear the click of the handle and when it swings open, she takes my breath away. Most of her hair is pulled back into a low bun at the nape of her neck, with a few stray pieces framing her face. Her black satin dress is fitted to every perfect curve. It hits her at the top of her thighs, revealing her long legs. She has on black heels, and the locket is around her neck. She does a little spin and reveals it's completely backless.

"What do you think?" she asks.

"I think we might need to skip the wedding," I say, moving in to kiss her. "You look absolutely irresistible, Pixie."

"You don't look too bad yourself," she says. Her emerald eyes rake over the suit I'm wearing. She runs her hands down my tie and kisses me again.

Pushing past me, she walks over to where a small black handbag sits on the bed. She clicks the clasp open and retrieves what resembles a car key fob and a tube of lipstick.

"I thought we were going to Uber," I say, looking at her hand.

"Oh, we are." She smiles at me over her shoulder. She pauses in front of the floor length mirror and applies the lipstick across her lips.

She walks over to where I stand and places the black and silver key fob in my hand.

"What's this?" I ask.

She takes my other hand and moves it along her thigh until my fingers brush up against the lace of her underwear.

"Lacey," I breathe out, letting my fingers tease her through the fabric. My hand stills and when I feel something, but I'm not sure what it is. With one of her hands, she clicks one of the buttons on the fob, starting a series of silent vibrations between her legs. She steadies herself with her hand on my arm and lets out a whimper. Her fingers dig into my shirt. I move my hand from her center and place it on the small of her back, holding her against me. She cocks her head, exposing her neck, and I place a slow tender kiss to her pulse point.

"You want me to play with your pussy all night, Pixie?" I up the vibration. "Want me to make you squirm in front of a room full of people?" I up it again and her whole body reacts.

"Yes," she says, breathlessly.

I grin against her and click the button, stopping the vibrations. She lets out a small groan in protest.

"It would be my pleasure."

"We have to stay within twenty feet of each other for it to work," she says. "Figured we could use it during the reception."

"I don't plan on letting you out of my sight all night."

"Good," she says. "Now let's go."

THE CEREMONY WAS BEAUTIFUL, BUT I WAS DISTRACTED BY THE girl sitting to my right. Lacey held my hand through the entire thing, and I was sure to squeeze her hand while Donovan and Enzo exchanged their vows, causing a smile to flash across her face and her eyes to get a little glossy. An unspoken promise that, one day, I will vow to love her in front of all of our family and friends, if she'll let me.

As much as I was tempted by the remote in my pants pocket during the ceremony, I haven't used it yet. Figured we should let our friends say their vows before I really started to wind her up, or we would be heading back to the hotel before the hors d'oeuvres were served.

We're standing at the cocktail hour waiting for the reception to start. Lacey is a few feet away from me, talking with Poppy and Wren. Tanner and Logan are going on and on about something, but I'm very distracted. My hand is firmly in my pocket situated on the remote.

I casually click the power button and watch as Lacey's body does a little jolt, sloshing her champagne over the edge of the glass. Her eyes shoot to mine and I throw her a wink.

"You good, Lace?" Poppy asks.

"Oh, yeah, I'm great," she tries to recover.

I click it off. My dick begins to strain against my boxer briefs, and I wonder how we're going to be able to make it through the night. Knowing I don't even have to touch her to make her react like that might be my undoing.

In a couple strides, I'm standing next to her. I tug on her hand, removing her from our group of friends and over to the side where she and I are alone.

"If we're going to do this, I'm going to need you to be a good girl and not give us away," I whisper against her ear. Her breath hitches and I hit the button again. "You think you can do that, Pixie?"

She nods her head. "I can do it." I up the vibration a couple notches and her forehead falls against my chest.

"I promise to reward you if you're good."

She immediately straightens up and steps back from me. I know this isn't going to last long. I watch as her throat bobs as she tries to swallow whatever she's feeling down.

"And if I'm bad?" she asks, smirking up at me.

Her words take me by surprise, and I clench my jaw. My dick hardens instantly. She slides past me before I can respond, and I up the vibrations one more time for good measure. Her body does a little shiver as she walks away and then I turn it off. *I'm so fucking screwed.*

A man on a microphone asks for everyone to make their way into the reception venue so dinner can be served. I catch up to Lacey and the rest of our group. We make our way over to the large pickleball themed seating chart adorned with monogrammed pickleball paddles and flowers. Only Donovan and Enzo could somehow make pickleball look elegant.

We all breathe a sigh of relief when we realize they squeezed all eight of us into one table. We find our seats, Lacey sitting on my right and Tanner on my left. I don't miss the break in his smile when Wren chooses a seat on the other side of the round table and Logan sits next to him instead. Without thinking, I place my phone and the key fob on the table between Tanner and me.

"I thought y'all Ubered here," he says, eyeing the key.

"Oh, we did." I quickly grab the remote and stuff it back into my pocket. "I brought my keys by mistake."

I feel Lacey's foot kick against mine under the table, and I try not to laugh. My phone pings.

PIXIE:

Careful J. Would hate to have to punish you for giving up our little secret! 😅

You wouldn't dare.

PIXIE:

Try me.

I inhale deeply and hear her stifle a laugh. The waiters begin to bring around food, and the room fills with conversation and music. About halfway through the meal, Donovan and Enzo make their way into the reception hall and everyone cheers. Both men are beaming and look so incredibly happy. Love looks good on them.

They begin to move around the dance floor and as they perform their choreographed dance, I can't take my eyes off Lacey. She sways to the music. I wish for a moment I had my camera because I never want to forget the way she looks right now. The glow of candlelight illuminates her soft features. Her eyes flit to mine, and like I did during the vows, I squeeze her hand, sending her another silent promise.

"Did you see my mom's painting yet?" Logan asks the table. He nods toward his mother, who stands in front of an easel to the right of the dance floor.

"No, but I'm dying too," Poppy says. "I tried to sneak a peek earlier and she wouldn't let me look. Told me to come back after the first dance."

"Painting?" Wren asks.

"Logan's mom, Gwen, owns an art studio in town, and on the weekends she does live paintings," Poppy explains.

"Poppy and I booked her as a surprise for the grooms," Logan says.

"Wow! She has my dream job," Wren beams.

"You don't like working at Dogwood Manor?" Tanner cuts in.

"Oh, no, I love what I do. But if I could do it all again, an art studio sounds like a dream."

The table is quiet for a moment and the music shifts.

"I get that," Tanner says. She offers him a shy smile. A waiter swings by our table and refills our water glasses. "Cake will be served shortly," he says before disappearing.

"Anyone need anything from the bar?" Tanner asks, standing.

"I'll take one of the signature cocktails," Gray says.

"Which one?" he asks. "The Tink or the Peter Pan?"

"Are they big Disney fans?" Chloe asks.

"No, the drinks are named for their dogs," Logan explains. "Or I guess I should say they were named for the ring bearer and flower girl."

"I think the Tink," Gray says. "That's the spicy margarita, right?"

He nods. "Could you grab all of us one?" Lacey asks. He nods again. Logan stands, following him and muttering something about helping him carry the drinks.

I rest my hand on Lacey's thigh, and she places her head on my shoulder. The other girls continue on about something that happened at work with a couple of the residents, who are now apparently dating.

Logan and Tanner return with their hands full of spicy margaritas. Each one is topped with a lime and a candied jalapeno skewered with a toothpick. On the top of the toothpick is a cutout of the grooms' English Mastiff, Tinkerbell, with a bow in her hair.

"Thank you," Lacey says, grabbing one of the drinks and sipping from the cocktail straw.

There is a lull in the conversation as we await cake and anticipate dancing. Lacey's hand moves to my thigh and comes awful close to grazing my cock. My jaw ticks, and I hear her laugh under her breath, obviously amused with what she can do to me in a second. But two can play this game, removing my hand from my beer, I slide it into my pocket and click the top button.

"The ceremony was so beautiful," Poppy says, looking longingly at Logan.

Lacey doesn't react immediately, so I increase the vibrations a level, which makes her shift in her seat.

"So beautiful," Lacey manages to choke out as I up the vibration to the next level.

"You okay, Lace?" Chloe asks.

I up the vibration again.

"Yeah, I'm great. Just thinking about how beautiful all this is and how excited I am for the happy couple." Her words come out in a rush, and she tries to take a large sip of her margarita.

"Yeah, what has you acting so weird tonight?" Wren asks.

"Nothing," she snaps.

Lacey crosses her legs and grabs my hand with hers. I reduce the vibration, slowly backing off until it's gone entirely. I don't want to send her over the edge—not yet.

"You sure?" Tanner asks.

"Yes," she says, a little breathless. I pull out my phone.

> If it's too much or you want to stop, you can tell me.

PIXIE:

> Are you kidding? This is so fucking hot.
> Whatever you do, don't stop.

CHAPTER 55: WE LOVE THIS SONG
LACEY

I t's official. I'm calling the wearable vibrator my best idea yet. After girls' night, the Good Vibrations coupon code was burning a massive hole in my metaphorical pocket and so I followed Gray's advice. It didn't take me long to find the perfect gift for Jace. *Or I guess I should say us.*

The look on his face when he discovered it was priceless, and when he opened that dirty mouth of his, one that could melt my panties right off my body all on its own, I knew I had picked the perfect thing.

The reception was a blast. Full of food, drinks, lots of dancing, and just the right amount of edging. I'm wound so tight that I'm pretty sure the minute his hands or his mouth finally touch me, I'm going to explode.

"You sure y'all don't want to come to the after party?" Poppy pouts outside the venue. Donovan and Enzo just drove away, and the remaining guests are huddled outside waiting on their rides.

"Yeah, I'm really tired," I lie, holding my black heels in my hand. My whole body jolts as Jace buzzes the shit out of my clit with the little vibrator hidden in my underwear.

"You sure you're feeling okay?" she asks.

"Never better," I answer through clenched teeth, crossing my legs as I stand. The vibrations stop as quick as they started, and when I peer over my shoulder, Jace is standing there looking absolutely delicious in the black suit he's wearing. His jacket is long gone and slung over his arm. The sleeves of his white dress shirt are rolled up, revealing his tattoos, and his tie is a little loose around his neck—a cocky smirk across his face.

"This is us," he says, nodding toward the black car turning into the parking lot.

"Have fun at the party," I say, moving quickly towards the vehicle and offering Poppy and the rest of our friends a wave.

Jace opens the door and I slide in. He joins me in the back seat, and it feels remarkably similar to the night after the bar. His hand finds the top of my thigh. He's inches away from touching me. *Fuck,* I want him to touch me. I *need* him to touch me.

I didn't get my way then, but maybe I'll get my way now. I slightly part my thighs and shift my hips. He leans in close, so only I can hear him. "My greedy girl. You want me to touch you?"

"Yes," I whisper. "Please."

"Is the music too loud?" the driver yells over the EDM song blasting through the speakers.

"Not at all," Jace answers. "Actually, would you mind turning it up? We love this song."

The driver shrugs and spins the dial. The base of the music vibrates the car, and while that would usually annoy me, tonight I'm thankful for the privacy it gives us.

He pulls the little remote out of his pocket and I watch as he hits one of the buttons a couple of times, turning up the vibrations.

I swallow a moan. I'm so close to coming it's almost unbearable. He flips it off. I shift my hips again and he places a kiss against the side of my neck. "Can you be quiet?" he asks. I nod frantically.

"I won't make a sound," I whisper.

The vibrations begin again, but this time he doesn't stop them. He slowly raises the intensity. My head lulls back against the headrest, my eyes slamming shut. His fingers tease the hem of my dress and my hand grips his thigh.

The vibrations intensify and he leans over. "Come for me," he whispers against my skin. His breath is warm on my neck, his hand firm on my thigh.

He increases the vibrator's intensity one last time and my fingers dig into his leg. Without warning, his lips find mine and he swallows the scream threatening to escape as I fall.

My head is still spinning when he breaks our kiss. I watch as he turns the remote off, making the vibrations disappear. Then, he slips the remote back into his pocket, as if nothing happened.

I glance up at our driver, who's bopping along to the music, completely oblivious to what we did in the back of his car. We ride the rest of the way in silence. Jace draws teasing circles on my thigh, and I match his movements with my own on his. Every now then, I let my hand graze his crotch. Each time I do, his jaw tightens and his Adam's apple bobs up and down. He's rock hard, and while I should be completely satis-fied, the toy left me wanting more. *Wanting him.* By the time we arrive at the hotel my body is aching for another release.

The tension that fills the air between us matches the tight-ness in my core. We step out of the car and practically sprint into the hotel. We manage to make it into the elevator before the tension completely bursts. He pushes me up against the wall of the elevator as soon as the doors close. The bag and shoes I'm holding fall to the ground. I wrap my leg around the back of his, pulling him into me. Our mouths meet in a heated kiss. Our tongues tangle and our teeth clash. His hands and mouth are everywhere, except for where I want them to be. My nails dig into his back. "Fuck, tonight was hot," he says. "You."

He kisses my shoulder.

"Are."

His tongue draws a line up the side of my neck. The feeling is dizzying.

"So."

His teeth graze my ear.

"Fucking."

His breath sends goosebumps across my body.

"Sexy."

His mouth finds mine again, and I lean my head back, letting him take the kiss deeper. The ring of the elevator door interrupts us, and he pulls away. His chest rises and falls with heavy breaths that match mine. I collect my bag and shoes. We make our way down the hall to the room, both looking a tad disheveled.

I fumble to find the card key in my bag. The door barely shuts before he picks me up, moving me toward the king size bed in the center of the room. My legs wrap around his waist, and I grind into him desperate for the right amount of friction. He sets me down and spins me around. His fingers trace along my zipper and he plants kisses along my neck as he unzips my dress. I let it fall to the floor.

Stepping out and kicking it to the side, I turn to face him in only my lace thong. His eyes darken as they rake over my body. My hands find his tie, and I begin to undo the knot. I work quickly, undoing the buttons of his shirt and his pants.

His lips find mine again in a desperate kiss, and when he's finally completely naked, I break away letting my eyes and hands explore his body. Every bit of this man is toned. My hands explore until I find his long, hard shaft. I take him in my hands and stroke, causing him to moan my name.

"Pixie," he says through heavy breaths. "Let me make you feel good." His voice is deep and rough. Dropping to his knees, he carefully removes my thong and the tiny vibrator, casting it aside.

"Eyes on me," he says. The glow of the moonlight barely seeps through the curtains into the dark room. He looks up at me and swipes his thumb over my most sensitive spot, causing my whole body to jerk. My fingers weave in his hair, my hips thrusting forward again as he presses his lips on the inside of my right thigh.

"You did so good tonight," he says in between kisses. My whole body reacts to his words and his praise. "Do you know how sexy you are when you come apart for me like that?" He plants another kiss on the inside of my left thigh. "How many times I thought about pulling you away and tasting you like I did in that bar?"

"I wish you had," I say.

He stands and pulls me onto the bed so I'm straddling him. His hands smooth over my hips, pulling me against his thick length and causing me to press against him. We both let out a moan. "You're so fucking wet," he says, grinding against me again. His hands move up my body and cover my breasts. He circles one of my nipples with his thumb and then pinches it gently between his fingers. My breath hitches.

"You like when I play with you like this?" he asks.

"Yes," I breathe out.

He continues to play while I grind down on him.

"Sit on my face. I've been craving your sweet cunt all night."

"Such a filthy mouth," I tease, moving up his body. I position myself over his face, grabbing onto the headboard in front of me. He takes my hips in both hands, pulling me down and covering my pussy with his mouth. His tongue flicks against my clit, and I grind into his face.

His hands grab my ass, and one of his fingers finds my asshole. He circles it gently. Surprised by how good it feels, I sit up a little straighter and unintentionally pull away from his mouth.

"Is this okay?" he asks. "If it's not, I'll stop." We both freeze.

"No, I like it," I say. "You just surprised me."

He chuckles. "You sure you like it because I don't have to touch you there," he assures me.

"Yes. I'm sure. I like it. It's hot."

"I need to hear you tell me it's what you want."

"I want you to touch me there."

"Good, now sit," he commands. "I'm not done with you yet." I grind my hips against his face as he laps up everything I give him. The roughness of his beard creates delicious friction. I lean into the feeling of his finger on my puckered hole and let him dip it inside. Between the slight pressure of his finger and his tongue on my clit, I come quick and hard. My whole body shakes as I come undone for him again.

"You think you got one more in you?" he asks as I move down and meet him on the bed. My body's draped over his lazily, and I'm not sure I do, but I want to watch him come undone too.

"I don't know, J. I barely can come once during sex, but three times?" I bury my head into his shoulder.

"You seem to come just fine with me," he says. "You've had three before."

"Cocky asshole." I laugh. "With you it's different."

"Then let's go for one more. This time I want to come with you."

He sits up and begins to move out of the bed. "Wait, I can do it. Where are you going?"

"I know you can. I'm going to get a condom." He smirks.

"You don't have to." I shrug, sitting up. "I have an IUD."

"You're positive this is what you want?"

"I want to feel you bare, J." My words are all it takes. In a split second, he has me on my back and he's positioned between my legs.

"You promise you're okay with this?" he asks again.

"Fuck me like a good boy," I smirk. He drives forward, and I take his cock all the way to the hilt. His hands smooth over my hips, pulling me against his thick length, causing me to grind against him.

The energy in the room shifts to something more delicate. It's no longer frantic and needy, but instead the kisses he plants are slow and meaningful. He pumps into me unhurriedly. His mouth finds mine and his touch is gentle.

Those three little words threaten to come out but I hold them back, not wanting to say them like this. Wanting to save them for another time. For the right time.

We continue to twist in the sheets, giving the other everything we have. He thrusts into me over and over again. His cock stretches me wide and fills me completely.

"I'm close," he says through heavy breaths. "Come with me."

My body tenses at his words and he begins to move more rapidly, creating sweet friction against my clit. I clench around him as he spills into me. His body collapses on top of mine and we lay there for a few minutes catching our breath.

"Told you," he says.

"Only with you."

He gives me one more kiss before rolling out of bed. He returns in his boxers and with a warm towel. Taking his time, he cleans me up and then helps me locate my underwear. I jump out of bed and head into the bathroom.

When I return, he wraps me in his arms and I melt back into him.

"Pixie?"

"Yeah?"

"I love you," he whispers the words against my ear. I flip around to face him.

"I love you too." His lips find mine, and he feels like home.

CHAPTER 56: AUSTRALIA
JACE

"**G**ood morning, Pixie." I place a soft kiss on Lacey's shoulder.

"What time is it?" she grumbles, pulling the covers over her head.

"Come on. Let's get up and get some breakfast." I tickle her sides. She tries to fight against me, but she finally gives in and fills the room with the sound of her laughter. "I could wake up like this everyday," I say.

She pulls the comforter down, revealing her sleepy face and messy hair. "How are you so full of energy after last night?"

"I don't know what you're talking about. What happened last night?" I smirk, grabbing her and pulling her on top of me. She sits up, straddling my waist.

"Let's see." She rolls her eyes. "If I remember correctly, we had mind blowing sex, you told me you loved me, we fell asleep, and then I'm pretty sure you woke me up a few hours later and made me come a fourth and then a fifth time."

"You weren't complaining last night," I tease. She bends down and presses a chaste kiss to my lips. "And I do love you."

"I love you, too, but you're insufferable," she teases, stretching her arms above her head and yawning. She rolls off the top of me and begins walking toward the bathroom. I grab her wrist, stopping her. "Come back to bed with me, Pixie."

She shakes her head. "I need to pee and I want a shower. Give me five and then come join me."

She walks across the carpeted floor and disappears into the bathroom. After a few minutes, I knock on the door. "Can I come in?" I ask.

She flips the door open, a sexy smile across her face. "Only if you promise to be good."

I pull her towards me, wrapping her in a hug. I lean down so my mouth is up against her ear. "I promise to be very very —" I begin, but I'm cut off by my phone ringing from outside the bathroom.

"Shit."

"Go," she urges. "It could be important. I'll be waiting for you." She winks, starting the shower.

I turn to walk out back towards my phone, adjusting myself in my underwear. I grab it and swipe up on the screen.

"Eli," I answer through gritted teeth. "It's Sunday."

"Jacks," she says. "I got a lot of people asking me about Australia and no one, including me, has heard from you. What's going on?"

"I know. I'm sorry," I begin. "I've been meaning to reach out, but I've been busy."

"So, are you in?"

"Actually, no."

"You're kidding?"

"I'm not. Things have changed, and while Australia sounds like an amazing opportunity and I'd love to do it, I can't. My life's here."

"What do you mean your life is there? They really want you on the team. This could be huge."

"I know." I sigh. "It's not that I don't want to do it, and I know I should have told you sooner." I pick my words carefully. I haven't told anyone about getting the job, and I want Lacey to be the first to know. "This summer things changed. Lacey and I are back together. I want to be here, not halfway across the world."

"I understand, and I'm happy for you. Disappointed, but happy for you. I'll let Ryan know we need to find someone else."

"I'll touch base with him this week and explain." I pause. "Maybe the next one if it's closer and I have time."

"Sure," she says. "I'll let you get back to your Sunday."

The line drops, and I flip around to see Lacey standing against the bathroom door frame, staring at me with her mouth slightly open.

"I thought we were grabbing a shower." I grin. My face falls when I realize I don't hear the water running anymore.

"No." She shakes her head. "I think we should talk."

"Talk? Everything okay?" Those five words make my stomach flip. Needing to talk is never a good thing. *Is it?*

"What's in Australia?" she asks, walking over and grabbing one of my shirts out of my bag. She pulls it over her head and then climbs on to the bed.

"A job. Can you explain to me what's going on?" I ask, confused. "Are you mad? You're worrying me." I keep my voice level, trying to process the sudden change in her mood.

"No, no," she says. "I'm not mad, but I overheard your call. I wasn't trying to be nosey, but I walked out to get my brush and I heard you mention my name."

"I was telling Eli that you and I were back together, that's all."

"That's not all, Jace. We said we were going to talk about things, so I think if you have an opportunity to go to Australia for work, we should talk about it."

I walk over and sit next to her. "You're right." I smooth

my hand over her hair. "I should have brought it up before now. I've been trying to find the right time to tell you."

"Tell me what?"

"I accepted a job with the Center for North American Wildlife Conservation in Atlanta."

"You accepted a job? Here?" A look that resembles relief covers her face.

"I did. I'll be the director of photojournalism. It's a lot less travel, more management. It'll allow me to be near you and my dad."

She sits there listening to me intently. "Okay, but why wait to tell me then? Why not turn down Australia once you knew you had the job?"

"I don't know," I answer honestly. "For starters, I saw this conversation going a little differently. Like maybe telling you over dinner or something special."

"And the Australia conversation?"

"I just hadn't done it yet."

She nods. "What's the job in Australia?"

"Six months or more photographing the Great Barrier Reef and studying the wildlife around it."

"And you don't want to do that? That sounds like a phenomenal opportunity."

"It does, but I got the job here in Atlanta. You're here. My dad's here. Tanner is here."

"You don't care where Tanner is." She laughs. "But you hadn't turned it down until a few minutes ago. I know you, Jace. Your job, discovering the Bix, traveling the world, that's your dream job. I think you hadn't turned it down because part of you wanted to accept it."

I run my hands down my face.

"I'm right, aren't I?"

"You're not wrong. Australia is a cool opportunity, but—"

"Okay, so why not go? Why not take her up on it?"

I move closer to her and pull her into my lap. "For so many reasons, Pixie."

"Well, I think you should think about it. Really consider it. I'm not going anywhere. I'll be here waiting and supporting you no matter what you decide. I meant what I said last night. I love you."

"I love you too." My lips brush hers and she pulls away.

"I know, and that's not going to change because you take a job halfway across the world. I don't want you to give up your dreams because you're scared I'll run away again. I've loved you for as long as I can remember. Even when I thought you broke my heart, I loved you. If this is something you even want to do a little bit, then I want you to seriously consider it. Take me out of it. We can make it work. We can figure it out. We're not kids anymore."

"It's not just you. It's Dad too."

"What do you mean?"

"I wasn't here when she died, Lacey. I did what I wanted to do. I found the Bix. What if something happens to him or you and I'm not here?"

She runs her hands through my hair and looks me in the eyes. "I know losing Annie was hard, and I know you've held that guilt for a long time, but she wouldn't want you to and he wouldn't want you to either. This job sounds like a really big deal. You need to take everyone else out of the equation. Really think about what you want."

"Okay, I will." I agree, knowing that nothing I could say in this hotel room would convince her that this is not what I want. I need to show her. I lean forward and press my lips to hers.

"You promise?" She holds her pinky up toward me.

"I promise." I wrap mine around hers and pull her in for another kiss. "So, about that shower?"

She laughs and leads me to the bathroom.

CHAPTER 57: YOU FUCK IN IT, YOU BUY IT

JACE

I miss you.

PIXIE:

You literally dropped me off at my apartment
thirty minutes ago.

What are you doing around 5?

PIXIE:

Nothing. Poppy's at Logan's again, so I
planned on reading. I thought you were going
to see your dad?

I am, but it shouldn't take long. I'll see you
at 5.

PIXIE:

What are we doing?

It's a surprise!

Lacey swings open the door right at five. She looks me up and down, eyeing my casual clothes. "Where are we going?"

"Wouldn't you like to know." I lean in and kiss her cheek. "Come on." I grab her hand and lead her to my Jeep.

"How was your dad?" she asks as I turn out of the parking lot and onto the road.

"He was good. It was a quick visit. I had to pick something up."

"What?"

"Just something small." I flip on my blinker and change lanes. "He told me to tell you hello. Asked about you and work."

"And what did you tell him?"

"That I love you." I grab her hand, and she smiles.

"I love you too. Did you talk to him about the Australia job?"

"I did." I don't tell her anything else. If I do, it'll ruin the surprise, and I can't. I want to see the look on her face when she realizes where we are. We pull up to a red light and I grab my phone. Swiping up on the screen, I send her a link. Her phone pings and she looks down.

"Jace?" she questions. Looking at her phone. "Why'd you send me this article?" Her eyes glance over to me.

"Click on it. Read it. We're almost to where we're going, and I need you to read it before we get there."

Glancing over in her direction, I watch as she exhales deeply and then clicks on the link to an AJC article titled *Photographer Jacks Jackson's Motivation For His Latest Discovery Might Surprise You*. I return my eyes to the road, and after a few minutes, I hear her begin to cry. I turn down the street to our destination and park along the curb. I watch as she continues to read, wiping away her tears with her hands, and when she finishes, she turns to face me.

"Did you know I Googled you? That's how I knew you found the Bix."

"You mentioned it."

"It was weird. Seeing so many articles and links pop up. I saw this one and almost clicked on it, but I didn't." She pauses. "I was so mad at you then and somehow knew reading it would make me forgive you for what I thought you had done. Would bring back all the memories of when we were kids, and I couldn't put myself through it."

"I wanted you to read it because I wanted you to know you've always been it for me, and at the risk of sounding like an absolute lunatic, everything I've done in the past decade was because of you. It was all for you, Pixie. When I walked into Poppy's graduation party, I was not expecting to find you. But it felt like fate. Like every wish I made had finally come true."

She wipes the tears from her cheeks. "You're turning me into a huge softy." She laughs. "Wait, where are we?" She looks out the window at the two-story home we are parked in front of. The exterior is covered with white siding and a red brick skirt surrounds the base of the home. The shutters and doors are painted dark green. An exposed fireplace that matches the brick skirt climbs up one of the sides of the house. The minute I saw it, I knew it had to be mine. *Ours.*

"Come with me." I exit the Jeep and round the front. She opens her door, and I help her down.

I lead her down the driveway and up the steps to the front door of the house. I grab the brass handle.

"Jace, what are you doing?" She grabs for my hand. "Aren't you going to knock?"

I flash her a wide grin and push the door open, revealing an empty house. Her eyes go wide. The entryway is framed by two large rooms. Polished hardwoods cover the floor in every direction. A staircase with a wooden banister leads to the second story. A beautiful iron and crystal chandelier hangs from the vaulted ceiling. Fresh, creamy white paint covers every wall.

"No one is living here?" she asks, looking over her shoulder to where I stand. "Wait, what are we doing here?" With my hand on her lower back, I gently guide her over the threshold.

"It's for sale," I say, casually. "I was thinking I might buy it." She flips around to face me.

"Buy it?" Her throat bobs up and down. "What do you mean buy it?"

I stifle a laugh and grab her hand. We make our way down the hall and into the kitchen. A small gasp breaks past her lips. Natural wood cabinets are topped with white leathered granite. In the center is an island that could easily accommodate four people. A large window sits over the kitchen sink, letting in natural light and giving the perfect view of the wooded backyard.

"What do you mean buy it?" she asks again, her hand running over the rough granite.

"This summer has been phenomenal," I begin, trying to find the right words. She spins around to face me.

"It has, but why are we here? What's going on?"

"A week and a half ago, I reached out to Donovan, and he got me in contact with Jaime, another realtor at his office. This house will go on the market tomorrow, and I'm thinking about buying it. She pulled some strings, as a favor to Donovan, and was able to get us in today."

"We get to tour it unsupervised?" she asks.

"For the next hour, it's ours. Perks of having a friend who's a realtor." I laugh.

"And why am I here?" Lacey's eyes move around the kitchen, taking it in. Her hip is propped against the island and her arms are crossed. I walk over to where she stands. Picking her up, I set her on top of the island. I move my body between her legs and push a piece of her hair behind her ear.

"When I came back in May, I was considering staying because of my dad, and then I walked into that party and saw you. I know things weren't easy at first, but I knew I wanted you from the moment I saw you." She smiles. "This morning, you asked me to think about Australia, and I love you for that. I love that you want me to follow my dreams, but you, Pixie, are my dreams. You are what I wish for on every star. I want to build a life here with you. I know we've only been doing this for a couple of weeks and that might sound incredibly crazy, but I'm crazy about you and I have been my entire life."

I place a soft kiss on her forehead, tears beginning to well in her eyes.

"Jace, I—"

"You're here because I want your opinion. For ten years, I had to live without you, and I don't want to live without you anymore. I want it to be your house too."

Our eyes hold each other's, and we're both quiet for a moment. "What's going on in that mind of yours, Pixie?"

She takes a deep breath. "In the occupational therapy world, we often have to find ways for our patients to modify their environments so they can become accustomed to their new normal. Some need new equipment to eat, some might need it to shower, and others need it to move. We find ways to make life easier for them, but it's never the same. No matter how hard we try to wipe away the difficulty or the disability, it never completely goes away. Life is always a little bit harder for them."

I nod and give her a look that encourages her to continue.

"I think, in a way, that's what I've been doing for the last ten years. I tried so hard to erase you because the pain was so big, and some days it was so debilitating I didn't think I'd survive it. So, day by day, I adapted to a life without you, but no matter how hard I tried, my feelings for you never went away."

Tears run down her cheeks, and I wipe them away with the pads of my thumbs.

"I want this too, J. The house. You. Whatever comes next. I want it so badly. I want *you* so badly."

Our mouths meet in a passionate kiss full of love and desire. Her legs wrap around my waist, pulling me tight against her. My hand weaves in her hair. I tug slightly, causing her to let out a moan. We get lost in each other, completely forgetting where we are. My hands run up her legs and move over her hips. I pull her towards me and she grinds forward. Moving up her body, I find the small strap of her dress and push it down her shoulder. I plant kisses across her collarbone, sucking gently on her pulse point. She lets out a whimper, her body erupting in goosebumps.

Her hands run through my hair and then down my back. My cock hardens as she grinds forward again. "Make love to me," she pleads through heavy breaths. "I need you. I don't want to wait until later. I want you now."

I let out a low chuckle. "You want me that bad, baby? Want me to fuck you in this house that's going to be ours?"

"Yes," she says. I plant kisses back up her neck and across her jawline until our mouths meet again. My fingers run up her thighs until they find the thin fabric.

"My god, you're so fucking wet. So ready for me." She leans back on both arms. The hem of her dress is bunched around her waist, revealing her sheer black underwear. I move them to the side and swipe up her center, making her shudder. Her head falls back and her eyes close. I push a finger in, hitting her most sensitive spot. Lacey's hips thrust forward.

"More. Give me more," she begs.

"So fucking needy," I say pushing a second finger inside. Her body clenches around me as I work her and she cries out my name. My thumb finds her clit and I rub slow, purposeful circles. Her hips jolt forward.

"You look so pretty letting me fuck you with my fingers like this," I praise her, and she lets out a moan. Her hooded eyes find mine, and I increase the pace. I press my thumb against the sensitive bud of nerves and then she falls. Liquid rushes around my fingers. I move my hand to her mouth and she cleans herself off of me. Her eyes stay locked on mine as her tongue swirls around.

"Good girl." Her lips tip into a sexy half-smile. Her hands work down my body, finding the button and zipper of my shorts. She undoes them quickly, pushing them and my boxers over my hips, so they drop to the floor.

I pull her forward, sliding her panties to the side again, and push into her. She takes me so well, the moan she lets out when I'm fully inside of her threatening to end our fun prematurely.

I drive into her over and over. Our movements are in perfect rhythm. The rise and fall of our breaths sync. My lips find her rapid pulse and I suck on her skin.

"Fuck...yes...Jace...god..." Her words are like a chant encouraging me to continue. My hands find her ass lifting her slightly to help us find more friction.

"I'm close. Come with me, Pixie." I push my hips forward, and we both find our release. Our mouths meet again as we ride out our orgasms together.

"Shit," she says, trying to catch her breath. "That was really fucking hot. We should definitely have sex in semi-public places more often."

I let out a laugh. "I didn't realize exhibitionism was a kink of yours," I say, stepping back and buttoning my shorts.

"It never was before, but I'm into it." She laughs and uses her legs to pull me closer.

"I love you," I say, kissing her.

"I love you too."

"We're going to need to get you cleaned up." I look

around the kitchen trying to locate paper towels but find none.

"There might be some toilet paper in the bathroom," she suggests.

"Good idea. Hold tight and I'll be right back." I move across the house. My footsteps echo throughout the empty space. I return with a roll of toilet paper and clean her up. Helping her off the counter, she stands wrapping her arms around my neck. She pulls me in for another quick kiss before disappearing down the hall. She adjusts her dress as she moves and then disappears into the bathroom.

"Fuck, Jace!" she yells.

I move toward her quickly, not exactly sure what she's freaking out about.

"You gave me a fucking hickey," she says, glaring at me as I enter the bathroom. She looks back in the mirror and examines the red mark on her neck.

I start to laugh. "Stop," she whines. "I have to work tomorrow." Her face breaks into a wide grin before she starts to laugh too.

"Can't you put some makeup on it or something?"

"Maybe," she says, looking at it again. She turns to face me. "So, you think this is like when you break something at the store and then you have to buy it?"

"What do you mean?"

"Like if you fuck in a house, do you have to buy it?"

"What they don't know won't hurt them." I chuckle. "Why, are you having second thoughts?"

She looks around the small bathroom. "I'm not sure about this wallpaper. I don't know if it's—"

I cut her off and pull her into my arms, placing a kiss to her forehead. "I will personally see to changing the wallpaper. This will be your place as much as it's mine. Come on, there is so much more of it I want to show you."

Jace grabs my hand and leads me out of the bathroom and to the staircase at the front of the house. We make our way upstairs to the large owner's suite.

"I thought this could be our room," he says. "We could put a bed there and maybe a dresser here." He points to different walls as he talks. "The owners recently painted almost everything white, so you can pick out whatever paint you want."

He leads me into the adjoining bathroom. It's stunning. A large chandelier hangs from the ceiling. The vanity is deep mahogany, and white marble covers every surface. The shower could easily fit both of us and has plenty of room for...activities. A large stand-alone tub is surrounded by windows that overlook the woods behind the house.

"I love the tub," I say, running my hand along the smooth porcelain.

"I knew you would," he says. "A bathtub that could fit both of us was on my list of non-negotiables I gave the realtor."

"And what else was on this list?"

"A large closet, a nice kitchen, a reading room, a—"

"A reading room? What's a reading room?" A grin overtakes his whole face, and he pulls me out of the bathroom and down the hall to another room.

"I was thinking we could make this a reading room. We could put a really big comfy chair in this corner, and then on these walls we could do built-in bookshelves for all of your books."

"A reading room was a non-negotiable?" I look at him with awe.

"You like to read," he says. "And I need somewhere to finish books seven and eight."

"I love you. I don't know what I did to deserve you coming back to me, but I love you so fucking much."

"I love you too. Now, come on, there is one more thing I know you'll love."

"Another part of your list?"

"No, but a happy coincidence."

He leads me to the third bedroom. It's a nice space in the back of the house, with plush tan carpet and white walls, but it's underwhelming.

"It's great it has three bedrooms," I say, taking in the room.

"It has four, but that's not what I want to show you." He tugs my hand toward the window. "Look," he says, pointing outside.

Outside is a carbon copy of the roof at my parents' house. It's *our spot*, but here. My breath hitches.

"Oh, Jace, it's perfect."

He wraps his arms around me from behind and rests his chin on my shoulder. His beard tickles the side of my face, and I melt back into him.

"So, does that mean you want it?"

"Yes, I want it, but can we afford it?"

"We can."

"Mr. Jackson, are you still here?" a woman calls from downstairs.

"That'll be the realtor," he says, checking his watch.

We walk back downstairs hand in hand. After some introductions, we talk through the next steps. I sit there listening to Jace talk through things. He doesn't let go of my hand the entire time she speaks to us.

"I'll get the offer paperwork all squared away and over to you tomorrow," she says. "Y'all have a strong offer and the sellers are motivated to sell it, so I'll be in touch." She smiles, shaking both of our hands.

We climb into the Jeep and it hits me that we're going to have to talk to our friends.

"When do we tell Poppy and Tanner we're moving out?" I ask. "Shit, I feel like such a bad friend. I mean, our lease is up next month, so she'd need to find a roommate. Do we wait until they accept the offer, or do we tell them now?"

"If we don't get this house, I still want to live with you. If it's not this one, then it'll be a different one, or we can find an apartment. Hell, I'd live in a tent with you. I think we have to tell them now." He squeezes my hand. "Is that what you want?"

"Yeah, more than anything."

"Okay, so we tell them now. It'll give them time to find new roommates. Didn't you say Wren said she might need a place to live? Maybe she can take over your lease."

"Oh, my god, you're right. That's good. Poppy is going to need a plan, so she doesn't stress. I'll remind her about Wren. What about Tanner?"

"Tanner will be fine." He laughs. "Half the time he doesn't even accept my rent payments."

"He doesn't accept your rent payments? What exactly does he do for a living?"

"Some type of office job with his dad. Honestly, he's told me before and I can never remember what it is exactly."

"He's like if Chandler and Joey from *Friends* had a baby."

"He really is." Jace and I both start laughing. I look over to where he sits. His smile takes up his whole face, and I know without a shadow of a doubt that I want to spend forever laughing with him.

"I'm really happy, J."

"Me too, Pixie."

We drive the rest of the short distance, and I tell him all the things I would want to do with the house. He doesn't say a word, just listens and nods. We talk about paint colors, furniture, and rugs. I take out my phone and start saving inspiration pictures, flashing them towards him as I talk.

"That would be great," he says. "I can't wait to make it ours."

"I like when you say that."

"Say what?"

"Ours. It has a nice ring to it. Don't you think so?"

"A very nice ring to it." He kisses the back of my hand and turns into the parking lot of my apartment complex.

"It's going to be okay. She'll understand," he assures me, pulling into a parking spot.

"I hope so."

"I'll see you tomorrow?"

I nod. He unbuckles his seat belt and goes to open the door.

"You don't have to walk me up. I need to get this conversation over with, and if you come up you'll distract me. Go home and tell Tanner. I'll text you later."

"I like to distract you, though." I slap at his chest, and he pulls me into a chaste kiss.

"I love you."

"I love you more," I tease winking in his direction.

"I love you most," he answers back. My heart skips a beat.

"You didn't think I forgot did you?" he asks.

"No, I..."

"I know," he says. After another quick kiss, I make my way out of the Jeep. He honks his horn when I make it to the door, and I turn to see him backing out. My nerves fully set in when I turn the key, letting myself into the place Poppy and I have called home for three years.

"You here?" I yell, walking into our apartment. She walks out of her room.

"Hey, how was today? What was the big surprise?" she asks.

"Can we sit?" I gesture toward the sofa and close the door behind me.

"Sure." She shrugs. "Is everything okay?" We both walk over and sit on the sofa, each taking our usual spots.

"Oh, yeah. Jace took me to a house today."

"A house? Like his dad's house?"

"No, he took me to see a house that's for sale."

"Oh, wow. So, he's staying? That's so great."

"Yeah, um, well, fuck," I try again. "He took me to see a house that's for sale because he wants us to buy it. He asked me to move in with him, and I know we've been here for a long time, and I don't want you to freak out about a room-mate, so I was thinking maybe you could talk to Wren and she could take over the lease for me when it ends next month. I mean she's not me, but I think she would be fun to live with."

Poppy laughs and tears run down her cheeks.

"What's so funny?" I ask, suddenly extremely confused.

"Nothing." She tries to catch her breath. "I've been meaning to talk to you about the same thing and I've been so scared. Logan and I've been looking for our own place. We've been considering it all summer, especially since the parent who almost got him fired lives across the hall from him. She's been fine, but running into her is getting hella awkward."

"You're kidding?" I begin to laugh too.

"No. Actually, the other day when you got home, I was

looking at places on my computer. I almost told you then, but I couldn't do it. As much as I love Logan, I love living with you."

"I know." I pout. "This is weird. We're going to be living with boys."

"Super weird. Although, Logan is a lot cleaner than you are, so it might not be that bad."

"You're hilarious," I deadpan.

"Wait a house? This is huge. What's it like? Do you have pictures?"

I grab my phone and swipe up. I show her the pictures I snapped while we toured the home that will hopefully one day be ours.

"Goodness, the island is beautiful," she says.

"Isn't it great? It's super sturdy."

"Do I want to know what that means?"

I snicker to myself then continue to swipe through the pictures. When I'm done, I set my phone back down on the coffee table.

"I'm so happy for you," she says, wrapping me in a hug.

"I'm happy for you, too, babe. Are you and Logan looking for a house? Maybe one will go up for sale on the same street?" I laugh.

"I think we might rent for another year," she says. "Finding an apartment that's decent is impossible though. Do you realize how good we have it here? Nothing is as nice, and if it is, it's like triple the price."

"Why doesn't he move in here?"

"Oh, my god," she shrieks. "You're right. It's perfect. You're moving out and he can move in."

She grabs her phone and starts typing away. Her phone rings and I wave her off. "Take it. Tell him the news." She jumps up and moves back toward her room, and I grab my phone again.

I swipe through the pictures, imagining what life will be like with Jace by my side. I click out and find his name.

Poppy and Logan are planning to move in with each other too!

JACE:

You're kidding.

Nope! I think he might move in with her here. How'd Tanner take the news?

JACE:

He's devastated.

Really? I thought you said he'd be cool.

JACE:

LMAO! He's fine. He said he'd start looking for a roommate.

Good. I really hope we get the house. It's perfect!

JACE:

Me too!

OMG! I think I have an idea. Hold on.

———

I think I figured out your housing situation!

WREN:

Please tell me Poppy is moving out and you suddenly need a roommate because I'm stressed.

No, I don't, but Tanner does.

CHAPTER 59: OURS
JACE

The last month has been a whirlwind of sorts. After Lacey and I put in an offer, the sellers accepted it, and we started the moving process. I also started at the CFNAWC. Most nights I spent over at Lacey's. Poppy was at Logan's, so it was nice to have a place to ourselves. We fell into a rhythm together, and if it's any indication of what life will be like with her at our own place, I can't wait to see how our future plays out.

Walking into our new home, I find her and most of our friends sitting on the floor of the kitchen. Moving boxes surround them. A stack of Bruno's pizza boxes are piled high on the island. Poppy insisted we could not celebrate move-in day without champagne, and Lacey agreed. It feels surreal seeing all of our friends sitting in *our* kitchen.

"The house is gorgeous," Gray says, sipping her champagne.

"A reading room?" Wren asks. "Talk about a dream come true."

I walk over, fill a paper plate with pizza, and grab a glass of champagne. Lacey stands and joins me. She wraps her arms around me from behind and rests her face against my back.

"The movers are gone?" she asks.

"Yep, I tipped the driver and they headed out."

"I can't believe it's all ours," she says. I spin around to face her.

"Ours," I repeat her words, leaning down to kiss her. She smiles against my lips.

"Have I told you I love you today?" she asks. "Because I like really fucking love you."

"I like really fucking love you too." I kiss her again. "Should I kick 'em out?" I whisper in her ear.

"Later," she winks. "I've got big plans for later."

"Deal."

"Careful you two," Poppy says. "We don't need the residents gossiping about another hickey on Lacey's neck."

Wren, Gray, and Poppy all burst out laughing.

"I swear, for being over eighty, those women have the vision of a toddler," Lacey laughs. "That was a month ago and they're still talking about it. 307 was offering me advice last week about how to properly cover one with makeup." She shakes her head.

"She's so funny," Wren says.

"I think she and 330 are talking about moving in with each other, too. I heard the office ladies talking about it the other day," Gray says.

"If they end up getting married, we better be invited," Wren adds.

"Right?" Lacey smiles.

She sips her champagne and laughs when Tanner says something stupid. She's wearing a T-shirt that she insisted on buying me. It's dark gray and on the front it says "Nice Tits" with two small titmouse birds sitting on a limb. Her black leggings hug every bit of her long legs. Her hair is pulled out of her face. She looks so happy. I walk over and grab my camera off the top of one of the stacks of boxes. I pull it to my eye and capture her happiness, telling myself I will do whatever it takes to make her this happy every day, for the rest of my life.

"Where's Chloe?" Logan asks, sitting down next to Poppy.

"Ava's sick, so she couldn't get away," Gray says.

"Ava?" Donovan asks.

"Her little girl," Wren says.

"I didn't know she had a daughter," Enzo chimes in.

"Yeah. She's super cute and absolutely wild in the best way," Gray smiles. "Dad's a piece of shit and long gone, so when she brings something home from daycare, Chloe's on her own."

"That's a shame," Donovan says. "I was happy y'all brought her to the wedding. She's a lot of fun."

"Oh, yeah, Chloe's a blast when she lets loose," Gray agrees. "She was bummed she couldn't be here, but she's going to try to help with Logan's move."

"When exactly is the move happening?" Tanner asks.

"Next weekend, and I expect you all to be there to help," Poppy laughs.

"And what will I get for helping?" Tanner teases.

"Pizza and champagne," Poppy deadpans.

Tanner grumbles something under his breath.

"What did you say, T?" Logan asks.

"Nothing, happy to help you move."

"Speaking of moving. How's the roommate hunt coming?" Logan asks.

"It's not," he says. I don't miss Wren's eyes shooting toward Lacey and then back down to her plate.

"If only we knew someone who needed a roommate," Lacey says, staring very obviously at Wren.

"Right?" Tanner says, oblivious to what my girl is suggesting. "All of you assholes"—he points at all the guys in the room with a mouth full of pizza—"are happily paired off and there isn't anyone left to take my spare bedroom."

"Doesn't have to be a guy. Wren needs a—" Lacey begins.

"So, how's married life?" Wren asks abruptly, cutting off Lacey and looking toward Enzo. "I know we keep saying it, but your wedding was stunning."

"What about Wren?" Tanner asks.

"Nothing," Lacey recovers, sending her an apologetic look. "Just that she won't be at Logan and Poppy's next weekend. Right?"

"I didn't know you couldn't come," Poppy says.

"Yeah, it's my brother's birthday," Wren explains. "Sorry. I thought I mentioned it."

"It's okay." Poppy offers her a smile. "How are you liking your new job, Jace?"

"It's incredible," I say. "I was nervous about having to manage people, but the group of photojournalists I'm overseeing are extremely talented, and I can already tell they're going to make my job a lot easier."

"That's great," Enzo says. "So, are you traveling anytime soon?"

"No." I shake my head. "There's no need. Part of my team is currently down in Florida studying the sea turtles nesting there, and next week they'll switch out with a few of the people who have been home. I'm working on setting up our next projects."

"And you're okay with that?" Logan asks.

I pull Lacey into a tight hug and kiss the top of her head. "Honestly, I don't miss it at all. I'll definitely have to do some small trips down the road, and those will be fun, but I know I made the right choice. I'm exactly where I want to be."

Lacey squeezes me tight before letting go. The conversation continues, and I let the happiness I'm feeling wash over me. There is a lot we need to do, but it can wait until tomorrow. For now, I want to enjoy our friends and my girl.

I clear my throat and everyone's eyes shift to me. "I'd like to make a toast of sorts," I begin. "I'm not very good at this sort of thing, but I wanted to say thank you for your help today." I put my arm around Lacey's shoulders. "It means so much to the both of us to have all of you here, so thank you for putting up with us the past few months. I'd like to think it was all worth it." I raise my glass and everyone sips their drink.

We finish off the pizza and the last of the champagne before everyone leaves for the night. I close the door behind Tanner, the last of our friends to leave.

"Ready for bed?" Lacey asks, standing at the top of the stairs. Her leggings are gone and she's wearing only my shirt.

"Where are we going to sleep tonight?" I ask.

"Come and see." She smiles.

I walk up the stairs and into our bedroom. The bed frame and box spring are leaned up against the wall, and our mattress is in the middle of the room. To my surprise, it's covered with sheets and a blanket. Two pillows sit at the head. Rose petals are scattered over the blanket. Fake candles are scattered around the room, giving the illusion of real ones.

"What's all this?"

"I wish I could take the credit, but apparently it's a house-warming gift from our friends."

"They did this?"

She nods, laughing. "There's even a note."

"What does it say?" She hands me a folded piece of paper and I open it.

You're welcome.

Love,

The Tortured Therapists Department and

S.H.I.E.L.D.

"Bunch of assholes," I laugh, setting down the note.

"Yeah, but they're our assholes," Lacey says smiling. I wrap her in my arms and pull her into me. Her body relaxes against mine. "You know, I'm not very tired," she admits, flashing me a wicked grin. "You?"

"Not one bit." I pick her up, causing her to let out a shriek. Climbing onto the mattress, I lay her down.

"I love you, Pixie."

"I love you, too, J."

LACEY - SEVEN MONTHS LATER

"I thought I'd find you in here," Jace says from the door of my reading room. He slightly pushes the door open and leans against the frame.

"I can't put it down," I say, holding up my e-reader. "There's just something about a second-chance romance, you know?"

"Definitely one of my favorites." He chuckles. "But I think we both know how it ends. Care to join me on the roof? I brought champagne." He holds up a bottle that I didn't notice until now and wiggles his eyebrows at me.

"Only you could make me stop reading." I laugh. I put my book down, grab the blanket, and walk over to meet him at the door. With his free hand, he pulls me in for a long kiss. His hand weaves into my hair and my core instantly begins to buzz.

"You sure you want to go out on the roof?" I tease.

"Come on, Pixie," he says, pulling away and taking my hand to lead me down the hall. He sets down the bottle of champagne on the floor under the windowsill and pushes it open.

We both climb onto the roof and are met by a chill in the

air. It's early March and the sun has already set. He sits behind me, pulling me back into his chest. I help him unfold the blanket, and we wrap it around the both of us.

I nuzzle into him. This has become our ritual over the past seven months. At least once a week, we come out here to talk. Just me, him, and the stars. It's by far my favorite day of the week.

"Where's Domino?" I ask.

"I put her in the crate so she didn't get into the trash again," he says.

"You think she'll be okay locked up?" I pout.

"I think she'll be fine," he assures me.

"I don't know how you'll ever outdo buying me a puppy for my birthday." I smile, thinking about the little black-and-white border collie puppy downstairs. He lays a kiss on top of my head. "Oh, I texted Colt earlier. We're all set to head to Austin in a few weeks to see him play. I know it probably didn't take much, but thanks again for convincing Mom and Dad to come with us. I think it'll be good for all of us to do something together."

"It was easy. Your mom loves me."

"Does she?" I laugh. "Not too long ago she was sure you'd break my heart. How did you get her to love you?"

"Well, love might be a strong word." He laughs. "She definitely really likes me. Is Colt excited about the season?"

"He sounds like it. I think he's nervous about getting drafted, but I think it'll happen."

"I'm glad."

I look over my shoulder. "You good? You aren't very chatty tonight."

"I'm fine, just thinking."

"About what?" I feel him move from behind me, so we are seated next to one another.

"I want to see you when I say this," he says.

"Say what?" His hands find mine, and for the first time, I realize he looks nervous. "You okay, J?"

He takes my hands in his. "Lacey, it took me ten years to tell you how I felt. And then for ten years, I had to figure out how to do life without you in it. Those were some of the hardest years of my life, but one thing remained true despite our distance. I never stopped loving you. I've loved you every day since I was eight years old."

My heart begins to race, and for a split second, I wonder if he's about to do what I think he's about to do, but there's no way, right? No way I wouldn't know.

"And then ten months ago, fate intervened and brought you back to me, and I've never been happier. You're my best friend and my soulmate."

"Jace? What's happening?" Tears begin to stream down my face and he wipes them away.

"Don't cry, Pixie. I promise it's good." He reaches back and pulls a small velvet box from his pocket. He opens it and reveals a stunning emerald-cut diamond ring. On either side of the stone sits a smaller emerald stone. It's all set in white gold. I recognize it immediately.

"Jace, is that your—"

"Yeah, it's Mom's." His eyes are glossy. More tears begin to fall, and I try to wipe them away. "The day I brought you to this house, I stopped by my dad's. I told him then that I wanted to marry you, and he didn't hesitate when I asked him for it. He told me my mom had always wanted it to be you, and he knew we would have her blessing." He chokes back a cry. Swallowing hard he continues. "Lacey Danielle Sims, I promise to love you for the rest of my days. Will you marry me?"

"Yes, oh my god, yes." He takes out the ring and slides it on my left ring finger. Tears cover both of our faces. Our mouths meet in a passionate kiss, and he wraps his arms around me, pulling me in tight.

"I love you," he says.

"I love you so fucking much, Jace Jackson."

He places another chaste kiss on my lips and stands, moving toward the open window. He reaches inside and pulls up the bottle of champagne. He pops the top, spraying a stream of champagne into the air. We spend the next hour sipping champagne straight from the bottle, stargazing, and getting lost in sweet kisses.

He checks his watch and places a kiss on my forehead. "Come with me. I have one more surprise."

We carefully make our way back into the house, and he pulls me down the hall. When we get to the top of the stairs, I hear hushed voices coming from below.

"You didn't."

"I did." He smirks. We hurry down the stairs and when we round the corner we are met with all of our closest friends and family.

"Congratulations!" they shout. Poppy, Gray, Wren, and Chloe tackle me in a huge hug.

I can't make out what any one of them are saying over their shrieks. They finally let me go, leaving Poppy standing there. Tears fill her eyes.

"I'm so happy for y'all," she says, wrapping me in another hug. Over her shoulder, I watch as the guys all congratulate my fiancé.

Poppy releases me. "Logan, take a picture of us," she says, throwing him her phone. We both put out our hands in front of us, showing off the diamonds that now adorn both of our left hands. "We're going to have so much fun planning our weddings together," she gushes. "There's no one else I'd rather do it with." She squeezes my hand.

Domino runs by us, wagging her tail, jumping up on me for attention. I bend down to scratch the top of her head. The crowd parts, revealing my parents and Jace's dad.

We make our way over to them, and my mom surprises

me by pulling me in for a hug. "Congratulations, sweetheart," she says, pulling away quickly and smoothing out her dress.

"I know you don't need our blessing, but it was an easy yes," my dad says, putting out his hand to shake Jace's.

"Colt wishes he could be here, but with the season starting he couldn't make it," Jace explains. "I told him we'd call him tomorrow."

"He already knows?" I ask.

"I had to get his blessing too." Jace smiles and my heart swells.

How did I get this lucky?

"Well, let us see the ring," my mom chimes. I put out my hand, and for a second, I think I see tears well in her eyes before she blinks them away entirely.

"Annie would be so happy you have it," she says, nodding her head. "It's beautiful."

"She sure would," Jace's dad adds, wrapping both of us up in a big group hug. "I'm so happy he finally popped the question. I've been on him for months," he jokes.

Poppy passes out champagne and we all take a flute full of bubbly liquid.

"To the past, present, and future," I say, raising my glass. Jace taps his against mine and then pulls me in for a kiss.

JACE

"I really don't know what I was thinking, inviting everyone over before we had a chance to really celebrate," I say, shutting off the downstairs lights.

"I'm glad they were here," Lacey says, looking at her ring as we make our way upstairs to our room. Domino trails behind us. "Have I told you tonight how happy I am?"

"I'm happy, too, Pixie."

She moves over to our dresser and begins taking off her clothes. I watch as she undresses. She's absolutely stunning.

She gets down to her lace bra and panties and turns around. "Should I keep them on, or are you going to come help me take them off?" Her lips move into a sexy grin.

I stride across our bedroom and meet her where she stands, only wearing my boxers. "Off," I say. "I want to make love to you tonight, and the only thing I want you wearing is that ring on your finger."

She steps forward and we collide into an emotional kiss. My hands rake down her body, unhooking her bra and tugging down her underwear. She meets my pace and pulls at my boxers. We both frantically kick off our undergarments. I back her towards our bed and lay her down on the mattress.

"Look at you, baby. You're so fucking beautiful." She gasps at my praise, and I move my hands down over her breasts, pausing to play with her nipples. She lets out another little breath when I pinch gently.

My mouth traces her body, moving down toward her center. She stops me, pulling me back to her mouth. "Let me," she begs. She sits up and I move to my back. Sitting with her knees tucked under her, she moves down my body, kissing and licking. She runs her hand down my shaft in one fluid motion. I let out a groan. She bends over, licking a bead of salty liquid from the tip. Taking the head into her mouth, she moves slowly down my length until I hit the back of her throat.

"Fuck," I let out, watching her as she takes me again and again. "Such a good fucking fiancée sucking my cock." She hums against me and the vibrations threaten to take me over the edge. Her mouth travels up my shaft and she sucks hard on the head, making a popping sound as she raises her head to find my gaze.

"Come here," I say, moving her so she's straddling me and facing away. "Scoot back, baby, and let me taste you."

She does as she's told and moves her body so that my lips find her center. I take my tongue up the middle of her slit, and she grinds back into me. Falling forward, she takes my cock back into her mouth.

We work each other in unison. My hands find her hips, pulling her down onto me. My finger gently plays with her asshole the way I know she likes. Her movements start to become frantic as she continues to work my cock in her hands and mouth. Her whole body tenses above me as she finds her release, and I lap up every drop she gives me.

She moves down my body spinning around.

"Do you know how good you taste? You're so fucking sweet," I say.

Leaning forward, she takes my mouth in hers. She lets out a moan, her hips jolting against my bare cock. With one hand, she reaches down and lines me up with her center. She lifts her hips, and in one motion she pushes down and takes all of me.

I rock my hips into her, our mouths still tangled together. I tug at her hair and she lets out another moan. Our hands explore each other. Every movement is full of so much passion and love.

I flip her around so she's now on all fours. My hands rake down her spine and over her hips. I drive into her from behind, causing her pussy to clench around me. She lets out a loud moan and my hands find her hair. I tug gently. She muffles a scream into the pillow.

"I want to hear you. Don't quiet yourself for me. I like it when you're loud." She screams again, this time letting me hear how much she likes taking my cock. "You like it when I fuck you from behind, don't you?"

"So much," she moans. She pushes her hips backward, taking me deeper. My hand makes contact with her ass in a playful slap.

"Fuck...yes..." she screams, pushing back into me as I thrust forward. My fingers find her asshole and I begin to play with her again, sliding one finger inside. I drive my cock into her hard, and she screams my name. She matches my pace—the view of her ass and the feel of being bare inside her taking me closer.

Her pussy tightens around my dick. "Come with me, J," she begs. We both find our release. She collapses underneath me, breathing heavy. "Such a good boy," she snickers.

She rolls out from under me. "I can't believe we get to do that for the rest of our lives," she says.

"Me either."

We get cleaned up and climb back into our bed. I pull her close and cover us with a thick blanket.

"Hey, J?"

"Yeah, Pixie?"

"You remember when we were at the lake last July and we saw that shooting star?" she asks.

"Yeah."

"Well, this is what I wished for. I wished for you, Jace Jackson, and I'm so happy it came true."

ACKNOWLEDGMENTS

If you made it to this page, thank you from the bottom of my heart for reading *When You Had Me Adapting*! I hope you loved Lacey and Jace's story, and I can't wait to share book three with you soon.

This story was special for me to write because I met my soulmate when I was sixteen years old. While it's not our love story—we never broke up or hooked up in a bar bathroom (yet)—it still feels like ours. I love you, babe! Thank you for your constant support. If anyone could make me believe in soulmates, it's you.

To my children, never be afraid to follow your dreams. You are incredibly capable of anything you set your minds to. Don't let anyone ever tell you that you can't do something. I love you both so much!

Kalie, this book challenged me in ways I wasn't expecting, and you were there every step of the way. Thank you for always being my sounding board and my shoulder to cry on. I'm so thankful to have you as a PA and friend.

Paige, the cover is gorgeous. I truly feel so lucky to get to work with you!

Kristen, thank you for all of your feedback and guidance.

To my alpha and beta readers, thank you for giving me your time. Thank you for your feedback and your ongoing support.

Lauren, Maya, and Rachael, thank you for answering all of my OT-related questions!

Sam, Ginsa, and Grayce, I will cherish the memories we made this year for my entire life. Thank you for every voice memo, writing sprint, and brainstorming session. Here's to reaching many more author milestones by each other's sides.

To the readers who have been with me since Speechless, thank you for sticking around and cheering me on! I will never be able to adequately express my gratitude, but I am truly thankful!

Lastly, to my family, thank you for supporting me in everything I do. I love you all so much!

ABOUT THE AUTHOR

Jess Christine is a speech therapist turned contemporary romance author who writes cotton candy smut: sweet, fluffy, and utterly irresistible. With low angst and high swoon, Jess crafts stories that feel like the perfect indulgence. Readers will quickly be lost in the warmth of unforgettable characters, light-hearted humor, delicious spice, and feel-good romance.

Jess resides in Georgia with her husband and two children. When she's not writing, she enjoys binge-watching her favorite TV shows, spending time with her friends and family, and getting lost in love stories.

If you would like to stay in the know about Jess' upcoming books, join her reader group: The Cotton Candy Collective, or subscribe to her newsletter at https://jesschristine.substack.com/subscribe

Sign up for my newsletter and snag your free copy of When She Said Yes - Poppy and Logan's Proposal Story!

<u>When She Said Yes</u> should be read after <u>When You Rec'd My Plans</u> to avoid series spoilers.

ALSO BY JESS CHRISTINE

Romance Rehab Series

When You Left Me Speechless - Poppy and Logan's Story

When You Had Me Adapting - Lacey and Jace's Story

When You Rec'd My Plans - Wren and Tanner's Story

Book 4 - Coming Soon

Fairytale Season Series

A Dance of Sugarplums and Power Plays- A Nutcracker Retelling